THE TWOFER COMPENDIUM

THE TWOFER COMPENDIUM

Edited by

Ruth Littner and Ann Stolinsky

Gemini Wordsmiths

CELESTIAL ECHO PRESS
ROSLYN, PA, USA
2020

Celestial Echo Press
An imprint of Gemini Wordsmiths
P. O. Box 1191
Roslyn, PA 19001
geminiwordsmiths.com/publishing
ISBN: 978-1-951967-36-9

Cover art and design: Kas Sweeney

Acquisitions and editing: Gemini Wordsmiths

Special thanks to April Luna

This book is dedicated to connections of all sorts—
between twins, between writers and editors, between
friends, and most of all, between all humans.

We're more connected than you think. ...

Contents

Foreword

Merry Jones

Maybe, like three percent of the world's population, you are a twin. Or, like only eight percent of that three percent, you're an identical twin. Cool.

The rest of us can only imagine what that's like. Does it sound like fun? Maybe it would be, now. But throughout history, all around the world, it hasn't always been.

Whether because of their likenesses or their differences, twins both identical and fraternal have evoked intense reactions from the singlets around them. Because they were inexplicable and unusual, they evoked curiosity, wonder, and often, suspicion and fear.

Here are a few examples. In the Middle Ages, European mothers who bore twins were accused of coupling with the devil and, along with their children, burned at the stake. Meantime, across the ocean, Native South Americans saw twins as proof of the mother's adultery or even demonic possession and, consequently, murdered or shunned the mothers and killed the younger of the twins.

In Old Peru, it wasn't just the mothers of twins who were punished. Both parents were forced to fast and endure the public humiliation of being led around in public with ropes around their necks. As for the twins? One or both of them were usually killed shortly after their birth.

Of course, not every culture killed twins and punished their parents. Some saw them as lucky, supernatural creatures who came from another world, a sort of "Twinland," and treated them with respect.

But even where twins have been allowed to survive—or even to thrive—their existence has drawn attention and inspired curiosity. Across cultures and time, they've been seen as embodiments of every extreme of human traits and behaviors, and show up repeatedly in history, literature, and religion.

In the Bible, younger twin Jacob tricked Esau out of his birthright. In Greek mythology, twins were the product of Zeus's lust and infidelities. Ancient Rome was founded by twins Romulus and Remus, who later fought over power until one murdered the other.

In many cultures, twins represented opposites. In Old Germania, the twin gods Baldur and Hoedr represented the extremes of beauty and ugliness. In Old Persia, Ohrmuzd and Ahriman stood for light and darkness. Hindus regarded Ashvins and Ashwini Kumaras as inseparable twin gods of sunrise and sunset, fertility and infertility.

Sometimes, at least in literature, "twins" have taken a different form, being contained within a single body. In the case of Dr. Jekyll and Mr. Hyde, the twins are opposing sides of a single person. With Dorian Grey, one twin is a façade, the other the man in the portrait.

Even in modern times, twins are said to share special bonds, understand each other's unspoken communication, speak their own languages, even possess powers of ESP. Their double-ness continues to fascinate the rest of us. Adored or abhorred, sheltered or shunned, twins have universally and perpetually aroused attention and curiosity. It was that fascination that inspired this collection of twin-themed stories. In fact, the force behind this anthology's publisher, Celestial Echo Press, is Gemini Wordsmiths, named for the constellation Gemini in which the twin stars, Castor and Pollux, shine together through eternity.

In honor of those heavenly twins, the stories were collected between May 21 and June 20, the astrological span of Gemini. In them, you'll find all matter of twins. The good, the bad, the fantastic, the fearsome, the magical, the envious, the secretive, the devious, and more.

The Twofer Compendium presents twins of all sorts.

As you read it, you might imagine that you are a twin. That you're one of a pair of people, being born together, being raised together, sharing all, starting in the womb. That another person is always nearby, at home, at school, everywhere, and that—no matter what his/her nature—he/she might look just like you.

Being a twin. Fun, right? Think about it. *What could go wrong?*

~~~~~~~~~~~~~~~~~~

Merry Jones is the award-winning author of twenty books, most recently, the domestic thriller *What You Don't Know*. Visit her at merryjones.com.
~~~~~~~~~~~~~~~~~~

Skippy

Danielle Ackley-McPhail

Kylie's screams shredded the air the way shards of glass cut through cobwebs. She jerked back, her hands shaking violently. Something cool and slimy flew off them and slapped against Don's cheek as he brought his hands up to steady her.

"Eww! Eww! EWWW!"

He didn't say a word, but Don agreed; whatever she'd flicked off her hand had slid down his face and was now heading inside his shirt. He lifted one hand off Kylie's shoulder to intercept it. His fingers rubbed across something the consistency of chilled jelly. Every year the haunted house changed. Whoever designed it this year had gone all-out.

The effort was not lost on his baby sister.

"No! No! I can't do it! I can't! I want to go back," Kylie whimpered. She continued to back up until she pressed tight against his chest. When he didn't move, she slammed herself into him and pushed, as if determination alone would send him the way they had come. Somewhere in the dark ahead of them rose a witch's cackle. Kylie jumped at the sudden sound and renewed her efforts with more force. Her little body crashed against him like a battering ram. He had to brace himself more than once as she pulled away and slammed back over and over. For all her fierceness, he smelled the acrid scent of her fear and responded.

"Shhh ... shhhh ..." With ten years between their ages, Don was used to soothing his twelve-year-old sister. They shared some link that made him particularly suited for it, a connection beyond the norm. He could not explain except to call it a mental ability. Not telepathy, not empathy, but something that allowed him to influence her. He could not *make* her do things, but if emotion clouded reason, he could clear it away, kind of like calming by osmosis. It worked best if they were touching, but that was not necessary.

His clean hand came off her shoulder and smoothed down her sandy curls so he could rest his chin on top of her head. As he did so, he brought both arms around her slender shoulders in a sheltering hug. He spoke because she expected it, though it was not what he said out loud that made a difference. "Come on, darlin'. It's OK. We're almost there."

"I want to go back." This time she braced against him and used her muscular legs to push him back. "I *want* to go back!"

Kylie was nothing if not stubborn. He could hear it in her voice. Intractable, unyielding ... she would dig in with both feet all night. Leaning forward to cancel out her nearly successful efforts, he chuckled and rubbed her arms gently.

"Sweetie," Don allowed amusement to edge into his voice. "Think about it—we're over halfway through. If we turn around now, you'll just have to go by the creepy stuff all over again."

She remained silent for a long moment. He could feel her scalp shift forward. In his mind, he saw the glowering pout so familiar to him. He gave her a little extra squeeze, another mental push. Growling, she slapped at his arms until he let her go.

"Never again! *Never* again, Donkey-breath!" She whirled as she spit the words at him. As she turned, artificial lightning cracked through the dank "graveyard" they stood in the middle of. The setting and the spooky glow made her glare downright ghoulish despite the silver tracks of tears glittering on her cheeks. If she weren't so young and his kid sister, Don would have been doing some serious backpedaling himself. Instead, he smiled.

"Come on, Ky, you say that every year. This was *your* idea, you know."

Her scowl deepened and her hands curled into hard little fists. He chuckled and grabbed them before she could bring them into play.

"Hey, find the way out and the caramel apple's on me."

Her fists stayed clenched, but the scowl lost all its heat. Kylie suddenly grinned as if she were six.

"A caramel apple *and* cotton candy," she countered.

Don let go of her hands, held out one of his own, and shook on it. He chuckled and waited patiently as she visibly gathered her courage to move forward. They weren't in any rush. The lady who tore their tickets told them they were the last ones for the night, so it wasn't like anyone was going to come upon them.

Ahead, the shrieks and laughter of those who had gone before grew fainter. Time to continue on or they would end up locked in for the night. They moved through darkness and shadow in a quick hustle. Canned shrieks and maniacal laughter kept pace with them while burning red "eyes" blinked from unexpected places. The occasional denizens of the dungeon leapt out, only to fade back once Kylie screamed. Near the end, the floor beneath the grate they walked on fell away to reveal the illusion of a raging inferno below, as if they were about to plummet straight to hell. Kylie simply clutched his hand a little tighter and plowed through, squealing as low-flying "bats" zipped by.

Finally, the moss-draped exit came into sight. Don barely registered Kylie's gasp as the door clanged shut behind them. He was too busy gulping hard. The exit had not led outside; it led to a hall of mirrors.

He turned to push back through into the haunted house, only to find that there were no handles on this side of the door.

"Wow ..." Kylie's tone came out hushed with awe. The wonder in her voice drew him back around. He struggled to force down his own less-eager reaction. For her, Don plastered a smile on his face. A strained grimace reflected back at him a thousand-fold.

Crap. This was not good. If he'd known this was here, he would have given in to Kylie's insistence to go back the other way. Something lurked behind the silver-backed glass, something hungry. Something primal instinct told him to avoid. He'd encountered it once as a child and had avoided mirrored mazes ever since. Hell, he avoided any mirror, if he could.

This time he had no choice; the way out led straight through that perilous maze. For the first time ever, Don wished his link with Kylie went both ways. The best she could do was hold his hand, but his ego could not stand the blow of letting her know how freaked out he was.

"Oh, wow! Will you get a load of this ..." Kylie started forward and it was Don's turn to dig in his heels. She turned to look at him, the memory of her own fear quickly fading. The corners of her mouth drew down and her brow furrowed as she grabbed his hand and tugged.

"Come on, Don Quixote, face your demons."

Internally, Don flinched. Demons. Apt word. Thousands upon thousands of them stared back at him. Each one wore his face. Literally mirroring his every move. In theory, he held power over them. After all, what could a reflection do but follow his steps? His forehead immediately filmed over with sweat. He gave in to his need to keep hold of her hand. He had learned long ago that reflections could be more than they seemed.

"Cut it out, Ky."

"Hey, it's just a maze." Her tone softened as she saw through his efforts to remain calm. "Let's go; we'll be through it in no time. I promise, this time I'll protect *you*."

Reluctantly, he let her draw him forward. He watched the thing with his face, waited for it to make its move. When he looked at it head-on, it matched him exactly, over and over in endless repetition. Except for the glimpses he caught from the corner of his eye. Those made him tense. Those expressions and actions did not exactly mirror Don's own.

He continued to let Kylie lead the way. Her reflection stayed true to form, never deviating. She came up against the mirrors and merely pushed away, continuing her search for the pathway out. That was how it should be. The natural order of things.

Don meticulously avoided the walls of the maze.

Kylie laughed and the sound tinkled off the glass. Hard to believe no less than ten minutes ago she'd been petrified. Don clutched her hand tighter. Without realizing it, his steps slowed. Their arms stretched between them. In the mirrors, his reflection reached for him. His eyes went wide and he shuddered to a stop.

"Whoa ... hello! My arm is attached," Kylie groused. "I'd kinda like it to stay that way. Come on, it's not funny anymore. What's up with you, anyway?"

He could not answer. She gave a tug and he followed. They left the corridor and found themselves in a huge, octagonal chamber with enough space to hold a small dance. The center of the maze.

As they stepped fully into the room, a sharp click sounded. The lights dimmed even further as the floor slowly rose and tilted like a low, wide top. Another click and a disco ball lowered from the ceiling. The spangled light effect combined with the shifting floor disoriented Don.

Kylie giggled and pulled him into the center of the

room. The floor continued to tilt, but not enough to make them fall. She grabbed him by both hands and with a mischievous grin she started them spinning. Her laughter rose bright and good. Don's terror ebbed and he told himself not to be silly. The nightmares he had had since childhood were not possible. What he half-remembered from that long-ago time in another hall of mirrors could not be possible.

His sister's joy and his own common sense chased back the demons. He smiled and put effort into spinning them even faster, leaning back, as Kylie did, to increase their momentum. The disco ball picked up speed, the floor tipped steeper. Don added his laughter to his sister's. The faster they went, the more their fingers slipped from each other's grip.

"Oh, shit!" Don reached frantically to strengthen his hold. What were they thinking? He had visions of them flying backward into the glass. Images of shattered, bloody shards flashed in his mind.

"No!"

He could not help it. His grip released and they both flew back in opposite directions, Kylie laughing all the way. She was still laughing when they landed. No tinkle of shattered glass followed.

Don hit hard, but not against the mirrored wall, though even with his eyes closed he could tell it was close. For a moment he could not move. When he could, it was only to roll onto his stomach. His body shook in delayed reaction and, in his thoughts, Don thanked the Lord that their stupidity had not had worse consequences. He rested his forehead on the ground and called out to his sister.

"Hey, Ky ... you OK?"

"Yeah." Giggles threaded her voice and he heard the faint scraping of denim as she picked herself up.

"How about you?"

"Just give me a minute."

Bracing both arms against the floor, Don looked up to see just how close he had come to disaster. He gulped as his hair brushed the wall. He blinked, eyes rising to the mirror. His dazed surface reflection stared back. Something else gleamed beneath it. Fear flooded to the fore. He scrambled to his feet too quickly. His heart clenched hard and he could not get a breath. He swayed and felt himself fall forward.

The mirror was too close. His choices were to brace against the glass or fall into it. Before he could decide, his hand came up in automatic reflex. Rested against the cool surface, it stabilized his balance in that critical moment. He blinked his eyes and drew a hard breath. Any second he expected his world to end. Nothing happened.

He laughed and the sound had an edge to it. What a complete spaz, letting a silly childhood fear tie him into knots. His forehead came to rest against the mirror. His eyes drifted closed. A moment to relax, to regain his equilibrium, that's all he needed.

That moment was all his reflection needed, as well.

A sharp tingle burned across his skin. Eyes snapping open, Don stared into his nightmares. The gaze that met his own in the mirror gleamed black with hatred, thick with jealousy. Venom whispered through his thoughts. It reminded him of his link with Kylie, only twisted.

'*Hello,* brother.'

What the hell! The thought formed, but Don knew he did not voice it out loud. That did not seem to make a difference. He struggled to pull back, to break contact, but the mirror held him fast, as if his flesh had melded with the glass.

'*You've been avoiding me. Time to get a little closer.*'

Don had no chance to respond. A shock raced over his skin. Then a second one, deeper still. His body buzzed.

He throbbed and ached with the sensation. It felt like two of him fought to occupy his skin. The world darkened and dimmed around him. He tried to scream. It sounded only in the silence of his mind.

What are you? He forced the thought past the pain.

'*Why, I'm your evil twin.*'

Don put every ounce of effort into pulling away. Agony ripped at him. A malicious chuckle tore through his mind as some force yanked him forward. He fought it with everything he had.

'*Behave, brother, it's my turn to come out and play.*'

You bastard!

'*Actually, I prefer Skippy.*'

Faint and far off, a sound drew Don's attention from the struggle. His heart clenched and a moan shuddered through him.

"Don, you OK?"

No! Kylie! But he could not answer. The demon had silenced him. It took everything he had to fight back.

"Hey, Don Juan, you're scaring me here. You hit your head or something? Or are you just busy making kissy-face with your reflection?"

An evil laugh drowned out whatever else she might have said. Don shrieked as a surge of power washed over him. Intense pain ... a tingle across his skin. He fell, his body passing through endless slivers of glass.

He landed hard. There was nothing left but agony and bright light. He forced his way past the torment. Scrambling to his feet, he turned and sought his sister. Panic nearly threw him down again. He saw her through a smoky haze, from every possible angle at once. Already disoriented, Don swayed. He closed his eyes against the sensation. Silence and darkness wrapped him tight. He stood stranded in a vacuum with Kylie trapped outside.

Don's eyes flew open again and he fought to focus

through just one view, to be in a single place at once. He stared into Kylie's face, but her gaze did not quite meet his. She smiled at the Don-who-was-not-Don as if nothing had changed. The love and trust in her gaze were tangible as she reached for his hand. For *Skippy's* hand.

No! Ky ... Ky! Don frantically tried to make her hear him. *Sweetie, run! That's not me!* His voice cracked and he pounded on the haze, desperate to shatter it. He fell.

Laughter sounded again in his head, in sharp, shredding jags.

'*There's nothing there for you to hit, dear brother— not unless I touch it from this side.*'

Skippy's malice rode the twisted link and hit Don hard. In reaction, rage shook him. He ground his teeth against another scream. He would not give the demon more cause to taunt him. Don's focus slipped and he saw his nightmare from a thousand dizzying views. Ky and Skippy moved off, heading for the second half of the maze. Determined, Don followed them.

His every step mirrored Skippy's. At first, he fought it, but the drain ate away at him. It stole his thoughts and his will until he could not remember why he fought at all. He was too new to the mirror realm to fight it. That added to Don's fury. Skippy's motions forced Don to follow, to watch, helpless as Kylie scrambled to keep up. The demon ruthlessly dragged her through the maze.

Don gave up on calling out to his sister. The place that trapped him also hedged in his words. Gritting his teeth, he locked his eyes on Kylie. He had to reach her. He thought of the link they shared, tried to sense if it still remained. The effort nearly floored him; would have, if he were not chained to Skippy's motions. His will struggled as if he were encased in thick glass. The mirror realm muffled everything, including the link between him and his sister. He could tell it remained, but only as a mere shadow of itself.

He called it. Willed all of his strength into it. Did something he had never done before: used it to make his sister anything but calm. He projected an image at her, one where she fought the grip of a stranger masked by Don's face. He felt, more than saw, as doubt and uncertainty took hold of her. Beginning wisps of fear drifted into her gaze. She no longer scurried to keep up.

Skippy shot Don a venomous look through the mirror's reflection but did not speak or slow his pace. If anything, his steps grew more urgent. Don roared and whipped his fist through the haze. He knew now what drove his evil twin: the exit. They were nearly out. And once they passed the threshold Don would lose his chance of escape.

'Yes! Yes, you will.' Skippy hissed in Don's thoughts. *'Once we go through, you are damned forever ... trapped forever.'*

Insanity tinged the demon's laughter. From the look on Kylie's face, she had heard it as well. She stumbled and Skippy jerked her hard to her feet, not even stopping.

Don thought the image at her again, stirring her doubt. He wavered with the effort.

Kylie instantly transformed. Her fear and confusion morphed into a familiar glower. Her free hand fisted and her feet planted firm and would not be budged.

Yes! Don knew his first glimmer of hope since he had been yanked through the glass.

Come on, honey, come on. Look at him, Kylie. See him! That could never be me.

Get away, Ky!

He watched as her gaze went from Skippy, to his reflection, and back again. She could not possibly hear Don, or see him, but did she begin to consciously feel him? Her brow drew down even further and she showed her teeth.

Yes!

That's it. You wouldn't take any of that from me ...

don't take it from him, Kylie. I love you, sweetie. Just get away.

Don gathered all his will and focused everything on the thought of his sister getting free, pictured her pulling away. His frustration built as Skippy dragged Kylie closer to the exit. One of the demon's hands reached for the handle, while his other jerked Kylie brutally, drawing her along.

Kylie growled and yanked back but could not break Skippy's grip. Don watched her yank again, throwing all of her body behind the effort. He continued his pinpoint focus on her, trying to lend her strength. He weakened and his world went several shades darker. He hardly noticed as Kylie slammed backward, dragging her hand from Skippy's. She collided with one of the mirrored panels. A spider's web of cracks fractured the silver-backed surface, the impact point smudged with blood; Kylie slid to the floor. She did not move.

Don cried out and tried to go to her, but he could find no way through the haze. His rage built and he no longer feared the demon. Not when he meant to tear it apart. He looked up and met Skippy's gaze. As earlier, his reflection showed him fear. This time not his own.

'*No! You cannot touch me!*' Skippy screamed in Don's mind. '*You cannot pass back. It's* my *turn!*'

Don just stared at him, as if memorizing a face he'd not seen before. He allowed his intentions to shine through. Skippy paled and backed away. Don just smiled an unpleasant smile. He also noticed something he had missed: the haze around him slowly thinned, like smoke escaping through a crack. Sound filtered through the fractured mirror—calliope music, the hawkers' last cries from beyond the exit door, and Kylie's moan, as she came back to herself.

The smile on Don's face took on a satisfied gleam. The moment he heard his sister's unmuffled moan, he knew. He mentally reached out to her. His suspicions were confirmed: The barrier was breached. The horror on Skippy's face clinched it. Don reached up and placed his hand against the haze, watched it shimmer and deepen to a silver sheen. Skippy scrambled back, colliding with a mirror on the other side.

This time Don purposely eased back his focus. He went from the singular point he'd clung to, to being everywhere at once. The tightness returned as Don stared into the madness of Skippy's haunted eyes. With a thought, he drew the demon to him with an unyielding grip. Again, Don's body held two of him. No agony, this time, but as he pushed through what felt like a stream of warm silk, he heard Skippy's tortured scream as the other fell back through endless slivers of glass.

Don landed hard with his senses still cloaked in a shimmery haze. Avoiding the glass, he pushed himself off the floor. He knelt in place, legs spread wide until he swayed no more. He raised his eyes to his reflection, braced for a glimpse of Skippy's hatred.

The mirror held nothing of the other. Don's reflection stared back at him from the glass, and it was him alone. Skippy was gone.

Only then did Don edge forward. He pulled Kylie into his lap and wrapped his arms around her. She stirred as he pressed his lips to the top of her head.

"Welcome back," she murmured, her voice faint as she sank into his hug. "Where'd you go?"

Don smiled down at her and whispered back, "You don't want to know, but for busting me out, you get *two* caramel apples."

~~~~~~~~~~~~~~~~~~~

Award-winning author, editor, and publisher Danielle Ackley-McPhail has worked both sides of the publishing industry for longer than she cares to admit. Her published works include six novels, seven short story collections and two nonfiction books. Danielle lives in New Jersey with husband and fellow writer, Mike McPhail, and three extremely spoiled cats. To learn more about her work, visit sidhenadaire.com or especbooks.com.
~~~~~~~~~~~~~~~~~~~

The Twofer Compendium

The Echoes

Gregory L. Norris

This morning at 6:30 I woke up, brushed my teeth, fed the cats, and checked my email. At 7:14, I put in a half hour on the treadmill—losing weight and staying in shape utterly bites the big one but is so important toward maintaining a long and healthy life. I drank a tall, cold glass of water with lemon, chased it down with my morning vegetable juice now that my mouth didn't taste like toothpaste, and showered.

I dressed for summer—shorts, a T-shirt, and my new sneakers with the electric green laces I saw at the mall and had to have. And then, at 9:00 on the nose according to the clock above my oven, I again saved the world.

⬯⬮⬯⬮ ⬯⬮⬯⬮ ⬯⬮⬯⬮

My name is Milo Guthrie Smith. I'm fifty-one and have been struggling with a spare tire since my twenties. I live alone with two rescue cats in a modest ranch house, though six months ago I met someone. He sometimes stays over. I'm a Taurus, I think I believe in God, and I hate liver. Oh, and I'm what you'd call a superhero.

Nine months ago, on what started off as the least remarkable night, I answered a knock at my front door right after sunset, and standing on the step was a lady made of light.

"Time is short," she said, though the words could have been spoken telepathically. "Will you answer yes or no?"

I don't remember answering the question, only nodding. I sensed my mysterious visitor's relief—and also fragments of the story as they washed into my consciousness. She and eight others like her, facing the ends of their lives, were tasked with the responsibility of either losing their incredible superpowers or passing them on to worthy recipients. The lady made of light felt I was one such candidate.

She said, "The Echoes," and reached for me.

An instant later I was on fire, though not being consumed. Every cell radiated with the cosmic energy of the Big Bang that first gave life to the universe. I was no longer a male being made of flesh, but a lady composed of light. I turned around and caught my reflection in the window glass—tall and feminine, clad in a white, formfitting costume and cape with a glowing, black, eight-pointed star emblazoned on my chest.

"Use your new powers in benefit of your world and its citizens," she said before going silent in my thoughts.

I promised I would, but there was nobody to hear. I blinked, and the effulgence of light and energy receded back into my core. Standing on the front step was a middle-aged man with a spare tire and wide, haunted eyes.

There were nine of us scattered across six of the seven continents—two in the United States and three in Europe. One month after our visitation by the Echoes, we formed the Allegiance and promised to work for the UN with government oversight. Not long after that, while patrolling the skies over the East Coast and keeping an eye on a chunk of space debris passing between the moon and Earth, I picked up an emergency call concerning a collapsed crane at a construction site in Boston.

My body of light soared down from its high position at the upper limit of the troposphere. In short order, I assessed the situation. The crane had blown over in heavy winds and hung precariously at the edge of the skeletal building frame. One man struggled to regain control, to prevent the inevitable. That crane was seconds from plummeting more than fifty stories to the pavement.

I raced down, trailing sunlight.

"I'm coming," I called and extended my arms.

He looked up and either part of me or the echo of the creature that had endowed me with its powers stole a double take. He was the handsomest man I'd ever met—dark hair, a scruff of five-o'clock shadow showing at eleven on a sunny morning, eyes so green behind his safety goggles they bordered on emerald.

The crane gave. He reached for me and I caught him and we rose in the air after shifting my composition to fast-moving photons capable of shouldering weight. On the glide back down to the roof, high above the city, our eyes connected, and a different kind of energy surged between us.

"Thanks," he said, his voice a manly growl.

"My pleasure," I said. And it was.

"Joe. Joe Galvin," he said.

"Allegiance 1, North American East Coast Guardian through to the continental divide," I said. Not very romantic, I know, but by our third date, I trusted Joe enough to tell him my secret identity. Because by then I was sure I loved him and that he loved me.

ᴵᴰᴵᴰᴵ ᴵᴰᴵᴰᴵ ᴵᴰᴵᴰᴵ

Locating, stopping, and neutralizing the proliferation of nuclear stockpiles had become mostly a European Allegiance task. Agents 3, 4, and 5 had done a remarkable job of dealing with Russian aggression and had resolved Chernobyl. Asia's Agent 6 often sought help from 2 but, nine months after the visitation, North Korea and Fukushima in Japan no longer threatened the rest of the planet.

I returned home from my patrol, landing on the front steps invisible to eyes and other tracking means, and coalesced into an older man in sneakers with neon-green laces. I opened the front door. Bongo and Fuzzy, my two cats, came bounding out of the living room to greet me.

The sound of the TV running on low volume alerted me to the presence of another. I tensed, transformed.

"It's only me," Joe said.

He padded out of the living room where the baseball game played. In T-shirt and blue jeans, bare feet—heavenly distractions.

"I used the key you gave me," he said.

I smiled and reached for him, knowing how much he loved this version of me, the female Echo swathed in light.

"No, Milo," Joe said. "The way you were. The real you."

I drew back, called the light into me, and stepped into Joe's emerald gaze. "Better?"

"Yeah," he sighed and pulled me into his arms.

ⅮⅭⅮⅭ ⅮⅭⅮⅭ ⅮⅭⅮⅭ

Under UN instruction, we nine had established the closest thing to world peace ever achieved. Two of us had traveled the solar system to map—and eliminate—the dangers posed by comets, meteors, and asteroids. Landings had been made on Mercury, Venus, Mars, and several of the major asteroids in the Minerva Belt. Landing plans were set for the moons of Jupiter and Saturn. No wars were being waged on Earth. Or so we thought.

In the early morning darkness as I nestled beside Joe and the cats lounged between us, a ghostly chill crawled over my flesh and I jolted awake, sure there was someone else in the room.

I tensed, froze, surprised at my reaction. I had diverted two hurricanes away from landfall and out to open ocean; had rescued one disabled airliner packed with terrified passengers by riding them down on a cushion of light; and had brought so many criminals to justice. And there I was, trembling in the dark.

"Who's there?" I asked in a voice barely louder than a whisper.

The dark presence answered with a dismissive laugh, confirming my fear.

Joe stirred.

"What's wrong?"

I unfroze and reached for the bedside lamp. An effulgence lit the room. In that moment, it was more powerful than anything the lady of light had conjured up.

"Milo, something wrong?" Joe asked.

I shrugged. "Not sure, babe," I said, scanning the empty room.

Whoever had been there was gone. But I never got back to sleep because I knew the encounter was real and suspected it for what it was: Our world had been gifted with superheroes, so it was only fitting that nature would strike a balance by cursing it with an equal number of supervillains.

ⅩⅪⅩⅪ ⅩⅪⅩⅪ ⅩⅪⅩⅪ

The nine gathered in secret atop Mount Helicon in Greece, mythical home to an equal number of goddesses. We held hands, formed a circle, and gave thanks to the cosmic powers that had turned ordinary people into defenders—and saviors—of the world.

"All goes well," said Agent 7, who guarded over South America.

"All?" asked Agent 3.

In the silence that followed, it was obvious that not all was as rosy as declared.

"Have any of you—?"

"A shadow?"

"A shadow, yes. As though I'm being watched. Watched by someone with intimate knowledge of who I am, where I live, my family and home life. Who I was before the light visited."

An internal shiver coursed through me.

"It's happening to me, too. Like I'm being watched by some malevolent force. An enemy."

"A villain," said Agent 2.

Silence again fell over us. Then the discussion returned to awards, accolades, and parades. So many parades now filled the world's focus.

"To the light," said Agent 9.

We all raised our arms in exultation and, in ones and twos, shot into the sky and returned to our districts in a world at peace.

ᴅᴄᴅᴄᴅᴄ ᴅᴄᴅᴄᴅᴄ ᴅᴄᴅᴄᴅᴄ

I paced the living room. A glance at the clock confirmed Joe was late. Ten minutes later, I called his phone.

"Leave a message," his recorded voice said on the third ring.

"Hey, it's me. You're probably on your way over, so I'll see you when you get here."

Dinner was ready—salads, steaks cooked on the grill to the perfect medium, and homemade potato salad, ideal for a warm summer night. For dessert, I'd prepared blueberry shortcake, Joe's favorite. I hadn't worked off that frustrating spare tire but figured, for one night, I could indulge. I also planned to ask Joe to make it official by moving in. My nerves were frayed. Villains were stalking us. No phone call returned. *Joe.*

I started to cover the steaks, but the nagging worry got the better of me. I dialed Joe's number again, set my phone on the counter, and transformed. As the call went through, I followed the signal at breakneck speed up, into orbit, back down to the cellphone tower, and far out to sea, ending at a rocky shoal upon which a lighthouse rose. I fluttered out of the sky on a column of light particles and caught the sound of the phone's ring above the crash of waves. Looking at the lighthouse filled me with a sense of dread. Its beam strobed through the darkness, one thin line against the night. Not lost on me was the analogy. I was that light, and the darkness surrounding me had abducted the man I loved.

I drifted over to the door and pulled. Locked. I shifted into electrons and slipped through gaps, coalescing on the other side. A dark, dark realm greeted me, one filled with the mechanized groan of the automated light system. Even in the guise of the lady of light, I sensed the same frisson of malevolence as that night in the bedroom when the super-villain first made its presence known. My panic over Joe's safety sent me charging up the staircase on a lightning bolt. I struck the door to the lantern room with enough force to knock it off its hinges.

I reformed and scanned the lantern room. Joe sat cuffed to a metal chair. I hastened over and wrapped my arms around him. One hand lasered the cuffs off his wrists.

"Joe, are you OK?" I asked.

He roused. "Milo?"

I kissed him, aware of his lack of focus. At first, I assumed it was because he'd been abducted, mistreated.

"He's fine," said the voice at my back. "He's not the one I have an issue with."

I straightened. Light pulsed in thickening bolos above my outstretched palms, ready to fly as weapons. Whirling, I saw a figure dressed in a cowled black robe with a white, eight-pointed star on the chest. The rest suggested my opponent was male.

"Who are you?" I demanded.

The figure in black broke out an arm and hurled an orb of dark energy at me. Even before it struck, knocking my light-form through the exterior of brick and mortar and out to the surrounding island, I sensed its source: the night, the void, of outer space. That explosion of shadows left me cold, shattered, and almost powerless.

Struggling to regain cohesion, I looked up at the night sky. The automated beam cast from the lighthouse strobed out to sea. Farther away, the same stars from which I'd drawn my new identity twinkled, seeming to urge me to fight on. I gathered in my powers and came back from the abyss. My adversary controlled all the powers of singularities—black holes from which not even light could escape.

Another salvo of dark energy hurtled toward me. I shot out of its path, circled around the living shadow now standing on the barren rock of the shoal, and unleashed a spree of raw tachyons. The faster-than-light superliminal energy pelted the villain's spine, knocking him off balance. He recovered, turned, and fired. I launched another attack. The two opposing energies collided, canceling one another out in a dazzling explosion that filled the air with a bitter edge of burnt ozone.

We faced off. The most powerful genies in the E-M scale crackled at my fingertips. My enemy postured, twin singularities dancing above his palms.

"I asked you—" I spat.

"Who I am. You don't know?" the darkness taunted.

And then his cowl slithered, shadowlike, down around his neck and I found myself staring at a mirror image of my face. Milo Guthrie Smith's, to be exact.

"How—?"

"Where do you think I go when you appear?" my twin asked. "I'm the echo of your echo."

"Impossible," I gasped. "No, this is a deception!"

The reflection shook his head.

"If you were really me, you'd never hurt Joe," I said.

"I haven't, wouldn't. *I love him!*"

"No," I said and readied to fire.

The shadow with my face followed suit.

"*Stop,*" Joe shouted.

We both paused and lowered our arms as he appeared beneath the strobing lighthouse beam.

"It's true," Joe said. "He didn't hurt me."

Joe stepped between us, the man I loved. And, clearly, the man my new archenemy claimed to.

"There are nine of you," Joe said to me—the light version. "And there are nine of them to make sure the Allegiance never abuses its powers."

"Us?" I said. "We would never do that."

"If you do, we're here to act," my twin said.

We faced off, with Joe between us. His eyes heavy, Joe looked from me to the living shadow, and I knew, I just knew, who he'd side with if forced to choose. With all the light and heat and power at my command, I willed the universe to avoid drawing that line. In the next instant, I silently prayed to whatever god was listening. *Don't—*

"Now that only leaves one question unanswered," my reflection said. "Joe?"

<center>~~~~~~~~~~~~~~~~~~</center>

Gregory L. Norris lives and writes in the outer limits of New Hampshire's North Country. He wrote "The Echoes" as part of *The Fortune Cookie Tales*, when he spent the entire month of December 2018 penning a story a day based upon the slips found inside fortune cookies. gregorylnorris.blogspot.com

The Twofer Compendium

Heir to Snow

Rose Strickman

It would not be long now, before the year's first snowfall.

Seated at her window, Gerda took a long, deep breath of winter. She tasted it—the cold, the icy river, the coming snow. Blizzards that would cover her city with an elemental whiteness. She drew winter through her lungs: its sharpness, its purity.

"Gerda ...?" She turned at her husband's voice. Kay stood in the doorway, still in his frock coat and office shoes. His expression was anxious as he looked into her face. "Gerda?"

"Apologies." She smiled. "My thoughts were full of snow."

Kay looked at the blue-gray dusk with hard eyes.

"You shouldn't have the window open." He strode over, pulled the window; it clicked shut, locking winter out. Kay drew the curtains and took a deep breath. "It won't last forever," he said, more to himself than to Gerda. "It'll be spring soon."

Gerda looked away, around her cozy sitting room. Her sewing fell from her lap; she had sat by the window for light, hours before, and become distracted. She picked up her work and laid it on the table. The fire's warmth glazed over her. Above her, the house was silent; below, she could hear the voices of the servants in the kitchen as they finished preparations for the upcoming dinner party.

"Why aren't you downstairs?" Kay asked. "I would have thought you'd want to make sure everything was perfect—this will be the first time you've seen Clothilde since—"

"Clothilde never cared about perfection." Gerda stood, white dress swaying around her. "I suppose I should change."

"As should I." Kay turned away. The firelight illuminated the lines on his weary face. "I expect you'll be glad to see Clothilde."

"I am," Gerda said. "She was a good friend." She smiled slightly. "I'm glad she's done so well for herself."

"Would you expect anything different from her?" Kay laughed fondly, and for a moment he looked young again: a playful boy, the skies of summer in his eyes, and the sunlight bright in his hair. "It will be nice to have a guest in the house."

"We've had guests. Just last week, your work colleagues—"

"You know what I mean. A proper guest. A friend."

Gerda did know what he meant.

"She'll make the house lively," she agreed.

Outside, unseen by Kay or Gerda, the clouds were gathering, black and invisible above the city, cloaked in dusky shadows.

⧓⧓⧓ ⧓⧓⧓ ⧓⧓⧓

It was too hot downstairs.

Gerda, laced into her wine-colored velvet evening gown, longed to open a window, but knew that if she did everyone else would be shivering within minutes. All the fires blazed; the light gilded the candle-filled chandelier and glimmered on the silverware. A centerpiece, topped by a pineapple, stood on the table; all was in readiness for their guest's arrival.

Kay stood by, tall, slim, and handsome in his evening suit. He sipped from his wineglass. He did not speak, but smiled, waiting. Her own figure, reflected in the black glass of the parlor window, resembled a ghost, her pale face washed out by the dark gown and the flashing necklace.

Outside, there came a clatter of hooves and a cry of "Holla!" After some spirited instructions to the ostler, punctuated by laughter ("And when you're done, get inside and drink some mulled wine—you look like an icicle!"), the door swung open. A dark-haired woman strode in, fur cloak swaying, pistols a-gleam at her hips, face rouged by cold.

"Clothilde Rothbart, sir, ma'am," gasped the maid, straggling in behind her as Clothilde swung off her cloak.

"Kay! Gerda! Marvelous to see you!" Cloak over her arm, Clothilde swooped upon Gerda, giving her a smacking kiss on each cheek. Her lips were frosty, sharp with ice. "You're looking lovely, Gerda; married life suits you. And Kay!" She delivered Kay his own kisses. "Who would have thought it? You look like a real man now!"

"I should hope so," laughed Kay. "Will you let poor Astrid take your cloak? And how about your pistols?"

"Oh, all right," snorted Clothilde. "You're so stodgy."

Later, at the dinner table, Gerda sat while Clothilde, warmed and flushed with wine, described her adventures to Kay's laughter and questions.

"—So, while India's profitable, I was very glad to get home. Far too hot there! The heat's a living thing there; it sucks at you like a mongoose does a cobra egg."

Kay gave a little sigh as he drank more wine.

"It sounds nice to me."

Clothilde grinned at him.

"Perhaps I'll take you next time, then. Both of you," she added hastily, eyes flickering to Gerda.

Gerda set down her fork.

"We'll see."

Clothilde finished her wine and set down her glass.

"So—enough about me! How have *you* been keeping?"

"We're fine," said Kay after a short silence.

Clothilde gestured. "Nice house you have here."

"Thank you—we like it."

"Plenty of space for your friends," continued Clothilde. "And your children, come to that. Any sign that some might be on the way?"

Another silence. "No, not yet," said Kay.

"Oh." Even Clothilde looked a little subdued at this. "Well, maybe it's for the best—terrible nuisances, children are. This way you get to go out as often as you like!"

"True," said Kay, after yet another pause. Gerda tried to remember the last time they had gone out together.

"Then maybe you can come to India after all!" Clothilde beamed.

Kay beamed back.

"Yes. Maybe."

Watching the pair—her husband and her old friend—smile flirtatiously at each other over her table, Gerda tried to feel something—pain, worry, betrayal. But she felt nothing at all.

☘☘☘ ☘☘☘ ☘☘☘

Perhaps it was Clothilde's presence that did it.

Gerda was surprised to wake up and find Kay in her bed; they hardly ever shared it anymore. It had been different once, she recalled dimly, in those first heady days of marriage, before the creeping frost of her heart had killed the springtime of their love.

"Gerda," came his soft, longing voice. "Gerda, please ..."

She did not resist his caress. But neither did she return it.

"Please, Gerda." She could not see his face, but she guessed that it was wet with tears. "Please, I miss you so much ..."

"I'm right here."

"No, you're not. You're gone, all the time. So pale—you never speak. Always, you look beyond me, like I'm not there! Please Gerda … come back to me."

"I'm sorry." Her voice was soft in the darkness of her room. "I can't."

"Why not?" Passion tore at Kay's voice. He sat up, dragging Gerda after him; his hands clutched hers. "Gerda, what's happened to you? You saved me from freezing in the Snow Queen's palace, but it's like you've frozen yourself! Every day, a little more of you turns to ice. I can't reach you anymore. Tell me how I can reach you!"

"You can't." Gerda climbed out of bed.

"Gerda!" She heard his sobbing voice after her, but did not pause on her way down the stairs. He did not follow her; perhaps he would seek consolation with Clothilde, Gerda thought. Perhaps that would be best.

Downstairs, all was dark and chilly. The servants were in bed; the fires had died down. No one observed Gerda creeping through the shadows to the front door, nightgown fluttering in the dark.

She opened the door to a blast of cold.

The first snow was falling, great white flakes drifting out of the vast darkness overhead, fluttering across the cobbles, icing the street. And there, waiting for her, just as she knew she would be, was the Snow Queen.

"Hello, Gerda," the Queen said, voice low and warm.

"Hello," said Gerda. The Queen had changed, she saw. Her snow gown still whirled around her, her ice crown still flashed; but her hair was turning from white to gold, her eyes a warm blue, a living flush spreading across her skin. Her face held expression now: hope, relief, happiness.

"You were human once," Gerda realized, eyes traveling over the Queen. "You're turning human again. You're turning into me."

The Queen laughed, and while the whine of the winter wind was still in it, her voice held a golden note of pure humanity.

"You can't visit winter's palace and return unchanged, Gerda. No one remains the Snow Queen forever. There must always be an heir."

Gerda nodded. For a moment, her life flashed by—a bright carousel of faces, places, events—and she felt a fleeting regret. Then the vision passed and with it, any sorrow.

The Snow Queen took off her crown. Hair flowing loose and golden, she placed it on Gerda's head.

Winter rushed into the empty place that had been Gerda's heart—all the power and deadliness and magic of the cold. The ice, the snow, the wind, the chill, all became part of her, the summation of her soul and being, while her skin froze over, her hair crackled white, and her gown grew into a blizzard.

Shivering in a thin nightgown, the woman who had been the Snow Queen stepped into the doorway. She turned, and the woman who had been Gerda beheld, for the last time, what had once been her own face.

"Goodbye," said the human woman.

"Goodbye," said the Snow Queen, her voice the high howling of a winter storm. And one last scrap of humanity caused her to say, "Take care of Kay for me."

"I will," promised the woman who was now Gerda, and she shut the door against the cold and went in search of her husband's warmth.

The Snow Queen watched her go. Then, with a cry, she whirled away, the winds lifting her up, a flake among snowflakes, up, up, into the winter sky.

~~~~~~~~~~~~~~~~~~~

Rose Strickman is a fantasy, sci-fi and horror writer living in Seattle, Washington. Her work has appeared in anthologies such as *Earth: Giants, Golems, & Gargoyles* and online ezines such as *Tell-Tale Press*. She also self-publishes on Amazon at amazon.com/author/rosestrickman.
~~~~~~~~~~~~~~~~~~~

- 32 -

A Pale Imitation

Dawn Vogel

I'm on the sidewalk, shrouded in a swirl of mist, while I look up at my twin sister, Soledad, a beacon shining in defense of the city, held aloft by the windstorm she's maintaining. The sunlight glints off Soledad's dark gray and celadon costume while we wait for Felix to access the cameras inside the bank and give us a report on the situation.

"It's Slayden. He's got goons with guns and knives at all of the ground level entrances." Our younger brother, Felix, is a super genius who runs our ops.

"All right, Mari, I'll go through a window," Soledad said. "If that pulls them off the back doors, head in that way."

"Got it. Grab my bag on your way," I said, summoning mist to whip around in the fierce winds Soledad had created. As the crowd of bystanders shielded their eyes, I headed for the back of the building.

A window shattered somewhere above me. And like clockwork, Felix announced, "Mari, we've got goons coming out the back door. You are not clear."

"And I'm engaged," Soledad said.

"Congrats," I quipped, ducking behind a dumpster. "I'll offer them in person as soon as I can get in."

A group of four of Slayden's goons clustered near the back entrance to the bank, all looking around. So much for me getting in unseen. Soledad's big entrance should have pulled them inside, but there must have been something else going on that kept them out here.

I weighed my options. I could blast them, but if they spotted me, they might realize there were two of us. So I decided to draw on a talent I've been developing. I yowled, a long, warbling sound meant to sound like a cat.

Two of the goons broke away from the door and headed in my direction. But they didn't seem like they were concerned about the welfare of a cat.

I hissed in response.

"What are you doing, Mari?" Felix asked.

"Trying to get the goons off the back door."

"By sounding like an old woman in pain?"

"It's a cat noise," I replied.

"Sure it is," one of Slayden's goons said, coming around the end of the dumpster.

Before they could fire their guns, I loosed lightning. If you hit someone with the right voltage of electricity, you can stun them rather than kill them. Look at me, science teachers who said I'd never make anything of myself. I did pay attention!

"Two down," I reported. "Two to go."

"Do you think you can get them without the yowling and hissing?" Soledad asked. "Because that's awful, Mari."

"I'm trying to expand my repertoire," I grumbled. Peeking over the top of the dumpster, I fired lightning at the remaining goons. They never saw what hit them. "Back door clear."

"Cops are en route," Felix said. "Mari, get in, but stay off the main floor. One of you should go out the window when you leave. Other one's going to have to lie low until the scene's cleared."

I flew inside to where Soledad waited on the stairs. "You wanna deal with the press, or shall I handle it today?"

Soledad shook her head. "I don't have a change of clothes with me. Do you?"

"That's my gym bag." I picked up the bag and peered inside, my nose wrinkling. "With last week's clothes I forgot to take out."

"Then I'll deal with the press. Have fun with your stinky gym clothes." Without warning, Soledad doubled over.

"Soledad, what's wrong?"

"Something's stabbing me," she gasped, clutching at her abdomen. "From the inside."

"Did you get glass inside your costume?"

"No. Slayden shot me with a pulse rifle, maybe, but it wasn't working right. I didn't feel anything."

I ran my hands over Soledad's stomach, feeling for dampness from blood that wasn't visible through her costume. "Your costume's not ripped."

Soledad slumped to the ground. "Felix, can you keep the cameras down while Mari talks to the press? I think I'm gonna lay low after all."

"Your vitals spiked," Felix said. "I'll have Doc Lyons come to you."

"That's not what I asked," Soledad grunted through clenched teeth.

"Yes, I can keep the cameras offline. What do you take me for, an amateur?" He paused. "Doc Lyons is en route. Mari, go talk to the nice people."

I set my gym bag where Soledad could use it as a pillow and kissed her gently on the forehead. "I'll come back as fast as I'm able."

⋈⋈⋈ ⋈⋈⋈ ⋈⋈⋈

Doc Lyons had arrived by the time I was able to disentangle myself from the clutches of the press. Soledad had curled up on my smelly gym bag, but her face was placid now.

"What's wrong with her?" I asked.

Doc Lyons doesn't look much older than she was in the photos we have of Mama and her obstetrician after we were born. It hadn't been an easy birth, and Doc Lyons was as much our Tia as she was our emergency physician, one of the few people entrusted with the secret of the Celadon Cyclone's identity.

We live in Cerulean City, which has had its fair share of superheroes over the years. Mama was the original Celadon when she was our age. At some point, when she didn't realize she was pregnant yet, a stray bolt of lightning fused with our DNA and made us born with powers. From the way she tells it, twins in their terrible twos with the power of thunder, lightning, and wind nearly drove her out of her mind.

As far as the world knows, there's only one Celadon Cyclone. That we both wear the mask is a secret we haven't had to work too hard to maintain. It would have been harder if we hadn't had a predecessor—a hero in the seventies called Duplication. It was actually three different people (one of whom was a woman) who made it look like there was only one of them, so multiple people as one hero was old news long before we were born.

"I gave her a sedative for the pain. But my preliminary diagnosis? Appendicitis. Sort of."

I blinked. "Sort of?"

"I can't tell much without an X-ray, but her stomach is as rigid as a board, and she's got massive inflammation throughout her lower torso. Appendicitis is the best name I've got for it, at the moment."

"So, what does this mean for Soledad?"

"We're waiting for the ambulance to take her to Cerulean Central for X-rays, and there's a good chance she'll have an emergency appendectomy this evening. She'll be back on her feet before you know it, Mari."

I frowned. "But I can't come with."

"No, not if you want to keep your identity secure," Doc Lyons replied. "But I'll be there, and Felix is bringing your mother. We'll take good care of her, Mari. Go home. Wash your gym clothes."

⋈⋈⋈ ⋈⋈⋈ ⋈⋈⋈

When we have to, Soledad and I have a way to be in the same place at the same time. One of us wears a Halloween wig and a lot of makeup, and we tell everyone we're the other one's cousin. It works for the most part, even though the wig sucks.

So I suited up to head over to the hospital, despite Doc Lyons' admonition against it.

As I stepped out of the elevator, glass shattered somewhere down the hall. It didn't take a super-genius to figure out where. I ran past the nurses' station, ignoring their insistence that I couldn't be there, and headed to Soledad's room.

Two people in ski masks and all black clothing were just inside the doorway, but beyond them, Slayden, wearing his high-collared black cape lined in red silk, like an old Count Dracula from the movies, hovered several feet above the ground, surrounded by more goons.

I moved out of his line of sight and stood outside the doorway, my heart thudding.

"Celadon Cyclone, now you are within my clutches." His booming voice echoed on the hospital room walls. "Get his earpiece, bring them both."

Something crackled inside, and my earpiece squealed. I pulled it out, reeling from the pain.

"What do you want?" Soledad asked.

"To stop the Celadon Cyclone. You've foiled my plans too often for me to allow you to roam the streets. Now I will be sure you cannot stop me."

Slayden, his goons, Soledad, and Felix were all gone by the time I recovered from the ear-splitting pain of Felix's earpiece being crushed on the floor. All that was left was the shattered glass of Soledad's hospital room window.

〖 ❉❉❉ ❉❉❉ ❉❉❉ 〗

I knew where Slayden would take Soledad, but I needed some information. So I called Doctor Justice, Cerulean City's premier science nerd-slash-superhero.

Her brother, Jack, answered the phone. "Mari? How's Soledad?"

"Slayden took her and Felix from the hospital. I need Doctor Justice."

Jack responded with a sharp intake of breath. "Well, that's straight to the point. She's out of town right now."

I sighed. "Are the Justicebots available?"

"Nope, they're with her." He paused. "What is it you need?"

"Slayden had a new weapon. Soledad called it a pulse rifle?"

He typed something. "Hmmm. It doesn't look like Doctor Justice has cataloged it yet. Can you give me any more clues?"

"It maybe gave Soledad appendicitis of the entire abdomen? Uh, didn't tear her costume, didn't draw blood. Maybe—"

"Sonic," Jack said, his voice flat.

I rolled my eyes. Of course, he had to say it first.

"Yeah, that's what I was about to say. Way to mansplain me, JJ."

"Ah, sorry, Mari. I forget you've studied this stuff, too."

"Yeah, it's Soledad who blew off our science classes, not me. Okay, so the right sonic frequency caused her internal organs in its area of effect to become inflamed. Which means, oh, yuck. There are other frequencies that could make things even more gross!"

"Yeah," Jack replied. "That's not the kind of weapon anyone should have access to."

"Okay, how do we counteract that? Counter-frequency?"

"That would work if we had the time to calculate it."

"Well, I need some sort of defense, because I'm going to get Soledad and Felix back."

"Can you get your hands on some foam tiles—some sort of soundproofing materials?"

I frowned. It was late enough that any stores carrying that sort of stuff wouldn't be open. But there are plenty of things that can be used for soundproofing in a pinch. "I've got an egg crate foam thing on my bed?"

"That'll work, I suppose. And avoid him shooting you."

"So, make myself a dress out of egg crate foam and try not to get hit?" I shook my head. "Okay, that sounds ridiculous. But it's expedient. Thanks, JJ."

⋈⋈⋈ ⋈⋈⋈ ⋈⋈⋈

Whoever thinks duct tape prom dresses are cool never tried to make one with foam added into the mix. If I walked, I looked like a drunk penguin. This dress was horrific.

It wasn't as bad as Slayden's house.

What used to be the house was now a burned-out shell surrounded by blackened skeletal trees. Maybe Firebrat was having a good day and had already taken Slayden out. But the more I looked at the remnants of the house, the less likely that seemed. Firebrat always had mutated lizards with them, and there weren't any dinosaur-sized tracks on the yard.

There were, however, blue tarps stretched over a portion of the foundation. I tried to lift one of them with a gust of wind, but it didn't even flutter. Coming in for a landing on the driveway that wrapped around to the garage behind the house, I peered at the edges of the tarps. There was a bit of light coming from underneath, but I'd have to get closer to see more than that.

I hovered a few inches above the ground. I couldn't be sure that Slayden, Soledad, or Felix were here, but I didn't want to tip anyone off. Slayden usually has a fleet of goons with him, and I was not in the mood to deal with goons tonight.

As I got closer to the tarped-over area, I caught glimpses of a basement below. All three of the people I was looking for were there, with no goons. I moved to another part of the foundation to hear what Slayden was talking about. No luck.

But I did spot a giant whiteboard covering one of the walls of the basement. Apparently, Slayden was a planner. An elaborate flowchart showed how he would catch the Celadon Cyclone, wipe her mind, and then set her free.

My breath caught in my chest. I couldn't tell how far along he was in his plan. Soledad might have already had her mind wiped. It might be too late.

But Felix wasn't listed on the flowchart, so maybe Slayden was reworking his plan. I scanned the rest of the whiteboard. Schematics, phone numbers, "stop the raccoon"?

That one gave me pause. It was all in lowercase, so I didn't think it meant some hero called The Raccoon. But it could have been. I took a couple of steps away from the house and pulled out my phone. Jack Justice didn't text much, but I wasn't in a position to call him. So I figured I'd try my luck.

"Ever heard of The Raccoon?" I sent.

It took five minutes before I got a response. "Not in any of my records."

The wheels in my brain had been turning while I waited. I opened up my WebTube app and searched "angry raccoon." Popping in an earbud, I listened to the noises and frowned. After the debacle with the cat noises, I wasn't sure I wanted to attempt sounding like an animal again. Maybe it wasn't the right direction to take my repertoire.

Instead, I cupped my hands around the base of my phone, turned the volume to the max, and wriggled my hands under the edge of the tarp with the speaker positioned toward Slayden.

As soon as I hit play, Slayden's head jerked up, his eyes narrowed into slits. He spared one glance at Soledad and Felix, before aiming a band on his wrist toward the tarp above him. Whatever held the tarp in place released, and he rocketed upward.

I shot up a couple dozen feet in response, leaving my phone behind. I wasn't quite fast enough, though, and Slayden spotted me.

"You?" he shouted. "Who are you supposed to be?"

"The Celadon Cyclone," I replied.

Before I could fire a lightning bolt in his direction, he swung a rifle toward me and fired.

I flew backward from the impact, which also knocked the air out of my lungs. And I realized maybe this wasn't the same rifle he had used on Soledad.

And me wearing a ridiculous homemade dress.

I flew up higher, chilling the air beneath me to create a foggy bank for camouflage, but he followed, continuing to fire pulses at me.

The good news was that aside from moving me away from him, the pulses didn't seem to be impacting me. But it took a few minutes between when Soledad got shot and when her internal organs rebelled against her.

Just in case, I thought I should bring the fight closer to the ground, rather than risk falling from a great height.

Slayden stayed above me, his stupid cloak billowing out behind him.

And revealing a thin wire leading from the butt end of the gun to somewhere on his back.

It took a tiny jolt of lightning to short out whatever power supply he had the gun connected to, rendering it ineffective. But before I could zot him into unconsciousness, my phone screeched, having moved on to a new angry raccoon video.

Slayden dove back toward the ground. He looked furious as he darted around above his yard.

He was looking for an actual raccoon.

I tried not to laugh. I almost felt sorry for him, for a second. But if he found an actual raccoon that was deviling him, that poor animal wouldn't stand a chance.

It was much more merciful for me to knock Slayden out and get out of here. I unleashed one more bolt of lightning, enough to render him unconscious.

That done, I wriggled out of my foam dress and dropped down into the opened portion of the tarps.

Soledad's eyes lit up as soon as she saw me. "Did you make those raccoon noises?"

I shook my head as I started untying her and Felix. "Please. I'm awful at animal noises. Let's get out of here before Slayden wakes up. Or before his sonic rifle catches up with me."

"Sonic rifle?" Soledad asked.

"Yeah, it's—" I began. "No, you know what, it's complicated science stuff. I found a way around it, maybe. But let's go, in case I'm wrong."

"So, how'd you do the raccoon noises?" Felix asked.

"My phone," I said, gesturing toward it with my chin as I untied the last knots.

Felix chuckled. "Ah, the angry raccoon channel of WebTube. Much better way to make yourself sound like an animal, Mari."

"Who knew your knowledge of the internet was so encyclopedic," I spat back. "But I'll let it slide, since I'm gonna need you to kill my phone ASAP."

Felix chuckled again. "Yeah, all right. But don't blame me if you find your new phone subscribed to all the animal noise channels on WebTube. Never know when that might come in handy."

~~~~~~~~~~~~~~~~~~

Dawn Vogel's academic background is in history, so it's not surprising that much of her fiction is set in earlier times. Her steampunk series, *Brass and Glass*, is available from DefCon One Publishing. She lives in Seattle with her husband, author Jeremy Zimmerman, and their herd of cats. Visit her at historythatneverwas.com.
~~~~~~~~~~~~~~~~~~

Double Exposure

John H. Dromey

Lenny was honest to a fault. Although that was seen as a commendable trait by many people, his penchant for consistently telling the truth was sometimes considered to be a liability—not a virtue—by his close relatives.

That's why Lenny was kept on the sidelines in ignorant bliss as his elder brother, Tony, worked his way to the top of the family business—an extensive criminal empire.

Following a downturn in the economy and a series of inept business decisions by the crime boss and his financial advisors, the family's legitimate enterprises developed a serious cash-flow problem. The gangsters needed a quick fix.

"We'll hit two diamond traders simultaneously," Tony explained to a select group of his henchmen. "Since our crews will immediately become prime suspects, we need a gimmick to confuse the witnesses, something to create reasonable doubt. Suspicion is one thing; proof is another. If we can muddy the waters for a few days, we'll have time to fence the swag, launder the money, and cover our tracks."

"How do you propose we do that?" an underling asked.

"We'll place identically dressed twins separately at the two crime scenes just before the robberies take place. Immediately after the dealers are held up, our stooges will exit the premises, change their clothes, and disappear."

"What if the decoys are found later on? They could be traced back to us."

"Not if their only contact was someone with *no* criminal record. Someone who's squeaky clean."

"We'll need someone we can trust. Where are you going to find someone like that on short notice?"

"Let's use my little brother as a buffer. As long as we conceal the details of the heist from him, he'll have no criminal knowledge. We can tell him it's an elaborate practical joke."

"Every detail will have to be exactly right. Any minor variation and the whole scheme will fail. Do you think your brother's up to the job?"

Tony glared at his lieutenant.

"Not only will Lenny jump at the chance to help us out, he'll follow my instructions to the letter. You should see some of the intricate model planes and cars he's assembled—not a single piece out of place."

"What if he hears about the robbery later on? Won't he put two and two together and squeal on us?"

"Lenny doesn't read the daily papers. All we have to do is keep him from watching the TV news coverage for a few days and we'll be home free. He'd rather watch movies anyway. I'll buy him some new DVDs."

Lenny was entrusted with a substantial amount of cash and dispatched to a theatrical agency. He also dealt with the tailor and the hairpiece maker.

⋈⋈⋈ ⋈⋈⋈ ⋈⋈⋈

"Who did you hire?" Tony asked his brother.

"Eric. I forget the other one's name."

"What does Eric look like?"

Lenny showed his brother a head shot. The face in the photograph was unremarkable. Add a bushy mustache and phony sideburns and the young man would be easy to describe, but difficult to identify once his disguise was removed.

Tony almost asked where the other photo was, but stopped himself just in time. That was the whole point of using twins.

"You did well," he told his brother.

⬕⬔ ⬕⬔ ⬕⬔

Finally, the two crews were assembled and rehearsed. With the exception of the twins, all of the participants were under Tony's direct supervision.

"Once we set the play in motion, there's no stopping it," Tony told his associates on the day of the diamond heist.

"Your brother's on the phone. Line one."

"Right on time," Tony said, as he picked up the receiver. "Hello, Lenny. Are your twins where they're supposed to be?"

"Yeah."

Tony gave the agreed-upon hand signal for the caper to commence. His lieutenants spoke quietly into their cellphones.

"There was a little problem, but I solved it," Lenny said, his voice dripping with pride.

"You *what*?"

Silence.

"Talk to me, Lenny. What did you do?"

"I rolled up the trouser legs on one of the suits."

"Why? You told me the suit fit Eric perfectly. The second suit should be an exact duplicate."

"It is," Lenny verified.

"Then what was the problem?"

"His twin sister's a few inches shorter than he is."

~~~~~~~~~~~~~~~~~~~~

John H. Dromey was born in northeast Missouri. He enjoys reading—mysteries in particular—and writing in a variety of genres. His short fiction has been published in *50-Word Stories* (Tim Sevenhuysen's site), *Alfred Hitchcock's Mystery Magazine, Mystery Weekly Magazine, Stupefying Stories Showcase, Thriller Magazine, Unfit Magazine,* and elsewhere. Visit goodreads.com/author/list/5294599.John_H_Dromey.
~~~~~~~~~~~~~~~~~~~~

Ian and Owen

M. Louis Lambert

Kenna Graham screamed. Neither the nurses nor her doctor were concerned, however. Great pain always preceded childbirth. Even if that pain compelled a woman to scream like a redheaded banshee.

Kenna's husband Stuart, or Stu as he was known by most, kept a calm, positive look on his face, despite Kenna's fingernails digging into his hand with each push. He locked eyes with his wife, mimicking the breathing techniques they learned in childbirth classes some five months prior.

"Hee hee hoo. Hee hee hoo," he breathed through a forced grin.

"OK, here comes another contraction," Dr. Robards announced, peering quickly at the contraction monitor to Kenna's left side, the small box displaying two lines converging into the peak of a steep mountain. "Now push! This should be the last one for this guy!"

Kenna erupted into a carnal shout that echoed down the halls of the hospital's birthing center. Agony and frustration filled her cries. She was denied the numbing epidural due to "complications with twins" as Dr. Robards called it. The doctor did not seem concerned when he suggested inducing Kenna a full four weeks early. When pressed as to why, he replied with vague, medical doublespeak, using terms relevant to convince the mother-to-be to agree to the early birth, yet not specific enough to cause any panic. And now, in her moment of triumph, Kenna announced to the world that her babies were coming and she was their mother: powerful, loving, and protecting.

"That's got it!" Dr. Robards declared. A second cry mixed with Kenna's exhausted pants. This was the cry of confusion and helplessness of a newborn child. "He's a boy!" the doctor declared, working efficiently to clear out the baby's airways with a small suction ball. The doctor's actions briefly muffled the baby's yells until the infant was placed on Kenna's upper belly so mother and son could be formally introduced.

"It's a boy, honey! A boy!" Stu's voice crackled with emotion as he stood beside his wife and wondered about this tiny little person who, just mere minutes before, did not actually exist separately from his mother. When the boy reached the warm, welcoming bare skin of his mother, he immediately stopped crying and looked directly into his mother's eyes. To this day, Kenna will swear on a stack of Bibles that the newborn smiled at her in that moment.

"Hey, little guy," Kenna's exhausted voice whispered. The baby continued to stare in awe at this warm and tender person on whom he lay. Stu gently stroked the baby's back as a welcoming gesture to his new son.

After a few more touching seconds, Dr. Robards said, "OK, Kenna, we have to get his sibling out now." Dr. Robards directed a nurse to swaddle the boy in some blankets and take the baby so the parents could prepare for their next arrival. "Just like the first time," the doctor said, again peering at the contraction monitor, noting its upward climb. With over twenty years' experience, Dr. Robards instinctively knew when Kenna should bear down.

Stu prepared his wife, too. He began to rhythmically breathe with her again and gripped her hand as she smashed his. The pressure in his hand told him when her pain escalated.

"OK, Kenna, now push!" Dr. Robards ordered. "Good! It's crowning! I'd say another five minutes or so and we'll have a set of twins on our hands." Dr. Robards looked up from his seated, observant position and grinned, engendering confidence and calm. Stu and Kenna exchanged a warm smirk, too.

But it wasn't five minutes. Upon the next push, the pain was not nearly as severe as with the first child. Dr. Robards moved quickly to catch the second baby, who arrived faster than even the seasoned doctor's prediction. Almost anticlimactic, the event ended. Kenna's moans subsided, punctuated by more labored breathing. But the sound that should have followed, did not.

In that moment, everyone froze. Kenna looked at her husband, who tried to see his second child over the doctor. Dr. Robards and his attending nurses swarmed over the baby, moving in a flash in an effort at resuscitation. All Stu could glimpse was a bluish leg. Stuart looked back at his wife and put on a brave face. His wife knew.

The crushing silence of the room made Kenna's realization of her second child's fate infinitely worse.

"No no no no no, please no," she pleaded through tears and weariness. Her wails escalated when Dr. Robards and the nurses rushed the silent child out of the room. Stu continued to project a strong exterior, while he crumbled inside.

Minute after crushing minute crept like slowly rising flood waters. Kenna burbled disjointed prayers through her sobs. Thankful for her new son, she pleaded for the life of her other child as well. Tears shone on Stuart's face as his expression deteriorated into horror and despair.

The doctor and his team arrived with two bundles. Kenna's heart lifted at seeing her two children, but quickly sank when Dr. Robards' face made the situation all too obvious. Her cries increased with this revelation and she pulled her husband to her, grasping at his clothes. She buried her face in his chest, desperately wanting to disappear from the world, never to return.

Stu squeezed his eyes. He, too, fiercely desired to escape. He eventually looked up to view Dr. Robards' sympathetic brown eyes looking back. Words were impossible for the new father.

"I'm sorry. We detected a heart irregularity while they were still in the womb. We felt getting the babies early may save both children, but the heart was too malformed to do anything about it. We did all that we could, but his heart just could not function properly."

"'He?'" Stu choked at his own words. "So, we had twin boys?" He tried in vain to hide his own sobbing. Kenna continued her inconsolable weeping.

"Would you like to hold both children and ..." The doctor's voice cracked with emotion. He could not bear to finish his sentence by adding, "and say goodbye." His nurses blinked at the wetness in their own eyes. Kenna removed her head from Stu's shirt. Her instinct was to scream. She wanted to scream and shout at the doctor, at the nurses, at the whole damn world for being cold and unfair and hard and full of pain, pain, and more pain. And despite it all, the world denied her even this one simple joy of having both children. Simultaneously thankful and lamenting, Kenna fixated her sorrow on the other son's passing.

Sensing the couple's paralysis of these events, Dr. Robards motioned to his nurses to give the newborns to them, without permission, for he believed they would be filled with a lifetime of regret if they did not have this little bit of closure for their stillborn son. Kenna's arms spread to receive the twins. One baby, warm and pink, rested in her left arm. The other, lighter and without color, lay in her right, his eyes permanently closed as if in a peaceful sleep.

The firstborn twin cooed in his warm enclosure. He marveled in silent wonder at his mother's kind face and another person's face, which appeared jagged and rough, less soft and rounded like his mother's, but just as kind. The baby noticed liquid came out of those kind eyes as both larger people regarded another smaller being on the other side of his mother. Though the baby could not possibly know the word for the scene that unfolded before him, he knew the emotion: sadness. He felt it. Only later as an adult did he know he was special.

And he felt something else: life.

Anything imbued with a life-force danced in his little mysterious mind like bright, animated constellations. The baby could feel his mother's mauve embers of light pulse with love and affection in swirling, soft curves. The nurses' essences similarly flowed around his thoughts like ethereal maroon waves of glowing substance. His father's life energy streaked with jagged intensity like fiery, red lightning. Dr. Robards' life substance cascaded upon itself again and again, flashing with orange sparks. Even the plants in the room communed inside his brain with small green bands of lighted energy. And his awareness of all this life became tangible to him; this was an energy he could control, for it was as natural to him as breathing. But there was one presence that lacked any such glow at all.

Before he knew the word 'brother,' he felt inextricably connected to this other little person on the opposite side of his mother. He also knew this person was the source of the sadness that poured from all the larger beings in the room. Specifically, he knew this little person's lack of life caused the despair. Simplistic as it may have been for an infant, all he wanted was to make her happy. Instinctively, he reached out with his mind to touch his brother's.

Darkness and serenity, like a still, motionless pond, reflected back to him. As if switching on a light, he effortlessly instilled some life-force from himself into the stillness of his brother. The blackness slowly flushed with hues of deep blues and yellows. Then something stirred inside the blank pool and shimmered.

The baby in Kenna's right arm twitched and coughed to life. Both parents jolted at this action and audibly yelped. The baby's breathing deepened, first gasping, then strengthened into a strong, even flow of air. The doctor, stunned by this medical impossibility, quickly moved to take the infant's vital signs, ordering the nurses to surround him and put the baby through some tests. The child began to cry, a wail that announced to the world he was not yet gone.

"It's a miracle! I don't know how this can be, but he lives. I, I can't believe it!" Dr. Robards, incredulous, and mortified at the thought of a misdiagnosis, stepped away from his examination to make sure he viewed a living boy who, just moments before, he had pronounced dead.

The newborn's parents, however, did not hear the doctor's words, nor did they care. Their babies lived. Reason need not be present for them. Their babies lived.

Nurse Tweedon, a young, blonde-haired girl just out of college leaned in toward the happy family.

"Do you have names picked out?" she asked. Her soft, Southern tone penetrated the bubble of joy surrounding Kenna and Stu.

"Yes," Jenna said through tears that flowed like rivers down her cheeks. She looked to her left. "Ian." Then to her right. "And Owen."

The boy newly christened as "Ian" felt the euphoria and warmth flow from his mother. This satisfied him. Soon he drifted off to slumber's playground to frolic among the life-forces he had recently discovered.

~~~~~~~~~~~~~~~~~~~~

M. Louis Lambert is a software training specialist in his day job. He lives in Ohio with his beautiful and patient wife, and their four boys. He writes primarily science fiction and fantasy, and is currently developing several short stories, a novella, and his second novel. Visit mllambertauthor.com.
~~~~~~~~~~~~~~~~~~~~

Dear Delilah

Hazel Humphreys

I'd like to say I hated you from the day I, we, were born; you, thirty-seven minutes ahead of me and already established in my new world. Inseparable, they called us. Well, actually, dear sister, I could never get away from you, from the womb to the tomb.

Delilah, the older twin, weighed in at a healthy eight pounds all pink and wrinkly as opposed to little Desdemona, younger by just over half an hour who entered life at a scrawny two pounds. "Like a bag of sugar" her father noted as she was whipped off to an incubator and her marginally older sibling wailed for attention.

That was the last bit of time to myself I ever got, sister dearest. And you even tried to ruin that.

Local Twin Makes Miracle Recovery

Little Desdemona Mayberry, of Black Rock, Massecuites, has finally come home from hospital to her family and twin sister after six months. Newborn Desdemona suffered a difficult birth due to being seriously underweight and the umbilical cord having wrapped itself around her neck, which restricted her breathing. Fortunately, doctors have confirmed that this has caused no lasting damage and Desdemona is at last reunited with her twin sister, Delilah. [Photograph: Reunited at last. Twin Sisters Desdemona and Delilah]. "I'm so delighted to have both my baby girls back with me," said Carole Mayberry, mother of the....

That was the last time my name ever came before yours. And you tried to strangle me, you little bitch.

We both endured a decade of matching fashion crimes. I kept my eye on you though. I knew you and I didn't trust you one little bit.

School was an eye-opener in the meantime. I had never realised how weird we are, two little girls looking so very alike (but if you knew us you would see I was slighter and she had more of a wave to her hair) dressed in coordinated and shocking shades of pink.

It was Billy McCall who started the rumour, that one about twins feeling the same pain. He strolled up to me during recess, with his little gang of minions, and asked me straight out, "So if I hit your twin, will you feel the pain?"

I wonder now what would have happened if he'd asked her instead. Or if he actually did ask her beforehand and she said "no."

I said "Yes."

I watched as Billy McCall walked up to my twin sister and punched her hard on the arm. She cried out.

I said "OUCH!"

And thus, a legend, in its own Elementary School Lunchtime, was born. I got a free milkshake out of it. As I drank, I winced, as it had really, *really* hurt, when it was just meant to be a joke.

You knew though didn't you, big sister? You knew that I had really felt the pain. And you wanted revenge.

So, you started starving yourself. It was subtle at first, leaving parts of meals, refusing biscuits. Biscuits I ate. At first I could match you with overeating, shovelling food down as though there were no tomorrow, neutralising your attack. I couldn't keep it up, as the more food I consumed to fight against your starvation, the more I felt sick of it all, so I stopped, but you didn't. As your face slowly became more skeletal, so did mine. Mum and Dad freaked. They took us both to a shrink, because I was getting thinner too (they presumed I was sicking up all those biscuits) and she couldn't find anything wrong with us, and charged Mum and Dad a fortune for her incompetence. They were so stressed about cash that we looked at each other and said (at the same time like the freaks we are), "Truce."

We got through junior high without incident, even combining our powers to combat anyone who dared mock us for our basic Twinnyness. In high school the problems started when we fell in love.

I spotted him first. His name was Rob and he was the coolest guy I had ever seen, but quiet and sweet and nice and nerdy with it. I met him at the library and he helped me find a book on the Nazis I had to study. He sort of bumbled about with his cheekbones and his eyes and his Edward Scissorhands hair and leather trousers, but he still came up with the goods. I took his number and he took mine, and I warned him about my evil twin (in case he mistook her for me). We agreed to meet at a coffee shop on Friday evening.

You watched me, sister dear, as I angsted over the right shade of eyeshadow and switched dresses three times.

He was early and nervous, which suited me. Over cappuccinos we chatted about films, books, and bummers, aligning ourselves subtly. And then came the million-dollar cliched question: "What's it like to be a twin?"

"I hate that question."

"Why?"

"It's like I'm not my own person and have to talk as part of two people. That's not fair."

"OK. Sorry. How do you think Delilah feels about it?" (I feel a shudder just because he says her name).

"Maybe you should ask us both at the same time. If you want to experiment on twins."

He smiled.

"Now that's dark."

"Welcome to my life."

It was a nice evening. We talked. We revealed our inner nerds. We chastely kissed goodnight.

That night I dreamed about him and me doing all manner of things together. I'd dreamt it before, but this time it was so intense I almost felt I was like losing my virginity in a dream.

Back in school on Monday and I'm hoping to see him straightaway, but have to hang on 'til lunchtime. He's not in the canteen as usual but I find him sitting under the big old yew tree on the grounds.

"Ashamed to be seen with me?" I jest.

He looks scared.

"Desi. I'm not sure I can cope with what happened last night. I mean it was wonderful, but it was too much."

"Last night?" I remember the dream. My mind starts racing ahead.

"Last night was my first time. And I think I need time to process that." He strokes my forearm gently. "I mean, you're an amazing girl, but you're way ahead of me and I need time to work out what I want."

I'm on her bed when she gets back from netball practice.

"You bitch!"

She shrugs.

"What do you mean?"

"You know! Rob! You slept with him. You bitch!"

She stretches and yawns.

"Oh, that! I guess I did you a favour. You don't want to waste your time on a guy who's so obsessed by sex."

I want to hit her, but what's the point? Instead I go to the bathroom and pick the razor blade out of dad's shaver and look at it for a long time before drawing the edge swiftly over my wrist. I hear her scream and I smile, quelling the wound with a flannel, which turns rapidly from white to red.

The door clatters open. She's deathly pale, clutching her wrist, blood bubbling through her fingers and staining the bathroom cabinet as she fetches bandage and scissors.

"Hold it out," she commands, and I obey, entranced, watching as she somehow wraps the cloth tightly over my numb arm and bids me to hold it tight whilst she compresses her own injury likewise, before finishing each makeshift dressing with a clean strip of sticking plaster. The trapped blood starts to throb and we both wince. "We can't go to hospital like this," she says matter-of-factly. "Have one of these, for the pain." She hands me a Vicodin and she pops one too. The combined effect goes to my head instantly and she grins. "Good eh? Let's have a drink!"

After the second shot of bourbon I start to laugh. She looks at me, raising her eyebrows.

"I mean! Processing! What an A-hole!" she catches my look. "Oh! He said it to you too?" I giggle into my empty shot glass. "We don't need trash like that," she says.

I wake up, wrist throbbing, in the late afternoon feeling like I had been beaten and half murdered. In the light of day, I realise I have to leave for my own sake. I pack the basics and move out.

Distance makes no difference, it turns out; in fact, oddly, it seemed to make us feel closer.

I transfer my studies north, house and cat-sitting for a cousin in Poughkeepsie; praying you won't follow me; self-medicating to numb the pain of separation that emanates from both of us. From booze and grass I move to blow and beyond. Somehow, knowing you are getting loaded too, whether you want it or not, gives me a grim sense of satisfaction. My weight plummets; you are back to your old tricks. I fight back with vast quantities of corn dogs and pizza and suck back thick shakes. Lesions form on my skin. What the hell are you doing?

I sit shivering over an assignment one wet November night when I hear a scritching sound and go to the back door to let the poor cat in. You are there, slumped in a heap, pale bony arms reaching out towards the threshold. I summon what strength I have and drag you into the kitchen, covering you in a blanket and quickly boiling up some soup. As you drink, I feel warmth returning to my own limbs, enlivening my body.

I set a makeshift bed for you on the sofa and hold you, whispering that I love you, that we will get help, that we will make things OK again, me and my beautiful sister. Finally, she lets sleep take her, her pale face relaxing with a faint smile. I take to my own bed, and as the cat kneads and purrs on my twitching feet, I slip into fitful and frightening dreams.

The covers and pillows lay crumpled on the empty sofa, the back door is wide open, and Delilah is nowhere to be seen. There's an eerie silence to the morning, a sense of blankness. And then I find the note, in a violet envelope, tucked onto my laptop, marked with a D. The message is scrambled and terrifying and there is no doubt about the doom-laden intent. There's a mention of the bridge and I switch on the TV news whilst I hurriedly dress. A mention of the Hudson Walkway draws my attention and stops my breath. Reports coming in of a young woman threatening to jump. Traffic held up, police negotiating with her. I'm about to dial 911, when I hear a series of groans, the anchor-man suddenly grim, "I'm afraid she appears to have jumped. There's police rescue crafts in the river below; let's just hope and pray to God they can get her out."

I fall to the floor, wind pushing past my ears, struggling for breath, the voices on the television suddenly muffled and distorted. Panic screams in my mind, "She's drowning herself; she's drowning us!" as blackness fills my vision.

Just as quickly, it's over; the room is peaceful again, other than the anchor guy.

"More on that potentially tragic story from Poughkeepsie as it comes in, but now over to Magda with today's weather." I switch it off.

I've never felt so alone. I can feel she's gone, and I'm amazed I'm still here, and then I remember.

Later in. Later out. I have just over half an hour before I join her, wherever she is.

~~~~~~~~~~~~~~~~~~

Hazel Humphreys is originally from Liverpool, England but lives in rural Essex where she runs a comedy night. She writes articles, short stories, and poetry for local publications and scripts for theatre groups. In 2019 her script was nominated for Best Original Script at the North Essex Theatre Guild Awards. Visit her at funnyfarmhazel.wordpress.com.
~~~~~~~~~~~~~~~~~~

The Chair

Peter Astle

We are identical twins, but we are nothing alike.

I like meat. Carl has been vegan for ten years. I like women. Carl prefers men.

It is a miracle we survived in the womb together.

Well, actually we didn't.

I hate the wheelchair.

You can dress up the funky slanted wheels with coloured wheel covers, but at the end of the day a wheelchair is still a wheelchair. People just see the chair when you're moving along sitting down.

Sometimes they look away, which is worse.

Cerebral palsy is not uncommon in twins. In fact, there is a higher risk with multiple births.

Twins have four times the chance of CP than single births and for triplets and quadruplets the risk is even higher. Often one sibling is affected and the other comes through perfectly formed.

It just so happened that I got the rough end of the stick.

Do I love my twin brother? You bet. Do I envy him? For sure.

I envy and admire him in equal measure. He has so much *drive*.

All I manage to do is sit in my chair.

Two years ago, Carl was a key player in the Fitness First initiative run by Derbyshire County Council, encouraging young people to be more active. Carl helped organise a half-marathon event that raised over two thousand pounds for young adults with cerebral palsy, while I just sat there, watching from my chair.

He got a full page spread in the *Derby Telegraph* and a segment on the local news.

I did nothing.

In the short, televised interview, he mentioned me because I am his identical twin. Identical, apart from the wheelchair, of course. He said I had been his inspiration and that I had helped a lot.

Lies. I did nothing to help with the campaign.

Carl has a supportive partner named Kevin. Two months ago, they got married. There were over a hundred people at the reception. I knew none of them.

I have no one in my life. Over the last couple of years, Carl and Kevin have tried to set me up on blind dates. Each time I bailed at the last minute.

We are thirty-five years of age. Sometimes we speak on Facebook. Carl has over four hundred "friends;" I have just twelve, most of whom I haven't spoken to for months.

Carl works for Scope, a national charity that aims to challenge negative attitudes towards disability. It used to be called the Spastic Society with a focus on cerebral palsy, but has since broadened its remit. Carl works at Derby College on Wednesdays and Thursdays, helping teenagers with a range of disabilities to accomplish their dreams.

I am on benefits because of my depression.

My therapist calls it 'survivors' guilt.'

Carl is a powerhouse. I am powerless.

Carl makes things happen. I just sit in my chair.

My chair does not have funky slanting wheels with coloured wheel covers like Carl's chair has.

My chair is an armchair. Not a wheelchair.

I came out of the womb perfectly formed.

Yes. I got the rough end of the stick.

~~~~~~~~~~~~~~~~~~~

Peter Astle hails from the U.K. He has had several short stories published in the *Derby Evening Telegraph* and *The People's Friend* and has contributed to a range of international anthologies. He recently won two book contracts with Clarendon House Publishing to publish collections of his short stories. You can find Peter at clarendonhousebooks.com/peter-astle.
~~~~~~~~~~~~~~~~~~~

Of Werewolves and Weretigers

Antaeus

In the time before man forgot about magick, there were born to the High King, Omnisire, twin sons. Their mother, Shanice, died to give them life. The first-born had golden hair like his mother, and the second-born had dark hair like his father.

The high king named the golden-haired one Dorado, which in the language of the time meant "Golden Sun." He named the dark-haired one Pascale, which translated to "Peaceful Night."

The high king's realm was vast. His kingdom encompassed most of the known world, and his subjects were happy. Omnisire's people enjoyed the gifts given them freely by the Earth Mother.

As the two boys grew, they were schooled in the arts and in the skills of warfare. The years passed swiftly, and the kingdom prospered. The young boys grew into strong, handsome men and became mighty warriors.

In time, Omnisire's sons became old enough and wise enough to be kings in their own right. It was in their twentieth year that their father called them to his throne room. He told them that he would be leaving on an extended pilgrimage to the sacred city of Lhasa. Since he would be gone for many years, he wanted to name a provisional ruler.

Tradition dictated that the elder son, Dorado, would inherit the kingdom, but their father loved them both equally. Ignoring tradition, the high king divided his realm equally between his two sons.

Neither brother was jealous of the other. For many years, all was well with the brothers as both kingdoms continued to grow and prosper. In time, Pascale married a woman named Elvira. This evil demon was really a succubus sent to him by the dark lords of the underworld. Every night while he slept, Elvira would feast on all that was good in Pascale.

It took many years, but soon there was no goodness left in Pascale. Once her transformation of the king was completed, Elvira left him and returned to her underworld palace.

With no light left in him, the evil ones found it easy to take control of Pascale's mind using dark magick. Pascale had become a pawn in the dark lords' plan to dominate the Earth.

When Omnisire returned from his pilgrimage to Lhasa, the dark forces prompted Pascale to kill his father. While the High King slept, his son crept into his chambers and slit his throat. Pascal offered his father's severed head in sacrifice to his dark lords.

... and the bloody war between the two brothers began.

⫘⫘⫘ ⫘⫘⫘ ⫘⫘⫘

King Pascale worshiped the evil gods of darkness. The "Dark King," as Pascale's subjects called him behind his back, rejoiced in the torture and mutilation of his enemies. King Pascale took great pleasure in performing many of these atrocities himself. Legend has it that he bathed in the blood of virgins so that he could live forever. His people suffered a great deal under his rule.

King Dorado was the opposite of his brother. He worshiped the gods of light and love. A kind man with a good heart, he was beloved by his people, who called him the "Sun King." This ruler took no pleasure in killing, even forgiving the assassins sent by his brother to kill him.

The Sun King was so forgiving that, after he won a

battle, he always gave the Dark King's men a choice: They could live in his kingdom peacefully or could go back to his brother's country. They always chose to stay and were the loudest of Dorado's subjects in their praise of him.

The gods of light blessed the Sun King's land, making it fertile and green. Its rivers were clear and abundant with life. His subjects prospered under this good king's rule.

The two armies fought hundreds of battles over the years. Being equal in number, one could never completely overcome the other. Soon the Dark King grew frustrated over his inability to defeat his brother. If he couldn't beat him by mortal means, he would use magick to defeat him.

Prompted by the dark gods, the Dark King ordered his wizard, Cloven, to summon up a shapeshifter from the underworld. A powerful being who could change at will into a ferocious animal to destroy his brother.

The obedient wizard made a pact with the forces of darkness. They would grant Cloven eternal life and help him create powerful allies for the Dark King in return for his soul. Fearing the wrath of the Dark King if the pact were not sealed, Cloven agreed to the bargain. Using powerful spells and dark magick, the mage summoned up a score of half-man half-beasts.

Ferocious in battle, these cursed creatures had a lifespan many times that of mortal man and an appetite for human flesh. Their wounds would heal almost immediately unless inflicted by silver. The beasts could not be killed save by the removal of their heads, or if a vital organ was pierced by silver. The wizard named his creations werewolves. "Were," which meant "man" in their language, and "wolf" for the animal that they became.

When the dark magick was done, the gods of darkness kept their promise. They bore Cloven alive into the abyss, where he would live eternally in suffering and pain.

The fiercest of the horrors conjured up by Cloven

was Magmas. He was the first of the werewolves to emerge from the cauldron of darkness, and he was the most bloodthirsty of all.

It was Magmas who taught his minions to tear out and eat the hearts of humankind, and it was Magmas that forced them to fight to the death in battle.

Legend has it that he had an appropriate punishment for any werewolf who didn't fight hard enough in battle. Magmas would chain them to a wall and devour their hearts. As it grew back, each lycan would take a turn ripping out the new heart and eating it.

Under Magmas' leadership, these "demons of the dark" devastated the countryside. They killed both man and beast without conscience.

◉◖◉◗◉ ◉◖◉◗◉ ◉◖◉◗◉

The Sun King's army was no match for these almost invulnerable creatures. Worse yet, those of his men wounded by these abominations became werewolves themselves. Thus, the number of monsters grew. Soon it became apparent to the Sun King that only the magick of light could defeat the magic of darkness.

The Sun King sought the counsel of his mage, Balain. Could he find a way to defeat these creatures born of darkness?

Balain fasted and meditated for fourteen days and nights before the gods of light gave him their aid. On the last day of his meditation, the exhausted and drained Balain was provided the answers.

The trustworthy mage immediately told King Dorado the information the gods of light had given him.

The werewolves were not invincible. Beheading would kill them quickly. The piercing of a vital organ with silver would kill each beast slowly. If a wound were inflicted by silver, the lycan would revert to human form, and it would only heal when the silver was removed. If a limb were removed by an object made of silver, it would never regenerate.

So it was silver, the metal named after the moon, that was the one thing that could hurt or stop a werewolf.

Silver alone would not be enough to entirely defeat the lycans, Balain told the king. For that, the gods had commanded him to create an army—an army of creatures who were stronger than the inhuman monsters. An army that would be able to hunt down and defeat the lycans, wherever they went.

King Dorado gave his mage permission to do whatever the gods asked of him. The next day Balain set to work, creating the beings the gods of light had instructed him to produce.

With his magick strengthened by the gods of light, the mage worked tirelessly, shaping and forming the beings the deities had designed.

Soon his spells and incantations became so powerful that they made the very earth tremble. From his blood, his sweat, and his very life energy, weretigers, the bane of the werewolves, were born. He named the powerful beings of good and light weretigers, after the animal that they could become.

The first to emerge from the cauldron of life was named Dunkeld, which meant "wolf killer." Being the first-born, Dunkeld was the strongest and wisest of his brethren. As a man, Dunkeld was light-skinned and stood well over seven feet tall. He was handsome and muscular in his human form. As a weretiger, he was pure white with mesmerizing blue eyes and unstoppable strength and speed, a powerful and dangerous killing machine.

Balain used his magick to pull two hundred weretigers from the cauldron of life before he collapsed. The king had the finest healers in the kingdom attend to the mage in an attempt to save him.

In the end, however, all magick, good or ill, has its price. The good king's mage had used the last of his own breath to give life to his creations.

So it was that Balain's spirit passed through the Gates of Ilium into the afterworld. When it arrived, the gods of light welcomed him into their number.

The Sun King, although saddened by the loss of his friend and mage, was grateful for Balain's sacrifice. As a reminder to always remember the sacrifice of their father, the king gave each weretiger a symbol of the House of Balain to wear. It was a pendant made of solid silver.

The pendant bore an oval eyelet that sat atop a crossbeam with pointed ends. This intersected a six-inch-long oval center post that tapered to a point at the bottom, like a knife.

▷◁▷◁▷◁▷◁▷◁▷◁▷◁▷◁

On the day after the funeral of Balain, the Sun King awoke to find hundreds upon hundreds of men standing in the castle courtyard. They were all former soldiers of the Dark King. The spokesman for the group was a tall and muscular man called Oman.

When the Sun King asked him what it was that they wanted, Oman told him that they were all volunteers. He said that if weretigers were anything like werewolves, a drop of their saliva in a non-fatal wound would turn a man into a weretiger as well. To a man, they wanted to fight for the Sun King as weretigers and defeat the Dark King's army of werewolves.

After meditating on it, the Sun King agreed. The next morning the weretigers disbursed themselves amongst the throng of men. Following Dunkeld's lead, the weretigers made a deep scratch on the right forearm of each man, and then licked the wound.

At first, the Sun King feared that once the weretigers tasted the blood of man, they would turn on the volunteers. He had nothing to fear. These were creatures of the light, and the taste of human blood was repugnant to them.

The volunteers fell ill for four days with high fever and delirium. The king's healers feared that they would all die. On the fifth day, the men began to improve. By the sixth day, they were on their feet. On the eighth day, they could transform.

While the new weretigers trained, the king prepared his mortal troops for battle. Needing more silver, he ordered his armorers to gather all the silver in his kingdom. When that had been done, he ordered them to melt it down and make weapons.

His smithies worked tirelessly, fashioning swords with a core of iron and an outer casing of silver. Their apprentices took the still-glowing swords from the forge and distributed them. Over half of King Dorado's soldiers now carried weapons that were lethal to werewolves.

⋈⋈⋈ ⋈⋈⋈ ⋈⋈⋈

On the day of the battle that would decide whether darkness or light would rule the Earth, the armies of the two kings met on a great battlefield. The army of the Dark King numbered in the many thousands. Most of them were werewolves.

The Sun King's army was much smaller and consisted almost entirely of men. Their contingent of weretigers numbered less than a thousand.

Only five hundred yards separated the armies when Magmas' men, their bloodlust up, shape-shifted into their wolf forms and charged. The Dark King's mortal soldiers hung back, not wanting to risk their lives when the werewolves were expendable.

The weretigers waited until the werewolves were

almost upon them before they shape-shifted. Having never seen the likes of the weretigers before, the beasts stopped their charge.

Roaring and slashing, the weretigers decimated the front ranks of the beasts. The Sun King's men, screaming his name, followed the weretigers into battle.

Sunlight gleaming from their silver swords, they stabbed and hacked at the fiendish creatures. The Sun King had instructed them to decapitate the werewolves whenever possible. Failing that, they were to try to pierce a vital organ or remove a limb.

This they did with abandon, and it was a bloodbath on both sides.

✂✂✂ ✂✂✂ ✂✂✂

Although the werewolves outnumbered the weretigers by almost a hundred to one, they were losing. The weretigers were bigger, faster, and stronger than the werewolves. They were decimating the ranks of the Dark King's accursed army.

Magmas fought like the demon from hell that he was. By chance, he learned that the way to kill a weretiger was to remove its still-beating heart. It was not an easy thing to accomplish. It took twenty werewolves attacking one weretiger to do it.

Led by Magmas, the werewolves quit fighting the humans and focused on attacking the weretigers instead. The weretigers fought valiantly, and although they killed fifty lycans for each weretiger lost, the fatalities began to take their toll.

The Sun King's men had pulled back to let the weretigers do the bulk of the fighting for the king. Once they realized what was happening to their allies, the men rallied to the weretigers' defense, and the tide of battle began to turn.

With their wounds made by the silver swords unable to heal, and their comrades falling headless around them, the werewolves soon lost the will to fight. Magmas tried to rally them, but it was to no avail. Even monsters are afraid of dying.

The savagery of the weretigers and the decimation of the werewolves demoralized the human portion of the Dark King's army. They abandoned the battlefield and fled for the safety of the castle. Magmas, now down to a fighting force of only one hundred werewolves, soon followed.

When they arrived at the castle walls, the werewolves found their entry barred and archers shooting silver-tipped arrows into their midst. Enraged, Magmas and his remaining men scaled the castle walls and killed every living thing inside. No one's life was spared—not the women, the children, or even that of the Dark King, himself.

⏾⏿⏾ ⏾⏿⏾ ⏾⏿⏾

Unaware of what had transpired before they arrived, the Sun King's army surrounded the Dark King's castle and awaited the arrival of their king.

It took four days for the Sun King to make the journey to his brother's castle. During that time, Dunkeld and a few of his men climbed one of the castle walls. They observed Magmas, his mate, Ursula, and the rest of the werewolves consuming the humans they had killed.

When Dunkeld told the Sun King what had taken place, the king was appalled. Saddened by the loss of his brother, the Sun King ordered his army back to his lands. Before he left, the king ordered Dunkeld to rid the world of the werewolves.

That night Dunkeld and his remaining 25 weretigers scaled the castle walls and attacked the lycans. In the ensuing confusion Magmas, his mate Ursula, and about a dozen other lycans escaped.

The descendants of Magmas and Dunkeld still battle today.

~~~~~~~~~~~~~~~~~~~~~

At the age of seven, Antaeus worked in a bar cleaning toilets. He wrote his first poem on a piece of toilet paper there. He is the author of *The Prepared Citizen*, a three-book series on how to react to and avoid dangerous situations and active-shooter attacks. Visit him at antaeus-books.com.
~~~~~~~~~~~~~~~~~~~~~

Blanket of Black

Kerry E.B. Black

Jaimie didn't fear the dark. In fact, she loved when her senses expanded to fill a lonely, deserted space. She imagined adding her heartbeat to the breath of the universe.

However, seldom was Jaimie alone.

Her twin brother, James, hated darkness, hated the loneliness it inspired. He disliked bold lights, too, and shied away from all company except the comfort of his twin. To her he clung as though she were a life preserver, and through her he navigated the turbulent rapids of life.

When the time came for higher education, Jaimie dove into the opportunity of an existence separate from her brother and his needs. On a busy campus she could blend into the mass of humanity, needed by none, free to explore individual thoughts and aspirations.

Guilt bogged her down at times but she sought solace in silence. When she closed her eyes after a grueling day of academia, she welcomed the blanket of black that settled over the campus. No nightlights marred her dorm room—heavy curtains blocked out streetlight glares and rowdy student nightlife, which allowed Jaimie to drift in blissful isolation until dawn.

Jaimie loved her twin. She understood his difficulty with interactions and fought the desire to chew her collar as he did his own to soothe himself. His anxiety electrified her and pulsed within her own wrists. His concerns echoed through her brain. To him, the world translated into bursts of glaring color, raucous sound, and overwhelming sensations.

She tried to share the escape of darkness, but he resisted.

"I'm not afraid of being alone," he'd shiver, shifting uncomfortably. "But when I'm in the dark, I can't tell who else is there with me."

Jaimie plunged into darkness and welcomed its cool, aloof embrace at every opportunity. As she grew accustomed to aloneness, it warmed her. She swam through its solicitous solitude with confidence.

Until James died.

Drowned.

Frightened by a dog or a wolf or a man imitating a werewolf, James ran until his feet splashed into a lake where autumn leaves obscured the surface. His terror drove him further from shore, deeper into the oblivion of water-filled lungs and oxygen deprivation.

James hated the cold, despised water. Even baths bothered him, yet in a lake on campus, he met his end.

From then on, Jaimie slept with a nightlight to hold the dark at bay. She added her voice to the cacophony on campus and ripped down the dorm-room curtains from their rods. She shivered atop a picnic table on the shore of the lake and whispered comfort and apologies to her wombmate, hoping somehow to receive succor and forgiveness in return.

Thereafter, she avoided the solitude brought by being alone, hoping thereby to avoid the accusations of those she couldn't see in the dark.

~~~~~~~~~~~~~~~~~~~~

Kerry E.B. Black writes in many genres and hails from the City of Steel, three foggy rivers, and about 450 bridges. Kerry's been published in many ezines and journals. Within the past year, she has put out two compilations of short stories, *Herd of Nightmares* and *Carousel of Nightmares*, and a novel, *Season of Secrets*. Follow her on Facebook, on Twitter at @BlackKerryblick, and on Instagram at Kerry_e_b_black.
~~~~~~~~~~~~~~~~~~~~

The Twofer Compendium

Final Call

S. P. Mount

Sam never intended to kill Sebastian . . . *per se*. He only ever meant to take an axe to his doppelganger's reckless ways so as to keep his shenanigans at bay. But things happen. Mistakes get made. And so, par for the course—just as was pretty much guaranteed about anything Sam Walker put his mind to—he'd gone way overboard.

'OCD . . . but in a good way.' Sebastian had always said about Sam.

Sam's overreaching tendency was the very opposite of Sebastian's fickle, full-on, high-energy endeavours in most everything; Sebastian's gregarious disposition flittering like an ambivalent butterfly wondering whether to nestle on a velvety leaf or get spattered by a speeding garbage truck.

Putting an end to Sebastian proved infinitely more difficult than Sam imagined, though. Even if he had all but severed his head—just like Mary, Queen of Scots, whose beheading took three swipes of an apparently blunt axe to achieve—Sebastian remained, somewhat annoyingly, not quite dead, hanging on by a tendril, enduring as a paraplegic echo of his former self.

As he considered his not-quite-successful attempt at doing away with Sebastian, the weak sound that escaped Sam's mouth could not quite commit to being a laugh. Neither could his reflection in the mirror be considered anything other than self-loathing because of the decision he'd made. He'd loved Sebastian. Hadn't he? Despite overshadowing his efforts as Sebastian had done in most everything, could he, Sam, even survive without Sebastian's vivacious personality to goad him into precarious adrenalin-fuelled situations?

The room in which he was getting dressed was better suited to a community theatre than a lower-ground-floor, three-bedroomed London flat of an erstwhile grandiose house for which it used to be its kitchens–and one Sam alone could not afford. The notion was a fabulous idea at the time, Sebastian asserting no better use of the underutilised third bedroom of the spacious apartment than to transform it into a fabulous dressing room such as actors got ready in before a show.

Framed by light bulbs 'of course,' the mirrors facilitated the application of cleverly applied 'man slap'–the term used for the unspoken *MacGyver* techniques employed by many males to subtly enhance a narrower nose here, a sultrier eye there, without the end result being so obvious it would call their masculinity into question–*MacGyver*, because they utilised anything that came to hand where cosmetics were not an option.

Sebastian was a master of duplicity, entering that room an above-average slate only to emerge with all the pizzazz of a movie star, his enhanced features looking as natural as the day he was born. But as Sam stared at his face then, trying to see something of Sebastian's in it and failing, despite it being identical, he wished Sebastian were there alongside him, g&t, ice and a slice, with just a splash of Rose's lime cordial in hand.

'But *just* a splash, mind!' he said, trying to mimic Sebastian.

Despite the fact their voices were exactly the same there was just no oomph when Sam said it. He failed to bring anything of Sebastian's effervescent flirtatiousness that told a bartender he needed to get it *just* right. There was no accompanying wink or held gaze to suggest, but only if they were good-looking enough, he might just take them home at the end of the night–which inevitably snagged him a free drink or two.

Sam frowned. Who knew he would miss Sebastian quite so much? He didn't know if he could actually bear the thought of never seeing his handsome face in that mirror again. He'd even tried to style his hair like Sebastian always did his, blowing it every which way before applying a light smattering of wax for a casual 'bed-head' look. But no, he'd tried way too hard; only succeeded in making him look as if he'd been dragged through a hedge backwards.

He could never possibly live up to anything of the ever-popular, carefree entity that was Sebastian. Not his look, and certainly nothing of his vibrant character. He suspected their mutual friends probably only put up with him because he was part and parcel of the Sebastian package. Identical, maybe, yet everyone always knew exactly who was who.

He hadn't decided what he would tell them all later when inevitably their friends asked where Sebastian was; he wasn't even in the mood to joke about it, and say something like, 'Well you know Sebastian; he ran off with the circus.'

Sam looked at a photograph of Sebastian's handsome face, so full of life, and thought it was strange how the twin thing worked. His own face only ever looked like death warmed up. They were exactly the same age, so why was it then he looked so tired and homely while Sebastian had hardly changed from their good-looking youth? In fact, Sebastian might even have become more handsome, more self-assured with age, rocking moderately current looks that somehow he always managed to make age appropriate. Yes, Sebastian definitely had skills.

Trying on the same look had seemed such a chore when Sam took a mind to dress up. The same height, build, face, *everything* except minor differences in how they styled their hair, yet Sebastian's sharp made-to-measure look hung on Sam something akin to a wet sweatshirt drooping from a wire coat hanger.

Sam's was a no-nonsense personality, according to Sebastian: 'A quiet, lone wolf type, as opposed to a *loner*.' And Sam described Sebastian as energetic, irresponsible, engaging, and witty with a blithe approach that sometimes got them both into trouble–like that one time in PJ's, their local pub, he pretended to have a slight German accent which transpired into a situation, meaning both of them had to keep the pretence up for months.

The guy who was chatting up Sebastian was, initially, only supposed to be in London on business for a few days, and so purely for a lark, Sebastian white-lied when he mentioned how nice his accent was–actually a soft Scottish brogue, lessened for having lived in England for years–that he was German. But it transpired the guy's weeklong stay extended to two months.

A sincere, intelligent person, it became increasingly difficult to admit that Sebastian's various conversations with him about a whole pretend-life of being German and moving to England had all been a bit of a joke that got out of hand. To confess it would only have been immensely insulting. And so it followed, if Sebastian were German, so too did Sam need to be, whenever they bumped into the guy.

It wasn't that Sam abhorred socializing – he didn't mind it – but he was only ever half-present sitting alone observing the crowd, smiling enigmatically at anyone who might happen to notice him despite the word 'unapproachable' stamped on his forehead. Such types impressed him, though—that level tenacity an admirable quality. Sebastian, on the other hand, ziplined across the chandeliers making sure everyone not only noticed him but zip-lined alongside him.

Despite coming to despise him, Sam always greatly admired Sebastian. He freely admitted that without him he might never have left the flat at all, or done many of the whimsical things in life he had without Sebastian's special brand of fearless bravado to encourage him—such as becoming a holiday rep in Corfu, and taking out a bank loan there was no way he could ever pay back.

And there were the people they'd met throughout their lives. Lifelong friends who loved both of them equally—albeit a motley crew that might not exist if it were not actually for the both of them. When all was said and done, the two balanced each other out—Sam definitely the yin to Sebastian's yang, reining Sebastian in, while in turn, Sebastian dragged Sam outside of his reticent tendencies.

He picked up an ornate silver photograph frame that showcased a photo of that self-assured smile Sebastian totally owned. In it, he was hanging onto Vanessa as she was to him—both Sam and Sebastian's BFF whom they met in Corfu. It struck him how young, slim, and joyful they both looked.

'*Naïve* more like,' he said.

He sighed. Why were there no photographs of him around? Everywhere he looked—except, of course, the reflection scowling in the mirror—it was Sebastian this, Sebastian that.

Whether he was pleased, or immensely sad that Sebastian would no longer be around, Sam couldn't quite make up his mind. The guilt and fear he felt for trying to get rid of him was both exhilarating and overwhelming. From then on he would need to go it alone, and that was a frightening prospect—especially as he'd just completed yet another decade.

Just what would life be without Sebastian to eclipse every single thing he did, persuading him to be irresponsible, encouraging him to let his hair down, stepping in to save him when he, Sam, inevitably faltered? But then, looking at the photographs, he did see himself there, after all. Certainly, there could be no Sebastian without Sam, either. He, Sam, had shared in all those memories, and he, Sam, cherished everything he and Sebastian ever achieved together from the very moment of their conception. Together they had been unique.

What consequence might there be for his actions, Sam had no clue. The answer would only come clear over time, but he knew he simply needed to try to live up to at least a modicum of what Sebastian had been. That much was evident.

Dipping his index finger into the ashtray to garner the slightest amount of ash that would 'undetectably' smoke his eyelids a little, Sam paused to stare at his reflection and wondered if it would be possible to 'channel' Sebastian at least *sometimes*.

'If not his infectious sparkle, then at least enough to put on a brave face to get through this party.' He mumbled, looking at his grey-tipped finger with disdain.

The ash was ridiculous. He'd long since thought so. So was the dark cherry lipstick Vanessa had left behind that Sebastian wiped his index finger over to 'undetectably' smudge a tinge of over his cheekbones and sometimes his eyelids so that only the faintest hint of what looked to be a healthy glow was evident. Sam sneered; he was too old to bother with such nonsense.

Involuntarily laughing, he examined his face in the mirror. It was handsome enough without MacGyver's help even if there were dark and ominous secrets skilfully concealed behind its countenance that, anyway, only someone as skilled as he, might detect. His aging teeth could use whitening though, he thought. Even Sebastian was having a hard time maintaining his 'Colgate smile.'

The clock behind him attempted to trick him into thinking it was 5:20 p.m., but he could not be tricked; he was Sam, not Sebastian, who might easily have been duped into having another drink or two, wasting even more time talking on the phone because he thought he had an extra hour to fritter away.

It was actually 6:40 p.m.; he had to get his skates on. He was supposed to arrive at PJ's by 7 p.m. But then, that would be made all the easier for going au naturel, instead of indulging in Sebastian's 'going out' regimen. He grabbed a Wet One and with a look of disgust wiped the ash from his finger.

'It's high time you stopped smoking, too.'

He cringed at the thought of going to the party. But even if Sebastian himself wouldn't be there, Sebastian promised weeks before on Sam's behalf that Sam most definitely would. Typical of him to make plans so far in advance for the both of them, never for one minute thinking Sam might not consent. It was just one more reason he'd needed to get rid of him.

Sam tried to convince himself not to care what people would think if he didn't show up either; it was, after all, what Sebastian would do without a second thought. Yes, he should just cancel, to hell with them all. But his bravado lasted only a split second.

He looked tired, miserable, *ugly*, all of a sudden. Had the man-slap really made such a difference, or had the effect simply been psychological? But then there were the pictures, and pictures lied only so much. He and Sebastian were identical. But as he considered the photographs and then his reflection, it was abundantly clear who was the movie star and who was the Average Joe. Or was it simply a lack of an engaging smile that made the difference?

One of them had to turn up. The party *was*, after all, in honour of their birthday. Sebastian's absence wouldn't be unusual; highly unpredictable, no one ever knew if he would make an appearance.

'But Sam . . . good old Sam . . . predictably reliable . . . would never let ya down.' His reflection sneered.

There was no way he could get through the evening pretending to appreciate it, though. His friends, most of whom were really Sebastian's, would soon start questioning Sebastian's absence, their initial excitement at seeing him fading quickly as Sam's lacklustre manner spread among them like a mysterious vapour and making them wonder why they bothered showing up—especially on a Sunday night. Sam was not who they wanted to celebrate. Not really.

Despite Sebastian being half-dead, Sam wondered if there was enough life left in him yet, so as to go to the party in his stead. But no, Sebastian's ectoplasm was already sticking to him; he didn't need to be haunted forever by allowing Sebastian to continually supersede his presence.

The phone rang. Sam shut his eyes knowing he had to pick up, otherwise it would ring repeatedly. They were checking up on him. He hated everybody and everything. He hated the phone even more so than Messenger and WhatsApp and any social media platforms that were all so very convenient yet so wholly intrusive these days. He had preferred it when it was just the phone; he could more effectively ignore that.

Sebastian, on the other hand, loved the modern world of keeping in touch. Technology had become his best friend; everybody knew where everybody else was and what they were doing at any given time in the history of the space-time continuum.

The number was private, and that always particularly irked Sam, but given the date—2nd June—even if he wanted to be left alone, he knew that was entirely unreasonable. It wasn't just about him that night; people had made an extra special effort to wish him, or Sebastian . . . whoever . . . a happy birthday.

'Sam speaking.' He said, doing his best to sound casual but was immediately aware his tone was overly curt.

No wonder people hate me.

'Where are ya, you old trout?' Graham's unabashed way of speaking with his south London accent demanded of him. 'You *better* not be in one of yer moods; the whole bar has been decorated in honour of *your* fortieth, so get your Sebastian 'ead on, and get yerself down 'ere . . . *pronto!*'

Sam stifled a snort. Despite his moodiness, his snobbery, only the people who knew and loved him not just for being Sam or Sebastian–the most obvious differing sides of his Gemini nature–but the many sides of him, could disregard his indifference and speak to him that way. Graham, in particular, was the most unpretentious person he ever knew, simply because he didn't have a clue how to be pretentious or even what the word meant.

'I take it you've changed phone numbers *yet* again?'

The tone in Sam's voice was enough to reprimand Graham for obviously getting into arrears with yet another telecommunications provider.

There was silence before Graham spoke again.

'Oh, FFS . . . Who the eff are ya tonight? Don't tell me it's boring old *Sam.*'

Sam snorted. Graham much preferred Sebastian in a social environment while respecting Sam more so when he needed advice. If he did turn up as Sam that night, Graham himself would inevitably do his best to make sure Sebastian made an entrance.

'Well, actually . . .' Sam said, 'I think, I prefer to think of myself as Sam Sebastian.'

'Whatevva the eff that means.' Graham said, never really able to comprehend Sam's alternating personalities even after twenty years. 'I don't care who the eff you are, just get yerself down 'ere.'

But suddenly Sam knew exactly 'wtf' he *did* mean.

'I'll see you in an hour. Mine's a pint of lager with a g&t chaser . . . ice and a slice with a. ...'

'Yeah, yeah, yeah, a splash of frikkin' Rose's. Just get over the miserable mood you're in . . . Ya *misog* . . . An' get down 'ere,' he said, quickly hanging up.

Instead of the snappy outfit he'd picked up in Rome and never had occasion to wear in his real life, Sam opted for a slightly distressed T-shirt and faded blue jeans. Special birthday or not, it was, after all, only a Sunday down at his local. He smiled into the mirror. His dark, slightly greying hair, not quite up to Sebastian's standard, suddenly looked great anyway. A demure sparkle commandeered eyes that were no longer dull and lifeless, but alluring and bright.

'Good to meet you, Sam Sebastian." He said, admiring his newfound persona with a level of modesty Sebastian himself would be proud of. 'You took your time getting here.'

'Sebastian put up a good fight,' his reflection said.

Putting a cigarette to his lips a la James Dean, a raised eyebrow Sam had never seen before appeared to judge him.

'*Ye–ah*, no. There will be none of that anymore. Now go flush them . . . and get rid of that filthy ashtray, too.'

~~~~~~~~~~~~~~~~~~~

Intrepid world traveler, animal lover, and perceived oddball, S.P. Mount's natural instinct is to 'go against the grain' in life. His lifelong friends both love and hate that about him. He adores the magic of technology, and in storytelling, yesterdays composed with the infinite possibilities of tomorrows inspire his artistic sensibilities. amazon.com/author/spmount.
~~~~~~~~~~~~~~~~~~~

You're Not Laughing Now

KM Dailey

Marie Weston let out the hair in her bun, sighing as she began to load up the dishes from brunch before Jack could get to them. It had been a long week for him. He deserved a break, but he wouldn't let her help him with his chores if possible. Good kid—if you could call him a kid at all. She'd ask Sophie to help, but Marie had enough of a headache without dealing with that inevitable fight.

She closed the dishwasher door and pulled back the curtains from the window over the sink. The sunlight illuminated the peeling yellow wallpaper, the marred wooden cabinets, the refrigerator covered with family photos she'd never gotten around to framing, the tiled counter and all its chips and stains.

Marie sighed and took a few steps toward the living room when she heard shouting and arguing coming from the dining room. Always, the shouting. She hung her head, closed her eyes, silently counted to ten, and headed back toward the dining room to check on Sophie and Jack.

Sophie's therapist had recommended that Sophie and Jack play some games, and given them a stack of simple games to try. For the past two months, they spent every Saturday afternoon playing one of these games. Seemed to Marie they had caused more argument than anything else, but at least they were spending time with each other.

"I did *not!*" Sophie shouted, throwing one of the game pieces down as she stood. "I did *this!*"

"You are such a bad sport." Jack's voice was calm, and he remained seated.

"You're cheating!"

"All right, all right!" Marie shouted over them. "What's going on?"

"I won and he's cheating!" Sophie shouted.

"How does the game work?" As far as Marie could tell, it was just a bunch of red circular counters.

"It's pretty simple." Jack gathered all the counters from his side and from Sophie's into a pile in the center. "You have all these pieces in the center of the table. On your turn, you can pick up either one or two. Whoever picks up the last piece loses. So you're trying to leave one tile at the end of the game, so that the other person has to pick up the last tile. It's just logic."

"OK, so what happened?"

"He *cheated*!" Sophie yelled.

"How do you even cheat at this game?" Jack turned to Marie.

"Sophie keeps winning. And every time, she laughs in my face."

Marie glanced from one wide-eyed face to the other. It never ceased to amaze her how her kids could be so mature in some ways and so childish in others. In some ways, it gave her hope—mostly, though, it was just exhausting.

"Play through a game. I'm going to watch."

The two quieted down, and the game began. Sophie's hand shot out to grab her pieces when she made her moves, while Jack's turns were slow, deliberate.

Four pieces remained, and Sophie's hand hovered above them. If she took one piece, Jack would take two, leaving her with the last one. If she took two pieces, Jack would take one, still leaving her with the last one. Checkmate.

Good. This would force her to lose, force her to learn to lose.

Sophie dropped her hand on the table, never taking

her eyes off the pieces.

"This game is stupid."

"Finish it, Sophie." Jack kept his eyes locked on the game.

Sophie brushed the four remaining counters off the table. Marie bent down to pick them up, but Jack beat her to it, dropping the four on the table.

Marie let out her breath, straightening up.

"Finish the game, Sophie. Yes, Jack is probably going to win. And it's OK."

Sophie dumped the pieces she had taken in earlier moves into the center of the table. "New game."

"No, finish this one." Marie brushed all of the pieces back toward Sophie until four remained in the center.

Sophie slowly fingered a single piece. She slid it over to her own side.

That was that. Marie shifted her weight and crossed her arms, bracing herself for angry shouting or demands for a rematch. At least Sophie couldn't claim Jack had cheated this time.

Jack took a single piece, eyeing Sophie's face. Marie breathed in to speak, to ask why he was letting her win, but let it out. She smiled a bit—she had underestimated him.

Sophie's eyes never left the pieces. She slowly took one piece. Then Jack took the last one, losing the game. Marie's heart swelled at his kindness.

Silence, as Sophie stared at the table before her. Perhaps his compassion had backfired—the victory was all too false. Sophie wrinkled her nose, then looked up to meet Jack's gaze.

Jack looked her in the eye and said, "You're not laughing now."

Ah. Not compassion.

"OK, that's enough." Marie swept up the pieces from both of their sides. "You've both been cooped up long enough. Both of you, go grab your skateboards, spend some time outside."

"Sure," Jack said, but his eyes never left Sophie's, and Sophie's remained fixed on his, until they both stood from the table and disappeared down the hall.

Slowly, Marie swept up the game pieces and dropped them into the bag. She had gotten it wrong. Sophie wasn't the one to keep an eye on. Sophie could be violent and temperamental—Marie had gotten four calls this month from the school principal about Sophie fighting with other students—but she was predictable. Unreasonable, angry, and tyrannical, but in the end, very simple.

But Jack. No part of Marie considered why Jack was always wanting to spend time with Sophie. It had seemed so obvious to her, second nature. She had projected her own familial emotions onto him, believing them to be part of the natural, universal human experience.

How could she have known better? How could she have guessed that every time she thought she knew what was going on behind those beautiful, round brown eyes, there would be a new surprise in store? Days when Marie would fight with Sophie for hours about getting her homework done, and Jack would convince her with a word. Moments when Sophie would randomly apologize for something, and Jack would deny having anything to do with it. Times when Jack's kindness punished Sophie more severely than Marie's parenting ever would.

Sophie yelled and nagged and fought while Jack was gentle and patient and calculating; and somehow, he always, always got his way. He wore emotions on his sleeve, but they weren't his emotions. Jack listened and obeyed Marie, and took care of his sister—but at what cost?

"Everything all right?"

Marie jumped, and turned around.

Ashton smiled and lifted both hands to half height.

"I should know better than to sneak up on you when you're staring off into space like that."

She let out her breath. His short dark hair was spiky from his shower, his face smoothly shaven. She wrapped her arms around him, breathing in his soapy scent.

Ashton rubbed her shoulders and pulled her in tighter.

"How's the cold?"

"Better. The sore throat is gone."

"Glad to hear it." Ashton let go and looked her in the eye. "How are the kids doing?"

"Um, pretty well, I think." Maybe she would talk to him about it later. Probably not.

He took a step back and held her at shoulder length.

"What's on your mind, Marie?"

Marie glanced out the open kitchen window. The twins coasted along the sidewalk on their skateboards, Jack remaining close behind Sophie. She laughed and he half-smiled, but neither spoke as they skated beyond view.

Marie sighed and shook her head.

"Nothing, dear. Headache is just acting up again."

<center>~~~~~~~~~~~~~~~~~~</center>

KM Dailey has been writing novels, short stories, and poetry since her preteen years. Her work has been published in *Daily Science Fiction* and *Deep Magic*, among other publications. You can find updates on her writing and other adventures at kmdailey.com.

Dating in the 5's

Matt McGee

SETH, MONDAY AFTERNOON

He's sitting in an Arby's when she walks in. Mid-50's, pushing 230, resigned to the elasticity of rayon. Beige slacks give room to breathe and digest lunch, and what girl doesn't want breathability? Judging by the cardigan and her choice of two-for-one roast beef and cheddar sandwiches, he imagines cats back at the house.

It's 4:56 p.m. Probably snuck out a few minutes early from her desk job in one of the medical back offices around the corner. It's Monday; a weekend's DVR'ing awaits, Purina cans need opening, litter boxes wait to be changed. First, a couple of familiar sandwiches like the ones her mother/father once bought on summer evenings, there'll be a diet soda in the fridge, and in the freezer, ice cream. Gonna be a few hours before that seal gets broken, though.

At her age, Seth is guessing 54, there are good memories of great partners but it's been years since she had a lover. And she's looked. Bars. Been out with office girlfriends on Friday nights. There's always Heather, the pretty one who attracts the guys. One will buy the drinks; he'll have a friend who will show a mild interest. But she knows he's just being a good wingman. She'll let him flirt, she'll smile, laugh at the right time, but as soon as he sees his buddy making his move the wingman will leave her with a handshake. God, she hates handshakes. No one who shakes your hand is going to rock your bed. Ever.

And it's Monday. There will be no signing on to a dating app or an early-week drink at a pub with a friend or co-worker, no matter how badly they need to talk. Just the two-for-one sandwiches, and off to bed with a binge-watch.

That's Seth's cue.

She takes her cup from the cashier and waddles toward the soda fountain. Seth's iced tea is half-full. Empty enough. He'll start a line; he's far enough away to not be creepy, close enough to be sensed.

"I'll be done in just a sec," she apologizes.

"No hurry." He'll watch her fumble a lid.

"I'm such a klutz."

"I see you like to drink. I like drinking, too. We should hang out."

It could be the most random thing someone has said to her all day, maybe for weeks. Her shoulders perk and there's a gentle thrust in her chest.

"Just getting my diet soda."

"Diet! Why do the pretty ones *always* think they need to lose weight?"

It is so bad. So corny. Almost dumb.

Two hours later the texting starts. An hour later she sends her address. He's lucky; her muscle memory isn't lost despite the years it's been since she's stretched out with a new partner. Fact is, no one asks anymore.

"Almost ten years," she says. It makes her all the more eager. She'll say she's doing it just for fun. But oh, the stories that will go around the water cooler tomorrow.

No, of course he doesn't give his real name.

AUBREY, MONDAY EVENING

The place is called Freddy's Steakburgers. They aren't cheap. It attracts a certain kind of guy. Guys who pay attention.

He's sitting at a table beside the ice cream cooler. Cakes and custard for hot days. The corner table gives him a chance to read. Oh, and he likes her chest. He's looked over twice. Perfect.

"Have you read all his books?" He looks up. She's pointing at the cover.

"Most. You like Grisham?"

"I liked *The Firm* like everybody else. Mostly I liked *The Pelican Brief*. Big Julia Roberts fan."

"I liked her in *Mystic Pizza*.'"

"Didn't see that one."

"It was a while ago. Her first film, actually." Aubrey lifted her cell. "Mystic Pizza," she typed aloud. Then she set the phone back down. His move.

"I like your shirt," he points. She had to look down. Sometimes, even a couple of hours after leaving the house she'll have no idea what she wore. The shirt has the Polaroid logo. The snug fit and horizontal rainbow stripes help the C-cups.

"It belonged to my dad." Lying. Actually, retro from Kohls. "My dad gave me one of those cameras when they first came out. You could snap pictures anywhere and not have to take film to the drug store."

"I'll bet that led to all kinds of naughty ideas." He smiled at his book.

"It did." She held up the cell.

"Now we have these. *And* the same naughty ideas." What gave him away, aside from his eating completely alone? The shaved bald head, the only haircut a guy his age could still have and look remotely badass. His maroon jacket was stylish 15 years ago. The belt pressing into the belly keeps it looking flat in his mirror. The rest of the world sees better.

"Let me get your number. We can talk about books sometime."

"Or watch *Mystic Pizza*."

"Sure! I think I still have the VHS in a box somewhere in the garage."

"You have a player?"

"Yeah. Haven't used it for a while, but ... yeah it's there."

"Well, text me." He's looking at his screen now.

"Number, please."

She's relieved when he doesn't shake her hand before leaving. God, she hates handshakes. He goes outside to a motorcycle. Triumph 900. Made to look retro for people who still want reliability. *Atta' boy, hold onto those* Easy Rider *roots.*

He texts around seven. *Loved chatting this afternoon. Found Mystic Pizza! Haven't seen it in forever! What day is good for you?*

How about now?

Pause. Then *Yeah, cool.* He sends an address. When he presses PLAY she leans against his forearm. The Triumph has kept them firm. It's Archie and Veronica in the theater; he 'stretches,' puts his arms around her shoulder. She leans a little harder and his hand goes right to the Polaroid stripes. Second base before the credits are done.

A few minutes later she's straddling, letting him pull the retro shirt over her head, helping him with his. There's a scar down the middle where a surgeon had his way. He's not bad in bed and she still doesn't know his name.

He didn't ask hers.

CARL'S JR., NEAR CLOSING

The dining room stays open late. Local homeless milk endless coffee refills before rolling packed carts into neighborhoods where locals don't roust them. Bar trolls quit early, and since it's Monday there's plenty of the Ones-and-Dones, the beer and game buddies, a quick drink with coworkers. A few have swiped right and took someone up on a free Monday night meal before claiming an early morning as a get-out of-here-quick card.

The one thing they all have in common is that they didn't eat enough.

Seth comes through the door at 8:58 p.m. He never got the office worker's name. He capitalized on all her pent-up energy, skills dusted off for the night. A great start to the week. He places an order, takes a number card. His favorite seat at a longer worktable is open, waiting.

Aubrey had wanted to hit the drive-thru, but something told her to park the car. The Freddy's guy had been snoring when she left.

She enters at 9:03 p.m., a dead cellphone and charger in hand. She places her order and sees only one other person at the worktable. He's in the corner. He looks OK. Too good-looking for her current tastes. She goes to the side opposite him.

"Mind if I impose on this end?" Seth waves, caught with a mouthful of burger. "Impose away."

She'd pulled a red hoodie out of her trunk and yanked it on just in case Carl's air conditioning was on the uncomfortable side. And it is. She takes a seat, pulls the hood down. It usually gives a certain off-to-grandmas, come-get-me, big-bad-wolf-look.

Seth, in his faded red Quicksilver flannel, had the look of a bricklayer on his day off.

"Look at us," she says. "We could be twinsies."

"I think we are. Yes. Glad you got the red shirt memo."

Aubrey peeks under the table for an outlet, plugs in the charger, and lets the green dial spin. She wouldn't be online soon.

"I hate going Amish."
"Amish?"

"When your phone's discharged. Amish." Seth raises a brow. Cute, but not his current taste.

"Oh, I see. I thought you were going to pull a white bib over your head and start plowing or something."

"No," she smiles, "the day's plowing's been done."

Seth wipes mustard from his fingertips.

"Being a total stranger, I won't ask."

"I'm not ashamed." When he doesn't respond, she asks, "How's your night been?"

Seth crumpled his empty wrapper.

"All the day's plowing's been done."

"You too, huh."

"Yep."

"Wife's birthday?"

"Not married. Even then, once-a-year nookie doesn't sound appealing."

"'Once-a-year nookie?' Is that a thing? Geez, I'm glad I never married."

"Nymphomaniac?"

"You wish. No, I was dating someone I was really into. Not gonna lie, he was hot. I wanted him pretty much all day long."

"Wore him out, did you?"

"I was well on my way." Aubrey shakes her head. "You know what good-looking people have more than anything?"

Seth raises a brow.

"Options."

"Yeah."

"Once he realized how many women were throwing signals his way, not just 'trying to be buds' as he put it, he started ... tuning in."

"Damn those good-looking people."

"You know what I learned?"

"What?"

"Not to date good-looking people." Seth smiled genuinely.

"So lately you've been …"

"Dating in the fives."

"Totally! And aren't they almost always down?"

"Always. Sad. I don't know how people go through life without love. And by love, I mean the touch of another human." Seth nods.

"I know how."

The cashier arrives with Aubrey's food, reclaims the plastic order card and offers ketchup. Aubrey says "no thanks" then slides a few fries from their sleeve into her jaws.

"You're into the Beyond Meat thing too, I see."

"Tastes just like it. I actually like it better than hamburgers. And I love hamburgers. You?"

Seth holds up the two empty wrappers.

"Continue," she says. "You were saying about being abstinent."

"For a while, I – "

The restaurant's side door slams, and a thin young woman appears. The rolled-up cuffs of her shorts almost expose her. A thin white top allows black lace to peek through.

She sees Seth and says, "Hey!"

Seth looks.

"Hey, Christy."

"You have such a good memory. How are you?"

"Excellent! What's new with you?"

She talks; he doesn't hear. He sees the caved-in cheeks, soot-stained fingertips, bulky male escort. Christy tells brief stories through smiles then excuses herself. Seth watches her enter the men's room. The bulky escort moves beside the door, hands clasped professionally.

"Someone you used to know," Aubrey asks, burger in her jaws.

"I used to help her out."

"Help ...?"

"Not my type."

"Young."

"She looks young but ... you know. The drugs are thinning her out. We all go through a party phase. Some people never come out."

"I get you. I –"

"Aubrey!"

A young man with a dirty, muscular swagger appears from the restaurant's other door. He wears a reflective yellow/green vest bearing his nametag and the logo of a local towing company.

"Sean."

"You remembered my name. I must make an impression."

She points at his shirt.

"Oh, yeah. How are you?"

"Not bad."

Sean spots the bulky escort beside the men's room.

"Cool. Be right back, yo; gotta use the little boy's room."

Seth and Aubrey watch as Sean makes eye contact with the doorman. Their hands meet quickly. Sean goes in. The escort looks Seth and Aubrey's way.

Aubrey looks at Seth. His eyes dip, and he sips his drink.

"I'm sorry."

Seth shakes his head. He shrugs.

"Not everybody knows how to accept help," she says.

"Some people accept it and move on to the next sucker."

"Hey. No one's a sucker for trying to help their friends." Seth rolls his eyes.

"Supposed friend."

"If she were a mechanic, and she opened a shop, would you patronize it?"

"What?"

"You heard me. Would you go into her shop to get your car fixed?"

"If she were a mechanic. And qualified. And wasn't going to break stuff. What does this have to do with anything?"

"It's hers to sell. I mean, shoot, I'm judging. I don't think Sean's the type who's gotta pay for it, but hey, his life, his body, right?"

"What's your point?"

"Her life, her body." She picks up her burger. "Your life," she says his way, "your body."

"OK, that's total crap."

"Look. We just met. I know your name because she said it. You're a good-looking man, Seth. Is dating fives a good use of your time?"

"Said the woman dating fives."

"And I've questioned myself long and hard."

"So why do you do it?"

"Honestly? Because some days you just need to feel better about yourself. And hooking up with some lonely guy ... it's like those two old women in *Arsenic and Old Lace*."

"They killed people and buried them in the basement!"

"Out of mercy."

"Is that the next step?"

"Killing guys? No. Of course not. But when it was time to go off to the booby hatch, they went happily along."

"So lemme get this straight. You're saying that dating fives is just some kind of lovely parade on your way out?"

"Maybe."

Seth looked at her sideways.

"Ooookay."

"There are worse ways to go than hooking up with a lot of people, a few of whom might actually remember me fondly."

"What do you mean? Where are you going?"

Aubrey looked away. Seth was smart enough to wait.

"What's near here," she begins.

"Here? Starbucks. McDonald's. Vons ..."

"Keep going ..."

"Church," he points, "hospital ..."

She points at him, then her nose.

"Are you saying you're going to start dating the terminally ill?"

"I'm saying I am the terminally ill."

Seth looked right at her. Mute. She threw her arms up.

"We all gotta go sometime!"

"What ... what is it?"

"It's cancer, Seth."

"Jeez."

"It's cervical. It's not good. OK? So, all that plumbing's going to come out soon. My treatments are up the street. That's how I know about this place."

"Wow. I figured you just came in here to meet dudes." She laughed.

"So, is it ... are you ...?"

"There's a fifty percent chance of survival. We didn't catch it very early."

"I thought ... I mean, don't you girls go into the gyno all the time?"

"Not all of us can afford to do that."

"Planned Parenthood?"

"Sure. Did I go? No. Do I regret it? Of course I do. I'd rather have the chance of living a long life. But as it stands it's fifty-fifty."

"Jeez. That's. I'm sorry."

"For what?"

"For everything. All the obvious stuff. The pain, for one."

Aubrey points over her shoulder.

"Any worse than the pain that *that's* giving you right now?"

"I'll get over that."

"Pain's pain, Seth. Mine's just more terminal." Aubrey slouches forward, elbows on the long table. Her phone said 17%. She could turn it on if she wants. She doesn't want to, yet.

"What did you mean when you said Christy's not your type?"

Seth has a little trouble regaining his balance.

"It means ... OK, it's like this all right? Guys, when we're young, like in our teens, we think we need to hook up with everything that walks. Getting turned down is like taking a meat cleaver to our egos. But what happens? We eventually figure out a crucial piece of Guy Wisdom."

She waits.

"We have Friendzones, too. And 97% of all women are going to fall into it. Of the remaining three percent, most of the time we're going to fall into *their* Friendzone. The trick is to not let getting turned down mess with your self-worth. I know guys who have literally gone nuts because they think women don't want them anymore."

"You just described my fives."

"Well ..."

"So where do I fall?"

Seth was caught in her headlights.

"Seriously?"

"Yeah."

"Total Friendzone."

"Based on ..."

"Seriously? If I thought you were hot I couldn't talk to you like this."

"Fair enough."

"I don't usually just converse like this with people."

"By 'people' you mean women."

"And there's attraction. You feel it or you don't. And it comes fast."

The men's room door opens. Christy steps quickly across the dining room, escort in tow. She doesn't say goodbye.

"Speaking of ..." Aubrey mumbles. "Remind me again why she isn't your type."

"It isn't obvious?"

"Too addicted?"

"Nope. Too skinny."

Aubrey shifts in her seat. Her eyes scan the tabletop. She collects her paper waste and tray. She heads for the trashcan.

"For the record," she says, "you're a three-percenter. You're better looking than the guys I date and far more in tune. But knowing how certain you are about the Friendzone, I know when to cut my losses. So, here." Aubrey reaches into her purse and slides a business card onto the tabletop.

"It has my email."

"And your cell."

She smiles gently, puts a hand on her purse strap, and turns toward the door.

"When you call, just say, 'Hey, it's your Five-Dating Twin.'"

"How will you know?"

She smiles." I'll know."

"Hey," he calls. She stops. He holds up two fingers, crossed.

"Fifty percent," he smiles.

She holds up two crossed fingers.

"Goodnight, twinsie," she says, turns and leaves.

Outside, the streetlamps beam down on her like a mild sun she remembers. It had once liked her, but that was back on easier days before things got so complicated.

~~~~~~~~~~~~~~~~~~

Matt McGee writes short fiction in the Los Angeles area. "Advice? It's easy to go weeks, months without being home and just live in fast food joints. Also, the best way to welcome yourself into someone's friendzone is to shake their hand." When not typing he drives around in a vintage Mazda and plays goalie in local hockey leagues. He can be found on Facebook: Matt McGee 7334.
~~~~~~~~~~~~~~~~~~

The Tyndarids

H. E. Casson

"Did you know it only takes eight pounds of pressure to rip an ear off?" Geri Gulcharan shifted her weight from one foot to the other, clutching the podium. "It's true."

Twenty-three people had come to her twin brother's funeral, almost all of them women. Two were looking at their phones. She pushed on.

"When Jerry and me were kids, we read it in one of those bookfair books. *One Hundred Crazy Facts,* something like that. Jerry had all of those books. *Guinness. Ripley's.* If there was a guy smoking a hundred cigarettes on the cover, Jerry had it."

Now three women were on their phones. Geri cleared her throat and looked at the door, hoping to see her mother. She didn't want to be alone when people started offering condolences.

"Anyway," she hunted for her train of thought, "after we read it, we got it stuck in our heads. How could eight pounds pull a body part right off? Jerry says, let's test it. He was already a scientist."

Two of the women looked up from their phones. The short one, wearing all black, even to her pantyhose, raised her eyebrows. This was probably more juice on Jerry than All Black Lady had gotten the whole time they'd dated; something new for her social media memorials and suicide-hotline meme posts.

"So, he was on the top bunk and I was on the floor and I just grabbed his ear and lifted my feet up off the ground and ... boy, the book was pretty close to right. There was so much blood. He was crying. I was crying. Our mom was screaming."

Again Geri checked the door, as though saying her title might summon her, like a demon.

"But the next day, he was all patched up. I was still so upset and what does he do? He gives me his bear that mom brought to the hospital, the one with the bandage on its ear. He says he never meant to make me sad. Make *me* sad? That's my brother. That's my twin. Jesus, Jerry. I love you. I'm sorry you're gone."

Geri retreated to a pew at the back to listen to All Black Lady sing a current pop song her brother wouldn't have known or liked. Halfway through verse two, Annette Gulcharan finally arrived, a ratty shoebox tucked under her arm. She paused, closed her eyes and crossed herself with her free hand, even though she wasn't religious. It was a move she'd seen on TV and churches always seemed to demand some kind of ritual. She did a wobbly bow at the minister, almost dropping the box, and turned left and right three times before she noticed her daughter.

"Excuse me." Annette managed to bump each person as she squeezed her way into Geri's aisle. "Excuse me. Excuse me. I'm his mother. I know. You're so sweet. He was an angel, I know. Excuse me."

Why hadn't her mother worn a dress or even a decent pair of tights? Instead she was wearing her familiar worn denim. For once she'd thrown on a blouse instead of a band T-shirt, but it had yellow stains around the armpits and collar. Though it improved her look, she still smelled of patchouli and pot.

By the time Annette plopped down next to her only remaining child, the minister had begun summarizing his eulogy. It was clear he'd never met Jerry, something Geri knew because she'd been the one to hire him.

Despite this, her mother felt the need to add in "So true," "That's exactly what I said," and "Amen!"

It was the last one that made Geri stand to go.

"Wait!" Annette grabbed her wrist, shoving the box at her. "This is for you!"

She wanted to thank her mother, promise she'd call, share a hug. If she opened her mouth, she knew, all that would come out were hateful words or uncontrolled howls. Biting back both, she walked out of the church, leaving her mother to deal with the mourners and the minister. *She'll probably enjoy the attention*, Geri thought.

Back at her bachelor apartment, Geri put the shoebox down on the table. She poured an entire bottle of tequila into a pitcher with some orange juice, and sat down across from the shoebox. It was from a pair of Jordans Jerry must have owned in high school. On it, written in faded Sharpie, was both of their names.

He had asked their mother once, after the third day of kindergarten — the third day they'd been mocked for having the same name — why she'd called them Geri and Jerry.

"I didn't know I was having twins! I only picked one name," followed by the ubiquitous laugh, the one that sounded like gargling sand.

It was the same laugh she'd given when they'd asked who their father was. Geri took three deep sips of tequila, ignoring the rubbing alcohol smell and enjoying the stream of heat down her throat. Shored up, she opened the box.

The first thing she saw was math. Her jaw tightened. Jerry lived for numbers and she'd dutifully tried to understand, but it was like magic to her. The box had her name on it, though, so this math meant something. Maybe it was the note. She wanted a note, an explanation for why Jerry had stood on a bridge and, rather than call her, let his body drop and break on the wooded path beside the highway. The math had one word scribbled on the top: Trajectory.

"Jesus, Jerry."

She pulled the sheet out and laid it on the table. One by one, she removed clippings, photocopies, scribbled scraps on the back of flyers.

The Yogi Milarepa, once a murderer, attained levitation by meditating on the third eye.

Saint Francis of Assisi could float three to four cubits off the ground.

Simon the Sorcerer, the Bad Samaritan, could fly at will.

Shirdi Sai Baba levitated in his sleep.

And along the margins, more notes she could not understand.

9.8m/s^2

Balducci

$\rho=PM/RT$

Daniel Dunglas Home

Under it all, a notebook with her name on the cover.

🧬🧬🧬

How much had she read and how much had she dreamed? She woke at 2:11, tasting vomit and tequila, trying to piece back together what she had learned.

Jerry thought he could fly.

In the notebook he told the same story she had told at the memorial, only he remembered it differently. In his telling, he had tried the trick first.

Geri sorted through her memories, trying to recall the experiment. Had he gone first, lifting up his feet and holding onto her ear? Had he really floated? Was she unharmed because he was able to do something that, even by his own theoretical framework, should be impossible?

In her memories she found a scratchy blanket with Smurfs on it, pilled from a hundred washes. There was the smell of the apartment, a cross between wet rot and new paint. She thought of the bunk bed, where they took turns lying on their backs on the bottom bunk and pressing their feet up on the top to give each other rides. The sound of plywood hitting metal bars. The feeling of foam-filled plush won at school fairs.

Jerry whispering conspiratorially, "Just let me try. If It hurts, I'll let go right away,"

Then, the dream.

She stepped off the bridge. It wasn't so much that she'd flown, as that she'd fallen slowly, willing a space between herself and the forest path, pressing up off the earth. Distraction would mean death. The space was a physical thing. Slowly she lessened it, like letting air out of a balloon. Then she was on the ground beside the highway. Cars rolled past, un-noticing. She tried re-inflating the balloon and was up by the trees. A leaf, still wet from the rain that afternoon, brushed against her cheek. It was real. She was real. She was flying.

"It only works when we're together, like our power is split in half." Jerry floated among the branches, "But if I'm gone ..."

With that, he fell, smashing tree limbs, tearing his clothes. His impact caused a too-quiet thud, like he was made of nothing at all.

Once she was sure she was awake, Geri grabbed the shoebox, jamming it into a used shopping bag, and slipped on her runners. The night was chillier than she'd thought, but she didn't go back for a coat.

What are you doing? His voice scratched at her brain.

Killing yourself.

"Or flying." She said it out loud.

She stood where the bridge met the road. College students were leaving the pizza shop, shouting, taking up space the way young men do.

Every other storefront was dark, but the streetlights made it feel like a movie set. Geri tried to steady herself. The tequila threw off her balance like a high fever. She fought with her eyes to keep them still, yet the bridge seemed to sway, caught in a wind.

Where had he jumped from? There were no footprints or crime scene tape. With no guide, she used the dream, spotting the tree he had fallen through on his way to the ground. Shoes squeaking on the wet cement, she wrapped both hands around the safety wires and used them to pull herself up onto the cement barrier. She pulled the box out of the bag and let the bag go. It was lifted by a breeze, circling her like a bug in summer.

Cars went by, full of people who could not fly. Geri took one step forward, sacrificing balance to empty air.

The ground had some small give. She had not anticipated that. It looked so hard from above. It seemed to wrap around her like a cocoon.

Fluttering down like autumn leaves were dozens of papers, all with notes in Jerry's hand. His theories, false beliefs spelled out in a manic scrawl, were now more litter on the side of the road.

You're not dead. Her own voice this time.

"I'm not dead." She repeated it out loud.

She rolled onto her side, pulled up on her knees and finally stood. She looked at the bridge and was overwhelmed with vertigo. How had she travelled so far so quickly?

Jerry couldn't fly. He was dead and gone. She screamed up at the bridge, pulling sound from the soles of her feet to the top of her head. She couldn't fly, either.

She couldn't fly, but she could fall.

She could fall and live. Her brother could dangle his whole weight from her ear and not tear it off.

The box had been crushed under her body, but the bag had landed, unharmed, nearby. She wiped her eyes on her sleeve, picked up the bag and started to walk toward the woods. She gathered pieces of paper, articles, theories, photocopies, all with notes written in her brother's hand.

~~~~~~~~~~~~~~~~~~~

H. E. Casson is a Toronto-based writer whose works have appeared in *Apparition Lit, Stonecrop Review, Room, Fireweed* and *Cricket,* among others. They value kindness, poetry, and coffee—usually in that order. This story is dedicated to their brother Pablo, who always survives to fly another day. Visit hecassonwrites.wordpress.com/about.
~~~~~~~~~~~~~~~~~~~

Lost and Found

Diane D. Gillette

Abilene was sweating inside her winter gear by the time she rang her mother's doorbell. For a moment she worried it was one of her mother's outing days, and she cursed herself for making her mother remove the spare key she used to keep under her welcome mat. The key Abilene had to her mother's house was at home in the kitchen junk drawer because Abilene had a bad habit of losing things. Keys. Mittens. Her phone. Her jewelry box had an entire section dedicated to mismatched earrings whose mates had gone missing. Her childhood cat. Her last two jobs. Every man she'd ever cared about. Ryan was simply the latest. She wasn't even surprised anymore. She supposed she'd be losing her mind next.

As thoughts of loss swirled around her now-pounding head, her mother cracked open the door.

"Sweet mercy, child, what are you doing here in this weather? It's colder than a well-digger's behind out there," her mother said as she pulled the door open and ushered Abilene inside.

"I had a doctor's appointment this afternoon, so I walked over when I was done."

"That must be at least three miles," her mother scolded. "Where's Ryan?"

"It's less than two miles. And he had to work." Abilene assumed she was correct on both counts.

"Well, sit down. I'll make you some tea and you can warm up some before Ryan comes to get you. He is coming to get you, right?" Her mother managed to give her a hard look over her shoulder while simultaneously filling the tea kettle and pulling a mug out of the cabinet. Abilene wondered if that level of multitasking was a general mom-skill or one specific to Gloryanne.

"I have some news about the baby," Abilene deflected.

The mug and the kettle both hit the counter, her mother's hands clasped tightly over her heart.

"Please tell me my grandbaby is healthy."

Abilene smiled. At least one person was excited about this pregnancy.

"As far as I know," she said. "But it looks like you're going to have two grandbabies."

Her mother turned, took two steps forward and gripped the back of the kitchen chair.

"Twins?" she said softly. "Well, I'll be." She smiled and Abilene tried her hardest to smile back, but instead she felt her bottom lip begin to quiver, with tears not far behind.

Her mother wasted no time pulling the chair closer to Abilene and sitting on it, pulling her daughter close and rubbing her back.

"Hush, hush. We should be celebrating. Twice the love, baby."

Abilene shook her head through a hiccupy sob.

"Twice the money. Twice the diapers. Twice the trouble."

"Oh, child. I remember the hormones. The crying jags. When I was carrying you I once sat on the kitchen floor and cried for a half-hour because of this little ceramic chick my grandma gave me for Easter when I was just a little girl. Must of had it for fifteen years before that day. Then all of a sudden it occurred to me that the chick didn't have a mama, and it made me so sad I just picked it up and cradled it, and had me a good cry. Felt like a fool afterwards, but that's just part of the deal when you're growing a new life. This will pass, and you'll see what a blessing this really is. I promise."

Her mother's story wasn't the comfort Gloryanne had intended, but by the time she wrapped it up, Abilene was down to just sniffling into a wadded-up paper napkin.

"Thanks, Mama. It was just a bit of a shock, I guess. Twins. It's still hard to believe there will be two of them."

Gloryanne had returned to making tea for the two of them.

"Well, it shouldn't be too much of a surprise. Twins do run in the family."

Abilene watched her mother pour steaming water over the tea bags and wracked her brain for a set of twins she was related to.

"How so, Mama?" she asked after a moment of thought that yielded no results.

Gloryanne paused with her back to Abilene.

"Well, I guess I was thinking of your daddy's family," she said after a moment. When she turned with a mug in each hand, she didn't look Abilene in the eye.

"My daddy's family?" Abilene repeated. Her mother rarely brought up the man who had walked out on them before Abilene's first birthday.

"Mmmhmm," Gloryanne responded as she cupped her mug in both hands and blew gently on the surface of the tea. "Back in Texas. He had a set of twin sisters a few years younger than him, I believe. I can barely remember now anyway. You want any honey for that, honey?" she asked with a laugh.

"If you can barely remember, why'd you say twins run in the family?" Abilene asked.

Gloryanne forced a laugh.

"Oh girl, don't read too much into what I blurt out when I get the best news of my life. I'm going to be a grandma twice over on the first shot. Can you blame me for not making any sense?" She stood up, suddenly went to the fridge. "You and Ryan want to stay for dinner?" she asked, peering inside.

"Why do I feel like you're hiding something, Mama? I can't think of a single set of twins in our family."

"Are you staying for dinner or not? Because if you are, I should probably get started."

Abilene sighed and decided she didn't have the energy to push deeper into whatever was going on in Gloryanne's head.

"I'll stay for dinner, Mama, but best not count on Ryan. I think he's picking up some overtime tonight." She stared down into her mug and hoped Gloryanne remained fixated on the contents of her fridge.

"He's been working a lot lately, but that's smart. Babies don't come cheap. But still, I don't think that boy's been around here for the last month."

Abilene took a deep breath and closed her eyes.

"You need any help with dinner, Mama?"

The two women worked well in the kitchen together. They'd been a team when Abilene was growing up, but on this chilly night, as Abilene chopped vegetables and her mother rolled out crust for chicken pot pie, the kitchen was largely quiet. Not an unusual state for Abilene, but she'd always counted on her mother's chatter to fill the spaces, cracks, and crevices around them. Something was obviously weighing on her mother's mind, but Abilene didn't want to poke at her too much for fear that she might poke back.

After dinner, Gloryanne laid out a fire in the fireplace and pushed another mug of herbal tea on Abilene, but instead of pouring her usual glass of wine, Abilene watched her mother mix up a Jack and Coke. She settled into her recliner and took a sip, closing her eyes as she swallowed.

"What's on your mind, Mama?" Abilene couldn't help herself. "You've been quiet all evening."

"Nothing but anticipation of a couple of sweet babies," she sighed.

"Why did Daddy leave?" Abilene found herself asking, without really planning to.

"Now why would you go and bring that up for after all this time?"

She shrugged.

"Maybe being pregnant is making me curious about my own parents, is all. You did OK raising me up, but I still wondered about him sometimes, you know? Besides, you're the one who brought him up earlier."

"I never should've said anything," Gloryanne muttered.

"But you did."

"He left because he was weak and couldn't handle it," she snapped.

"Couldn't handle what, exactly?" Abilene prodded.

"None of it. Being a daddy. Being a husband. Not all men can, you know. I'd warn you to keep an eye on Ryan. He's got that bolting look about him."

Abilene looked into her mug.

"He's already gone," she finally said. "Has been for a month now."

Her mother set her glass on the end table.

"Oh, sweet baby girl. I'm so sorry."

"Please just tell me why my own daddy left. Maybe I can understand why Ryan would leave his babies, too."

Gloryanne leaned back in her recliner and closed her eyes. Abilene held her breath as she watched the shadows from the fire dance over her mother's face.

"Well, now, I hesitate to even bring it up," Gloryanne finally began, eyes still closed. "I guess I should have told you a long time ago. You had a twin brother named Austin."

Abilene sat up straight, placing a hand on her own stomach. "I what? Why wouldn't you tell me this before?"

Gloryanne shrugged.

"Well you were only nine months old when it happened. You both got a nasty cold, but it turned into pneumonia for Austin. You were both small for your ages, having been born early and all. We just didn't know how serious it was until it was too late."

Abilene listened to her mother in disbelief.

"But why wouldn't you have told me when I got older? Don't you think I had a right to know I had a brother?"

When Abilene saw the tears rolling down her mother's cheeks, she immediately felt bad for snapping at her. She handed Gloryanne a tissue.

"Of course you did. But no matter how much time passed, it never got easier to talk about. Didn't help that your daddy took off not long after. I think losing Austin broke something inside him."

Abilene reached over and covered her mother's hand with her own.

"Don't you dare make excuses for that rat-bastard. If he was so brokenhearted over losing one child, how could he walk out on another?"

Gloryanne just sniffled into her napkin and shrugged.

"Living with me after that couldn't have been easy, either."

Abilene narrowed her eyes at her mother, but figured a scolding could wait.

"Where's Austin?" she asked softly instead.

"Buried over in the Rosemont," she sighed. "I'm sorry I never told you."

Abilene nodded and looked out the window. Snow had started to fall. She stood up and peered out further. The sidewalk was already covered.

"Do you mind if I stay the night here?" she asked.

Gloryanne nodded.

"This is still your home, sweetie. You never have to ask. Why didn't you tell me about Ryan sooner?"

"Maybe it didn't feel true if I didn't say it out loud."

Gloryanne nodded and squeezed her hand.

"I know. Please don't be too mad at me for not telling you about your brother."

"I'm too tired to be mad right now. Probably later," Abilene said.

That night as Abilene lay awake in her old bed, it occurred to her that she must have shared this room with Austin for the few short months they had together. Her grandparents had bought the house for her parents as a wedding gift and her mother hadn't lived anywhere else in twenty-five years. Abilene closed her eyes and wondered if she could summon some kind of twin magic and feel her brother in the room with her. But all she felt was the draft from the old window, and she snuggled deeper under the quilt. She wondered if she had felt the absence of her brother her whole life and didn't realize it.

Abilene worked her hands up under the old T-shirt she'd worn to bed. She pressed them into her abdomen as if she could feel the two babies growing there, though it was far too soon. Here, alone in her childhood bedroom, she tried to feel something other than worry about the lives inside her. But all she felt was the cool flesh of her palm pushing into the soft cushion of her belly. She turned onto her side and peered through the break in the curtains to the falling snow beyond. Several inches had built up. It was soothing to watch the flakes, fat and fluffy, drift past her window when she was so warm and safe. In that moment, with her mother's soft snoring drifting through the thin walls, Abilene felt that maybe everything might be OK.

The next morning, Abilene ate the hearty breakfast her mother insisted on cooking for her and then waved Gloryanne off as she left for her yoga class at the rec center.

"Are you sure you don't want me to stay? Or at least give you a ride home?" Gloryanne asked.

"No," Abilene assured her. "I'm going to maybe use your computer to apply for some jobs, and then I'll head on home."

Gloryanne finally hefted her yoga mat onto her back and trudged through the snow to the driveway where her car was slowly warming up, exhaust steadily piping into the atmosphere.

Once her mother pulled out of the driveway and disappeared down the road, Abilene settled down with Gloryanne's laptop. She did start out looking for jobs that had been posted since yesterday, but soon found herself looking up facts about pregnancies with twins. She perused forums where other mothers posted about their experiences and learned about "lost twin syndrome," where one of the twins is simply absorbed somehow and disappears completely. Abilene pressed her hand to her stomach once more and sucked in her breath. The thought of losing a baby so easily, with no warning, no pain, no suffering – it didn't seem like it should be possible. It seemed almost unfair. She thought of all her lost keys and earrings and rejected the idea that a baby could just vanish in the same way. Maybe she hadn't asked for twins, planned for them – or even one baby for that matter – but for the first time, Abilene realized she wanted them. She wanted them both. She closed the browser on the laptop and clicked the laptop shut with a little more force than necessary.

Abilene sat clutching her mother's laptop for a moment before she set it on the coffee table and went to gather her winter gear and her purse. She left the ultrasound picture her doctor had given her the day before on the kitchen table where Gloryanne would find it and coo with renewed joy as she was reminded of the double bundles of joy she'd be grandmothering in a few months.

Outside, Abilene did not head for the bus that would take her home, but instead walked a few short blocks to the bus that would take her to the Rosemont Cemetery. Luck was with her as a bus pulled up mere seconds after she reached the stop.

Abilene stared out the window at the snow-covered world. What had been gray and dirty the night before was fresh and clean now, but by nightfall, the purity of the snow would be marred once more. Everything was so fleeting.

She disembarked at the cemetery stop and made her way into the small office building inside the cemetery gates. The man at the desk typed on his computer and found the spot where Austin was buried. He showed her on a map of the cemetery and asked if she needed assistance locating the grave. Shaking her head, Abilene replied, "No, I'll find him."

The going was slow through the snow, but Abilene was in no hurry. She felt like she'd been waiting for this moment her whole life, but just hadn't realized it until it was upon her. She savored the anticipation.

At first Abilene walked right by the spot, but turned around when she realized she'd gone too far. Nestled between two headstones was a space with no apparent marker, but it was where Austin was buried, Abilene was certain.

She set to work clearing the snow and was rewarded with a small flat stone set in the ground. Its engraving was simple:

Austin Lee Henley
Little Lamb Called Home
Beloved Son and Brother

The dates of his short life were at the bottom and Abilene pulled her glove off to trace her own birthday and her brother's name.

"I've found you," she whispered. "I've found you."

Abilene sat crouched in the snow longer than should have been comfortable, but she couldn't tear herself away until her toes were numb and her calves and thighs protested the position. She stood up stiffly and stared down at the place where her twin brother rested. She tried to imagine what it would be like to have a brother, a twin standing beside her, but that was lost, and she knew there was no way she could ever capture it. Her brother was still nine months old, and Abilene was grown, about to be a mother. Still, she couldn't help but feel that some missing piece had been restored to her.

Abilene reached in her pocket where her house keys should have been, readying herself to head home and make some decisions, but not surprisingly, they weren't in her pocket. She wondered if they had fallen out on the bus, or if they were buried in the snow that lay disrupted around Austin's stone, but she couldn't bring herself to search. Little lost things were replaceable. She could go back to her mama's house and make decisions there. She pressed her gloved fingers to her lips and blew Austin a kiss. Her other hand gently covered the new lives growing inside her.

~~~~~~~~~~~~~~~~~~

Diane D. Gillette lives, writes, and teaches in Chicago. She is a founding editor at *Cat on a Leash Review*. Her work has appeared in over 50 literary venues including the *Saturday Evening Post* and the *Maine Review*. You can find more of her published work through digillette.com.
~~~~~~~~~~~~~~~~~~

Multiple Loves

Carolyn Geduld

Steph had gone from one bad boyfriend to another, always in trouble because of her inattention to the most obvious red flags. She had been with a series of addicts, cheaters, petty criminals, jerks, and losers. From now on, she vowed to be more choosey. She would find out about a guy before falling for him instead of falling first and then finding out how weird or disappointing he was.

A dating site would allow her to read a guy's profile and find out about him before meeting up with him. She wondered what kind of profile she could write about herself that would attract someone normal, for a change. The only job she had had was in Housekeeping for a nursing home, and she had managed get fired from it. Some achievement! She had no pets or hobbies. She had never travelled. Unless she mentioned the bad things she had done, she was totally boring.

"I have a big heart, and I like hanging out, movies, and good coffee," she wrote. That seemed like a good description of her positive qualities, she thought. "I want to meet a man with a sense of humor and a job."

For the profile photo, she chose one in which she had posed wearing her sister's red prom dress. This was before she gained weight. After posting her profile, there was nothing to do but wait, since she felt shy about messaging men on the site.

Several weeks went by without any messages expressing interest. Then, at last, there was one from a guy named Ray. His profile photos revealed what Steph would call an honest-looking face—clean-shaven, wide-set blue eyes, a good-natured smile. Like her, he had only posted one photo.

"I am looking for an open-minded woman who wants a long-term relationship. My personal qualities are harmony, curiosity, and spontaneity. I am looking for a girlfriend who is understanding, adventurous, and tolerant. Who can be the woman of my dreams?" he wrote.

She decided to message him back. There was nothing to lose. After all, he was a decent-looking man. She could be attracted to him, if she were ready to go there. She chose a reply from the tips on the site.

"It seems like we are a good match. What kind of stuff do you like to do on weekends?"

"I'm sort of an adventurous couch potato. Like you, I'm for hanging out, movies, and coffee shops. Would you like to meet for a coffee and see how we do in person?"

An adventurous couch potato? Steph wondered what that meant. It would take a personal meeting to sort it out, she thought. Having coffee after a single exchange of messages went against the advice of the dating site, which was to exchange emails and have phone conversations before a live meeting. But Steph couldn't think of anything else to write or ask.

"I don't mind if we meet for coffee," she messaged.

At the agreed-upon time, Steph arrived at the coffee shop first. A few minutes later, a man who looked like the profile photo came in, looked around, and smiled when he saw her.

"Steph?" He asked, advancing toward her.

"Ray?"

"Roy."

"*Roy?*"

"I'm Roy. Glad to meet you, Steph. Can I get you a coffee?"

Steph had a moment of concern. Either she had misread his name on the dating site, or he pronounced "Ray" as "Roy." She looked at the swirls in the latte he brought to the table for her. It would be unfair to judge him for his pronunciation. She would give him a chance. He did most of the talking. Later, she would realize that he had spoken in a roundabout way, without a lot of detail. He said he had a desk job, but never mentioned the company. He mentioned previous girlfriends, but not their names. What Steph focused on was that he said the previous relationships had not worked out.

"How come?" she asked.

"Their expectations were not in line with mine."

"What do you mean?" she asked.

"Relationships have two parts," he said with apparent authority. "One part is about comfort. Someone to eat dinner with every night. Someone who becomes part of your routine. The other part is about what I call cohesion. It is about having someone who can make your life easier and more productive. Someone who can help smooth out the bottlenecks. The people I've dated have not been good at both. I'm looking for someone good at both."

"I don't understand the difference between comfort and cohesion," she said.

"Comfort is the part that is easier for most women. It is about affection, companionship, being interested in each other. Cohesion is about doing what you can to make the other person's life easier," he said.

"You mean, like, doing favors for them?"

"That would be part of it," he said.

"That doesn't seem so hard," she said.

"Good. Maybe you will be the one," he said.

They made a date to have another coffee. In between, he sent her emails repeating his wish that she would be the one he had been waiting for. He hoped she would be open to the two parts of the kind of relationship he required. He hoped he was the kind of man she could be interested in getting to know better. He wanted her to give him a chance. Maybe if the second coffee date went well, they could do something the next weekend.

He signed his emails "Ray." She figured it was his pronunciation that made it sound like "Roy." But the second time they met, he called himself "Ray." She clearly heard him say an "a" and not an "o." She felt shy about asking him about it. Perhaps it was her error. It was a minor matter, she decided.

Just as he had done the first time, he arrived a few minutes after her, and bought her a latte. Ray did most of the talking on the second coffee date. He told her again that he had an office job and talked about previous girlfriends who had not worked out. Then he talked about the two parts of relationships in the same way he had talked about them on the first date. In fact, nothing that Ray said was any different from what he said the previous time. Steph felt like she was in a time machine, re-experiencing the first date all over again, except for the way he pronounced his name.

He ended the date by saying, "Good. Maybe you will be the one."

The next weekend, "Roy" invited her to see the Wonder Woman movie. The weekend after, "Ray" invited her to see the same movie. When she said that they had just seen it, Ray said he wanted to see it again. Steph went along with what he wanted, not knowing if it was comfort or cohesion. He seemed pleased no matter which it was.

Despite advice to wait from the dating site, Steph and Ray had become intimate—twice. She was not surprised that his lovemaking was exactly the same each time. She didn't care because, as unwise as it probably was, she was falling for this guy who repeated himself. He was weird, but in a predictable way. Whatever he did, she knew he would do again. All she had to do was make sure she did everything the same way as well—so that he did not have to worry about variations. This was what he seemed to mean by cohesion. She would make things easy for him to do in duplicate, something his previous girlfriends probably did not like. It was no big deal for Steph. She had been through a lot worse than a little repetition.

This continued for several weeks. They spent every weekend together, and often saw each other during the week as well. They texted several times a day and spoke on the phone in the evening if they were not hanging out in person. Steph began to dream of a future with Ray.

She thought it might be soon be time to change her Facebook status, although she dreaded the awkwardness of explaining Ray to her family. Had she fallen for another weirdo?

Then, Ray said he had a surprise for her. He asked if he could bring the surprise to her apartment. Was it a gift, she wondered, or maybe a ring? Finally, there was a knock on the door. There he was.

"It's Ray," he said, kissing her.

A few seconds later, another figure entered.

"It's Roy," he said, leaning forward to kiss her. She took a step back.

"Oh, my God," she shrieked. "There's two of you."

Steph slid to the floor, shaking and taking rapid shallow breaths. She was dizzy. She might have been having a heart attack.

Ray kneeled down. "You are having a panic attack," he said. "Slow your breathing down and take deep breaths. That will help you feel better."

Roy said, "Don't worry. It's not a heart attack. You will be fine. We've seen this before."

They picked her up and helped her to the sofa. Her breath was slowing down. The room stopped reeling. Ray and Roy sat on either side of her. She kept looking from one to the other. They were exactly alike! Slowly, it came to her. The repetitions were not repetitions. They were not because one person was doing everything twice. Two people were doing everything once the same way.

"Oh, no. My God, no," Steph said.

Roy and Ray each put an arm around her.

"We're identical twins, Steph," they said in unison.

Steph pushed their arms away and stood up facing them, so she could see them both. Her hand covered her mouth. They were wearing the same clothing, had the same haircut, and were sitting the same way. She couldn't tell which was Ray and which was Roy.

"I don't know which one I'm in love with," she sobbed.

"We are both in love with you and you are in love with both of us," one of them said, reasonably. "Now come and sit down so we can talk."

The talk lasted several hours, broken up only by Steph's crying spells and panic episodes. Both men were kind and caring throughout, bringing Steph water, crackers, ice packs, aspirin, wine, Xanax, and weed. They were sympathetic listeners while she raged at their deception and wept.

When she finally calmed down, she was able to listen to them.

"We are the same person, Steph. We are clones. That's what identical twins are. Clones. Some twins are not as alike as us because one gets more nutrients than the other in the womb or one catches a virus in infancy and the other doesn't. But we were exactly the same weight at birth and neither of us ever had an illness that the other did not have. Our parents dressed us alike, fed us the same food, bought us the same toys, made sure we always had the same teachers, and treated us as one. We have never wanted to be anything else," one said.

"The only thing that could separate us is two different girlfriends. Different girlfriends make us different—or we make the girls the same as each other. There is always resentment and jealousy and a bad ending. That is why we are looking for one girl who can treat us both as one," the other continued.

"Why don't you go and find identical twin girls?" Steph asked tearfully.

"We tried. We've made our request in twin clubs and on twin online sites. Most twins have separate identities, either because they are not exactly the same or they were raised to be individuals. They are no better than sisters," one said.

"We love you, Steph. We want to be exclusive with you. We want to plan a future for the three of us," the first said.

"Remember 'comfort' and 'cohesion?' Cohesion really means making things easy for us to be as one. You can call us Ray or Roy. Whichever you choose. Because if you agree to have a relationship with us, you will never be able to tell which one is with you. It will be just like having a singleton boyfriend," the second said.

It was very late. Steph was drunk, high, dazed, and sleepy. She asked the guys to leave. They agreed to meet again the next day. She fell asleep on the sofa and woke up with a headache. There were hours of confused thinking ahead of her.

On the one hand, how could she pretend to forget that she had two boyfriends? If she had two goldfish, she would always know they were two even if they looked exactly alike. Or two potatoes. Ray and Roy might say they were one, but in her mind, there would be two. She might spend the rest of her life trying to tell them apart or figuring out which she loved more.

On the other hand, if she had to choose just one, which would she choose? Maybe it wouldn't matter since there was no difference between them. Up until then, she had been with both separately and it had not been noticeable. What if it continued that way—she would never know or care if she was with Ray or Roy. The important thing was that they be exclusive with her. That was what they said they wanted.

Another factor was that no one else showed interest in dating her. Ray and Roy were decent looking, devoted, and employed, for the same company as it turned out. She might not get another chance for months or years. And her family might accept her again if she showed up with a regular guy for a fiancé. No one need to know there were two fiancés. If they fooled her, they could fool her family.

With considerable uncertainty, Steph decided to move ahead with the relationship and see what would happen. Roy and Ray were delighted. It was decided that she should call both of them Ray from then on. It would help her to put out of her mind the fact that there were two of them. She would introduce one of them—she would not know which—to her family as Ray and leave it at that.

It was explained to her that they could not introduce her to their family. As unusual as their family was, there was no way they could account for their choice of one girlfriend for both. And because of the pressure they were always under to be alike, their family would insist that each son have his own fiancée. Never mind that having two women had always ended in disaster. Roy and Ray were convinced that the best course was to pretend to be single for the rest of their lives. Steph did her best to be accepting. She wanted to try to do the "cohesion" part of the relationship well.

The comfort part of the relationship began to go smoothly. Steph and Ray or Roy behaved like other romantic couples. They walked hand and hand in public. They spent every spare moment with each other. They were affectionate and kind. Although unease gripped her now and then, Steph thought she had lucked into a good boyfriend. Her family liked him. Steph found herself enjoying talk of bridal dresses and venues. She gave up her apartment, which she could no longer afford, and moved back into her old bedroom in her family home. If she visited Ray in his apartment, only one of him was there.

After many months of preparation, the wedding day arrived. Although Steph had become accustomed to her unusual arrangement with the twin brothers, she did wonder which one would show up at the altar. She worried that when she walked up the aisle on her father's arm, she would find both standing there next to a very puzzled minister. When the moment came, however, there was only one—which one she thought she never would know. At the end of the ceremony, she was married to either Ray or Roy, but not both. Unless they could be regarded as one person, as they insisted they were.

The one she married accompanied her to the wedding reception, unless the twins had switched places. Together, she and the one with her listened to toasts, fed each other wedding cake, and were the first of the guests to dance. Then it was time to board the limousine that was to take them to their honeymoon hotel suite. Steph was happily nestled against Ray's chest, not thinking of which one he might really be.

Nevertheless, she was not too surprised to see the other twin waiting for them in the hotel room with a bottle of champagne. She hadn't been with both men since the day she agreed to have the three-way relationship. But that night was an exception, Ray or Roy said. After a glass of champagne to celebrate, one would leave. There might not be another occasion when all three were together again.

Steph was feeling soft-hearted by the joy of the day and by the several glasses champagne.

"Maybe, like, the three of us can get together, you know, sometimes. Like on our anniversary or on your birthday, I mean, if you want."

The brothers beamed at her.

"You are the woman of our dreams," one said.

Just then, there was a knock on the door.

"I'll get it, "Steph said, "One of you better hide."

Strangely, neither moved as Steph opened the door.

"Hello, Steph," a man said, "I'm Rye. I'm your legal husband."

~~~~~~~~~~~~~~~~~~

Carolyn Geduld is a mental health professional in Bloomington, Indiana. Her fiction has appeared in *The Writing Disorder, Pennsylvania Literary Review, Persimmon Tree, Not Your Mother's Breastmilk, Dime Show Review, Dual Coast* (Prolific Press), *Otherwise Engaged,* and several other literary journals. Contact her on Twitter at twitter.com/CarolynGeduld.
~~~~~~~~~~~~~~~~~~

Circadian Rhythms

Frank Kozusko

Luka was an insomniac, a chronic insomniac, a desperately tired-all-the-time insomniac. His insomnia had cost him jobs, friends, and, finally, his wife. It hadn't always been that way for him, and he couldn't recall when his sleep became so troubled. In his youth, Luka was quite energetic, able to work all day, party at night, and sleep a solid six hours to arise fully charged in the morning. Maybe it started with the job that rotated him through the day, swing, and graveyard shifts, upsetting his biological clock.

Maybe it was the interlocking stresses of being breadwinner, parent, and husband that forced him awake in the middle of the night with a mind that raced from one seemingly unsolvable dilemma to the next. Even his dreams became a mishmash of quandaries, relief coming only when his subconscious demanded he awaken.

He tried different over-the-counter and then prescription medications that helped at first, until his body fought back against the forced sleep. He lost job after job falling asleep at work. When the debt grew so large that he had to declare bankruptcy and he lost the house, his wife filed for divorce.

Luka tried to create a life around his sleeplessness. He found a job where he worked from home processing medical bills and records. As long as he met his quota, he could work any time for long or short periods until sleep seemed possible. His bedroom was a storage closet with no windows where no daylight could penetrate to challenge a false nocturnal slumber. His clock operated without illuminating the room. A clap of his hands would turn on the red numbers that would quantify his misery.

Tonight he clapped and saw 12:33. Was it day? Luka was never sure when he woke in his blackhole sanctuary. When he focused, he saw a dot indicating a.m. He had been asleep for only 45 minutes. After 27 minutes of fruitless tossing and turning and no sleep, he got up. It was 1:00 a.m. in the "City That Never Sleeps." Well, that might be true in Manhattan, but Luka's New York City was Brooklyn. He lived on the edges of the dock area and his neighborhood was quiet, asleep. Why couldn't *he* sleep?

He was too tired to work; his mind would not concentrate. Yet he needed to work. He was falling behind in his quotas, the third time in the last six months, and the company was threatening to drop him. He decided his only hope was to walk to exhaustion, so he could sleep and then maybe catch up on his work. He dressed and stepped out into the stillness of the summer night.

Luka made his way to the piers where there would be no traffic and few lights. He wanted to eliminate as many sensory intrusions as possible. Soon he was alone with his footsteps. He should've been afraid to be in an isolated area; for some reason, he wasn't. The flashlight he was carrying wasn't needed tonight. The full moon was shining clearly, bright enough to cast thin shadows on the potholes that dotted the street. At the waterfront, he was greeted by random slaps of waves on the pilings and the damp smell of the bay. Walking south, he had the water to the right, warehouses to the left.

His body was fatigued. His mind was fatigued, filled with anguish. He stepped up onto the seawall and looked out over the East River. The ripples glistened in the moonlight.

The tide is going out. If I jump in now, my body would be carried out to sea. Nobody would know. Nobody would care.

Luka slid his feet closer to the edge, leaning forward, his head bent, staring at the water below. At the moment he might have given into his despair, but his thoughts were interrupted by the sound of drums. *Dida boom dada, Dida boom dada. ...* He stepped back, nearly losing his footing on the slippery wet timber.

Shaking from the reality of what he had nearly accomplished, Luka decided to follow the drumming. He walked along the piers until he came to a dark narrow alley. A faint light, oscillating with the drumbeat, escaped from an opened cellar door. His heart beat faster as he cautiously approached. The smell of incense rose from the opening; gyrating shadows from below stretched across the narrow steps leading downward. He hesitated, inhaling the smoky fragrance. Bending forward to lower his gaze, slowly, silently he descended, bracing himself with arms stretched to his sides, touching the cool stone walls.

From the bottom of the steps, he advanced only enough to gain a view into a grotto filled with dancers and drummers. The dancers, in white robes tightened at the waist each with a red cord, whirled with outstretched arms alternating clockwise and counterclockwise. They orbited around a statue of what might have been a larger than life-size human figure, save for the huge wings rising from its back. The drummers in reverse colors, red robes with white waist cords, beat their drums with heavy carved-wood sticks that curved into a spherical fist.

Staring transfixed, concentrating on the ceremony, Luka was not aware when he was approached from behind. A firm hand on his shoulder spun Luka around to face a tall, red-bearded man who was dressed as a dancer. Luka's fear prevented him from uttering a sound. It was Red Beard who spoke first in a deep commanding voice.

"What are you doing here?"

"I am sorry, I don't mean any offense. I was taking a walk and I heard the drums."

"You're out for a walk in the middle of the night?"

"I couldn't get to sleep tonight. I thought if I went for a long walk, I might get tired enough to sleep."

"Oh, I see, trouble sleeping," said Red Beard.

"Yes, all the time."

"Ah, it is Somnus, God of Sleep and Dreams, that brings you here to join us. On the night of the full moon, we gather to beseech him to bring us sound sleep and pleasant dreams. We dance around the image of Somnus to relax mind and body, then we will individually make our petitions to him," said Red Beard as he loosened his grip. "What's your name?"

"Luka."

"I am Dimerus, Keeper of the Night. So, Luka, would you like to come in, ask Somnus for sleep?"

Luka turned his gaze from Dimerus to the dancers while thoughts of fear, disbelief, and desperation bounced around in his head. Turning back to Dimerus, he nodded his head slightly, quietly saying, "Yes."

"Then come, join; the procession is about to begin."

Dimerus escorted Luka inside the chamber and dressed him for the ceremony. Luka joined the end of the line and watched as each ahead took turns standing in silence before the statue of Somnus, looking to the face, palms up, and taking their place in the circle. Luka, afraid of the strange covey surrounding him, participated for his own wellbeing and to prevent offense. When his turn came, he went through the motions. Without really believing, he did allow himself a small prayer in his head: "Somnus, give me sleep."

When the ceremony was over, Dimerus took Luka aside.

"The locations of meetings are different each time and known only to the members. If you want to join, you must stand before the Council. I am on the Council; I can sponsor you, evaluate your eligibility. If you are accepted, you must choose a member name. We are an anonymous group; true identities are known only to the Council members. When I joined, I took the name Dimerus, meaning "two parts." I am a Christian, yet I pray to Lord Somnus for my sleep."

"Yes, I would like to join," Luka replied

"Good. Give me a contact number."

Luka gave Dimerus his cell number. Dimerus didn't allow Luka to exit the grotto until all the other members had dispersed. He waited, and when Luka went north, he went south. By the time Luka got inside his apartment, the sun had risen in the cloudless blue sky, the sunlight streaming through his east-facing windows. Completely exhausted, Luka retreated to his catacomb. For the first time in years, he slept well. The next night, and the next, and the next, he slept well. He was gradually adjusting his sleep cycle to a normal day/night schedule.

As the days passed and the next full moon approached, Luka waited for a call from Dimerus. He was anxious to join the Somnulists, wanting to continue the blessing of sleep. Dimerus' call registered as an unknown number on Luka's cell.

Dimerus instructed Luka: "Meet me at the corner of Fourth Avenue and 14th Street in Manhattan at midnight tomorrow."

ЖФЖ ЖФЖ ЖФЖ

The next night, Dimerus arrived at the rendezvous corner by a yellow cab. He flung open the back door and called to Luka.

"Get in." As the cab pulled away, Dimerus handed Luka a sleep mask. "Put this on." The drive was long enough that Luka couldn't really estimate the length of distance they had traveled. He heard the sound that tires make when going over the treads of a bridge. Gradually the traffic noise diminished. When the cab stopped, Luka was led out of the cab by silent arms.

The air is damp. We crossed a bridge. Are we back at the Brooklyn piers?

He was ushered a short distance before ascending a few steps.

Ascending, so it's not the grotto.

"Stand here." Luka recognized Dimerus' voice. "Remove your blindfold."

Luka found himself standing before Dimerus, with two other men and one woman sitting at a table facing him. Each was dressed in dancer garb.

Dimerus spoke first.

"Is it your desire to join the Somnulists?"

Luka replied, "Yes, it is."

One by one the council members questioned him about his sleep, his personal, and his professional life.

Dimerus advised the board, "I have done a background check and recommended Luka for trial membership." Luka was asked if he was ready to take a vow of loyalty and secrecy. Once again, he replied in the affirmative. Dimerus administered the oath and declared Luka a postulant of Somnus.

"Postulant Luka," said Dimerus. "You will be invited to the next full moon ceremony where you will be formally inducted and asked to choose your Somnulist name."

Blindfolded once more, Luka was returned to the rendezvous point.

⋈⋈⋈ ⋈⋈⋈ ⋈⋈⋈

Next month, as instructed, Luka arrived at a warehouse on Staten Island at 11:00 p.m. on the night of the full moon. He brought with him a small gym bag for carrying his robes home and the $1,000 in cash for initiation and annual member fees. He received a brief indoctrination before he was presented to the assemblage by Dimerus and asked to renew his vows. Then he was ceremoniously dressed in his dancer robe.

"Now Postulant, what name have you chosen?" asked The Keeper of the Night.

"Zoticus."

"Ah, Zoticus: full of life," said Dimerus, nodding approvingly. "Somnulists, I present Zoticus."

Luka, now Zoticus, turned and bowed to the north, south, east and west, while the congregants applauded. Zoticus participated in the dancing ceremony he had witnessed as an outsider a mere few weeks ago, once again beseeching Somnus for sleep and dreams. When the ceremony was over, each member changed back into street clothes and exited the warehouse carrying a gym bag.

⋈⋈⋈ ⋈⋈⋈ ⋈⋈⋈

Luka never missed a Somnulist meeting over the next two years for which he was rewarded with solid restful sleep. He had abandoned his closet sleep sanctuary long ago and moved his bed into the bedroom. Now he enjoyed waking with the sun. He kept his work-at-home job because of the flexibility it offered. Luka even started dating.

In those two years, a power struggle had developed in the council. It looked like the group would split in two. Recent meetings were strained by the factions trying to win over members. Dimerus led one faction and expected Luka to side with him. Luka felt a loyalty to Dimerus, but his meetings would be held too far outside the city.

Luka decided that his only choice was to abandon the group. He became so confident in his sleep, he wondered if he needed to attend their full moon gatherings anymore. Why did he need to be in the group to ask Somnus for sleep? He decided he didn't. He had seen the ceremony; he had participated successfully many times. He would create his own grotto to Somnus in the same closet where sleep once tormented him.

Luka searched the cult shops in lower Manhattan to get the makings of his shrine to Somnus. He settled on a small altar from a Buddhist shop. He ordered a statuette of Somnus on the internet. He could only guess at the incense that the Somnulists had used, so he settled on Buddhist wares there, too. On the night of the full moon, he ignored the invitation from the Somnulists and held his own ceremony in his own secret chamber.

✕◗✕◖✕ ✕◗✕◖✕ ✕◗✕◖✕

Dimerus noted Luka's absence from the full-moon meeting. He called Luka's cellphone the next morning. It went to voicemail.

"Luka, this is Dimerus. You missed the meeting; I hope you are OK. Members are not allowed to skip a meeting without informing their sponsors. I need to know why you weren't there."

After three days of unsuccessfully trying to reach Luka by phone, Dimerus decided to check on him personally. He went to Luka's building and rang his apartment buzzer several times. There was no answer. Turning to leave, Dimerus saw a man taking the garbage to the street.

"Excuse me, are you the super?"

"Yes."

"I am a friend of Luka, in 2D. We had an appointment three days ago, but he didn't show. I haven't had any luck reaching him on his cellphone. Have you seen him recently?"

"No, but I rarely see him."

"Can you let me in the building, so I can knock on his door?"

"OK. I'll go with you."

When they got to Luka's floor, they could see three days of newspapers in front of Luka's door. Dimerus knocked loudly several times but no answer.

"Something's not right. Do you have a key?" asked Dimerus.

"Yes."

"Can we go in and check on him?"

The super unlocked the door and opened it slightly.

"Mr. Hanson? Mr. Hanson?" called out the super.

Fully opening the door, the pair entered.

"Wow, it's cold in here," said the super, shivering and rubbing his arms. "Mr. Hanson?"

Walking across the living room, Dimerus turned off the noisy window air conditioner and said, puzzling out loud, "The heat wave ended two days ago; it's cold outside."

A quick check of the two other small rooms yielded no sign of Luka and nothing to arouse suspicion of foul play. Dimerus went down a short hall to the bathroom door, knocked and entered; nothing. He opened a small closet door across from the bathroom. There on the floor lay Luka, dead in front of a small altar. On the altar was a winged statue and above a sign that read **SOMNUS.**

The super stuck his head through the closet doorway.

"That's Mr. Hanson." Looking at the altar, the super opined, "Somnus? I guess that is the guy in the statue."

"No," said Dimerus, looking down and shaking his head. "Somnus is the God of Sleep and Dreams. That is Thanatos, his twin brother.

"He prayed for sleep to the wrong god. He prayed for sleep to Thanatos, God of Death.

"Thanatos granted his request. He sleeps for eternity."

~~~~~~~~~~~~~~~~~~

Frank Kozusko is a retired U.S. Navy submarine officer. After the Navy, he spent 20 years as a university math professor. Third beat: Writer. Frank writes short stories in many genres. His work has been published in *Pilcrow & Dagger*, *Ariel Chart* and *Bewildering Stories*, and anthologized in *Bubble Off-Plumb*. Visit him at circadianrs@yahoo.com.
~~~~~~~~~~~~~~~~~~

Conjoined

Sharon Frame Gay

I stop for the tenth time today, touch my shoulder where she often rested her head. My fingers trace the rough patch of skin along my side where surgeons detached us from each other, my sister Lena and me.

I still walk with a lurching gait. Physical therapists tell me this can be corrected. With some effort I can learn to walk normally. I listen, nod, then go about my day, carrying the invisible weight of my twin. To change would be a dishonor, I think. One more way to let go of my other half.

We were born in 1956, conjoined twins. This was a rare event. When Mom and Daddy brought us home, a great throng of visitors waited to catch a glimpse of two tiny girls wrapped in a single blanket.

Lena and I were attached at the abdomen, omphalopagus twins. We each had our own hearts and other organs, four legs and arms. But we shared a liver, and our intestines were entwined. There was great concern about the risks of detachment surgery in the 1950s, so Lena and I lived seventeen years before it was decided to separate us. Even then, it was a call made out of necessity.

How can one explain the experience of being conjoined? It is like no other. In the beginning Lena and I knew nothing different, nor understood our unique situation. We took our breath in tandem, eyes peering into one another's as we searched our faces for the familiar, little hands touching heads and bodies in wonder. We ate, slept, rolled and crawled together, winding across the floor in a tumbling fashion. If one of us became ill, so did the other, rivers of snot, tears and saliva basting one another in odors and sensations that bound us together.

One cried, the other slept. The crying twin woke the sleeping one, the hungry child demanding food despite the sated belly of the other. At first there were tiny circles under our eyes, as neither got much rest. Our poor mother jumped in and out of her bed each night, soothing, cleaning, diapering, chaffing at a job that saw no end.

Once we defied gravity and stood upright, life became an adventure. We leaned toward each other like poles in a makeshift teepee, four legs going in opposite directions as we tried to move, spider-like, across the room. Eventually we learned to walk in a coordinated effort, but often forgot, and ran pell-mell toward things to explore, resulting in an uncomfortable pulling and tugging sensation, and our ultimate fall to earth.

Lena learned to compromise first. As the smaller and weaker twin, hanging onto me was her best strategy. She often went along without a whimper, for the ability to touch, feel, put into mouth, rub into hair. I was not a benevolent dictator, but rather an imposing little czar, lurching in the direction I wanted to go, dragging her along, my determined head jutting out like a bull as she flopped along like a rag doll.

Of course, Mom had double duty with diapers and rash cream. She tried to train first one, then the other, to sit on a child's potty in an orderly fashion. It took patience; each lesson learned was a hallmark, a passage, as we grew together like dandelions. Mom found joy in even the biggest challenges and taught us to do the same.

Our father was not as involved as Mom in our upbringing. He loved us fiercely, but the entire notion of twin girls, not to mention conjoined twins, was overwhelming to him. Daddy, a chemical engineer who put in hours of overtime to support his unusual family, found it easier to hang back and let his wife navigate the waters that seemed to swirl into an eddy every day.

On Sundays, Daddy held himself in check toward the back of the church as we entered, the congregants' heads swiveling to catch a glimpse of the awkward ball of girls lurching down the aisle. Mom surged ahead like a tugboat, making way to safe harbor, Daddy a following sea.

The subject of separation was never far from anyone's mind. Surgeons and specialists examined us thoroughly. In their wisdom they decided surgical separation was possible, though not without considerable risk. The obvious conclusion was that since Lena was the weaker twin, she faced the higher likelihood of complications. Each year after our examinations, the doctors conferred with our parents. And each year, it was decided to wait, in hopes of new techniques and tools on the horizon.

We lived in a small town. By the time kindergarten started, folks had grown accustomed to seeing us, and we no longer turned heads. The children accepted us the way children often do, and the first years of school were a joy for Lena and me.

When we entered high school, however, things changed. I wanted to be a cheerleader. Lena had her heart set on singing in the chorus. Clearly, cheerleading was an issue, so I reluctantly accompanied Lena every day to the music room. I lip-synched while Lena belted out song after song with enthusiasm. She even sang a solo, standing before the microphone in the auditorium in front of the students, me next to her as though she were a puppet and I the ventriloquist.

I was more outgoing than Lena and made friends easier. Girlfriends came to our house for sleepovers on weekends. We sat in a circle, braiding each other's hair, giggling about boys. Lena listened, but seldom participated in our chatter.

In the spring of our sophomore year, students were buzzing about Spring Fling, our formal dance. One by one, girls were asked to the dance. Excitement was mounting in the halls of Jefferson High School.

Our friend Josie walked up to us one day after lunch.

"Hey girls," Josie said. "Guess who I just talked to?" She looked at us expectantly.

"Who?" we asked in unison.

"Jon Blake," Josie said. "I asked him if he had a date for the dance and he said no. We discussed girls who didn't have dates yet, and your name came up, Lorna."

"Mine?" I could barely breath. I had a big crush on Jon.

"Yeah. He said you were really cute, but ... well, you know ..." her voice trailed off.

I flushed with humiliation. I felt ashamed, as though I had taken a needle and thread and sewed my sister to my abdomen for the hell of it. I didn't know what to say. I turned toward our locker, dragging Lena with me as her toes pedaled at the ground, trying to gain her balance.

That night I stopped talking to Lena. Like a dog hit by a car, I snapped and growled at everything in my path. I was deeply upset, and the target of my anger was attached to me like a tentacle.

"Lorna, what's wrong?" Lena asked me again and again, until I yanked at her hair.

"Nothing!" I screamed at her.

What good would it do to tell her how angry I was because a boy didn't ask me to a dance? Or that I'd never shake pom-poms and do somersaults at a football game? What good would it do to blame her, when I am half of the same entity? It was not our fault that our bodies wove together as they formed in our mother's womb. There was no answer. There was never an answer. So I remained silent for days, brooding, until one night I heard Lena crying into her pillow and my heart softened.

The next morning, I reached over and stroked her face.

"Sister, wake up. Let's be friends again," I offered.

"We were always friends," Lena said, rubbing my forehead. "I understand. What value am I but an appendage that you're forced to carry through life?"

Her tears started in earnest and we held each other, wrapped around our bodies in the womb of our bed, crying in unison and tasting the salt of each other's tears.

In the fall of our junior year, Lena decided to cut her hair short and spiky, adding kohl-rimmed eyeliner and mascara. Overnight, she became a solid hit at school. Kids paid attention, sought her out. Lena bloomed. The budding popularity boosted her confidence. She joined the debate team. She also continued singing and studied hard to get into a good college.

The thought of college was daunting. I didn't apply myself in school and had lukewarm grades. Lena was determined we would go, even if she had to drag me along, the way I dragged her for years.

Lena was to compete in a debate our senior year. We paced the floors, discussing what topic to speak about in the dawning era of women's liberation and equal rights. Finally, she decided to talk about abortion.

"Abortion?" I asked. "Really? That's a touchy subject. Was it on the roster?"

Lena nodded enthusiastically.

"Yep. I'll be debating a girl who lives in Dayton."

"Are you debating for or against it?"

Lena looked at me in surprise.

"Against it, of course."

I stared at her in disbelief.

"Are you kidding me? I mean, Lena, just look at us!" I ran my hand along our bodies, like a hostess on a game show, displaying a consolation prize that nobody wanted.

Lena turned her head, so she was staring straight into my eyes. Hers were soft and gentle. She touched my cheek, a feathery motion that resonated to my soul.

"Yes, Lorna," she beamed, "just look at us."

That night I lay in bed with eyes wide open while Lena slept. It was humbling that I never saw us the way Lena did. We were a gift! A blessing. A strange irony of sperm and egg, a twist of fate. Yet, we were more than enough. Life was sweet despite our situation. I pressed my lips against her cheek and whispered, " Just look at us, dear sister." My heart filled with gratitude.

ⅮⅭⅮⅭ ⅮⅭⅮⅭ ⅮⅭⅮⅭ

When the flu hit our town, it hit like a fist wrapped by a brass knuckle. Kids were falling like flies. Fevers were high and spirits low as half the school fell ill.

Lena and I became sick within hours of each other, taking to our bed in a tangled mess of sweaty sheets and crumpled tissues. We coughed and wheezed in each other's faces. Mom and Daddy scurried into our room hour after hour, bringing juice and aspirin and piles of magazines to keep us company.

Within a week, I was feeling better. But Lena continued to cough. She was unable to clear her lungs, even when she gripped my shoulder and barked as hard as possible, her face a sheen of sweat from fever.

Doc Porter came to the house, as it would have been too exhausting to raise us from our bed. He gave me a perfunctory once over, then turned his attention to Lena.

"Hannah," he said to my mother. "The girls need to go to the hospital. I want Lena on fluids, antibiotics, and oxygen. I think she's developed pneumonia."

Off we went to the hospital, twenty-five miles away in Cleveland. We were scarcely placed in our room before doctors and nurses appeared at our door, monitoring Lena. They poked and prodded us with serious expressions.

Lena moaned with fever, lips dry and cracked. When I spoke to her, she barely answered in a raspy voice.

I was frightened. Lena was terribly sick, and it appeared that the doctors thought so, too, as they were spending a great deal of time outside in the corridor talking among themselves, and to Mom and Daddy.

As she worsened, thoughts struck me like a thunderclap. If she died, would I die too? Would the illness that swirled through her body bring me down with her, pulling me toward death like an undertow? I panicked and called out for Mom. All she could do to comfort me was stroke my hair and say things would be OK. But her eyes betrayed her.

It was close to two o'clock in the morning. The hospital was quiet. The only sound I heard was the monitor that recorded Lena's breath and her heart rate. Lena lay as still as I had ever seen her, face waxen and pale despite the oxygen and the antibiotics pumping into her. Despite everything.

I touched her face with my thumb and her eyes opened. She held up her fingers and I grasped them in mine.

"Just look at us," I said, gazing sadly around the hospital room. I brushed strands of hair from her sweaty face. "I can't wait for us to get out of here."

Lena grimaced, made an effort to speak.

"I love you, sister. You're my other half. But you have to let me go now," she whispered.

"No!" I cried. "Stop talking like that! You're going to be fine. *We're* going to be fine. It'll just take another day or so and you'll be feeling better. I promise!"

Lena shook her head, closed her eyes. Her skin was cold and clammy, each breath tortured. I reached for the call button. Almost immediately a nurse materialized, along with Mom and Daddy and several doctors. It was as though they were sitting out in the corridor, waiting. A doctor moved forward, listened to Lena's chest, looked up at the others sadly. They nodded. Mom let out a soft sob. Daddy put his arm around her, hung his head.

And then I knew. I knew they were going to remove Lena from me, as though she were a withered tree limb. I raised up from the bed, tried to climb out, thinking maybe if I ran away down the hall, dragging my sister with me, we might escape this nightmare. I wanted to rescue Lena, save her, save myself.

"No!" I screamed over and over. The nurse came forward and poked my arm with a needle as Mom and Daddy tried to soothe me through their own tears. I felt Lena's last breaths on my face, and then a great darkness overtook me and I floated away.

When I woke up, I was alone for the first time in my life. I could not bear the thought that Lena had died. For days I refused to eat or drink. They finally put a feeding tube in me and forced nutrition. In a rage, I ripped out strands of hair, raked at my skin until it bled, and cried until my eyes were swollen and my vision blurred.

I grieved night and day, refusing visitors, even my parents. My body continued to heal, dare I say thrive, without Lena attached. But my mind remained with the ghost of my sister. Weeks went by in a fog of sorrow. Seasons changed outside the window, but I barely noticed.

⋈⋈⋈ ⋈⋈⋈ ⋈⋈⋈

One Saturday morning, I finally came home from the hospital. Mom and Daddy wanted me to sleep on the couch, or in the guest room. I refused and walked to our room. The door opened with a sad sigh, and I stepped in.

The room looked the same. Our favorite blanket was on the bed, my teddy bear on the pillow. Lena's stuffed dog sat on a bench in the corner. The walls were messy with pictures, photos of us at the prom, at Lena's debate in Dayton. Posters of boy singers were taped on the ceiling, awards and ribbons placed around the room. In the dresser drawers were hair clips, ribbons, and nail polish, the detritus of young womanhood.

At the bottom of one drawer were brochures for colleges that Lena had pored over. She wrote notes and drew stars or little flowers with happy or sad faces on them as she scrutinized each school. One brochure stood out, a small college in New England. Circled in bright red ink were the words "THIS ONE!" I held it in my hands and rocked back and forth, crying. I traced the glossy photos with my thumb, and pictured Lena walking about the campus, clutching books to her chest as we scrambled through the autumn leaves. I imagined her grin as she'd say, "Just look at us, sister!"

⋈⋈ ⋈⋈ ⋈⋈

Two years later, after I had healed, I went off to college. I chose the one Lena picked, and worked hard, determined to make Lena proud of us, and graduated with honors. I begged the college to put both our names on the diploma, using Lena's as my middle name, and they did.

My husband, Ron, and I met at school. We married and settled not far from my childhood home. We see Mom and Daddy often. Their old house echoes with the spirit of Lena, and our seventeen years together.

ⓧⓧⓧ ⓧⓧⓧ ⓧⓧⓧ

Now I sit at my kitchen table watching the lilac trees turn bright with blossoms, bees flitting from bloom to bloom. It's a lovely spring morning, full of promise.

The monitor next to my elbow emits a sound, and I rise and walk down the hall to a brightly painted door.

She stands in the crib, sturdy on two feet, no appendages. Her little face is flushed from sleep; chubby hands clutch the rails. When she sees me, she smiles.

"Hey there, sweet Lena," I say, then pick her up, press her close to my chest. I inhale the sweet smell of her hair, her skin. Then I transfer her to my right arm, hold her against the scars, and place her head right where it needs to be.

I look across at the photograph on the dresser of my twin sister and bring the baby closer to the picture. She touches the frame with a tiny finger. I see our reflection in the glass, all our faces blending together, and whisper to Lena, "Just look at us."

<div align="center">~~~~~~~~~~~~~~~~~~</div>

Sharon Frame Gay has been internationally published in anthologies and literary magazines, including *Chicken Soup for the Soul, Typehouse, Adelaide, Fiction on the Web, Literally Stories, Thrice Fiction, Crannog, Literary Orphans* and other literary journals. She has won awards at Owl Hollow Press, The Writing District, WOW! Women On Writing, and Rope and Wire, and has twice been nominated for a Pushcart Prize. On Facebook: Sharon Frame Gay-Writer, at Twitter at @sharonframegay, and on Amazon.

Twenty-three Feet

M. Louis Lambert

Ian

My brother, Owen, could be a selfish jerk, but no matter how much he pleaded, I would not let him die.

When we walked through the door of the house belonging to my girlfriend Trinity's cousin, the overwhelming wave of life energy flooded my mind like I was suddenly immersing myself into a hot bath. I took a moment to soak in the delicious colors and intensities the energies formed.

And I felt Owen, too. His was a familiar presence. I no longer had to concentrate on giving him energy. I had been doing it since birth; it was as mechanical as breathing. And no matter how much he protested, I resolved to give it to him no matter the cost.

I coughed. Searing pain flared in my lungs, then faded.

Trinity led me through a sea of humanity. I brushed shoulders with others as we passed, and my senses exploded with the intimate details of each person's energy.

A girl on my left swooned at her boyfriend, and I felt the orange flow of her sexuality. A brooding man on my right exhibited the deep purples and grays of addiction. A drunken man bumped me, and I felt several hundred cells in his brain blink out of existence with the surge of alcohol washing through his system.

Ear-piercing squeals burst from my girlfriend as she released her grip and embraced another girl similar in stature and personality. After brief introductions, Trinity reattached her vise on my hand and began an unintelligible conversation with her cousin, Catie. I distracted myself by sending to all the houseplants in the room iotas of life-force, enabling their full vibrance. I also reached out to feel for Owen, as was my habit; I felt him near and then resumed my plant enhancement.

Something big smashed into my back and my shoulder suddenly felt wet.

"Hey, watch it!" I yelled, spinning around. My annoyance from a wet shoulder made me say some unkind utterances. I would have taken them back, had I seen the confrontation's source. Easily 6'5", a man scowled and held an empty glass. If Orson Welles and Yul Brenner had a child, he would be it. His head gleamed an impressive shine, and he wore a black, Under Armor shirt that deformed from his bulk.

"You gotta problem?" He snarled. Jagged, maroon energies of aggression flowed from the man. I soaked in the aggression, and my heart raced with its intensity.

"Yeah, my shirt's wet because of you!" I blurted, immediately regretting it.

"Oh, boo hoo," the behemoth said. "Someone bumped into me, so get over it." The maroon pulses intensified and I could tell he was one insult away from exploding.

"Listen," I softened my tone. "Let me get you another drink, and—"

From another room, a girl screamed, "He's dead!"

The deafening din of the party quieted. I couldn't see anything past the enormous frame of my drink-less friend. Inwardly, I reached out to feel for the tendril that linked my brother and me. None could be found.

OWEN! He must have exceeded our twenty-three-foot limit. I freed myself of Trinity's hand and edged my way between the Welles/Brenner love child and rushed toward the source of the scream. Another shriek burst from the same direction. *Need to get closer*! Someone grabbed at my sopping sleeve. It was the black-shirted gorilla who held me.

"Hey, what about that drink, wise guy?" He sneered, inching me closer to his face.

"Dude! My brother's in danger! I have to go to him!" I yelled, grappling with his fist.

"It's probably some girl who thinks her passed-out boyfriend is dead. C'mon buddy, you said you'd get me that drink, now let's have it."

"You want it?" My chest ached from my pounding heart. I didn't have time for this! I drank in the powerful elixir of his hostility and imagined my fist into a giant hammer.

"Yeah!"

"Here!" A quick uppercut into the giant's jaw opened both his hands, releasing me and sending his glass to the floor with a crash.

"Ian!" Trinity called behind me as I fought my way through the crowd growing outside a bedroom door.

To hasten my mission, I announced, "Make way, I'm a doctor!" I slid between bodies to the opening of the bedroom door. Fiery pain from within my chest worsened with every person I squeezed past. What I saw surprised me little.

A girl knelt on the floor, sobbing uncontrollably. Lying next to her, Owen's body did not move. Regardless of the fact that we were now within twenty-three feet, if our connection had been broken, I would have to make a conscious effort to reach out with my energy and revive my brother. Another sharp pain in my chest fought for attention over my focus to 'jumpstart' Owen. I ignored the pain and concentrated.

He twitched, startling the girl next to him, stopping her hysterics. A moment later, he drew in a deep breath and groaned. Only a minute, perhaps two, had passed during his "death," so I knew his brain would be fine.

Cold sweat beaded on my forehead and I felt the need to sit on the bed. Owen lifted his head and met my glare.

"Hi," he said with a sheepish grin. I nodded with displeasure.

Behind us, shouts and insults announced another's arrival. I turned to see the black-shirted man storm into the room.

"Where is he?!" He bellowed and noticed Owen. "Hey, it's the guy who bumped into me, too!"

I snapped my head back to Owen so fast I nearly developed whiplash. Pieces of tonight's events quickly flew together in my mind. Owen, noticing the crowd and my preoccupation with Trinity, decided to find a drunk girl, push some monster to distract me further, and try to get far away. In other words, he just tried to kill himself.

Before I spoke a word, the enormous man sent a giant fist into my face. My chest crushed in upon itself, and I succumbed to the pain on the bed, unable to fight back. I struggled to stay conscious. If I blacked out, it was all over for Owen. Keeping him alive was a subconscious effort, even in sleep, but a concussion would turn off everything in me except breathing and heart rate.

Dark red energy flashed through my brain and through my blurred vision I witnessed Owen rush the stranger. Sounds of bodies exchanging blows exploded from all around. I gripped my chest; the pain now travelled through my left arm, and I could only wheeze.

A gasp sneaked past the tumult of Owen's scuffle. I recognized Trinity's energy—pink with glowing, lilac edges.

"Ian!" she shouted. I felt her hand grip mine, but I couldn't reciprocate. "Someone get an ambulance!" She screamed louder.

Immediately, the fight stopped, and Owen came into my skewed view. "Ian?"

Owen

I cursed myself with scathing insults with each pulse of Ian's heart monitor. *Beep.* Idiot. *Beep.* Moron. *Beep.* Imbecile.

I still couldn't believe that my impulsive plot to kill myself almost took my brother's life, too. Just another blight on my record as a worthless human being. The weight of my brother's burden in keeping me alive had been a constant thorn in my side since we were teenagers. But it wasn't until tonight that I realized the burden was physical as well.

I knew of my brother's gift for helping living things early on and I knew all too well that my life literally depended upon him. As we grew, it was at first a treat to be constantly around my brother, sharing in everything. But, as time went on, Ian's gifts grew into a litany of achievements and abilities. He played piano at age six. He wrote his first novel at age eight. The more we matured, the larger and darker his shadow became, under which I was forced to roam. Youngest Eagle Scout in our state. Winner of our library's poetry contest three years in a row. In our junior year of high school, recruiters started calling. Harvard. Yale. West Point. They all wanted him and having to care for me held him back.

He insisted that I shouldn't think this way, but I couldn't help it. His was an amazing mind, within a beautiful person. Who was I to deny the world of his potential to enrich it? Bitter tears snaked down my face.

"What's wrong, Owen?" My brother's voice broke my silent desperation.

I hadn't noticed he awoke. "You need your rest," I said. "Go back to sleep."

"Owen ..." my brother pleaded through slightly knit brows.

"Hey, Ian," Trinity said from the other side of the bed.

"Hey, Trin," Ian rasped. They shared a smile. "Can you give us a minute?"

"Sure," the girl said, maintaining that smile that betrayed an underlying sadness. The smile faded when she looked at me as she left the room.

"What's up?" my twin asked.

I sighed heavily. "Same argument."

"Meaning what?"

"My life has denied your life of so much," I started. "And now, apparently it's killing you."

"Nah. It's just a little heart thing. The doctors said I'll be out in a couple –"

"Twenty-four-year-olds don't have heart attacks, Ian!"

That shut him up. There had only been a half-dozen times I could silence my brother with a remark. Usually, he would retort with something wise and logical, but not today. Today my logic was unmistakable.

"Enough is enough," I said.

"Now I know what you meant by the 'old argument.'"

"If we continue down this path, Ian, we would both die. What would that solve? At least without having to keep me alive, you would be able to finally live the life you deserve—unobstructed, free, with boundless potential."

"I don't care!" Ian blinked the wetness in his eyes. I supposed it was unfair of me to take advantage of him in a drugged state, but I couldn't back down now. Logic was on my side.

"Really? Where would you be now had you gone to Harvard? Or Yale?"

"Without a brother!" He was practically screaming.

"So what?"

"So what? I can't believe you're saying this. You have worth. You matter to me. I don't care about Harvard or Yale. I care about *you*." His monitor quickened to an audible pace. His face vacillated between pleading and anger.

This was where I usually backed down and became the emotional one in the several arguments we've had about this subject. But his life was never part of the discussion until tonight. "And I, you. What sense does it make for both of us to die?"

"You don't know that either."

"Cut the crap, Ian!" This time, I was shouting. "Your life-giving during all these years has been slowly killing you. I can't believe I didn't see it before. You've always been rail thin. You tire easily. You've had a cough for the past six months. And now this! Your heart can't handle the strain anymore!"

"So, you're a doctor now?"

I ignored his condescension and glared at him, expressing disappointment at his pathetic attempts to dissuade me. We shared several moments of burning silence. He soon looked away.

A vase of half-dead roses sat on the windowsill to his left. The stems pointed the spent blooms toward the floor. Ian raised his hand with outstretched fingers. As if on strings, the flowers straightened, revived, and opened into their full glory.

"Ian ..." I said. "Don't waste your energy. You're still recovering."

"Flowers are easier than people," he said, still turned from me. One rose, after widening its bloom, seemed to stiffen considerably, and appeared to glow. My brother then shifted his focus to me. "Every life is precious. Who am I to deny you yours, simply because I possess some extra gifts?"

"Who are you to decide who should live?" I knelt beside his bed and grabbed his hand. Tears erupted from my eyes, no longer able to contain them.

"Who are you to decide who should die?" he replied.

"I wasn't supposed to live to begin with." My voice had dropped to a whisper. "If you continue, you'll die, then I'll die anyway." We both wept and stared into each other's identical light eyes. "Please, brother. I want this."

"I love you too much," he said.

"Then release me from this prison ... this walking death."

The bond twins share is not a thing of myth. I felt his sadness and pain, but also a particle of relief.

Finally, Ian said, "OK."

Ian

We arrived at Sterling Lake just when the sun crept over the horizon, bathing the countryside in a brilliant glow of golds and reds. I basked in the glory of this environment, from the flora to the fish, down to the simple microorganisms that swam within the water.

We scaled a small hill that overlooked the lake, which possessed a serene stillness like a mill pond. As was my habit, I reached out for a fish that patrolled the center of the lake for food and sent it a burst of energy. Predictably, it leapt from its watery confines and splashed back a moment later.

"You always liked doing that, didn't you?" Owen said.

"Yeah," I sighed. I still couldn't believe I was doing this. I hoped he would forgive me. Owen reached for my arm.

"Let's get this over with. I've waited long enough," my brother said.

"Are you sure about this?"

"Yes." He never looked more serious. "Do you have the story straight?"

"Yes. We came here. We went for a swim. I tripped and hit my head on the shore while you went in first without noticing. When I came to, it was too late."

"Right."

My eyes stung from the overwhelming sadness that welled up inside me. I was always the strong one. The smart one. But now my world was about to fall apart.

"It'll be OK, Ian," Owen said. He displayed a strength I hadn't witnessed in him before. That's good. He'll need it.

"OK." I exhaled and steadied myself as we grabbed each other's shoulders.

I closed my eyes as my mind touched his life-force. I slowly withdrew the energy I had always provided to him and felt darkness creep into him. His hands softened their hold on me and he teetered from side to side a bit.

Then I opened up everything.

Bright, pure life energy burst from me like a cannon. Owen's grip tightened like steel cables, digging into my deltoids. He inhaled violently as wave after wave of my life poured into my brother, filling him with the power and the magnificence of the energy from every cell. I permeated his body with the very essence of my being. All that I was, I now gave to Owen.

"Ian, what are you doing?" I heard Owen ask as if at the other side of a tunnel. That same darkness I sensed in him now bled around the edges of my own shrinking reality.

Like straining to inflate a balloon with your last breath, I continued to push the energy out and push some more, beyond the point of no return. I held nothing back. Consciousness faded from my mind, now nothing more than the burnt ember from a lit match, and my last thought was the tiny hope that Owen would understand.

Owen

My insides burned. Just before I felt death's calling, something shot into me and I've been feeling this fire ever since. Ian slumped into a ball on the ground. Every fiber screamed as I bent to put him on my lap.

"Ian!" I shouted. Over and over I shrieked his name but got no response. What did he do to me? This wasn't how it was supposed to happen! Why am I the one alive and he seems dead?

Wait.

My last thought made no sense. It was impossible. Is he dead? I felt for a pulse on his neck but detected none. If he's dead, then how can I be alive? How?

I turned toward the lake and felt the presence of hundreds ... no ... thousands of tiny animals, all swarming gently beneath the surface. A multitude of colors from each creature reached out like invisible threads into my psyche and I felt all of them, all at once. The sensation overwhelmed me and I lashed out through those threads, reacting defensively. The sudden rush of energy sent all the lake's residents bursting through the water's surface simultaneously, sending a loud hiss of splashing through the air.

Was this how Ian felt? Could I now have the power that Ian possessed? Did he somehow give me this lifeforce ability? If so, then could I bring him back and sustain him in life, just as he's done for me?

I had to try.

I faced my dead brother and concentrated. I beheld nothingness within him. I reached out with my mind and wove a conduit between him and myself. With our connection in place, I willed some of my own life through the conduit to be placed into Ian. It trickled at first, ebbing in small pulses of blue light.

My brother twitched. Seeing this, I increased the flow until a pool of light churned with activity. My brother drew in a long breath and startled awake.

"Hey," he said with a dry throat.

"Hey," was all I could reply.

"You figured it out."

"I guess I did."

"It's your turn now."

The realization of our situation made me think of the flower that glowed in the hospital. Ian already had the idea of giving me his gift and experimented with the flower. Even with my last request, he still stuck to what he believed to be right, at the risk of losing himself. He hoped I would feel his power and understand.

My twin brother can be a stubborn jerk. But I guess I'll keep him around.

~~~~~~~~~~~~~~~~~~

M. Louis Lambert is a software training specialist in his day job. He lives in Ohio with his beautiful and patient wife and their four boys. He writes primarily science fiction and fantasy, and is currently developing several short stories, a novella, and his second novel. Visit mllambertauthor.com.
~~~~~~~~~~~~~~~~~~

The Twofer Compendium

She's Here!

Rod Marsden

Rose grew up with a friend no one else could see. This friend said her name was Helen. When Rose told her mother about Helen, her mother got upset over the name. For years and years Rose wasn't to know why. It was a secret. Rose's father thought having someone invisible around was a game Rose had invented. He told her not to do it anymore.

By the age of six, Rose stopped talking to her parents about Helen, but Helen was still there. She wouldn't go away even when urged by Rose to do so. What's more, Helen was Rose's twin. They looked at each other in the mirror and they were the same. As Rose developed, so did Helen. They continued to look alike as they grew.

In primary, on the first day, Rose could have been hit on the head by a soccer ball kicked by a bad boy, but Helen told her to duck, so it flew right past her. In class, the same bad boy tried to dip one of her pigtails in an inkwell but she turned around in time to prevent him from doing so, then told him off. Soon other children discovered it was not possible to take Rose by surprise. They wanted to know why but she kept quiet about Helen. She said she had good hearing.

At age ten Rose took up martial arts and, thanks to Helen, she was good at it. Helen told her when she was getting it wrong and also what she should do to improve. It was like having a second martial arts instructor.

Since her parents were Scots who had migrated to Sydney, Australia, Rose took up Scottish dance. This she enjoyed and, when she was old enough, she performed with other girls at the Celtic festival that took place at Berry on the south coast of New South Wales every year.

When she was in high school, Rose was tested for ESP. One of the tests was a card game in which she had to say what card was in the tester's hand. Thanks to Helen, she could have gotten every card right, but both girls were canny enough not to go that way. Instead she got every card wrong. This baffled the tester, since anyone without much, if any, ESP should get at least a couple right through random guessing. She suspected Rose of holding back but did nothing about it.

Science was both Rose's and Helen's favorite subject. Helen helped Rose find plants and birds to study. This meant Rose left high school with high marks in what she wanted to study at Sydney University.

With her long, red hair and ruby lips, Rose had no problem getting dates. She just had to make sure she didn't talk to Helen when she was on one. It got a bit awkward when she did. No one wanted to go around with a loony.

There were moments when Helen was frustrated at not being seen by anyone other than Rose.

"It's so unfair," Helen told Rose one night. "I want to be able to dance in front of a crowd the way you do and I'd do just as well, too." Still Helen didn't have to eat, drink or sleep so there were advantages in being the way she was. Her pacing during the hours for sleep, however, did get on Rose's nerves. She also didn't care for Helen's singing in the middle of the night, especially when it was a sad Highlander song.

One day Rose was walking in Hyde Park when she came upon a large dog that growled at her. She sensed it was going to attack and she didn't know what to do. Then Helen appeared in front of it and the dog left Rose and chased her twin instead.

"So, some animals can see Helen," said Rose to herself. "She isn't just something out of my mind but, in her own way, real." This was some revelation. Of course, the dog couldn't sink its teeth into Helen. She wore the animal out by running while Rose strolled home.

Rose came to work for a branch of CSIRO, a government-funded science organization. Her specialty was in insect-resistant plants. The trick was to create wheat, barley, and corn crops that still produced an edible yield for humans, but insects didn't care for. Thanks to the internet, she was in touch with scientists elsewhere in the world who were tackling the same problem.

One day she was discussing her latest findings with two young American men from Ohio who happened to be twins, when something strange happened. They knew her name but wanted to know who the young lady beside her was, the one who looked a lot like her but hadn't spoken. Rose was taken aback. It was late at night and the only people in the lab were herself and someone no human, apart from herself, had ever claimed to have seen.

"Helen," stated Rose. "Her name is Helen. What does she look like?"

"You, of course," said one of the lads. "But she's poking her tongue out at me. I don't know what that's about."

"She can be frightfully cheeky," mused Rose, "but not everyone can see her."

"That doesn't make sense," offered one of the lads.

"No, it doesn't," agreed Rose, who decided to get back to discussing her findings with them.

At the end of the conversation they said goodbye to both Rose and Helen. This encounter led Rose to thinking more about twins and how they generally come about.

She contacted the Ohio lads on other occasions and discovered that when the lab was full, Helen could not be seen by them but when Rose was supposedly the only one around, Helen was also visible to them.

One weekend when she was in her late thirties, Rose visited her parents and approached her mother for the first time in decades on the subject of Helen. Her mother was most uncomfortable about the subject, even after all these years, but it was time the truth came out. Her father also thought it was time.

"I gave birth to two girls," said Rose's mother. "One lived and the other had too weak a heart to survive. There is a tiny grave in Botany for my Helen. She would have been your twin, your sister, had the doctors been able to save her."

"She still is," stated Rose who, to Helen's approval, kissed her mother on the forehead. Her mother also felt a second kiss that seemingly came from nowhere and an invisible hand placed for a moment on hers. It was a warm hand.

~~~~~~~~~~~~~~~~~~

Rod Marsden was born in Sydney, Australia. His stories have been published in Australia, the USA, and Canada. He is a contributor in the Canadian anthology *Grey Matter Monsters – Takers of Souls*. Many of his short stories have been published in *Night to Dawn* magazine. You can visit him on Facebook at Rod Marsden.
~~~~~~~~~~~~~~~~~~

Different Strokes

Peter Astle

Gary and I are identical twins, right down to the two small moles on our backs.

We both share a talent for painting. For me it is landscapes and old buildings. For Gary it is bodies and faces.

Different strokes, I suppose.

On our fourteenth birthday our parents took us to Montmartre, Paris. We both sat cross-legged on the streets watching in wonder as artists created magic on their canvasses. We were equally spellbound. Our parents had to practically drag us away.

Gary kicked up a fuss one afternoon when they said it was time to go back to the hotel.

He was intensely drawn to one particular dark-haired female artist wearing a bright red beret. She painted caricatures of customers in the centre of the square with a simple charcoal stick. Long, tanned legs, glistening with oil.

There was a small queue and quite a crowd. Both Gary and I shared a look. She was very pretty. At dusk, Gary rushed to get her signature as she packed away her tools. She smiled when she handed a scrap of paper to him with her name scribbled in cursive. Her name was Marcella Bonnet.

▷◁▷◁▷◁▷◁▷◁▷◁▷◁

Many people have tried to encourage us to be individuals, but it has never worked.

At school the headmaster separated us into different classes. That was fine. But the inevitable happened, of course. We played the game and switched classes every now and again just for the fun of it.

We were seventeen when we started dating girls.

Just like we swapped classes, we swapped dates. It was no big deal.

Only our art was different. We would often take our sketchbooks out to Derby City Centre, dressed in exactly the same clothes, find a bench somewhere and sketch. Thinking about it now, we must have looked pretty weird sitting there. I cast my eye high and sketched the magnificent rooftops of old banks and department stores, while Gary sketched the blur of people passing in the streets.

Bizarrely, he'd often sketch people as animals.

The trouble started in our mid-twenties when we finally started out on our journalism careers. I worked for the *Derby Telegraph* and Gary worked for the *Nottingham Post*. We'd both graduated with identical honours degrees in journalism.

We did our best to keep our love lives separate. Honestly, we did. There was no question of us messing around with one another's dates like we did in our early teens.

Gary fell in love before I did.

Selina had just joined the Nottingham newspaper and she happened to catch his eye. Can't say I blame him. Jet-black hair, piercing brown eyes, perfect lips. Pretty much like Marcella Bonnet in Montmartre sitting on that wooden stool when we were fourteen.

Selina was bright and pretty and full of energy. When Gary introduced me to her in a pub in Nottingham, I do admit to a twang of envy.

I dated many women, but none of them were like Selina. They didn't have that fire.

Gary married her. I was Best Man at the wedding and made an appalling speech.

Trouble started five years into their marriage when Selina wanted to start a family.

Selina was a planner. Life mapped out in stages. She was twenty-eight when she decided it was time to have kids.

Problem was, nothing happened.

They went for tests. It wasn't good news.

My brother cried on my shoulder when he told me he was infertile. I offered to help. Donate sperm, whatever. But that was out of the question as far as he was concerned. At least to begin with. In the end, I went for fertility tests and discovered I was fine.

I swear he hated that fact.

Selina approached me on her own in tears. It was a dangerous move.

I was pretty shocked by her direct approach. I was single at the time and Selina was an attractive woman sitting right next to me on my settee. She knew I'd had the tests done and she knew I was fertile.

Gary held his head in his hands when he agreed. Selina said she'd deal with the doctors and booked an appointment with a specialist at the hospital. I donated my sperm and the IVF treatment began in less than a month.

Selina got pregnant on the first shot. Gary said he was happy for her, but I knew there was something very wrong by the way he'd said it.

I knew my brother.

I met Gary at a pub in Derby close to the hospital when Selina was in labour. He was crying. Unshaven. Unwashed.

"I can't do this," he said. "It feels wrong."

"We've been through this, Gary. It's your child. You'll be Daddy."

He shook his head. "It's *your* child. We both know that. Selina knows that."

"We're identical twins. The kid will share our genes. He'll resemble you."

He blew out his cheeks.

"Maybe."

"Not maybe. Definitely."

Finally, he met my eye. "OK. Let's go see."

⋈⋈⋈ ⋈⋈⋈ ⋈⋈⋈

Jake was born a healthy eight pounds and one ounce.

Gary held the baby in his arms and cried. He passed the crumpled red-faced infant to me, but I held my palms flat towards him.

Gary insisted.

I took the baby in my arms.

Selina touched my shoulder before I handed Jake over to her.

"Thank you," she said.

Gary left the room.

Selina and I exchanged a glance, one transmitting a thousand unspoken words.

But worse was to come.

Much worse.

⋈⋈⋈ ⋈⋈⋈ ⋈⋈⋈

I'd decided to leave them alone for a while to gel as a family.

It tore me up to not be in daily contact with my brother, but I knew he needed his space. Five days without contact just about killed me. That Friday night Selina came to my house in a flood of tears. Gary had vanished.

And so, too, had baby Jake.

⋈⋈⋈ ⋈⋈⋈ ⋈⋈⋈

We called the police.

By the time the two uniformed officers got to my flat Selina had calmed down enough to tell her story.

She was asleep when it happened, exhausted from all the demands a new-born baby brings, sleeping on the settee.

When she awoke at around five o'clock that Friday afternoon, Gary was not in his armchair.

Jake was not in his cot.

No one at *The Post* had heard from Gary.

The Peugeot was gone from the driveway.

To begin with, the police officers weren't overly concerned.

I filled them in on the background. Somehow that got their attention. When they asked for a full description of Gary, I said, "You're looking at him."

Once it was established that my brother was a potential risk to an infant, they pulled out all the stops. Detective Superintendent Bradbury from Derbyshire CID led the case.

Gary's passport was missing from the top drawer in the bureau. That was significant. Worrying, I put my arms around Selina, held her close.

Another dangerous step, but what else could I do?

Bradbury put the wheels in motion. In the haze of it all I heard phrases like "automatic number plate recognition" and "airport checks" and just after three o'clock in the morning we learnt my brother had taken a flight from East Midlands Airport to Alicante at ten past seven on Friday evening.

He was travelling alone.

❊❊❊ ❊❊❊ ❊❊❊

And so it began:

The media circus.

Mum and Dad didn't know what hit them when the reporters from the national newspapers started knocking at their door, ringing endlessly.

Mum was scared.

Dad was angry.

I was furious.

The problem was, it was a great story. A child had been abducted. Not just a child, but a baby. The abductee was a twin.

And a baby had vanished.

⋈⊲⊳⋈ ⋈⊲⊳⋈ ⋈⊲⊳⋈

It was established that Gary had made it to Spain on his own.

He'd arrived at nine-fifty local time. They had CCTV of him leaving Alicante airport but that was all.

Bank records showed that Gary had taken just short of ten thousand pounds from his savings account over the last three weeks and had not used his credit or debit card since his disappearance.

The Sun and *The Mirror* initially flashed Gary's face on their front pages like a Wild West wanted sign.

Selina was beside herself. I had no choice other than to stay with her.

Bradbury stayed close, but there were no leads. The story was still headlining in all the major newspapers weeks after Gary's solo flight to Spain and the consensus was that baby Jake was probably dead somewhere in England.

I refused to believe it.

Week three and Gary still hadn't used his credit or debit card. Bradbury assumed he was spending the ten grand he'd withdrawn from his bank account. Gary could be anywhere in Europe by now.

I was scared for my brother, but terrified about Jake.

He was, after all, my son.

Selina and I fell into one another's arms and cried together, shaking and quivering and sobbing like babies.

And then, well, the inevitable happened.

It was one of the most beautiful – and most painful – moments of my life.

᚛ ᚛ ᚛

The world had pretty much turned upside-down for me by week four.

The media circus was closing its tent.

I was sleeping with Selina but most nights I couldn't sleep.

I started wandering the house in the middle of the night, searching for answers.

According to Selina, Gary continued to paint right up until his disappearance. A cupboard in the basement was where he kept his works.

I wondered why he'd hidden them away.

There were dozens of paintings. I sat cross-legged on the floor one night and held each one to the light.

The first twenty or so were all variations of Selina. Gary had made inscriptions on the back with a black charcoal pencil: "Selina in Armchair," "Selina Lounging on the Grass."

"Selina Pregnant."

I stared at that one for quite some time. It wasn't his best piece.

There were portraits of other people, too. Caricatures. School friends painted like animals.

And then I found something interesting.

It was a watercolour portrait of a young blonde woman in a yellow dress sitting at a kitchen table. A salt and pepper pot and a bowl of fruit before her. Mid-thirties maybe. A complete stranger with corn-yellow hair. In her arms she cradled a life-sized doll. On the back of the canvas Gary had written, "Alison Without Child."

The date attached was just over a year ago.

I woke Selina, showed her the painting.

She didn't recognise the blonde woman, but she thought the picture with the life-sized doll was strange.

I thought it was downright creepy.

We logged onto Gary's Facebook homepage and scrolled through his friends list. It took less than five minutes to find Alison Mead.

I should have called Detective Superintendent Bradbury but instead I called Trevor Clarke.

Trevor was the school computer geek. He now worked for some high-tech software company in London designing computer games and knew his way around the internet. I cut to the chase. Told him what I knew about Alison Mead. Within thirty minutes he called back with an address.

Alison Mead lived at number twenty-four on the second floor of a block of flats in Alvaston. When she answered the door, she didn't look too surprised to see me.

The kitchen table was exactly as Gary had painted it. The salt and pepper pot placed side by side next to fruit bowl. Alison's hair was the same corn-yellow Gary had captured with his brush.

Jake cooed softly in a highchair next to the kitchen table.

"I was only looking after him," she told me. "I know he's your child."

"I should call the police right now."

"You won't do that," she said. "How did you find me?"

"A painting. The internet. It doesn't matter. What happened?"

Alison explained she could not have children.

"Gary liked to paint me," Alison said. "He knew me through the Portrait Project. I've been bringing a small group of students there for the last five years, every Wednesday afternoon."

I knew the police had interviewed all volunteers at the Cherrywood Community Centre in their search for Gary weeks ago. I wasn't so sure whether they'd spoken to the visiting schoolteachers.

"Wednesday afternoons are what we call 'electives' at our school. The kids get to choose to do an extracurricular activity. Most of them choose some kind of sport, some choose film club, some dance. A handful choose the Portrait Project."

Jake was less than three feet away from me. I wanted to grab him, get out of there, but something told me I had to hear her out.

"Gary was good with the kids," she continued. "Mostly he taught basic portraiture. Sometimes he taught caricature. For the most talented of all, he taught what he called 'comparative physiognomy,' turning faces into animals. Some famous painters introduced the idea hundreds of years ago."

"Giambattista della Porta," I said without thinking. "Charles Le Brun, too. Gary was crazy about that stuff when we were kids." I glanced across at Jake. "What has this got to do with my son? The abduction?"

Alison held my gaze. She didn't seem at all fazed. "I knew this time would come. I just needed time with him. It was important to me. Gary understood that. An illusion maybe. But sometimes illusions are magical. If only for a while. If you want to report me to the police, that's fine. But I know you won't do that."

"And why wouldn't I do that?"

"Because if you do, you will never find your brother."

ᛝᛝᛝ ᛝᛝᛝ ᛝᛝᛝ

Selina broke down in tears when I returned home with baby Jake in my arms. He was safe in his cot, thank God.

But I was in turmoil.

Gary was still missing. Only Alison Mead knew where Gary was holed up and Alison Mead refused to tell me where my twin brother was until she was sure she would not be in any kind of trouble.

We came up with a solution. It was clumsy and frankly ridiculous, but it was a solution nonetheless.

I rang Detective Superintendent Bradbury at seven-fifteen the next morning. Halleluiah. A miracle. Baby Jake had been left on our doorstep all warm and cosy in a sturdy cardboard box, swaddled in warm blankets, returned anonymously.

Did Bradbury buy it? I very much doubt it. He studied me for a long while when he questioned me. He knew.

So did my parents. So did the tabloid media. So did my colleagues at the *Derby Telegraph* who interviewed me for the story.

I let it stew a couple of months before calling Alison Mead.

We sat in the July sunshine on the tables outside a greasy spoon café on the corner of East Street in Derby City Centre. The story of missing baby Jake was ancient history by then.

I'd brought Jake along with me in his stroller.
Alison smiled.
"You kept your word."
"Of course. Now tell me where Gary is."
She told me.
I should have guessed.

⋈⊏⊐⋈ ⋈⊏⊐⋈ ⋈⊏⊐⋈

Le Café du Peintre, on the corner of the artist's quarter in Montmartre, Paris, was tiny but the exhibition outside extended well into the street. Tourists milled around in that lazy way tourists mill around in mid-summer.

My brother's canvasses lay bold and flat on the ground, brilliantly lit in the summer sunshine. I was astonished to see how much he was charging for his works. Famous actors and actresses, politicians and popstars, historical and holy figures had all been transformed into animals—eagles, monkeys, lizards, bears, snakes, tigers, leopards, giraffes. It was Gary's hand. The same hand I'd known since we were kids.

A slim, attractive dark-haired woman with olive skin was selling the pictures to tourists. I had the idea that she was more than just a working partner.

Gary sat on a wooden stool in front of his easel, his hand raised in a flamboyant manner as he transformed the tourists into creatures in his sketches. I joined the queue. Gary had grown a scraggly beard that was greying at the sideburns. He worked fast, his eyes keen, completing each picture in less than five minutes. When I sat facing him on the stool opposite his easel, Gary just stared at me. He blinked twice and placed his palette on the ground.

ЖЖ ЖЖ ЖЖ

The woman's name was Gabrielle. The three of us sat inside Le Café du Peintre drinking coffee and brandy. Gary's fingers were caked in paint. The corners of his eyes were damp.

"How did you find me?" he asked.

"Alison Without Child."

"Is Alison OK?"

"The police won't be pressing charges," I said. It was telling that he'd asked after Alison rather than his wife.

"Jake's safe with Selina now. I explained you'd left him with a friend. A friend who doesn't read the newspapers."

Gary sipped his brandy.

"You look a mess," I said.

"You look smug."

Gabrielle raised a palm.

"Calm down, boys. Or I'll set mother onto you."

I had no idea what she meant by that, but we calmed down anyway.

"Good to see you again."

Gary raised his brandy glass.

"Tell Selina I'm sorry. I won't be coming back."

Gary's paintings were still spread outside the entrance to the café. Gabrielle excused herself to deal with customers who still wanted to purchase his works.

I explained I was with Selina now.

"Makes sense," he said. "We always did have the same taste in women."

I watched through the café window as Gabrielle Sellotaped brown paper around another animal canvas.

"Looks like you've done all right for yourself, too."

Gary grinned.

"She's a work of art." He leaned forward in his seat. "I've tried to get her to wear a bright red beret, like her mother used to do."

~~~~~~~~~~~~~~~~~~

Peter Astle hails from the U.K. He has had several short stories published in the *Derby Evening Telegraph* and *The People's Friend* and he has contributed to a range of international anthologies. Peter recently won two book contracts with Clarendon House Publishing to publish collections of his short stories. Find Peter at clarendonhousebooks.com/peter-astle.
~~~~~~~~~~~~~~~~~~

T Wins

Neal Wiser

I don't know what I'm doing.

I mean, I can see what I'm doing. I can feel my footsteps. I can hear myself breathing. I know The Plan, but I can't stop myself, and that scares me.

I'm walking down the hall at District Southern Middle School. It's Cheerleader Appreciation Day, which is stupid. As if cheerleaders aren't worshipped enough, we have to have a whole day in their honor? I mean, I don't hate cheerleaders. They're cute in their uniforms. But they get so much attention already. Especially Lani Lincoln.

Lani's captain of the Cheerleader Squad. Straight-A student. Rich. Sweet. Funny. Everyone's best friend. Life for Lani is effortless. She has her own fan club. I'm not kidding. Her YouTube channel has like ten million subscribers and she's got a contract with some big makeup company from New York. I know. It's crazy.

But I love her.

There, I said it. No point keeping it a secret anymore because in about a minute, everyone's gonna know. Might as well scream it.

I. LOVE. LANI. LINCOLN.

"No duh, shit face. Keep moving."

Uh, oh! T heard me.

Crap.

OK, I didn't scream it out loud, just in my head. So you might think it's weird that someone heard me, especially T. But it's not. T can hear what I think, even what I'm telling you now.

Who's T? Oh, right. T's just a nickname I gave him. T's Timmy, my twin brother. But he's not in school. T doesn't go to school. He can't. He's a Bubble Boy.

"Shut up, you a-hole! I told you never to call me that!"

I think back at him, *Sorry, T. I didn't mean anything by it. Chill out, 'kay?*

"Don't tell me what to do. You're not the boss of me."

I tune T out. It's not easy. I have to think really hard and he never really goes away, but it lets me think for a minute.

So, T's my twin. He can't go to school which is a good thing because he'd freak everyone out. T's really sick. He's got something the doctors call Severe Combined Immune Deficiency Syndrome. You might think it's AIDS, but it's not. There's something wrong with his DNA and he gets sick real easy. A paper cut could kill him, so he's stuck at home in the Spaceship like an astronaut.

The Spaceship? That's what I call the rooms in our house that my parents built so T could have some space to move around. It's actually kinda cool. It's got an airlock. Filters keep his air clean. Stuff like that. But that's not what would freak everyone. T's different. Really different.

"Shut! The! Fuck! Up! Shut up! Shut up!"

I grab my head. It hurts when T screams at me. He doesn't like it when I talk about what he looks like—

OK. OK, I think to T. *I'm sorry. Can I just go to class*?

"No. You're going to do this. You need this."

I need to go to class before I get into trouble.

"You need to grow a pair. The bell's going to ring in a minute. Let's do this."

I don't want to do anything especially something that T wants me to do. His plan's going to get me in trouble. I mean real trouble, like getting suspended or expelled.

Or arrested.

So, I'm walking down the hall. It's between classes, and it's packed. I get bumped by kids trying to squeeze past me. Everyone's rushing. They don't give us a lot of time, so I have to hurry.

There's an intersection up ahead where the hall forces you to turn right or left. It's a prime hangout because you'll see almost everyone as they're going to class. And that's where I catch a glimpse of her.

Lani Lincoln.

I gasp. She does that to me whenever I see her. She takes my breath away—

"Keep moving, loser. You've only got a ten-second window after the bell rings."

I really want to go to class, but T pushes me forward. And while I can block T's thoughts, I can't stop him from controlling me. I'm like a drone on remote control. And that scares me. I mean, T could make me do anything, like this stupid plan of his, and I can't stop him.

So, I keep walking.

Toward Lani.

Lani's hanging with her crew, the Cheer Squad. But you can't see them because they're surrounded by kids who aren't cheerleaders but who want to hang with Lani like everyone else does. They form three circles, what I call The Three Rings of Death.

The Outer Ring are the Wanna-Bees—kids who have classes with the other kids but aren't really friends. They want to be friends, but all they can do is just buzz around like bees desperately trying to get into the Middle Ring.

The Middle Ring are the Hangers—kids who are actually friends of some of the cheerleaders, but not cheerleaders themselves.

The Inner Ring is the Cheer Squad. They surround Lani like her own freaking Royal Guard protecting their queen.

And in the center, Lani. The Queen Bee.

A gap opens as the kids move around and I see her.

Lani's hair is thick and curly, but not tangled. Her skin's a soft brown; not a single zit. She's a little taller than me, but that's because she's a girl and Mister Mackie, our Health teacher, says girls hit puberty before boys, but that we'll catch up.

Lani catches a glimpse of me through the gap. She smiles.

I freeze.

"*There she is.*" T thinks at me. He feels like an animal on the hunt.

The gap closes and Lani disappears.

"*OK, get ready.*" T thinks at me. "*Remember, when the bell rings you'll have about ten seconds before she heads to class, too.*"

I swallow hard. I just know I'm going to get into big trouble. I really wish Mom and Dad weren't such assholes. They're scientists and when Mom was pregnant, she gave herself shots that she thought would make me and T smarter. I'm OK, but T? He got screwed. Oh, he's super-smart and all that, but if he were just a normal kid, he wouldn't be able to control me, there wouldn't be any plan, and—

The bell rings.

T yells in my head, "*Go! Go! Go!*" He starts a countdown, "*Ten seconds. Nine ...*"

T drives me into the loose Outer Ring. That's an easy one because kids drift in and out, scared they'll be late for class like I'm going to be.

T continues, "*Eight seconds. Seven...*"

I push into the Middle Ring and the Hangers. They're slower to break up and tougher to push into. A lot of them are my friends, but they guard their positions, scared that someone will get closer to Lani than they are. I really just want to go to class.

"Six seconds. We're running out of time. Keep going."

Another gap opens and I see her.

Lani.

She notices me. She faces me. She looks at me!

"Five seconds. Move!"

Holy shit! I gotta go. I gotta get to class, but T won't let me stop.

"Three seconds."

T drives me through what's left of Lani's Royal Guard.

"Two seconds."

Lani's eyebrow arches. Curious as I step toward her.

"One second."

I stop a foot away from Lani. She smiles at me.

I melt on the inside.

"Zero. Do it! DO IT!"

"Hey, Huckster," she says.

Lani started calling me Huckster earlier this year. I have no idea why. She knows my name's Fred.

"What's do'n?" she asks.

She's talking to me. I can't believe it. And I can't believe I'm doing this. I'm terrified. I'm frozen. I can't breathe. My hearts slams in my chest like a nuclear bomb.

T screams in my head, *"What're you waiting for? Now's your chance!"*

T pushes me forward. I close the gap between us. Lani's surprised, or maybe just amused. But she stands her ground. Brave girl.

T lifts my arms. I ball my fists, but I can't stop him. T makes me grab Lani. I pull her toward me and—

I kiss her!

Holy shit! I'm kissing Lani Lincoln!

Lani's Royal Guards freak out. They scream. One of them grabs me, but T has me locked on Lani so the Guards can't move me. Then I realize something. Lani's not pulling away.

She's kissing me back!

Oh, my god!

Her lips are warm and soft. I can feel them move—

Then something happens. Something I never expected. Something I could never have guessed would happen when T came up with his cockamamie plan.

Lani's lips part. She slips her tongue into my mouth.

I. Am. Going. To. Die.

Her tongue is sweet. Tastes like strawberries. But there's something hard. She forces it into my mouth.

It's her gum.

More hands grab me. It takes four Guards to pry me away. Our lips separate. The Royal Guards scream at me, but I can't hear a thing because T's screaming at me, too.

"You did it. Hot damn, you did it! You are now a man. Mission accomplished."

I look at Lani. She slides her pinky across her lip and wipes away the saliva. Then, she smiles at me.

AT ME!

I can't help myself. I smile back.

Lani glances at her Guards. Her smile vanishes.

"Sorry, Huckster," she says. "Don't take this personally."

She moves in slow motion. I think she's doing one of her cheer moves.

Lani spins. Her foot comes up. It's a blur. I don't even see it as it crashes into my nose.

ⵌⵌⵌ ⵌⵌⵌ ⵌⵌⵌ

An hour later I'm sitting on the bench outside of Principal Nadar's office. I'm wearing handcuffs and I've got bloody wads of surgical gauze sticking out of my nose. My nose hurts like hell, but the nurse said nothing's broken.

Lucky me.

I hear screams through Principal Nadar's door. My mom and Lani's mom are going at it. I can't make out much of it, but I hear words like "suspension" and "assault" and "expulsion" and "arrest."

I think to T, *I told you. I'm in trouble.*

T thinks back at me. *"Don't worry. Everything's going to be fine."*

Easy for you to say. I—

The office door opens. Lani and her mom step out. Lani's mom is furious. She gives me an evil side-eye. I think she's going to hit me, but she snorts like an angry bull and marches down the hall. Lani pauses in front of me.

"Sorry about the nose," she says. "Gotta hold up appearances and all that. Can I have my gum back?"

T screams at me, *"Don't give it to her. I want it."*

Shut up, I think at him. I was going to keep the gum as a souvenir, but I guess I'm in enough trouble. It's hard to pull it out of my pocket wearing handcuffs, but I manage.

I hand it to Lani with both hands. The chain between the cuffs makes a little clinky sound.

"Those handcuffs are badass," she says and pops the gum back into her mouth.

Lani's mom screams from down the hall, "Lani!"

Lani rolls her eyes. She looks at me, wipes her lip again, and licks her finger.

"See you around, Huckster," she says. Then she follows her mom.

My mom, Principal Nadar, and a police officer step out of the office. They surround me. Look down at me.

Moment of truth.

The police officer speaks. "All right, Freddie. Missus Lincoln isn't pressing charges, so you won't need these anymore."

He removes the handcuffs.

"You're not going to make a habit of this, are you?"

"No, sir." What else am I going to say?

My mom looks like she's about to have a stroke, not that I know what that looks like, but I hear it's bad.

ⅮⅭⅮⅭ ⅮⅭⅮⅭ ⅮⅭⅮⅭ

I'm riding shotgun next to my mom. Now I know I'm in real trouble. She never lets me sit up front unless she's really happy or really pissed. And since she's been screaming nonstop since we left school, I guess she's pissed.

"You have no idea how lucky you are," she screams. "It would have been bad enough if you got suspended, but do you know what would happen if Child Welfare gets wind of this? They'd want to inspect our home. Our home, Frederick! They'd discover Timothy and our secret would be out. Your father and I could go to jail. Jail—"

"Diane, do you ever shut up?"

Mom hits the brakes. My seatbelt keeps me from hitting the windshield. Cars skid around us. Their drivers curse and honk at us. Mom looks at me.

I freeze. I can't believe I said that. Well, T said it, but it came out of my mouth.

Mom's face is cherry red. I think she's in shock. Shit.

"What the hell did you just say?"

T has me face Mom. She looks weird. Kind of shiny. I see my reflection in the car's window behind her. What's with my eyes? They're glowing. What the—

T speaks through me again. "Listen Diane, I didn't ask you to bring me into this world, but you couldn't freaking resist. Congrats, you got your genius-boy. But since you're not smart enough to fix my immune system, someone else is going to have to cure me so I can go freaking outside and have a life. Got it?"

Shit, I think. *T, what are you—*

My Mom's veins are pulsing on her temples. She's so pissed she stutters over her words.

"You ... You little ... You piece of shit—"

T puts my hand on my Mom's. She stops talking. She just stops. Then, she shivers and just like that, she starts driving again.

T thinks at me, *"Finally! Do you know how long I've been trying to get her to shut up?"*

I don't speak. I can't move.

Mom glances down at me and smiles. She smiles. She talks like nothing happened.

"When we get home, I want you to go right upstairs and play with your brother. OK? It's not fair that he can't go outside."

I don't say a word.

⋈⊏⋈⊏⋈ ⋈⊏⋈⊏⋈ ⋈⊏⋈⊏⋈

Fifteen minutes later we pull into our driveway. Mom gets out of the car and walks to the front door. I notice she's singing.

I think to T, *What just happened?*

"Just get your ass up here."

I get out of the car and walk toward the house. I try to stop. I want to run, but T has me again. Just like at school, I can't stop.

I go inside, head right up the stairs, and go into T's rooms.

I'm in the outer airlock. It's filled with air tanks, medical equipment, hazmat suits, and other stuff. The walls are thick plastic sheets and glass. Something moves inside. It's T. He rolls up to the glass in his motorized bed. T can't use a wheelchair. He's got too much equipment keeping him alive—more air tanks, IVs, a dialysis machine, and computers. Lots of computers. Google would be jealous.

I look at T and can't help but feel sorry for him. He's a dick, but he's still my brother and he's right. He didn't ask to be born. T thinks he can cure himself in a couple of years, and maybe he can. After all, he started speaking at three months, though you couldn't understand him since his vocal cords weren't ready, and he was doing calculus on his first birthday. He invented his own math when he was two and then got into genetics. By the time he was three he was already in my head, so who know what he'll be able to do by the time I graduate high school.

So, I look at T. He's tiny, the size of a five-year-old. His limbs are skinny and twisted. He's got an ergonomic head-brace that holds his head upright. It's made out of metal because T's head is huge. Well, his brains are huge—all three of them. I can see them through the glass helmet that takes the place of his skull. If it weren't for the harness, his neck would break, or his head would tilt over and he could suffocate. For some reason I keep forgetting that. Maybe I should write it down—

T's laughing as he rolls up to the glass. He talks out loud.

"Dude, that was awesome. I could actually taste her gum. But you were supposed to keep it."

"She wanted it back," I said.

"I needed the DNA in her saliva." T sighs. "All right, we'll try again in a few weeks."

"Are you kidding? I almost got arrested. I'll never get within fifty feet of her again."

T looks at me with three of his six eyes.

"She likes you, Huckster. You'll get another chance. Besides, you've got a rep now. You're going to need that. Can't be a dweeb once you get into high school. You need to man up. I got plans, big plans, for you and Lani."

"What if I don't want to be in your plans?"

T's eyes glow. Like mine did in the car with Mom. T makes me walk toward him. I lean over his bed. He looks me right in the eye.

"You don't have a choice."

T lets go and I step back. I take a breath.

"One of these days," I say, "I'm going to get you out of my head, even if I have to kill you."

T glances at me with a side-eye. He snorts.

"Yeah, you keep telling me that. But that day isn't today. Come on, we have work to do."

I nod. What else can I do? With T in my head, I'm his prisoner. T wins again. T always wins.

~~~~~~~~~~~~~~~~~~~

Neal Wiser is an actual twin. He's also a screenwriter who focuses on writing genre-based dramas with depth, heart, and a touch of humor. He writes cautionary tales that are in tune with the zeitgeist and puts his characters through Hell, but they thank him later. Follow him on Twitter at @NealWiser.
~~~~~~~~~~~~~~~~~~~

He Knew How to Keep Christmas Well

Joette M. Rozanski

"Happy Krampus Day!" Mom and Dad shouted.

Allison just rolled her eyes.

Allison's twin sister, Ashley, smiled and carefully hung the Krampus ornament on the Christmas tree, something Allison had done every December 5th morning until she realized how stupid the tradition was now that Great-Aunt Ida was dead.

The ornament depicted the Christmas Devil sitting with his sack-full of bad children on his back, his long red tongue dangling across his chest. Allison's mother didn't like it very much, but Great-Aunt Ida had brought it back from Austria years ago, and her kids adored it.

She, Ashley, Mom, and Dad sat in the living room of Great-Aunt Ida's house. Cold light from the big picture window glittered on the tinsel that covered the big fake Christmas tree near the unlit fireplace. Everyone wore red and green plaid robes and fuzzy green slippers. They had finished breakfast, done this stupid ritual, and now Allison wanted to go to her room and read.

Great-Aunt Ida died last week; Allison and her family were here to go through her effects and pay her final bills. It was winter break for Allison and Ashley, and their parents had a lot of vacation time to use up. Allison and her family were the only close relatives Great-Aunt Ida had left. They lived six hours away and so decided to stay for a week, until Cousin Stan arrived. He was interested in buying the house, which would make getting rid of it so much easier.

"I saw Krampus last year," Ashley said quietly. "When we visited Great-Aunt Ida the week before Christmas."

"You did not," Allison said. "There's no such thing."

Allison despised the fact that her sister believed in things like ghosts and monsters. Ashley watched all the ghost-hunting shows on television and believed herself an empath, whatever that was. She liked to wear dramatic makeup and styled her blonde hair like a certain popular medium. Ashley embarrassed Allison to no end. Allison felt that she, at least, was on the edge of sophomore popularity and she didn't need a weird twin messing up her chances.

Dad laughed.

"Maybe Krampus was the one who broke into George Little's mudroom last night; he stole poor George's greatcoat, boots, scarf, and stocking cap. Oh, and mittens, too."

"Nothing else?" Mom asked. "I thought George kept hunting gear in there—expensive stuff like scopes."

"Nope. Just clothes. The guy smashed through a rear window. Nobody heard anything because the bedrooms are toward the front of the house."

"Oh, dear. I hope that story doesn't scare Stan away."

Allison stood up.

"I'm going to my room. See you later."

She had no interest in listening to her mother and father debate alarm systems for the next half-hour.

⊠⊠⊠ ⊠⊠⊠ ⊠⊠⊠

Later that day, near sunset, Allison heard a soft knock on her bedroom door.

"Come in." She lay on the bed and put aside the book she'd been reading, *The Castle of Otranto: A Gothic Romance.* Allison had found it on a shelf in the spare bedroom and thought it sounded interesting, especially the romance part. However, the story was hard to follow and when Allison flipped ahead trying to find the juiciest scenes, she saw mention of ghosts and spirits and a giant helmet that squashed a guy. This was definitely an Ashley kind of book.

The door opened and her sister entered. She went to the bedroom window and drew the curtain.

"Maybe you better keep this closed."

"Why?"

Ashley hesitated and then said, "I saw the Krampus out there last year. I was staying in this room. Remember?"

"Oh, stop it, Ashley. We all know there's no such thing as Krampus."

Ashley sat down on the bed next to Allison.

"I swear I saw him Ally, and so did Great-Aunt Ida. It was the day of that really big snowstorm, when you and the others were shopping in Lansing and had to stay overnight. I was in here talking to Ida and looking out at the snow, when I saw something moving near the woods."

"Bigfoot!" Allison cried.

Ashley made a face.

"I'm not kidding, Ally. I was really scared but Ida told me not to worry, that she had him figured out."

"Who? Krampus?"

Ashley nodded.

"She said that as long as we kept up the traditions, Krampus would stay away."

"What traditions are you talking about?"

"Celebrating Joshua Whiting's birthday at the crypt. Christmas, too."

"Why would we want to do that? He's not family."

"I don't know. Anyway, I'm going to the crypt tomorrow afternoon to wish Joshua happy birthday. You can come along if you like. Until then, don't look out the window. I don't think the Krampus would hurt you, but he is kind of spooky."

She left Allison's room and Allison picked up *Otranto* again. Ashley and Ida sure liked fantasizing together. Allison was glad she didn't have to share a room with her sister while they were here.

Allison knew Mom and Dad wouldn't let Ashley go alone to the crypt, so she was resigned to indulging her younger twin sister in yet another idiotic adventure.

⋈⟨⟩⋈ ⋈⟨⟩⋈ ⋈⟨⟩⋈

That night Allison had a strange dream. She heard footsteps crunch across the snow outside her room. Curious, she grabbed her glasses, got out of bed, walked to the window and pulled the curtain aside.

A tall man walked near the woods, a couple of hundred feet from the house. He wore a greatcoat, boots, and stocking cap. Allison couldn't see his face, which was almost hidden by a big scarf, but she noticed no breath coming from his mouth.

He stopped for a moment and moonlight glowed upon his shoulders like a cape. His left mitten fell off, revealing a skeleton hand. Allison gasped. Almost as if he heard her, the man bent down, picked up his mitten, and continued walking toward the woods.

The next morning Allison woke up leaning on the windowsill, glasses sliding off her face. She didn't say anything to anybody about what she saw, or thought she saw. People didn't like hearing about other people's dreams. Especially stupid Krampus dreams.

⋈⟨⟩⋈ ⋈⟨⟩⋈ ⋈⟨⟩⋈

After breakfast, Ashley called Allison into the library. It was a small room, its lilac-colored walls lined with white oak shelves gleaming in the light that spilled from the single large window in the eastern wall. About a hundred books and periodicals lay scattered on these shelves: "Reader's Digest" specials, do-it-yourself and crafting books, a few classics like Dickens' *Great Expectations* that looked as if they'd never been opened, and lots of home improvement magazines.

Great-Aunt Ida had self-published a few memoirs and local histories; these were kept in the corner behind the rocking chair that sat opposite the door. Ashley, still in her pajamas and robe, gave one of these books to Allison.

"This will tell you more about Joshua."

Allison looked down at the book in her hands. It was only about an inch thick and its cover was burgundy in color. The title was stamped in gold and read, *Solstice Legends: He Knew How to Keep Christmas Well.*

"Ida got the title from Dickens' *A Christmas Carol.*"

Allison walked to the seat beneath the window.

"I'm going to get dressed," Ashley announced, pushing her glasses up her nose. "Will you be ready for our trip to the crypt by one?"

"Sure. I'll see you at lunch."

Allison opened the book. She learned that Joshua was born on December 6, Saint Nicholas' Feast Day, on a particularly cold morning in 1885, in a farmhouse that had previously occupied the land where she now sat. Joshua had thirteen children, three of whom died before they reached their teens.

Joshua loved Christmas above all other holidays. He kept it—and kept it well, according to the newspaper clippings reproduced in the chapter—from his birthday until Epiphany, or January 6. The rest of the year's leisure time was spent planning for the Great Holiday.

Joshua enjoyed playing Father Christmas and re-enacting Dickens' *A Christmas Carol.*

Joshua served ably in various local government positions until his sudden death in 1925. The family buried

Joshua on his beloved farm rather than in the church cemetery two miles away, where all the other Whitings were laid to rest. None of his remaining children wanted to work the farm and so it was sold to Allison's Great-Uncle Samuel and Great-Aunt Mildred. Ida was Mildred's sister.

One of the terms of sale involved Joshua remaining in the crypt in which he was buried. This didn't bother Great-Uncle Samuel in the least since he was a practical man who wouldn't let a dead body get in the way of a good deal. He tore down the farmhouse and built the current home, which was renovated several times over the years.

⋈⋈⋈ ⋈⋈⋈ ⋈⋈⋈

Another clipping showed the crypt itself. The small building was built for Joshua, his wife Esther, and Joshua's parents. Unfortunately for Joshua, his wife and parents outlived him and joined the rest of the family in the graveyard of the First Christian Church. Esther wanted to be with her family. Joshua alone inhabited the little stone structure.

Vagabonds swore they'd seen Joshua's ghost, wearing the traditional robe of Father Christmas, wandering across the snow during the month of December. Nobody took the stories seriously.

"Not so simple!" Ida wrote in the right margin of one of these clippings. "Harder to settle him than originally thought. Likes both birthdays and holidays."

Allison wondered what she meant. She closed the book and put it back on its shelf.

⋈⋈⋈ ⋈⋈⋈ ⋈⋈⋈

Later, around one o'clock, Ashley and Allison went to see the crypt. The air was calm and almost warm in the near-winter sunshine. They saw blurred prints in the snow near the woods, but whether human or animal they couldn't tell. The wind had almost erased them.

At last they reached the little crypt. Snow drifted against its walls, but remained shallow at the door, as if someone had swept it clear. The stained glass in the little window prevented them from seeing inside.

Ashley reached inside her anorak and brought out a plain doughnut from breakfast.

"Why'd you bring that?" Allison asked, annoyed that her little sister was about to waste a perfectly good doughnut. "Are you giving it to the birds?"

Ashley bent down and placed the pastry on the crypt's threshold.

"No. I saw Great-Aunt Ida put one here a couple of years ago. It's Joshua's birthday, you know, and Saint Nicholas' Feast Day. She wanted us to celebrate with Joshua somehow."

"Great-Aunt Ida was nuts," Allison stated. A few stray snowflakes had caught in her hair.

The tattered remains of a Christmas wreath, clearly several years old, hung upon the door. As a breeze whistled by it lifted the dried-up pine branches and banged them against the door. It almost sounded like someone was knocking from inside.

"Let's go," Allison said. "I'm getting cold."

◄◄◄ ◄◄◄ ◄◄◄

On Sunday the entire family visited the First Christian Church for their Winter Holidays program. The day was sunny and the temperature in the low forties, so everyone dressed in jeans and layers of sweaters and jackets. Ashley's jacket was purple denim and she carried a matching purse sprinkled with sequins.

Sunshine poured through the clear glass panes of the huge windows in the nave, warming the interior of the church. The pews were plain, without cushions, and songbooks were piled in each corner. People would join in the Christmas carols midway through the program.

The choir had taken their places behind the pulpit. The church was nearly full. Allison's family sat down near the front. Everybody fit in a single pew, but there weren't enough songbooks.

"Allison, there are books on the racks in the vestibule," Mom said in a low voice. "Get us a few more."

Allison, who sat on the end of the pew, slipped out into the side aisle, making her way into the vestibule.

She found the rack with the hymnals and grabbed two. From the corner of her left eye she noticed a man's tall figure. He wore a greatcoat, mittens, and boots, but something warned her not to look at his face. A terrible musty odor, like an old, dank basement, filled the air.

They stood together like that for several moments. Allison was too scared to move. She heard the soft dripping of water as snow melted off the man's coat and onto the wooden floor.

A feeling of awe gradually wore away at the fear. She still didn't want to look at the man, but she wasn't terrified of him. This was no ordinary person; the prickling of her scalp and the goosebumps on her arms convinced her.

She remembered something Ashley had told her about people who hung around too long on the earthly plane. She took a few moments to work up the courage to speak.

At last Allison said, "You should move on, Joshua. Move toward the light."

If this wasn't Joshua, Allison was going to feel really stupid.

The man said nothing. Allison had a feeling that he couldn't say anything. She ran back into the church and into her pew.

She didn't listen to a single carol for the next two hours. She tried to understand what she had seen or rather, not seen. Someone—or something—wanted to come into the church but knew he shouldn't. He was considerate, and that thought made Allison sort of like him.

After the program, Allison and her family filed out of the church. The vestibule was empty. She returned the two songbooks to the rack and walked outside to the nearby cemetery.

⋈⋈⋈ ⋈⋈⋈ ⋈⋈⋈

Allison went to Great-Aunt Ida's grave first. Ida's photograph had been embedded into her headstone, which lay flat against the frosty ground. Ida's dark eyes regarded Allison fondly, and her soft lips curved up into a winsome smile.

Allison said a prayer and then decided to visit the Whiting graves. The plain white headstones were precise and proper, much like the Whitings themselves.

As Allison gazed down at Esther's grave, a flicker of movement near the church caught her eye. For a brief moment she saw a tall figure dressed in a long gray coat disappear into the woods across from the cemetery. A gleam of sunlight fell across the gray woolen hat on his head.

Ashley came and stood beside her.

"You saw him, too, didn't you? I always knew you had the gift."

"I saw a guy in a coat, that's all. I don't have a gift. You better not tell anyone at school that I do."

"I want to go back to the crypt tomorrow. I made a new wreath for the door. Joshua would like that, I think."

⋈⋈⋈ ⋈⋈⋈ ⋈⋈⋈

The next morning, Allison, Ashley, and their dad walked to the crypt. Snow showers had dusted the grass with another inch of snow, leaving the path unbroken by anything but ripples of wind-driven white. Ashley carried her wreath, a circle of pine boughs decorated with small silver ornaments.

Dad didn't want them going by themselves at this early hour, and Allison was happy to have him along. She didn't know what she would have done if a man in the woods waited for them, a man who hid his face in his scarf.

The sun had risen above the trees. In a few hours the snow would melt, but for now everything looked touched by glitter. Allison almost believed they moved through a Christmas card.

When they reached the crypt, Dad removed the old wreath, then stood aside.

Ashley stepped up to the door, lifted her wreath and hung it on the hook beneath the little stained-glass window. A soft noise came from inside the small building, like someone rolling over in bed.

"Did you hear that?" Ashley breathed.

They all listened for another minute but heard nothing.

"Let's go," Dad finally said. "Mom wants to go shopping today."

They walked away fast, leaving just time enough for one backward glance, but nothing remained except the crypt, the wreath, and the silent woods beyond them.

⬤⬤⬤ ⬤⬤⬤ ⬤⬤⬤

Cousin Stan arrived in the afternoon, which meant that Allison and her family could finally leave this place.

As they waited in the car while their parents said goodbye, Ashley said, "Do you think Joshua will come back next year?"

Allison thought about this question for a moment, then shook her head.

"I think he's settled now. And he has you to thank for that."

"What do you mean?"

"Joshua just wanted someone to tell him that everything was all right. You know what?"

"What?"

"Your ghost shows aren't so stupid after all. Maybe we can watch them together."

Ashley looked overjoyed and Allison hoped she wouldn't regret making this decision, but she figured spending more time with her twin was a good idea.

After ten more minutes, they started on their way home, and Allison looked forward to them keeping their own Christmas well.

~~~~~~~~~~~~~~~~~~~

Joette Rozanski lives in Toledo, Ohio, where she works as a freelance desktop publisher. She enjoys photography as well as writing science fiction, fantasy, horror, and humor. Joette has had stories published in these anthologies: *Sword and Sorceress 13 and 26, Such a Pretty Face, Strangely Funny,* and *Tomorrow's Cthulhu.* @sippinghouse.
~~~~~~~~~~~~~~~~~~~

The Twofer Compendium

The Branded Shadow

Nicole Fratrich

Frantic, Ben rushed through the saloon's swinging doors and headed toward the bar to meet a familiar figure wearing a black leather hat and vest.

"I just got your wire," he said as his brother downed a glass. "Blake—"

"Another whiskey," Blake told the bartender and then turned to his brother. The men locked eyes as they each gazed into a mirror of themselves, although one's cobalt eyes emitted winter while the other's radiated spring.

Meanwhile, Sam, the bartender, slid Blake his drink and asked Ben, "Sheriff, what can I get you?"

"Maybe later, Sam. I'm on duty." Ben eased himself onto a barstool and folded his hands neatly on the counter. "The warrant landed on my desk this morning. Everyone is going to be looking for you."

Blake shook his head and picked up his glass.

"Had to shoot 'em, I had no choice."

"Why? Old Man Buck was your competition, sure, but to kill him and his brother? The whole ranch will be chasing your hide, especially his son."

"You think I don't know that?" Blake snapped. "That's why I skipped town and rode until I got here. But fifty miles to a different town ain't gonna be enough."

"No," Ben agreed, staring at the counter. "But why, Blake?"

Blake got to his feet.

"I don't owe you no explanation! Here I thought my own twin brother, my flesh and blood, would help me instead of grilling me. But I guess I was a fool to think beloved Sheriff Ben Duvall would help me." He threw money on the counter and stormed out.

Ben trailed after him and caught up with him out in the Nevada heat.

"Where do you think you're going to go with a bounty on your head?"

At this, Blake slowed his pace in realization of the truth, and Ben pushed him inside the stable. Ben wasn't leaving this stable until he knew the whole story.

"Now, why did you kill Buck and his brother? Did you shoot to kill?"

Sighing, Blake took off his hat, revealing Ben's identical straw-colored nest of hair. He wiped his forehead on his sleeve and prepared to open up to his brother.

"Buck stole two hundred of my cattle. One of my ranch hands noticed some were missing and we found them in Buck's fields."

"Your brand on them?"

"It was clear to see."

"There was no way that your cattle could've gotten loose?"

Blake hated Ben's skepticism. He always felt that Ben never gave him any credit, thought he was stupid.

"You think I would shoot without having all of the facts?"

"Your perspective isn't the only one that matters. You could've missed something. Don't forget that Buck's men are probably on their way right now. Besides, you still haven't given me your reason to kill him."

"Reason? Ben, he pulled a gun on me. I shot in self-defense."

"And Buck's brother?"

The brothers looked at each other again and knew exactly what the other was thinking.

"You did it before his brother could retaliate," Ben narrated Blake's thoughts.

"But his gun was pointed at me."

Then they were silent a moment, Blake thinking about what he did and Ben thinking about what he should do now.

"You should leave," Ben said as though he were in a trance. "I'll pay for the horse and supplies."

Blake was taken aback.

"You're just gonna let me run off? You want me to be a fugitive for life?"

"I need time to think and get the facts straight. Stay low around the state border and I'll meet you there as soon as I can."

Now Blake was fuming.

"You still don't believe me! You think I murdered them both in cold blood! You never understood me. Why don't I add theft to my record? My name has already been dragged through the mud." Blake led one of the horses out from the stall, mounted it, and tore out of town, not daring to look back at his brother.

Ben paid for the horse, and he went back to his office to process what all had happened. *Who am I to believe, my brother or the law?*

✕◻✕◻✕ ✕◻✕◻✕ ✕◻✕◻✕

Rosemary knew that she shouldn't have bought those extra two sacks of flour. She was only halfway home when her wagon wheel broke, but truthfully, she figured that the wheel and flour weren't directly related. Whether they were or not, she was stranded outside of town, and the only luck she had was that the wheel broke right by a huge tree. She was too far from town and too far from home, so she decided to wait it out until someone passed by.

After an hour or so, she heard the sound of a horse's hooves growing louder. Looking over her shoulder, she spotted a lone rider coming closer. To make sure he saw her, she climbed onto her buckboard and waved her hands wildly. At first it seemed as though he wasn't going to stop, but the horse finally slowed down and she recognized the pair of eyes that met hers.

"Ben, I'm so glad you found me. This no-good wagon wheel—" The man was just staring at her, and she realized that this wasn't the sheriff. After all, he didn't have a badge. "Ben?" she asked to make sure. Again, he only stared at her. "Forgive me," she said as she smoothed her dress against the wind, "I thought you were a friend of mine."

"You know Ben Duvall?" Blake looked down at her.

Rosemary nodded and Blake said, "Course you do. Then you're coming with me."

Puzzled, Rosemary stood her ground.

"I'm not going anywhere with you! Who are you and how do you know the sheriff?"

Blake quickly pulled out his gun and pointed it at her. He didn't have any intention of hurting the lady, but his anger for his brother was bottling up at a fast rate. Just to spite him, Blake decided to take Ben's friend hostage.

"Take one of your horses and let the others run free," he commanded.

Rosemary was in no mood to comply with this man, whoever he was, but she did so anyway at the expense of her life. She wasn't about to fall prey.

As Blake watched the horses run off, Rosemary began to slide her gun out of the extra bag she kept in the wagon. But when Blake turned his head back in her direction, she closed the bag and hid it under her dress.

They rode side by side in silence. Blake had his brother on his mind and Rosemary was thinking about how she could escape. At the same time, she was also curious about who he was. He didn't seem to be a criminal at heart. He didn't match the stories of criminals who constantly kept a gun pointed at their victims. He didn't even say anything when she periodically glanced over her shoulder. It was like he didn't know he had a hostage.

Finally, Rosemary broke the silence.

"I think I have a right to know my kidnapper's name."

Blake saw no need to hesitate.

"Blake Duvall, your honorable sheriff's twin."

"Gee," Rosemary said, although she wasn't completely surprised, "I never knew Ben had a brother."

"Wouldn't expect you to. Nobody ever knows who I am." He paused as a sickening thought crossed his mind. "But I guess now everyone will, with the warrant and all."

"What did you—"

Bang. A gunshot rang out behind them.

Whirling his head around, Blake was still able to distinguish the blurry figure of Earl Buck, the son of the rancher he'd killed, riding with a group of men. Ben was right: The whole ranch would be after him.

"Giddyap!" Blake urged his horse, and Rosemary did the same to keep up.

"Just turn yourself in," Rosemary persuaded. "You can't run from them forever."

"We'll see about that." Blake urged his horse to run even faster.

Blake soon directed them through every narrow path he knew so they could shake the mob. But Earl Buck didn't give up that easily. He and his men followed as fast and as close as they were able.

The fugitive and his hostage rushed through the trees and stopped in a cluster of thick bristlecone pines. Blake drew his gun and scanned his surroundings, ready to pull the trigger again if needed. This back road took them off course, and he wanted to continue the path they were on previously.

"I don't think you can escape them," Rosemary said, finally drawing out her own gun in case she needed to defend herself.

Blake glanced over at her.

"How long have you had that?"

Rosemary smiled faintly and Blake nodded.

"I see. Thanks for not shooting me."

They became silent again and listened intently for any rustling. Just as Blake sighed in relief, he heard a tree limb rustle, and he cocked his gun. Rosemary did the same.

Suddenly, Earl Buck emerged from the trees and stood in front of them, gun also ready. His eyes and lips were hardened, and he was in no mood for games. His broad, towering figure was prepared to move at Blake's slightest flinch.

"You ain't making it outta here alive," he said sternly. "My father and uncle are dead because of you, so that reward money is mine."

"Your father was nothin' but a thief and a liar!" Blake aimed his gun directly at Earl's chest.

But Earl was no fool.

"Make one more move and this bullet will knock you off your horse." Then he realized Rosemary was there. "You won't be needin' that, little lady."

"I'll take my chances."

Earl's laugh was dark and rough, just like his stare.

"You better drop that gun before you get hurt."

Rosemary wasn't going to be told that she was weak and vulnerable. Out of the corner of her eye, she saw that Blake was getting ready to pull his trigger. Earl noticed this too, but Rosemary was too quick. Earl almost fell off his saddle when Rosemary's bullet pierced his arm. He hit his trigger as a reflex when he fell backward, and his bullet grazed Blake's shoulder.

Just then, there was a commotion of shouting and gunfire beyond the woods where Earl's men waited. Earl tore off to find his men allowing Blake and Rosemary to escape. They headed down the back road that Blake didn't want to take. As they scurried away, Blake heard a familiar, distant voice.

"Carson City Sheriff! Drop your guns! Where's Earl Buck?"

But Blake didn't turn around. He kept on going.

By nightfall, they were heading in the right direction. They camped by a stream, where Rosemary cleaned and bandaged Blake's wound with a ripped patch of Blake's shirt. Blake built a small fire and they cooked a rabbit they shot along the way.

After they ate, they were both wide awake, so they stared into the fire.

"Why did you save my life?" Blake asked. "I'm a criminal."

"Are you?" she asked softly. "You don't act like one. A wanted killer wouldn't be so nice to his hostage."

Blake hadn't thought of this. He chuckled to himself and realized that he didn't even know this woman's name.

"I suppose you got a point, ma'am. You know, I never got your name."

She smiled and tucked loose strands of her auburn hair behind her ears.

"I'm Rosemary. I was on my way home from town when my wagon wheel broke."

"And where'd you learn to sling a gun like that?"

"My pa taught me when I was younger. You see, it was just me and him on the big ol' farm in the middle of nowhere; he wanted me to be able to defend myself."

"Well," Blake looked down at his bandaged shoulder. "Your pa taught you right."

They grinned at each other, but Rosemary wasn't sure if she should ask the burning questions that had been on her mind for a while. Needing to know, she took a chance.

"Blake, what're we doing out here? Did you really kill Mr. Buck and his brother?"

He hesitated, but as he gazed into the soft glow of her hazel eyes, he had a feeling that she would believe him. So he recounted the story as he had told it to Ben.

After hearing the story, Rosemary took a second to digest it. Slowly, she said, "It sounds to me that it was all self-defense. But Mr. Buck's brother ... did he ever pull a gun?"

Blake sighed.

"Yeah. We were arguin' about what happened, and the next thing I know I shot him."

"I think you have a good case of self-defense. Is your brother going to help you?"

Shrugging his shoulders, Blake said, "He paid for the horse and he's supposed to meet me at the state border. But after what happened today with Buck's gang, who knows when he'll show up. Or if."

Rosemary was confused.

"Why wouldn't he come? He's your brother. He's your twin brother. You're like one."

"No, we ain't!" Blake stood up, enraged. "We may look alike, and we may sound alike, but we are nothin' alike." Panting, Blake tried to calm himself down.

Rosemary was patient. She knew he had a lot to say.

"Ben thinks he's better than me," Blake continued. "I've always lived in his shadow. I never mattered! He became Mr. Good Guy and I'm just a lowly ol' rancher. He's a faster shot than me, he's more liked than me ..." Blake trailed off, running out of steam.

The fire continued to crackle as they both stared into it again.

"I don't think you're a murderer," she said confidently. "I can't tell you how many thieves and murderers rode onto our farm when I was a child. Pa and I saw a lot of black souls and icy hearts. You're not one of them. If you weren't like your brother, then you wouldn't have a heart. You would've killed me hours ago and you would've shot down your brother if your hatred and anger were that strong. You're clearly a man who cares about your ranch, your property. Ben is passionate about justice and you're passionate about your cattle. Blake, from what I see, you don't live in your brother's shadow, even though you look like him. You take control of your own shadow."

Blake, who hung his head between his knees, lifted his eyes to look at Rosemary's warming and gentle smile. *How does she see all this good in me?*

"Miss Rosemary, I thank you for all you done for me. I haven't been shown that kinda kindness in a long time."

All of a sudden, the trees behind Blake rustled, and he shot to his feet. He slowly pulled his gun from his holster, and Rosemary grabbed hers as well.

"Drop it," a voice commanded from the trees, and a figure emerged from the darkness into the campfire light.

⋈⋈⋈ ⋈⋈⋈ ⋈⋈⋈

Earl Buck rode proudly into town, although his arm was in a sling from Rosemary's shot. Ready for vengeance, he neared the sheriff's office. His ranch hands followed close behind. Blake was already standing in the middle of the street, waiting for his opponent.

"I got your message," Earl said, still on his horse. "So, you want to settle this once and for all?"

"You won't make it outta here alive," Blake said as Ben stepped out of his office with Rosemary right behind him. They didn't move any farther than the porch of Ben's office.

Earl jumped off his horse and stood a distance apart from Blake.

"Well, Ben, I can't believe you're gonna let this wanted murderer try to shoot me down," he said smugly.

Ben shook his head.

"It's just a shoot-off between two wanted men."

"What?" Earl shouted, hoping his ears were deceiving him.

Nodding, Ben smiled.

"You see, Earl, I did my own little investigation. It seems that you're wanted for several counts of cattle theft, under different aliases of course. But it's your face on the posters, and you don't have a twin."

"I—how—" Earl was speechless. He thought he had covered all of his tracks in the past few months. Irate, he pulled his gun and shot.

But Blake was faster. Earl fell to the ground and nursed his new non-fatal wound.

Ben and Rosemary rushed over to Blake.

"You won't get away with this," Earl growled.

"Actually, I will." Ben, who was dressed in Blake's vest and hat, put his gun away, and Blake handed him his sheriff's badge.

"You're nothin' but a yellow-belly," Earl sneered at the real Blake. "You couldn't shoot me yourself."

Blake shrugged.

"I only shoot in self-defense."

Ben's deputy hauled Earl off and the ranch hands slowly left the scene.

"Your name's clear, Blake," Ben said as he put a hand on his brother's shoulder. "It seems the whole Buck family was in on stealing your cattle. I'll make sure you get them back through a court order."

"Thanks," Blake said. "Ben, I'm sorry for treating you the way I did. It's not easy to be your own self when there's someone else that looks and sounds just like you."

"And I'm sorry for doubting you," Ben admitted.

They shared the same grin until Ben exclaimed, "Come on, I'll buy you a drink."

"I'll be right there," Blake said. He turned to Rosemary. "I thank you again, ma'am."

"Rosemary, please."

"Well, Rosemary, you're the fiercest hostage I've ever seen. You're welcome to visit anytime."

"I sure will," she answered quickly.

Blake started to turn away, but she said, "My wagon is still sitting by that tree."

Thinking for a moment, Blake said, "Come on, I'll buy you a drink. We'll settle that later."

As they headed for the saloon, Blake felt like his shadow had finally been lifted.

~~~~~~~~~~~~~~~~~~~

Currently a student at Saint Vincent College in Latrobe, Pennsylvania, Nicole Fratrich has been published in *Mystery Weekly Magazine* and the Johnstown *Tribune-Democrat* newspaper. She has won various local contests over the past few years. She has a novel in progress and can be found on Instagram at @nicolefratrich_author.
~~~~~~~~~~~~~~~~~~~

Girls of the Sun

Chitra Gopalakrishnan

Siya is twelve years and six months old. So am I.

We clatter noisily outdoors, on a late afternoon in June, when the temperature in New Delhi has crossed 48 degrees.

Running in hurried, excited circles around our huge banyan tree, we sunburn our arms and legs to a crisp brown, uncaring of the *loo*, the strong, dusty, gusty, hot and dry summer winds, whose each puff feels like a blast from a furnace, or the sunbaked earth beneath our naked feet, stepping on which feels like walking on burning charcoal.

We loop, swoop, and whoop in an ecstatic stupor around the thick woody trunks of the banyan that is indistinguishable from its main torso. The dizzying spaces between the trunks and many undiscovered tree hollows hasten the flow of blood in our veins and the spirit within our souls.

It emboldens us to yell, "We are part-elves, part-spirits, and part-girls." We both read enough of the same things to know what we talk of.

We invent games with carefully agreed-upon rules. We have our own language, our very own signs. Our movements are so well synchronized, our clothes and their colours so similar, that people forget that we are two girls. And we ourselves believe that we are one and goddesses of our little world.

Now in our blissful aimlessness, we get to our feet to run past our garden with its balding grass, as our gardeners have cut it as close to the earth as possible saying only then will it grow long and lush, to the patch where the trees of *amaltas* (laburnum), *champa* (frangipani), and *parijat* (the night-flowering jasmine) have spurted out of the cracked earth to suffuse us with their scent.

We can feel the brightness and the sting of the sun's leaking light on our backs. Our calves now ache with our unbridled running.

Yet we go on, past the tree thicket to the shaded area, to where the shrubs of *mogras* (jasmine), *madhumalthis* (Rangoon creeper) and *raat ki raani* (queen of the night) climb stern stone walls. We mean to look for snakes. We have read that they, in this kind of heat, slither away from their underground homes and from holes within walls in favour of cool, fragrant places. We both agree this is the place they will choose to cloister. As we sit and wait, we feel the moistness of this grove creep into our bones. We shiver happily in our brave desire.

We see no snakes but are instead bitten by a sea of small, buzzing cicadas. All we see is a clutch of high-pitched common babblers rummaging at the bottom of a hedge, perching on shivering creepers and pestering squirrels with repeated dive bombs. And one large, fat, crow pheasant that chases away all other birds in sight, its beady eyes surveying us with distrust, its black beak ready to peck if we dare go closer.

Our home is in the city's outlying part, one that our parents built after our stay abroad for some years and after deciding against staying in an apartment in downtown Delhi. They have built elongated pools along one side of the house, not to swim but to grow umbrella palms and lilies and, in particular, to breed fishes as a way to keep away mosquitoes that attack us virulently through the long summer months.

Siya and I head towards one of these long, rectangular waterbodies paved with spring green tiles to spray each other with its murky water. Our game is one that is long and full of giddy gaiety.

We then take our time to pluck at the spongy, springy moss beneath, soft green growths that sway with liquid grace. We plan to lay the moss out on the tufty grass. We do this in the way we have seen our gardeners do. They dry these wet stalks in the summer sun for a few weeks to line up and dry the pits of winter vegetables.

Our final wickedness is slotted for the very end. We jump into the forbidden pond waters that only cover us 'til our waist, our thin, awkward bodies reflecting our brownness in the sun, our clothes ballooning up comically. We slip on the moss, fall over in what we call "a sunny-side-up style," giggle helplessly at nothing in particular, at everything in general, our hands linked, and our eyes saying to each other that life at this moment is very livable.

Our conspired merriment tinkles past the banyan tree's large, leathery, glossy green leaves, our gardens, shrubberies and limpid pools and through the wet lattices of the aromatic thatch curtains of a brown jungle grass called *khus-khus* that run through the entire length of our home's long porch. These grasses cut off the rays of a razor-sharp sun, let the breeze pass through and render our home to something close to an agreeable cool.

I am sure the many staff members, herded around in various nooks of the porch, so that they are in a position to answer to the calls of our *ma* (mother) and *nani* (maternal grandmother), can hear us over the simple water-pumping mechanism that keeps the dry grass damp, and the clamorous noises of the hot winds.

But I suspect they choose to ignore our chittering in this languid hour, lulled as they are with the somnolent lapping of moist breezes against the webbing of the woven grass.

They do not report us either to *ma,* who sleeps on in the air-conditioned comfort of her room, as we should have done in ours. Or to *nani,* who keeps to her quarters and sleeps on a sparse cot with only a ceiling fan, using her hand-held bamboo fan to kick up an air storm for her face.

We have both, that very morning, been warned "not to step out of our room during the day."

Our father, with a face like a shut gate and with a certain fondness for crisp, gleaming, well-ironed, white *pyjama-kurta,* has read us a news report from *The Times of India,* in his clipped, carefully cultivated voice, of the "the capital's bitumen-lined roads melting" and of "how stepping onto them is like walking on molten lava." He has shown us pictures of congealed bitumen bumps and of city hospitals filled with people hit by sunstroke and in some cases, delirium.

We have heard the word "doom." The sun-bleached hullaballoo reported in the papers seems close to that. We fear its quiet menace.

But somehow our dread vanishes the moment he leaves and we sit down to do our math homework at the wide window ledge in our room, the air conditioner whirring away. More so, as we moonwalk around percentages, areas, volumes and measures and start on Zoe Sugg's vloggings and Jeff Kinney's Wimpy Kid series, we put our heads together as we read and laugh and laugh and read.

As our morning decelerates and as the fearfulness of our father's words completely dissolves, we stick our legs through our room windows to graze our feet over the tall, yellow sunflowers alongside them, those that *nani* prizes above all. We love the feel of their petals and their prickly undersides.

Nani knows that we do this regularly, opening our windows while keeping the air conditioning on, and has warned us repeatedly, "Both of you will find yourselves dead one day, dropping off petal after petal, like these flowers, as they, like us, were humans in their previous births."

We laugh every so often over this image of our drop-off deaths 'til we are weak and helpless with the tears running down our cheeks. We then mock her, saying, "We will die but like the sunflower be awakened daily by sunshine."

We know our white-*sari*-clad *nani* well enough, with her aromas of warm camphor and mustard oil, her comforting lullabies, to know she does not mean to cause us our death. She loves us to distraction.

We don't mean any harm, either. We love her too much for that. We love her when she reads our textbooks with so many inaccuracies and an appalling English accent just to show us she knows and understands as much as we do and when she pretends hurt when we laugh. But we love her most of all when she tells us her endless stories of our family, of births and rebirths, even though they are chipped away by repetition.

Ma, however, tries to never let her finish her stories, telling her that we do not understand her toothless stories told minus dentures. But *nani* always had the last word.

"My gums are capable of cracking nuts and I have been telling them these stories from the time you have birthed them so it is in their systems as are my genes and secrets."

Anyway, it is only after *ma,* still in her clinic clothes (she is a doctor), serves us our lunch of rice, lentils, potato curry and curd that we indulge in our sun antics, and muddle through slush and grass and muckrake to allow soil and soul to mix. Things I have described earlier as well as my memory serves me. And as much as with my imagination, at least 'til the point it allows me to keep to the truth.

The evening passes in a blur as we wash up. Vani, our household help, tuts-tuts with horror as she sees our sun-splotched skins and rubs a mixture of chickpea powder, cream and turmeric to take away the angry welts and soothe away the burn we feel. And in a wave of rare anger and candour, she calls us "black devils."

The sky, as usual, turns fluid at dusk to help the night skies bleed into it.

It is on the next day that our world changes. All the sunflowers die. And so does *nani*. We are told it was the sun in flames, ruby red in its anger, which did it.

Over the next few days, *ma* does her best to clothe the pain of all at home in gauzy gentleness. It does not help. It does not help that others say, "We are sorry to hear about Siya." What about her? It does not help that I do not know. They talk of hospitals, delirium, ventilators and the end, as if I should know of it. As if it happened.

It does not help to look in their disbelieving eyes when I say she is right beside me. It does not help when our room is shifted and Siya's clothes disappear. It does not help that we do not know why this is being done. There is talk of encephalitis that Siya has been inflicted with. It does not help to not know what that is. Or why it has chosen her and not me, or both of us.

It does not help that it rains without mercy in the afternoon of the sunflowers' and *nani's* death. It does not help that none of us can remember when Delhi had such intense rains, showers that completely drenched and flooded our home. There are convulsed puddles everywhere and the roofs are leaking. And there are people and more people with leaking umbrellas, looking fearfully upward at the cacophonous thunderbolts as if they are messages from the heavens. Everyone blames the unseasonal rains on climate change. And our *karma* for the collective deaths at home. It does not help that I don't know what climate change means other than the definition learned by rote at school. Or what *karma* has to do with death.

How can our lives change so much in one day? How has it melted like dew? It does not help not to know.

What Siya and I do know is that our lives are different now. That we had a life before the death of *nani* and the sunflowers and now there is the life after.

As sleep and wakefulness pull at us from different ends for days, we realise that our life, which once moved like a cyclone, has slowed down immeasurably. Both Siya and I seem to be trapped between the needles of a slow-moving clock, in a much-lessened life with the rhythms of our earlier life lost to us.

I know I falter in the telling of our tale at this point but I cannot do better with the loss of my sense of time and with my always being in a place of waking sleep.

All I can say is Siya and I would wake up often to the long shadows of midnight, to dancing patterns on the floor, still spiked with sleep, wondering where the day went. Where our certainties went.

On some days, I would see Siya struggle alone in a pool of light, her hair shiny and her eyes clotted with sleep. On other days, I would watch a mass of mosquitoes perform a ballet. On yet others, I would listen to the whirring wings of a bat flitting outside the window, not silently, as it usually does, but with sounds loud as an airplane.

Our heads would think something, our tongues would say other things. A dull resentment had come to settle within us. Our hearts would ache. Our muscles would be listless. Our blood would congeal. Our heads would be hugged by dark secrets.

So, we would indulge in silence. We would talk only to one another. How could we not? We had to try to make sense of life and death. Of how *nani* tried to live, somehow only to die. Like we will, too.

We would try to fill the empty spaces she created by making drawings in her honour. Our staff would ask me why I sign for Siya. I would grunt. A noise, an ambiguous one, which could mean anything. It would turn to annoyance when they would refuse to see Siya standing right by me. Or signing her own paintings.

Siya and I began to think of the sun as their undoing as well.

My parents prove to be no different. Ma has suddenly begun to look older; her eyes have become veiled and there are many newly formed creases on her neck. I see her and Pa wandering in the house at all odd hours like Siya and me, leaving the fridge in the kitchen open and the lights on. Things they had never done before. I see the shades of gray in our living room gather a hold over their lives making them detached, emotionless. Quite like the cold, studded diamond earrings my mother wears.

And they keep saying to me I must go on without Siya. What on earth do they mean? They look at me fearfully, as if I have turned into something frightening, when I ask why. It is tempting to call them all mad and painfully repetitive. Going on and on about a missing Siya when she is with me all the time.

Strange as it seems, over the last two months, I have the distinct sense that I must not contaminate their lives with reminders of Siya. So I don't. I need to keep the balance of our house going, through silence and pretense. So I learn to keep Siya's presence a secret. It takes effort at first and then it happens effortlessly.

These days, I find myself armed with the secret of peaceful co-existence.

Today, when alone with Siya, I croon the lines of Emily Dickinson to her from a book of poems I have found in the library. In a steady, rhythmic whisper.

I'm nobody! Who are you?

Are you nobody, too?
Then there's a pair of us – don't tell!
They'd banish us, you know.

For the first time in many months, she giggles.

In the cold of December, when the air is so chilly that our blood could condense, we sit together at our new window ledge to gaze at a perfect sun, in perfect peace and oneness.

Tomorrow, we will be thirteen years of age.

~~~~~~~~~~~~~~~~~~

Chitra Gopalakrishnan is a journalist by training, a social development communications consultant by profession, and a creative writer by choice. She willfully exploits all genres to tell a story. Visit her at chitraaa.com.
~~~~~~~~~~~~~~~~~~

ReBorn

Lee F. Patrick

December 23, 2012

The dilapidated bus was beyond full. The four of them squashed into a seat that usually sat three very close friends. Normally Terry didn't mind having a girl on his lap but after two hours on rutted dirt roads he couldn't feel his legs. The surrounding trees vanished, heralding their arrived at the site. He wished he'd brought earplugs to guard against all the different noises: bus horns, music blaring from at least three stages, guides shouting for customers. "At least there won't be any dangerous animals around," he muttered. "They must be twenty klicks away by now. Maybe more."

He realised that the buses he'd seen were the tip of the iceberg as they reached the parking area of the site. Except there wasn't any ice around, unless the drink stands had some in their coolers. There were thousands of tourists, each festooned with video cameras, come to watch someone else's version of the end of the world. Maya-style this time. The whole Y2K thing had been a bust, he vaguely recalled, all hype, hand-wringing, and pundits foretelling disasters of all kinds. He and his twin brother Kerry had been nine. He didn't think this one would be any different. For one thing, it wouldn't have the continuous TV coverage as the world sighed in relief that the banking and communication nets hadn't gone down at 12:01.

"Where do you want to go first?" Terry yelled into his brother's ear. Kerry shrugged, one shoulder shorter than the other because of the girl hanging onto him. Terry had a similar girl on his arm, though she let him lean on her as his legs thankfully realised blood flow had resumed. Karen and Anne, who were twins as well, had insisted that they leave the beach and the waves and come to Chichen Itza for the dawning of the new cycle. It would be something to tell their children. The few parking areas not occupied with buses had dozens of souvenir stands and lots of young women in what might be traditional garb for vid opportunities. For a price, of course. Either their fathers or husbands took the money while the women smiled.

The mobs pouring out of the buses buffeted against them and the air was still full of voices. At least it was December, so even far away from the Caribbean breezes, the temperature was bearable.

"I show the senors and senoritas all that they wish." A guide appeared in front of them, dressed in moth-eaten furs and drooping feathers. "Very cheap. I tell you all the wonders of this place. Take you to best place to see ceremony. Yes?" The man had a smile that nearly split his face in half, white teeth against honey-brown skin.

"Yes," Karen said. She was Terry's. Anne was Kerry's. "You tell all, we see all."

"How much?" Kerry asked.

Terry let his brother negotiate the fee down to fifty U.S. dollars. He looked at the brochure they'd been given as they boarded the bus – a little of the history, and more importantly, a map of the site – just in case the guide decided to play any stupid tricks on the stupid gringos to encourage them to increase his fee.

"Twenty now, thirty when we come back to the bus," Kerry was saying. "In U.S. money. And if you give us a good tour, maybe a tip."

The bill disappeared into the shorts almost hidden under the tattered furs. "I am Pakal Hernadez, senors and senoritas. My people built this place and it is now my pleasure to share our history with you. Come this way first;

fewer touristas this way. Get video cameras ready for beautiful pictures." A smile and he waved them toward one side of the complex, away from the buses and vendors. Buying souvenirs on their way back to the bus sounded a lot better than having to carry them all over the site with them.

Terry had to admit that Pakal was a good guide. He hardly ever stopped talking, even as he led them up steep temple stairs. Terry liked the stories about the twins who saved the world back in the dawn of time. He wondered if Pakal had a different set of stories for those who weren't twins, but it did seem to be a big part of their religion.

Karen was interested in the carvings on the top of one temple. Terry thought that she'd come up with a great excuse for a break. A Stairmaster couldn't prepare anyone's legs for the kind of up and down they'd been doing. Up here the music and chatter were far enough away that it was easy to hear Pakal and the other guides.

"And these carvings, senorita, you see here are the Hero Twins, about to be reborn from their father, the grain god. ..."

Terry tuned out the patter and gazed at the crowds of people below. This complex was way bigger than he'd thought. The temple at the other end of the site looked small. He knew it wasn't. It had more steps than the one they were on. He'd counted.

Pakal stopped the lecture and looked up at the sun. "It is nearly time. Come, we must go. Ceremony starts when sun reaches highest point. Cannot miss this. Many pictures to take." He started down the steps, gesturing and describing the carvings as he went. At least going down used different muscles, and they had gravity on their side.

"This is the ball court," Pakal said as they approached a small temple covered with more carvings. Terry's ears caught the word "ball."

"What kind of game did they play?" he asked.

"Soccer is somewhat like, senor, but no one really knows," Pakal answered. "Their ball did not bounce like those we have today. But, senor, see the paintings here. They show the game. Many of the carvings are damaged by time, as I have said, so one of my cousins with the scholars did this to show what it was like." A brightly painted canvas stretched along the outside of the temple, showing extravagantly costumed men bouncing a ball off their hips or diving under it to keep it from touching the ground. Terry looked at the ballplayers, then back at Pakal, recognizing his outfit.

"You ready for a game?" Kerry asked. Pakal smiled and shrugged apologetically.

"See the padding they wear, senor? It is not a safe game to play. The Hero Twins, they played for their lives and those of their father and uncle and for the whole world."

"What's that man doing out there?" Anne interrupted and they all looked into the ball court. An old man, mostly hidden under a multicolored cloak of feathers, had set up a table in the middle of the court.

"Is a ceremony to honour the Hero Twins. He is supposed to be here," Pakal said. "He is Itzam, a priest in the old tongue. Hired to amuse the senors and senoritas on this day of the changing cycle."

"What's he doing?" Karen asked. "Burning incense? Cool." She aimed the video camera at the table and started recording.

"Is resin of the copal, senorita. The ancient ones say the gods are nourished by the smoke and smell of the burning resin. We collect it as sap from trees and let it grow hard to store it. My cousin's stall has some. Will take you there once you wish to leave."

With Karen and Anne in the lead, they and perhaps ten or so other tourists with guides converged on the old man. Pakal went into a harangue in Spanish, but the old man didn't respond to it. He was lighting cornhusks probably full of the copal resin and the smoke from them billowed around the tourists. Two started coughing.

A sapling was tied at each corner of his table and the four uprights were tied in the centre to form an arch over the whole thing. Shells with long spines, pottery bowls with dried corn heaped to overflowing, and gourds were piled around the legs of the table.

A noise came from underneath and Kerry leaned over to see what it was. "It's a couple of chickens," he whispered. "They must be his lunch."

The old man suddenly looked over at them, then shouted something that Terry didn't understand. Pakal moved in front of them. "Do not worry," he said over his shoulder. "The old man is mad. It is all smoke and shouting, that is all."

"You bring them to here," the old man said in accented English. "Hunahpu and Xbalanke have returned as we were promised." He lit more cornhusks and left the table to wave them around us. They all started coughing and Anne rubbed her eyes.

"I am invited today," the old man said with solemn dignity. "To pose for the touristas." He made a grand gesture marred by some of his cloak's feathers fluttering to the ground.

"That misbegotten son of my sister's old age has done something wonderful for a change." Terry heard the old man mutter as he picked up a nice red one.

"You all take places," he continued in his normal tones. "The senors here and here and the senoritas between them. Please, rest to sit with touristas." He shooed the others away with the red feather as if they were chickens. The other tourists walked slowly away, one walking backwards with a video camera.

"I don't get it," Kerry said. "What do we have to do

with this? Why us?"

"Twins. Very good omen for future. Very good for pictures," the old man said after a moment. "Lots of video cameras." He made a wide gesture. "See, they all come now. Be still. No movings." More and more tourists were coming into the ball court and being directed into the seats. The guides tended to stay near their tourists but down on the grass. A few came towards the altar area. Terry wasn't sure all of the people from the buses would fit. Maybe most of them would stay on the temples so they could watch with binoculars and not get smoked.

Anne turned and scanned the crowd. She waved, and a girl who Terry recalled seeing from the beach came down from the bleachers and took Anne's video camera with a long-suffering look.

Pakal and several others, dressed in the same type of ratty furs and drooping feathers, now carried smoking bowls of incense around the open area. Other guides joined them to waft the billowing smoke over the crowd with fans made of large leaves.

"We make ground holy again for ceremony," one shouted when the tourists started to cough and wipe their eyes as the smoke billowed around them. "No allergies."

Terry tried to shift his feet but couldn't move. The same with his arms and head. He couldn't speak, either. All he could do was stare at the table, the incense rising from the corners and from a huge pottery bowl in the centre. Candles added pinpricks of light through the haze of the incense and he felt more and more lightheaded.

A couple of uniformed officials came up to the old man and one pointed at them. Terry didn't think they were police officers, but part of the site administration. After several minutes of low-voiced argument, the one who had pointed at them came over.

"Did you all agree to this?" He sounded mostly

puzzled, but there were hints of anger in his voice. "If you want to leave, better do it now, before the old faker gets into his stride."

"We want to be here," Anne said, eyes bright. "I just hope we get some great pictures. A friend of ours has our video camera so we'll have a great view."

"And the rest of you are all right?"

They all nodded. Terry tried moving again and felt all the tension in his body flowing out like water. "We're fine, sir. Thanks for asking," he heard himself say. "It's a great opportunity."

The officials left with a shrug and the old man marched around the four of them and the table with more incense, all the while calling out in what Terry assumed was Mayan. He could recognise enough words in Spanish to realize that wasn't what the old man was speaking. Wait, wasn't Mayan supposed to be a dead language?

The big bowl of incense was placed back on the table and Terry couldn't hear any noise from the crowds, just the sounds of the wind. The old man reached under the table and brought out the pair of chickens, feet tied together and wings bound close to their bodies. They clucked sadly, as if they knew what came next.

The old man took them one at a time, passing them over the still-smoking incense and sprinkled them with dried corn and water. Their throats were cut with single strokes of a black-bladed knife that caught the light from the candles and reflected it into Terry's eyes. The blood sprayed onto the burning incense and a new cloud rose, one that stank and made Terry's stomach roil but he couldn't vomit, only stand there like a statue.

"Hunahpu, Xbalanke." Terry couldn't make out any of the other words the old man said as he circled them with the blood smoking in the large incense burner. The fog of incense hurt his eyes and he lost sight of the others and of the table in front of him. It went on for a long time. Then he started to hear other voices, one in front of him and another across the table where Kerry stood. Two men were singing in that same language. The old man was silent, or had gone away. One of the men's voices was right in front of him but still he could see nothing but the smoke from the incense. Then the voice started to come out of his own mouth. In English.

"Do not fear. You have been chosen for my rebirth. My soul shall dwell with yours until a new vessel is created. Then you shall be my father and I shall honour you as my brother as I did honour my first father, Hun-Nal-Ye. But for now, you will not remember my coming, as your brother will not remember my brother coming to him. Wake now, and greet your bride."

Terry's eyes opened and he blinked. The fog of incense had largely dissipated, showing the tourists still intent on the old man, now brandishing a red hatchet decorated with red and yellow feathers as he paraded around them, shouting in that archaic language.

He was giving thanks, Terry thought. But for what, he had no idea. He'd be glad when the old faker finished up, so they could find somewhere to sit down and maybe get something to eat. The girls smiled broadly, obviously thrilled. They'd probably insist that Pakal get a huge tip for getting them altar-side seats for the end of the world.

Big deal. It hadn't ended, it had just started all over again. Like all the times before.

~~~~~~~~~~~~~~~~~~~~

Lee F. Patrick lives with her writer husband and four cats in Alberta, Canada, writing short and long genre fiction. Lee's imagination travels to a multitude of fascinating worlds to meet interesting characters with problems they never foresaw. This results in an overfull hard drive of tales seeking an audience. (ReBorn was originally published as The Hero Twins in *Fantasy, Folktales and Fairytales* <Chaos Manor> in 2000). You can find her on Facebook.
~~~~~~~~~~~~~~~~~~~~

Buried Beneath the Gallows

David C. Strickler

Auguste Catron was about to see his final days. He was infected with a new kind of influenza; almost the whole world was. Most believed that it spread through sneezing and coughing. No one survived long enough to find out.

The Ernest O. Lawrence Institute where Auguste worked had shrunk from five hundred and twenty-two employees down to a skeletal crew in a matter of nine months. The Physics Department building itself was large— eight major research facilities, which included an electron storage ring accelerator, a center for materials research, and a whole wing dedicated to X-ray diffraction.

"Hey, hey, wuddya' say?" Auguste said in his usual friendly demeanor. It was how he greeted most of his coworkers, even though some of them were pompous and boring.

Auguste's assistant, Dr. Leo Chadwick, had arrived to help where he could, bringing boxes of canned foods. Just enough to keep Auguste's energy level up.

"You have enough to get by? I brought you more baked beans."

Once the grocery stores shut down, Leo had to get creative when it came to finding their next meal. FEMA had done most of the work of finding safe homes for him, spray-painting 4-part X-codes on every house. Each of the quadrants had a meaning, using shorthand letters and numbers to ID the rescue squad and the date of their arrival. The bottom quadrant indicated the horrors inside. If it had a "1" followed by a "2," for example, it meant there was one survivor left and two dead in the house. Looters typically broke into the homes with "o" as the first digit. It was easier that way.

Leo didn't mind taking care of his mentor. Auguste was all he had left. He no longer had any friends or family, because they all had died. Besides, where else could he go that would be less lonely than here?

The old man spent all of his time focusing on his computer, manipulating mathematical equations that Leo still had trouble keeping up with. No matter how hot the equipment got in those labs, Auguste spent his remaining time toiling away in a hazmat suit. In his mind, he believed it would prevent further spread. When his body was fit to collapse, he often slept on the breakroom couch.

"Herr Catron ... Auguste. Take off that ridiculous outfit. If I'm not infected by now, I probably never will be."

Auguste had already scolded Leo for what he called his excessive stupidity, but finally conceded.

"You need to find someone in immunology," he said, as he peeled away the suit. "See why you're still kicking. You might have to do your own blood work, though." His response came with a heave, as if a toxic cloud of ammonia had filled his lungs. He hacked and sputtered until he was purple before putting on his wrinkled button-down shirt and tan khaki pants.

⋈⋈⋈ ⋈⋈⋈ ⋈⋈⋈

Leo had been driving to Georgia when he learned about the pandemic on his radio. What everyone took to be the common cold turned into something far more deadly. There was always that possibility of contagion, which is why he decided not to fly. Leo never liked to fly. All that recycled air. Petri dishes with wings.

At a gas station, a man approached from behind his car. The closer he got, the worse he looked. His teeth chattered, his face was covered in sweat, and he was shaking. As he fumbled to put the nozzle back into the pump, everything Leo learned in microbiology came flooding back. Leo plunged his hands into his pockets, looking for a napkin. All he could find was a long receipt from the CVS, which he pressed against his nose and mouth.

"Please help *me...*" the man gurgled, ". . . *hospital.*"

Leo shrank from his reach before the man hit the ground. Those were his last words.

ᗑᗑᗑ ᗑᗑᗑ ᗑᗑᗑ

A week later, Leo peeked his head into Auguste's office, with one foot still in the hallway. His boss held his phone tight to his ear, then hung up without blinking.

"Is everything OK?"

Auguste shook his head *no.* It could be something less significant than the deaths of four billion people, but Leo doubted it.

"We have some serious business to address." There was a slight shake to his head that was barely noticeable. Leo was perceptive, but not good with interpretation. He was aware that Auguste wasn't one to keep his cards close to his vest, but it would have been nice if he didn't leave him hanging with so many long dramatic pauses.

"My friend on the inside, Rao, said they found the smoking gun. All seventeen U.S. intelligence agencies concluded it isn't just any old plague, the result of microbial variation in nature. He said human tinkering was involved."

There had been rumors. The world population had hit ten billion people, and with it came climate change, water and food shortages, rampant disease, and political unrest. What started as a joke at one of the G10 summits quickly spiraled into something far more despicable. It was a Russian oligarch—he compared the masses to drooling cattle, saying life would be far easier if they were somehow able to thin the herd.

"Those bastards ... those immoral bastards," Auguste wheezed. "The One Percenters."

As was typical, those with obscene amounts of money wasted little time on long-term solutions. Everyone had a price. They found a scientist, a Dr. Teichert, who was willing to go along with their scheme, which they nicknamed Thin the Herd. He created a highly virulent flu strain that nearly halved the world population, but before unleashing it into the environment, they secretly manufactured a vaccine that guaranteed their survival. By the time unwitting researchers could mass-produce their own vaccine, the earth's population would be down to a more manageable size. They even kicked around the idea of making it themselves, for some extra cash.

"Their decisions depend on what's best for them. They knew our insatiate hunger for resources would never cease. I scold myself for not picking up on all the signs sooner."

Leo rested his hand on Auguste's shoulder, the same kind of gesture he would use for his closest friend.

"You all right?"

"One last thing I want you to do before you're dismissed," he mumbled. "Even though it wasn't listed in your job description."

"Yes?"

"When I die, stick me out back with a bone up my ass. Let the dogs carry me away."

"Oh, come on," Leo replied with a catch in his throat, "You'll bury us all."

He always reran in his head what he had already said out loud, wondering whether or not it was appropriate. He was weighed down by PC culture. Was it gallows humor? People were overly sensitive these days. Guess it didn't really matter anymore.

"What can be done? Now that we know ... they can be arrested."

Auguste knitted his eyebrows together.

"Are you kidding? We're to the point where these pigs have so much wealth they can stand above the law."

"...and the wheels of justice turn slowly as it is. I wish there was something we could do."

Auguste looked at him dead in the eyes. Another drawn-out pause. He then shuffled over to a storage room with sliding racks, picked out a black body suit, then hung it back up just as quickly, his hands doing all the thinking. Most of the researchers knew what the suit was to be used for, knew it at first sight. The thought of activating it caused him to take a step back, as if he were the pilot on the Enola Gay, buckling under pressure to drop his payload. He wasn't its inventor; it was the work of many men and women over the last one hundred-and-fifty years. The project had been around so long, it was barely top secret.

"There is something we can do. Something *you* can do: the Leap."

Leo shook his head in disbelief. No human being had ever made the Leap, but similar, smaller outfits were utilized on animals with mixed results. Lesser creatures, like chipmunks and mice, rodents with not a lot of mass.

"We can make Teichert disappear."

Leo pressed his forehead against the table. He held his breath and closed his eyes. His hands rolled back and forth over his knees, and he thought about all the animals that returned dead. Three out of ten. Nobody ever liked those odds. The larger the test subjects, the worse their chances. Not one was ever bigger than a cat or a dog. They came back as bags of mash. Gray-brown in color. Homogenized throughout. Amorphous. Not one ligament, no muscle tissue, not even one tuft of fur was recognizable.

"So, if I'm to believe we're on the same page, you're saying I'm supposed to go back in time and take out Teichert. You want me to take him out before he becomes a genocidal lunatic?"

Auguste nodded.

"No. No. I don't want anybody's blood on my hands. I'm sorry. I'm not a murderer."

"No, you're not a murderer. You're a savior. You're going to save billions of people."

"I don't know. I don't think it would be the right thing to do."

"The right thing to do?" Auguste hobbled over to his touchscreen and tapped in P-L-A-G-U-E and B-U-R-I-A-L and hit "enter." A video opened of a bulldozer pushing piles of dead bodies into a mass grave.

"Think of all the pain and misery Teichert caused."

Leo took a deep breath and clasped his hands together. The cadavers rolled over top of one another, like rubbery mannequins into a landfill.

"Can you tell me why I'm the one you're volunteering for this job?"

"Why does anyone do the things they do? Why do I collect *Mad* magazines?"

Auguste buckled over into a coughing fit. He plucked a tissue and pressed it to his mouth, hacking up green-brown phlegm.

"OK, good. Looks like I have a bacterial infection as well."

He closed his eyes and let out a few residual hacks.

"Don't worry. I'll do everything to ensure your safety. Matter is finite. You're not meant to be there. All the forces in the cosmos of the past will boomerang you back."

Leo rubbed the oils on his forehead with nervous agitation. Sure, he would come back, but would he come back alive? And that's after killing someone. Could he live with himself?

What did they talk about in college over the occasional bong hit? Killing Hitler that one time, its ethical implications, the anti-Semitism already set in motion that might have put someone else in his place. Erasing Hitler was no guarantee that World War II and the Holocaust would've never occurred.

"What happens if I set off another reality? How do I know that my actions will remain in our timeline?"

Auguste bent down and gathered up all his three-ring binders with a smirk.

"All the non-falsifiable statements we'll have the pleasure of discussing upon your return will make your trip all the more memorable, now won't it?"

❈❈❈ ❈❈❈ ❈❈❈

Leo stood in the tunnel, staring into the control console. His skin was warm and slick against the suit; his feet slid in his footies. His stomach hurt, like he had eaten a bag of cement.

He sniffed the air. The scent of hot metal hung in his throat—an odor that was pleasant. It clung to his lab coat and trousers whenever he got on the train after work. He would pull his collar up to his nose and inhale deeply. It smelled like science. It smelled like progress.

"I forget how the stopwatch works."

Auguste pointed toward his wrist.

"Slide from left to right up your forearm. The digital display should blink on."

Leo mimicked the gesture for a couple of swipes until a box of red dots appeared.

"Again, by my calculations, you should have fourteen minutes and seven seconds before you bounce back. Set it for fourteen minutes, to be on the safe side."

Leo loathed having to figure out technology on the spot, but managed.

14:00
"Come back to me alive, OK?"
Leo shook his head.
"I certainly hope to."
"Leo?"
"Yes?"
"I'm sorry about what I said in last year's evaluation. I was unusually cruel."
"You were, Herr Professor, but I generally keep that opinion to myself."
"You're definitely getting a better evaluation this year, I promise."
Without a conscious effort, both men gave each other warm smiles.
Wires of every color ran along the ceiling over Catron's head, like vessels in an extraterrestrial robot, a giant invader from some distant planet. A computer screen cast a cold, blue light across his glasses.
"Is it worth it? Is it worth risking everything?"
Auguste flicked some switches and activated the software patch he wrote to make up for the lack of staff. He shook his head, thinking of all the possibilities, pausing to scratch his scalp.
"I'll let you know when you get back. Or at least some version of me will. See you real ..."

◞◐◟ ◞◐◟ ◞◐◟

Long waves of electrical shock vibrated through his bones, making him unsure of his footing. When his eyes finally focused, he realized he was on a street. The name TEICHERT was glued in crisp plastic letters down the wooden post of a mailbox. He was in the suburbs of Toronto.

Census data and Catron's calculations out to the nineteenth place—along with the perfectly timed bursts of dark matter—all converged on the right x-y-z coordinates. In the past.

It was night. He was so far from home. His parents were still alive and he wanted to contact them. Give them a warning about what was to come. He looked at his watch.

13:21

There wasn't enough time.

Leo ran along the side of the house—and pushed open a window. Leave it to the Canadians to never lock up their homes. He thought about what he would do if he were caught. He didn't have to. He was in the nursery, before the crib, clenching a pillow he found on a nearby chair. It should do.

Except the young Teichert wasn't a he. Teichert was a girl, a baby girl. The sight of her gave him an immediate stab of sadness. He stared at the delicate hair on the baby's scalp, and tried to imagine all those faces, four billion dead, an image he couldn't even see in his mind. The future of the world was etched upon her cold heart.

He wasn't going to do it. It wasn't right. It was easy to release his hands from the pillow.

Maybe it would be easier if he treated her like a wounded bird, a poor, delicate creature that had fallen prey to the whims of a local cat. Put her out of her misery, except it wasn't her misery he was dealing with. It was the misery of all those who had to suffer, choke, breathe their last. It was there in his hands, the power to make the dead walk again.

Auguste was deemed by *Time* as the Einstein of his day. The journal he kept as a child included the quote, "If science is to ever evolve, we must no longer stand on the shoulders of giants, but instead illuminate new ideas from the ground on up." By the time he was thirteen, his paper on wormholes and general relativity was long regarded as "radical" until the experiments backed him up. Not so long ago, the subatomic particles behind dark matter were only a theory, until Auguste came along and unlocked their mystery.

Teichert.

If Auguste hadn't gotten ill, he probably would have produced another twenty years of advances. *Fucking Teichert.* She will not rob humanity of Auguste's genius.

In that moment he filled his lungs with air. He wished he had on black leather gloves, but then he realized he was being ridiculous. No one would be able to make sense of his fingerprints. In the silence that followed, he heard the faint squeak of mattress springs in the next room. He looked at his watch and knew his time was limited.

Forgive me.

The vertebrae cracked between his fingers.

He gritted his teeth. He saw the red behind his eyes. He couldn't stand the silver-clear strands of snot pouring from his nose and wiped it on his shoulder. *What a horrible fucking life.* Tears rolled down his cheeks. He bit his tongue to keep from whimpering.

He straightened up, studying the room. Was she dead? The black-purple color of the child's face made the white sheet underneath much whiter. He held the railing and waited for the feeling of nausea to pass.

And then he saw it. The bassinet. Something moved under a pink blanket covered in white stars. It was another baby.

A twin.

Auguste made no mention of there being a twin. What if he killed the wrong Teichert?

Leo was beyond the point of regret, and he was ready. The die was cast.

0:00

Space-time shifted his direction, as if gale-force winds pushed upon every molecule in his body.

"... soon. Hey, hey, wuddya' say?" Auguste said. He was feeble now, barely able to keep his head up. Already, Leo was getting teary eyed. Only a second had passed and Leo wasn't sure if anything had changed.

He got his friend to his feet and heaved an arm over his shoulder.

Auguste felt better not opening his mouth, instead conserving his energy for the brief walk to the break room. He was sorry to be a hassle and felt a wave of relief when his body gave way onto the couch, his deathbed.

Leo said nothing about the twin. He sat on the edge of a plastic chair, holding Auguste's fingers in his closed hand. His boss had the pleasure of knowing and befriending many people, but when he took his final breath, it was Leo who was closest. So it was Leo's face that he could see, turning into a white static apparition, as his life, and his life's work, drained away. ...

~~~~~~~~~~~~~~~~~~

David C. Strickler is a writer who lives in the suburbs of Philadelphia. The screenplays co-written with his friend, Tisha Garcia, have garnered Screenplays of the Month on Triggerstreet.com. Since they don't involve superheroes, he expects them to be thoroughly rejected by Hollywood in the not-too-distant future. Also, his birthday falls on May 24, which makes him a Gemini. Visit him on Facebook.
~~~~~~~~~~~~~~~~~~

Magdalen and Matilda

Bruce Meyer

In the end, it did not matter whose body it was—they were both dead. Magdalen's face turned toward Matilda's, and Matilda had raised her right arm and laid it across Magdalen's breast in comfort and, perhaps, to cease the beating of the one heart they shared. The undertaker stood over the sisters and shook his head in despair, not grief. He did not have a coffin wide enough for the two, and the local carpenter had recently passed on. The undertaker had buried him.

Southern had not always been an undertaker. He had set his heart on becoming a blacksmith like his father. But when his father fell on hard times, the forge had been sold, tong and bellows, and the sound of clanking that may have been the first thing the sisters had heard when they entered the world was gone from the village. He turned to Magdalen's husband, Jacob.

"They could have done so much for this village," but the grief-stricken man put his hands over his ears. He would not hear a word the undertaker said. "Can't you see their lives were framed by nothing but grief? They died as they lived, shut away from the company of others, speaking their own language when they did not want anyone to know what they were thinking."

Magdalen's husband closed his eyes. Their wedding night had been hideous. While his wife embraced him and stroked his face, her sister beside her uttered curses against the man. Magdalen tried to hush her sister, speaking to her in words only Matilda could understand. Nothing would calm the twin who, for the first time in her life, felt cut off from her sister, isolated, and alone. Love was not hers. It was her sister's.

Love, the village parson had told Magdalen and Jacob on the eve of their wedding, was what brought people together, what made man and woman one. The vicar begged Matilda to bless the union as vehemently as he had begged Magdalen to forego marriage for her sister's sake. Magdalen had replied that she was her own person; she was not her sister, although God had made them partially one being, of two minds. Magdalen wept. She could not live without her sister nor could she live without love. In the end, Matilda consented but stated that she would do everything in her power to ignore Jacob.

The vicar said, "What God has brought together, let no man put asunder," and then he added, "and no woman," as he stared directly at Matilda.

Matilda loathed Jacob. He remembered how his namesake from the Book of Genesis had wrestled with an angel. The Biblical Jacob had won. Scripture gave him a place for all time for his strength and perseverance. For Magdalen's Jacob, there would be no twelve sons. There would always be the dark angel annoyed at having been woken in the night, a spirit in the gloom of midwinter hours before dawn, lying next to him, hating him, and wishing him dead. How could love survive in such circumstances? The vicar asked Magdalen and she had a simple answer: Jacob loves me, and I love him.

Jacob met Magdalen when he came to the girls' house to repair a crumbling chimney. He had grown up in the village without knowing the sisters lived there.

At the insistence of their father, the twins were never permitted outside of the house. The girls' father had heard the legend of the Biddenden Maids, conjoined daughters like his own who had lived hundreds of years before in the twelfth century. The father of the Biddenden Maids did not hide them from the world or consider them freaks, but looked upon his daughters as gifts from God, the instruments of divine intervention whose lives could be put in the service of charity.

The Biddenden Maids, joined at the hip, made their town famous: They drew visitors from far and wide, and the money charged to see them and the souvenir biscuits they sold, stamped with the image of the two girls on them, was used to purchase a parcel of property that became known as the Bread and Cheese Lands. An endowment from the Bread and Cheese Lands generated alms that continued into the time of Magdalen and Matilda.

Even so, their father insisted they stay indoors. "I'll have no circus in my home. They'll have no spectacle about them."

An old woman who lived in a broken-down half-timber house claimed that Magdalen and Matilda were the reincarnations of the Biddenden Maids. She predicted that the two new sisters, who shared one heart but had their two legs each, were destined to live longer than the Biddenden Maids of folklore.

By locking his daughters away from the world, Magdalen and Matilda developed their own language, as twins are apt to do. It was their means of keeping secrets, of sharing a comprehension of the world that was peculiar to them alone. The girls understood that while everyone else could come and go as they pleased, their world, their lives, were based entirely on agreement and compromise. One could never do what the other did not want to do; that was the case until love entered their world.

In the course of making the repairs, climbing his ladder, tuck-pointing the mortar, and securing iron braces around the chimney, Jacob asked to come inside the house to examine his repair work from within. Magdalen peered around the corner of the kitchen doorway and smiled as

Jacob drew his head from the flue. The windows of the house were open to a spring morning. A cuckoo echoed in the distance. A vine of wisteria around the window frame brought an ethereal perfume into the room. Magdalen and Jacob stared at each other and both said later, they felt as if they were the only two people in the world. Perhaps it was love at first sight, but Matilda denied it. She said she felt nothing for the man and despised him from first sight.

Nonetheless, Magdalen and Jacob's courtship began and she fell in love with him despite her sister's protests. He tried his best to ignore his beloved's other half but it was, needless to say, difficult. She was always present.

One night as the three sat on a settle by the fireplace, Jacob stroked Magdalen's hand and said, "Can you be the one to complete me?" In contemplating Jacob's proposal, Magdalen told her sister that although they shared one torso and one heart, they did not share one mind. She would have her own way. Even on their deathbed, Matilda never forgave her sister. As Jacob wept over Magdalen, who died first of a hemorrhage in the brain, Matilda lay beside her dead sister, terrified, anticipating death, and cursed Jacob for having loved the woman who was part of her.

For Jacob, the death of Matilda was as harrowing as Magdalen's passing, a second grief, a second loss of the beloved, for in losing Matilda, Jacob lost the last vestige of Magdalen. The last night of her life was terrifying for Matilda. In a final moment, Matilda turned to look at her sister. She stroked her sister's face, then put her hand over her sister's mouth and could not feel the familiar breath that had been as constant and as ubiquitous to her as her own. Then she said nothing. She stopped weeping. In her final hours, Matilda was alone in her own head, perhaps alone for the first time in her life. Jacob said the last sister died of loneliness. That was only his guess. Matilda refused to speak to Jacob. She no longer had Magdalen with whom to share their private language. She had no one she accepted as an ally of the spirit to allay her fears.

Whenever Jacob told his story of the sisters, he always began by saying that their lives were framed by grief. Their mother had died in childbirth. Delivering twins was hard on any woman, but delivering conjoined twins meant certain death. The story that everyone in the area knew was that their mother, a beautiful woman named Elizabeth, had married a carter who was beneath her station, and her family had cut her off.

Elizabeth did not consider that her daughters could be conjoined. She was certain that she would deliver two healthy babies. The midwife told her that all was well. Around midnight, the girls' father sent for the doctor. It would cost him all the money he had, but he was determined that at least one of the three should be saved. After examining Elizabeth, the doctor broke the news to her husband.

"These things should only be decided by God," the new father had whimpered. But God was not present, at least not with the possibility of a miracle, and in a moment of despair and fear that no one would look after him in his old age, the father of the two girls chose them over the woman he loved more than life. He exchanged one life for two. The father had stood in the doorway to the birthing room, leaning on the frame with one arm, his other hand gripping the white porcelain doorknob as he wept.

The doctor said that the merciful way for Elizabeth to give life to her daughters while losing hers in one procedure was to bleed her to death. That way Doctor Hallins could say he had tried to save the mother's life. When the last breath passed from Elizabeth and her body lay as pale as the sheets in which she died and would be buried, the doctor reached into the dead woman's belly and drew out Magdalen first and then her sister, Matilda, who was clutching at her mother's open wound as if refusing to give it up. The door through which the sisters came into the world was death's door, and every time someone uttered the phrase in the house, Matilda would cast a dark glance at her sister and her sister would clear her throat.

The girls were born on the 22nd of May 1806 as the sun entered the zodiac sign of Gemini, representing twins. A former clergyman who had been forced to give up the cloth because of his profound fascination with astrology studied the positions of the planets at the time of the twins' birth, and announced the girls were true Geminis in every sense of the word. In a cradle built specially for them, they would tug in opposite directions, neither satisfied with what the other wanted. But in the evening as each fell asleep, they would turn their heads toward each other, and cry with hunger until the wet nurse arrived to feed them.

The nurse did not feed them one at a time as is the case with most twins. A strong farm woman who had lost her husband and infant son to measles in March of the twins' birth year would hold the girls in her strong arms with their heads cupped in her palms and their faces planted against her nipples. Equal suck to both.

"God gave me two breasts," she said to the girls' father, "so He must have known the two infants would need them both equally."

Their father and the nurse tried to speak to the girls, to point out words for things in the house so that the sisters would learn to speak correctly, but they spoke only to each other. They would babble and then laugh. No one else knew what they were saying. The haunted syllables troubled their father who thought the devil was speaking through them. He would shout at them whenever he heard their strange language, so they learned to communicate only in whispers, and then in finger taps, softly drumming out messages to each other that only they understood.

The vicar, who was young at the time, paid them weekly visits in an attempt to school them in the arts of reading and writing. He despaired when they showed no progress. They refused to write anything in the King's language.

Then, one day, he followed them up to their room after their studies had concluded. There he found reams of paper with their cyphers as he called them, scrawled in lengthy passages. Against their protests, he gathered up the papers and took them away in an attempt to decipher the strange code they had developed. He soon realized that the girls had written stories where there were two narrators.

The stories described a faraway place, a land comprised of two islands side by side, situated far from any known land and surrounded by stormy seas. On each island lived a princess, sisters to one another like Philomela and Procne of classical mythology. They had been separated and longed for each other's company. What kept them apart was love. Procne had married a king and had borne him a son, but when she realized that her husband had abducted her sister and locked her inside a tower, and cut out her tongue so she could tell no one of her ordeal, Procne went to Philomela's assistance. They hatched a plot to feed Procne's husband his own son as retribution for the mutilation and violence against Philomela. When Procne's husband discovered what the sisters had done he chased them with a sword and intended to kill them, separating them with the blade of death. But the gods took pity on the sisters, changing Procne into a swallow and Philomela into a nightingale. It was a story that had been taken, almost verbatim, from Ovid's *Metamorphoses*.

But how had the girls found that text? He had not shown it to them. There was not even a copy in the vicar's study. It was considered lurid, a book that a parson should neither own nor keep on display. It was the truth of a violent world especially to those who found their lives defined as remote islands in a stormy sea.

By rights, and because there were two minds behind the stories the girls had written and the story that became their lives, there should be two very different narratives, but there is only one. Language is to blame. One heart, thought Jacob as he read the astrologer's transcription of the girl's works. One mind. The heart governs the spirit behind lives; if there is only one heart there can be only one life.

The more he thought about the sisters, one who loved him and the other who did not, the more he listened for the distinctions that separate things in the language people use. By nature, things, thoughts, sensations, all want to connect to something. Nothing stands alone. Love itself when it is described is a matter of similitude: "I love you like the spring loves flowers," Magdalen had told him. "I hate you like the wind hates blossoms," Matilda had hissed.

Words can connect separate things, and if they do, they fuse them into one entity with a simple "and," so that the world is inhabited by conjoined thoughts, joined and enlarged by the power of a conjunction where two beings become one life. The English language is a tongue of binomials, though that word had not been invented when Jacob sat in the garden of the girls' home one afternoon during his elder years. He remembered when he had been part of a couple, a part of another who was attached to his wife and who turned her face away. To be a widower, he understood, was to lose the power of "and."

A cherry tree the twins' father had planted in memory of their mother was in full bloom. It appeared to flower as the sun shone on the garden and the warm air embraced everything around him, the way the breath of lovers shares a secret when they are close, a secret no one else should know or understand.

And as the sun disappeared behind a cloud and the air cooled and the sky became grey as it does before it rains, a wind came and plucked the new blossoms that had hardly opened from its boughs. The hard waft carried the petals away as if they had been enticed to leave by having learned a secret that denied the flower but longed for the fruit to come.

And if the world is seen through words where so many diverse things are conjoined and made one, whether asked to be joined or not, maybe everything is connected to something else; once that connection is made, the way mortar joins bricks until they become a chimney or a wall, they cannot be unmade. "What God has brought together," the vicar had once told him, "no man could put asunder."

~~~~~~~~~~~~~~~~~~~

Bruce Meyer is the author or editor of 64 books of poetry, short fiction, flash fiction, nonfiction, and literary journalism. He lives in Barrie, Ontario. Find Bruce: @bruce.meyer57 and on Facebook.
~~~~~~~~~~~~~~~~~~~

In My Image

Gerri Leen

The call comes in as I'm getting ready for the opera. It's not one I can ignore, so I put down my makeup brush and answer it.

"Yes?"

"Got a job for you, Leslie."

"Now?"

"Yes. Just sent you the details."

In my line of work, conversations on open lines tend to be terse and vague. The details come via encryption I don't understand to a laptop an ordinary person can't buy.

"Fine." I hang up and slip out of the new red dress I was hoping I'd get to wear first this time. I pull on my standard, boring all-black outfit before yelling, "Manny?"

I hear the heavy steps and smile at how fast my assistant shows up. "What's up, Boss?"

"I need her," I say, handing him the dress. "Can she do her makeup yet?" Not in general, but the way I would apply it.

"I think she can."

I take his word for it. Manny's more than a little bit obsessed with me, and he notices details. Like how much the current clone does or doesn't imitate my style.

This one—I call her Dorothy Four because I'm not going to call her by my own name and I still resent having to watch *The Wizard of Oz* a gazillion times with the mother who left Dad and me for her tennis instructor—seems to be picking up a lot of things fast.

"You were looking forward to this opera." He moves closer. "I was looking forward to seeing it with you."

He's also my bodyguard when I'm in public, so he pretty much does everything with me. "Them's the breaks." I look at him pointedly—no way I'm going to crack open the email until he's good and gone. I trust him but I don't let him in very far. And frankly, the distance I maintain works for me: as long as I keep him at arm's length, he'll want me, and he'll be loyal.

It's bad enough having a revolving line of clones; I really don't want to have to train a replacement for him. He knows what I do and he makes it easier for me to do it.

I steal things. Things important people want. Things that I will never be suspected of stealing because *I* will have been at the opera with him.

That's the beauty of a clone. Especially if Manny does his job and keeps her from spending too much time talking to anyone. Clones are like impressionist paintings: great from far away, but a big old mess if you get too close. So he'll keep her from interacting too much with anyone, and I'm so aloof when I'm out that no one will expect her to be welcoming. I'm not the kind to invite others into the box I love but rarely get to actually use.

She'll sing parts of the opera tomorrow. She does that to piss me off, I think.

It's what I would do, if I were my clone. Which maybe should bother me? Is she becoming a problem?

ↂↂↂ ↂↂↂ ↂↂↂ

Next day, sure enough, she's in the hallway, humming the closing aria.

I smile as I walk up and she doesn't seem to realize the expression isn't sincere. Her smile back goes all the way to her eyes.

"What are you humming?"

"Do you mind? Manny said you loved this opera. I thought you'd like hearing it since you had to miss it."

It's actually sweet. Which is a relief, because I've only had her a few months, and I don't want to have to send for Dorothy Five just yet.

Since she's not showing the annoying tendency to start questioning why she's obliged to stand in for me, I chalk the humming up to an eccentricity unique to this clone. They're never completely identical. They come to me and then learn—but our interactions are never the same from clone to clone. For some reason, this one is more musical—who knows why?

I'm not going to worry until she shows more definite signs of becoming a problem. Sending in a version of yourself for termination once the new clone is ready, even if that version is a thing you own, isn't always easy. Not that my enemies would believe that. They think I have no soul.

Some of those enemies don't play nice. Dorothy Three's demise wasn't my idea—she may have been the best clone I've had yet. Losing her was beyond inconvenient on so many levels. Fortunately, Manny was there to make it look like she was hanging on to life—and it was up to me to "recover" in a very exclusive clinic where the doctors play along however I need them to.

Did I mention I'm rich? I mean I get paid for the jobs, but really I steal for fun. For the thrill. Because I'm good at it. Because being able to find anything, no matter how well hidden, is a rush. There's honor in that—honing your craft— isn't there?

Trouble is, I've honed it too well. Nothing is challenging anymore. Including the job last night—I could have done it with my eyes closed. I considered doing it that way, but I don't get paid to be stupid.

Dorothy pops into her room and comes out with the dress. She hands it to me with a little grimace. "You know that red's not our color, right?"

"Of course. But people don't forget a woman in crimson, which is why we wear it."

"But why would we wear something we don't look that good in? Seems out of character even if it gets us what we want. Don't you care that we'd look better in something else?"

I study her. What's with this "we" shit? "How about you let me call the shots for what I wear."

"But I'm you, too," she goes on, her tone set on stubborn mode and my benevolence toward her starts to fade. "So I should have a voice."

I make the game-show buzzing sound my ex used to do to me. "I'm sorry but that's the wrong answer."

She looks as pissed off as I probably used to when he did it to me. "Is not."

I refuse to get into an "is not, is too" argument with her. "You're not 'me,' toots. You're 'mine.' Big damn difference."

"Some days I hate you."

"Well, by your logic you'd be hating yourself. So I guess it's a good thing your logic is wrong. You aren't me. You just look like me."

She looks down.

"Are you unhappy with your life, Dorothy?" Clones are illegal and she knows it. I might get fined for having her, but she'd be destroyed if discovered. It's the only incentive any Dorothy has needed to behave. Born or replicated: everyone has a basic need to survive.

And the clones are too innocent to see a loaded question when they get one. Dorothy One and Two gave me an earful on how unhappy they were with their lives—right before I had them terminated.

"No." She meets my eyes. Hers seem untroubled. "I'm unhappy with your color choices."

"Fine. You can pick out the next dress."

"Really?" Her smile is brilliant.

It's the little things that keep a clone happy. "Just don't make it yellow or orange."

"As if." She laughs and heads for the laptop she's allowed to use, the parental settings turned up to "Maximum restriction."

"That was nice."

I whirl, startled that I didn't hear Manny approaching. "Yeah, well, it's just a dress."

"But it means something to her."

"So does getting to pick the way we wear our hair for the day. Big deal."

"Don't you ever feel like she's a ... sister or something?"

"No, I feel like she's a copy." I move closer to him. "What the hell is with you?"

"Nothing, I just... I see a lot of you in this one."

"Isn't that the point?" I laugh and motion to where she's sitting. "Go be Mister Moneybags for her. Just don't let her buy me something ugly."

"I won't. I know what you like."

For a moment there's this weird silence between us, then he turns and walks away.

Her face lights up when she sees him, no doubt at the one-time credit code he'll give her to use.

We're pretty when we smile so guilelessly. Too bad that's a look he's probably never seen on my face.

⋈⋈⋈ ⋈⋈⋈ ⋈⋈⋈

The dress she's chosen for us is an icy blue. I let her try it on and murmur, "Very nice."

It pisses me off a little how good it looks on us. I'd have never picked that color—I'd have considered it too soft.

"What makes a person?" she asks as she slips out of the dress and hugs it to her. "What makes you the only you? Why aren't I you? We look the same. We sound the same."

"Memories. Experiences. The fact that I commissioned you, not the other way around."

Clones are spawned and raised in a clean facility with no idea who made them or where they are, happy affirmations playing everywhere they go: "I will serve willingly. The orders given to me are for my own good. I play an important role." You can hear them murmuring the affirmations to themselves when you tour the warehouse, like some kind of weird-ass choir.

They're drugged before they're delivered, so they wake up in a new home with no idea how they got there. In Dorothy's case, a very nice home—her life doesn't suck the way some clones do, like the ones who are used piece by piece for replacement parts.

"Manny doesn't let me do much when I stand in for you. But I could. I could be more useful to you."

"You're useful the way you are."

"I could be more so. If you'd let me. But you don't let anyone in, not really."

I study her. She's watching me with very little emotion in her eyes. She seems to be just...curious. "No, I don't. People will hurt you." It's a lesson I had to learn over and over when I was young. There were more wicked witches in life than there were happy lions or brainless scarecrows.

"But I'm not people. I'm you. If you can't trust yourself, then what kind of person are you?"

I laugh. "That's a good one."

"I'm serious. I could do more. I *want* to do more." I hear frustration this time, even though her expression is even. Generally, I trust my hearing more than what I see.

She's becoming a problem. None of the other Dorothys have ever wanted to be my ... my what? Partner?

Friend?

"The dress is pretty," I finally say.

"I know, but this isn't about a dress. Leslie, let me in." It's clear she realizes her mistake when she sees my expression. She holds her hand up, murmurs, "I'm sorry," and walks away quickly.

I text Manny to come see me.

It takes him forever to show up.

"You have something better to do than help me, Manuel?"

"No. No, I don't. What's up?"

"It's time to get rid of Dorothy Four. She ... she wants too much."

"Okay." He meets my eyes. "Now?"

I nod.

"That means you'll be without a clone."

"I don't care. Something's up with her. I haven't stayed alive this long by ignoring when my hackles go up, and she's got them doing the Charleston."

He doesn't smile like he usually does at my crazy sayings. "Can we ... can we have dinner when I get back? Just ... spend some time?"

"You're with me 24/7, Manny. How much more time do we need to spend together?"

"That's work." His eyes are searching. "Don't you ever think about how much more we could be? Closer. Happy, even."

I can sense he's serious, so I touch his cheek gently. "You know so much about me already. There's no one closer to me than you."

"So let me in, Les. This isn't enough anymore."

I smile as gently as I can. "That's not what I need from you. And trust me: it's better this way. You wouldn't like me if I let you in."

He exhales and meets my eyes, holding the gaze for a long time, as if I'll change my mind if he just stands there long enough. "I had to try." His smile is the one I'm used to. "I'll get her out of here."

"Good." I stop him as he turns. "I do value you, Manny. I don't trust people easily, you know?"

"I know, Boss. I know." His expression's a little sad, like he pities me or something.

I hear the car start up a while later and try not to think how useful a clone who actually wanted to help me might have been. It would never have worked.

I know myself too well.

𝇇𝇇𝇇 𝇇𝇇𝇇 𝇇𝇇𝇇

I wake up the next day, expecting to see Manny at breakfast, but he's not and when I check his room, the bed hasn't been slept in. I text *WRU?* and wonder why I didn't notice he wasn't here earlier. Anything could have happened.

No reply.

Hours later, the phone rings with his tone. I grab it and answer on the first ring. "Are you all right?"

"I'm fine. And so's Dorothy Four."

"Good. I was imagining all kinds of disaster if you two had been in a car accident."

"I'm sure you were." His tone is off, like he's pissed. "Were you worried about me or about being discovered?"

"Uh, both."

"Yeah, sure. Listen, I put in the order like you asked." Again he sounds just wrong.

"Why aren't you here?"

"See, when I said she was okay. I mean ... she's alive. She's ... with me."

I sit in stunned silence.

"Boss, I know that sounds bad. I get that you're pissed off. But ... she's not going to be a bother. We've dyed her hair and it's cut different, too, and she's got glasses on. She seriously looks so little like you now—no one will know. You can go on with Dorothy Five and we'll stay out of your way."

"You *stole* her from me?"

"You didn't want her anymore. I did. I ... I love her."

"Oh my God, you love me, you idiot. She's not me." If she was, she wouldn't love him. She had to be playing him.

It's exactly what I'd do if I were in her place and he was my only hope. Her smile for him—it hadn't been about a damned dress. What the hell was wrong with me?

"Boss, please calm down. I've got a few guys that could take my place. Real trustworthy men. I left their contact info on your desk. This doesn't have to be a big deal."

I grab my phone and check the tracking chip's code—every clone has one.

Except this one, apparently. "You disabled her tracker?"

"Les, I can't have you finding us. I don't want us to fight over this. But I'll do what I need to—to protect her."

"You're supposed to protect me."

"I am." There's noise in the background, then he says, "She wants to talk to you."

I don't want to talk to her. I hate her so much right now I'd kill her myself if I could get to her.

But she's yammering in my ear no matter what I want. "Leslie, please. Just let us be happy."

"Happy?"

"I could have gone to the police, if I'd really wanted to screw you over. I think Manny would have done that for me if I'd asked. But I didn't ask him. Because I don't want to hurt you."

She isn't anything at all like me if that's true.

She also sounds like my mother, on the phone from her new husband's house, trying to tell me how she didn't mean to hurt me or my dad.

No one who hurts you ever seems to want to.

"Sure. No harm, no foul. You go on and enjoy your life—what are you calling yourself now? I'm sure it's not Dorothy or Leslie."

She laughs. "Like I'd tell you."

That sounds more like me.

"This isn't over is it, Leslie?" she asks.

"I don't know. You're the expert on us, Dorothy. You tell me."

"Yeah. This isn't over." She hangs up.

I send an encrypted email to the clone factory putting the order for Dorothy Five on hold. I ignore the list of Manny's recommended candidates and call someone I've always had in mind—just in case.

And then I sit down and start researching.

Finally, something challenging to steal.

~~~~~~~~~~~~~~~~~~~

Gerri Leen lives in Northern Virginia and originally hails from Seattle. She's passionate about horseracing, tea, ASMR vids, and creating weird tacos. She has work appearing in *Nature, Escape Pod, Daily Science Fiction,* and *Cast of Wonders,* and is a member of SFWA and HWA. See more at gerrileen.com.
~~~~~~~~~~~~~~~~~~~

How Could You Leave Me?

Gabriella Balcom

Hearing the distinctive call of a whippoorwill coming from the nearby woods, Ivette blinked hard, trying to hold back her tears. It didn't seem to matter where she was or what she did. Reminders turned up everywhere. Wiping her eyes, she turned around and went back inside, letting the screen door slam shut behind her.

"Would you—?" Mom trailed off when she saw Ivette's face. "Oh, honey," she began. "I ..."

But Ivette didn't want to talk. She didn't want to listen, either. Running upstairs to her bedroom—*their* bedroom—she flung herself on her bed. Sobs racked her body. She heard footsteps on the stairs, and locked the door. Just in time, too, because the doorknob rattled seconds later.

"Are you all right, dear?" Mom asked from out in the hallway. "Can we talk?"

Ivette chose not to answer. The woman meant well, but her sympathy only made things worse, and it didn't matter how many times she insisted, "I understand." She didn't. Yes, she'd given Ivette and Hannah a home and lavished kindness and what humans called "love" on them, but she wasn't really their mother. She hadn't given birth to them. The universe had. And she also had three other children to focus on, so her grief wouldn't eat her alive.

It *did* gnaw away at Ivette. Constantly. Hannah was her *real* family. Her sister, but much more. They were twins and connected in a way no one could understand. They'd spent all of their lives together—centuries beyond count—and they'd always been there for each other.

For a long time they'd studied their surroundings and watched others' lives pass by. But they'd grown bored. Visiting other places had seemed like the perfect plan, and that's exactly what they'd done—Mars, Orion's Belt, Saturn, Neptune and its rings, Venus, the moon and the sun, and they'd gone to other solar systems.

Eventually going to Earth had been inevitable. They'd hidden their true identities, adopted different personas, and dived headfirst into one adventure after another all over the world. White-water rafting the most dangerous waters. Sky diving. Bungee jumping. Mountain climbing. Donning scuba gear to visit ocean and sea wonders. They'd also indulged in karate, wrestling, gambling, shooting, bull-riding, and visiting ghost towns, the Seven Wonders, and more. If anything had sounded exciting or interesting, they'd done it.

Ivette, using a different name, had experimented with romance, making quite a stir with her blue eyes and blonde hair, and garnering dozens of admirers. Hannah had done the same, but as a green-eyed brunette.

But the newness and excitement had worn off, and they'd decided to try something different. After studying a specific group of individuals—children—Ivette and Hannah had transformed themselves into the young of the human species. They'd carefully modified their bodies to allow aging and development.

Walking down a rural Texas road by themselves, they'd been seen and picked up by police. No one had questioned when they'd claimed to have no memory of their parents or prior home. The authorities had concluded they must have been about eight years of age, placed them in foster care, and given them names. They were adopted. It hadn't taken them long to conclude that Lorna and Dave Jones, their adoptive parents, were good people and the best planet Earth had to offer.

Being children had been everything Ivette and Hannah had hoped—and more. Although they'd originally planned to remain only a year, that had turned into eight. They'd experienced living in a family, going to school, making friends, and even having pets, although they'd communicated with animals on a different level than those around them. From day to day, they'd been frantic to learn and feel and do.

They'd read—devoured—book after book and material on the internet in the human way rather than by just magically absorbing things. Trees had fascinated them, along with plants, animals, snakes, bugs, and everything else, and they'd briefly merged with some life forms. Birds had been their latest focus, and they'd learned each variety's distinctive chirps and whistles. Whippoorwills had been their favorite, and they'd taken turns responding each time they'd heard one.

They'd found their new "family" fascinating, too, especially in how deeply they'd felt love and caring. In fact, the twins weren't in any hurry to leave.

But everything had changed eleven days earlier as they'd walked home from school. A passing bus driver had lost control of his large vehicle after a blowout, and plowed right into Hannah. In the blink of a eye, she'd been motionless on the ground, her blood pooling around her.

Ivette had spoken to her sister, shaken her, and screamed, but Hannah had remained silent. Ivette had tried to touch the other girl's mind, but her efforts had been in vain and she'd felt sheer nothingness. Even after watching Hannah's body go into the ground a few days later, Ivette hadn't accepted that. She'd concentrated on her twin as hard as she could again and again, but she hadn't been able to detect Hannah's consciousness anywhere.

They had never imagined anything like that happening. Neither had suspected her life would end, or *could* end.

"Honey," Mom said now, tapping on the door. "I put together a plate of food for you."

Ivette cleared her throat and forced herself to respond. "I'm not hungry—but thank you."

"You have to eat, Ivette. Our bodies need food."

"I know, Mom. Maybe later."

"All right, dear. If you change your mind, though, the food will be in the refrigerator."

"Thank you." The very thought of eating nauseated Ivette. She hadn't felt hunger for days, even though she and Hannah had eaten regular meals throughout their years on Earth. Doing so had seemed normal and they'd reasoned someone might've noticed if they hadn't. But they'd wondered if modifying their essences had made food necessary.

Thinking about it again, Ivette realized they *must* have needed food, because her parents had told her several times lately that she'd lost weight and she'd confirmed it on their bathroom scale.

For maybe the thousandth time, she reached out mentally for Hannah but shuddered when she still found no trace. Agony shot through Ivette. She felt bereft—hollow— and like a part of herself was missing.

The following night

Ivette's stomach churned.

Dad reached over, squeezed her shoulder, and she saw how troubled his eyes were. "Losing someone you love hurts, sweetheart," he said quietly. "But our bodies require food to be strong, and we haven't seen you eat much of anything for days."

"I'm fine," she replied automatically.

"No, you're not," he insisted. "Either your mom or I will take you to see the doctor today. We love you and don't want anything to happen to you."

"Thank you for caring." Ivette knew he had no idea how very much she meant it. She and Hannah had discussed that very thing. Being loved by their Earth parents had been new for them, because they'd never shared a true bond with anyone but each other, and they'd felt astounded at the depths of their own feelings for their adoptive family. Ivette gazed at her father now, then her mother, read the worry in their eyes, and forced herself to eat a green bean and a bite of dinner roll.

Three nights later

Lying on her bed and staring up at the ceiling, Ivette felt listless. Not tired to the point of falling asleep even though it was well past bedtime, but *blah*. She'd felt like this all day long. Nothing was interesting anymore. She normally enjoyed school, but lately her brain had seemed foggy, and she hadn't done any work in class or at home. Music she usually liked had lost its appeal. Movies, too. She just didn't care about anything.

After tossing and turning awhile, she gave up on sleep. Creeping down the hall and stairs so she wouldn't wake up her parents or siblings, she went outside, roamed the front yard, then the fenced one behind their home, and finally lay on the grass in the backyard. Staring up at the stars, Ivette wished Hannah were beside her. If only they could go back in time and—. But that was one thing they'd been unable to do.

Minutes passed, then an hour, as Ivette remembered her life with her sister. She finally sighed, stood up, and felt lightheaded. As she collapsed, everything went black.

She awoke in the hospital the next day with an IV in her arm and her family around her. No matter what direction she looked, she saw worried expressions. Mom burst into tears. Dad's eyes were wet, and Ivette's brothers and sister made a genuine fuss over her.

When she returned home that evening, though, she felt as bad as she had before. Nothing mattered, and she imagined pulling her covers over her head and drifting away after Hannah. At supper, she managed to force down two bites of mashed potatoes and one of cantaloupe, but she threw up soon after eating.

In her room, Ivette stared at the empty bed across from hers and whispered, "You weren't supposed to leave me." Tears rolled down her face and she cried into her pillow. She dozed off but woke, thinking she'd heard a faint sound. Looking around, she saw nothing, but could've sworn Hannah's pillow was in a slightly different position than how it had been earlier.

When she fell asleep again, she dreamed her sister was beside her. "How could you leave me?" she demanded. "What about all the things we'd planned to do?"

"We're still going to do them," Hannah replied, her green eyes blazing as she studied her sister.

"*How*?" Ivette wailed. "You're dead!"

Hannah frowned. "Am I?" She seemed confused.

Ivette awakened with a shriek, sat upright, and gasped. For just an instant, she thought she saw Hannah standing nearby, making no sound although her lips moved. Ivette blinked and saw nothing. Obviously, her wishful thinking was playing tricks on her.

An hour later, she switched TV channels one after another, but nothing caught her interest. A creaking sound came from the direction of Hannah's bed as if someone had climbed onto it, but no one was there. Shaking her head, Ivette stared wide-eyed at her sister's bed and wondered if she were going crazy.

She left the room to go to the dinner table, ate

nothing, and felt awful when she saw the fear in her parents' eyes. They urged her to at least drink a nutritional shake, and she accepted one so they'd feel better. But she flushed it down the downstairs toilet. When she walked into her room afterward, she froze. A book—*The Sword of Shannara*, Hannah's favorite—lay on her bed, and it hadn't been out earlier.

Two days later

"I've lost it," Ivette muttered. She'd continued to catch glimpses of her dead sister, which made her loss even worse. Other inexplicable things had occurred, too. Once she'd heard Hannah's voice and responded to it before remembering her sister wasn't around.

That evening, she couldn't force herself to eat even one bite. She hadn't eaten anything for a while now. Accepting a shake again, she planned to dispose of it later. She no longer felt nauseated at the thought of food. She felt nothing. Not only about food, but everything.

Hearing a ringing in her ears, Ivette shook her head and hoped the sound would go away. She wasn't aware of anything when her body toppled to the right, then fell onto the ground, and she didn't hear the alarmed voices around her.

Within seconds, she found herself looking down on her body lying on the floor and saw her parents frantically trying to revive her.

"Of all the places we chose to go, *this* was the best one," Hannah commented. "We couldn't have chosen a better family."

Ivette saw her sister in the air beside her, also studying the scene below, and answered automatically.

"Yes. We won't forget what we learned here."

"Their love was the best part."

"It was," Ivette agreed. Then she demanded, "How

could you leave me? We always agreed we'd be together, no matter what. And we're supposed to be immortal, comprised of energy that lasts forever."

"We *are* immortal. But I think when we took human bodies and gave them the ability to age, we changed ourselves more than we'd realized."

"Losing you *devastated* me and was worse than anything I've ever felt." Ivette's voice shook. The agony she'd experienced had been horrendous. "I couldn't feel you. Why didn't you talk to me? Mentally at least?"

Hannah pulled her into a tight hug and whispered, "I'm sorry." Ivette sobbed bitterly and Hannah cried, too. "I tried to communicate with you but couldn't," she said. "I could see you and hear you, but it was like I was trapped in some kind of thick fog. But it's gone now and everything's back to normal."

"Is it?" Ivette asked, stepping backward a few inches. "I'm afraid I'll wake up and find out I've only been dreaming."

"This isn't a dream. It's real."

Hannah raised both of her hands into the air and held them at shoulder-height, palms facing outward. Ivette did the same. Walking toward one another, they put their palms together. A blinding light appeared, enveloping them. Energy rippled through the air, built up around them, and exploded with fragments flying in all directions. Ivette and Hannah merged into one, then divided into two separate, glowing beings.

Holding hands, they spoke together, their voices ringing. "We are two and we are one. Joined in energy. Joined in purpose. Forever. We are Gemini."

She-Who-Had-Been-Ivette glanced at She-Who-Had-Been-Hannah, and their eyes shone. Silently sharing their thoughts, the twins studied the humans who remained unaware of their presence, agreed they'd miss their family, and agreed on something else, too: They channeled energy into the motionless body on the floor, and within seconds a completely human Ivette opened her eyes, to the happiness of her parents and siblings.

"We will never forget," the sisters agreed.

Feeling a joy all their own, Gemini shot upward through the air leaving Earth, to resume their position amid the stars. Perhaps they'd travel again someday—maybe even return to Earth—but not today.

~~~~~~~~~~~~~~~~~~

Gabriella Balcom, who is from Texas, writes fantasy, horror/thriller, romance, sci-fi, and more. She likes traveling, music, photography, great stories, history, and movies. Gabriella loves forests, mountains, and back roads. She has a weakness for lasagna, garlic bread, tacos, cheese, and chocolate. Check out her author page on Facebook: GabriellaBalcom.lonestarauthor.
~~~~~~~~~~~~~~~~~~

The Twofer Compendium

- 286 -

A Bayou Tale

Steve Carr

It's been a long time since I've been back to the bayou. Some people say it's the mysterious happenin's that occur in the Louisiana bayous that explain how I've gotten to be 112 years old and am as healthy as a man of thirty and don't look much older than that. I was born and lived in a shack surrounded by cypress trees dripping with Spanish moss in the Bayou Manchac until I was seventeen. I had some experiences and saw some things that, lookin' back on it, were mighty unusual, but I don't know if any of it should be considered a mystery or how it might have cast some spell on me. That I'll have to leave to you to decide.

Although I ain't talked Cajun in probably a hundred years, sometimes I wake up from a dream in the middle of the night and realize I was talkin' Cajun to Nightsong or Morningsong, twins I was friends with when I was young, and who I dream about a lot. Everyone called 'em Night and Morning, which was easier. They were the same age as me, born in a shack on the other side of the swamp.

Night was born first, an hour before sunrise, while the woods were still blackened by darkness, and Morning was born an hour after sunrise. Ma and Pa said it was one of the hottest mornings anyone in that stretch of the bayou could remember.

In almost every respect the twins looked identical, except Night had black hair and Morning had blonde hair, which given how the first thing a lot of us notice about someone else is their hair, I guess that's a significant difference. But they both had the same slightly turned up nose, high cheek bones, piercing dark green eyes, and the same crooked smile, as if they were always about to do something mischievous.

They didn't attend school or go to church so my memory of them before we became teenagers is kinda spotty. When they were five their parents died within a few weeks of each other, during an outbreak of fever that considerably lessened the population in Bayou Manchac. Their mother's sister, a widow from a bayou so remote no one ever bothered to name it, came to live with the twins and raise them as hers.

It was rumored she had had six children of her own that all died soon after they were born owin' to her being a practicin' witch and using spells that backfired, but as I said, that was the rumor. The girls and everyone in the bayou called her Auntie Grunn. She was a short woman, around four feet tall, and stout like a bulgin' pickle barrel, but when she spoke it was like thunder was comin' out of her mouth. She kept a tight rein on the twins, so they had to sneak away and take the rowboat across the swamp to play with me, or any of the other kids who lived nearby. The few times I went to their shack, Auntie Grunn stared at me so hard I could feel her vision burning right through my skin.

Because swampy bayous typically smell like everything in them are slowly decayin', and swamp water is as thick and stagnate as a bucket of pig's blood in some places, you'd think that in the bayou time moved at the pace of a dead chicken. But time there was pretty much like time everywhere else; it doesn't stand still long enough to let you linger for very long on what is happenin' at the moment. It's not until the twins and I were sixteen going on seventeen that I really remember them and what happened shortly before I left home, in the summer of 1924.

◼◁◼◁◼◁ ◼◁◼◁◼◁ ◼◁◼◁◼◁

Toothache was about the meanest and most cunning alligator in Bayou Manchac. Pa told me that Toothache had been around since he was a boy and was always the same monstrous size with that same evil look in his eyes, like he'd been hired by the devil to snatch a few souls and pull them down to the fiery pits of hell. Toothache's favorite place to hide to catch deer or wild pigs while they were getting a drink of water, or an occasional fisherman who refused to listen to the warnings, or a child who just didn't know any better, was just beneath the surface of the water between the bank on my side of the swamp and the bank on the side where the twins lived.

It was early morning and a thin layer of hazy fog hung over the swamp. Toothache was submerged with only his eyes above the water. Ma had invited the twins to our house to teach them how to do a star design quilt and I volunteered to meet them at the swamp. I stood on the bank and watched as they first threw into the rowboat their bundles of quilting pieces, collected from months of going to every shack in Bayou Manchac and beggin' for old clothes and bed linens, and then climbed into the boat.

As always, Morning sat in the front and Night sat in the back. I had spotted Toothache but wasn't sure if they had.

I put my hands to my mouth, forming a kinda megaphone, and shouted, "Toothache's waitin' for ya." Morning waved.

At that moment a ray of bright sunlight broke through the branches of the cypress trees and illuminated her just like she was being lit by hundreds of candles. Her blonde hair glowed. At least I like to think that's how the sun shone on her that morning, but I can't swear to it actually happening that way. The first stirrin's of love – or what felt like it for a few moments – does strange things to a fella's eyesight. The light stayed right on her as they pushed away from the shore and rowed in the direction where Toothache lurked. When they got near the alligator it rose out of the water and opened its mouth, displaying its jagged, sharp teeth, and then suddenly it closed its mouth and submerged beneath the murky water.

A few moments later it resurfaced and gently swam up beside the boat. Morning leaned over and patted it on the head like it was a pet. Toothache stayed beside them the rest of the way across the swamp with Morning petting his head. He went back under the water and swam away as soon as the tip of the boat hit the bank.

"Why'd Toothache let ya do that?" I excitedly asked Morning when she stepped out of the boat.

"Ain't nothin'," she said.

She handed me a bundle of quilting pieces and we walked side by side all the way to my place. If we talked at all I have no memory of it. I do remember feelin' as if my feet weren't touchin' the ground. It never occurred to me that those were mighty strong feelin's to have for a girl I rarely saw.

Night walked behind us with a scowl on her face.

〉〈〉〈〉〈 〉〈〉〈〉〈 〉〈〉〈〉〈

While Ma and the twins sewed the squares of their quilts together, I went into the woods with Pa to check on the traps he had set the day before. The watery moss that covered the ground was sponge-like beneath my shoes. It was as quiet as when you hold your hands over your ears, as if the swallows, woodpeckers, and hawks had all been told to hush. I walked behind Pa, carryin' the burlap sacks to hold whatever was found in the traps. He carried his shotgun on his shoulder, lookin' for the marks in the trunks of the cypress trees that he had carved in 'em as a way to remember the way to the traps and back again.

We were an hour into the woods when I spotted Auntie Grunn standin' between two cypress trees about ten yards away. She had her arms crossed and she glared at me with eyes like burnin' embers. I stopped in my tracks.

"Pa!" I said in a whisper, feelin' as if there were hands clutchin' my throat.

The moment he turned Auntie Grunn disappeared.

"What is it, boy?" he asked.

I thought my eyes had been playin' tricks on me.

"Nothin', Pa. I just thought I saw a deer but I was mistaken."

We continued on, checking the six traps he had set. All of them had been sprung, but there wasn't an animal in any of 'em. When we returned to our place the twins were standin' outside. Pa nodded to them and went inside.

"We hoped you'd get back in time to walk us back to our boat," Morning said with a smile that would charm the quills off a porcupine. I had never noticed before how perfect her teeth were behind that crooked smile. "Your ma has invited us back next Saturday to work some more on our quilts. Ain't that somethin' to look forward to?"

"Only if Auntie Grunn says it's OK," Night added, and then stormed off toward the direction of the swamp.

Morning grabbed my hand and held it all the way to the boat. If someone had told me that I was bein' eaten alive by a swarm of mosquitoes I wouldn't have noticed a single bite. My entire body felt warm, like I was lying naked on a riverbank on a summer's day.

"You'll be graduatin' from high school next year," she said. "What are ya goin' to do after that?"

"I turn seventeen in a few weeks. Pa and Ma said I can drop out of school and go to New Orleans and find a job workin' on one of the fishin' boats. One day I want to own a fishin' boat of my own. I don't need a high school diploma to do that," I answered.

We were at the bank when she said, "Maybe I can change your mind about going. I'm sure Auntie Grunn wouldn't mind at all if you wanted to court me."

I gulped.

"Court you?"

"Well, you did hold my hand," she said and gave me a quick peck on the cheek and then leapt into the boat.

Night kept her head down as they pushed away from the bank.

I stood watching them as they rowed the entire way across the swamp. My cheek where she kissed me felt like it was on fire.

Toothache was nowhere in sight.

"Them girls talked to each other without sayin' a single word out loud," Ma said that night during supper. "They passed things back and forth to one 'nother just as if they were askin' it to be done, and broke out in giggles at exactly the same time."

"Twins are born with special abilities," Pa said. "I knew a couple twin boys when I was growin' up and they could light somethin' on fire just by lookin' at it, like they were human matches."

"Imagine what an influence livin' with that witch Auntie Grunn must have on 'em," Ma said.

"She's a strange one, all right," Pa said. "That bayou she and the mother of the twins comes from is about as scary a place as you'd ever want to visit."

❊❊❊ ❊❊❊ ❊❊❊

The bullfrogs were making a real ruckus during the twilight when I rowed across the swamp. The purple and red in the sky also spread across the bayou, changin' the browns and greens of the swamp and woods to unnatural colors, like those you see in some modern paintings. With every stroke of the oars I kept a lookout for Toothache, who a few days before had grabbed Pierre Moon's huntin' dog off the bank and made a meal of it.

Although it was sweltering hot, I was wearing my Sunday going-to-church long-sleeve shirt and a tie. I could feel the rivulets of sweat runnin' down my spine and from under my arms. The bunch of foxglove and purple aster that I had picked and tied together with a bright yellow ribbon Ma gave me, lay on the seat beside me, wilting.

"How come you're so suddenly sweet on Morning?" Ma asked as I combed my hair for the hundredth time just before goin' out the door.

"She's mighty pretty," I said.

"So is Night," Pa said. "But you shouldn't make plans to stay around here for neither one of them. There's no real life for you here in the bayou."

"I know, Pa. I'm just going to call on her once to say goodbye."

I reached the bank on the side of the swamp where they lived, tied the boat to a post stuck in the mud, and began the walk down the path to their shack. The insects began buzzin' and hummin' louder than I ever heard. You could throw a rock the distance I was from their place when Auntie Grunn and the twins appeared out of nowhere, floating in a circle a few feet off the ground, their hands linked. They whirled about in mid-air before Auntie Grunn turned her head and saw me standing there, my mouth agape. In that instant they stood on the ground as if they had never left it. I shook my head, checkin' for loose nuts and bolts.

"What are ya doin' here?" Auntie Grunn bellowed.

"I'm leavin' the bayou and came to say goodbye to Morning," I stammered. I raised the wilted flowers. "I brought her these."

Morning sauntered over to me and glanced at the

flowers.

"How can you leave? I thought you loved me."

"I never said such a thing," I replied. "I like you. I like Night, too."

Momentarily her face changed, takin' on Auntie Grunn's leathery brown skin and fiery eyes. She stepped up to within an inch of me.

"Get away from here before I turn you into a dragonfly," she hissed. Her breath smelled like swamp water.

I dropped the flowers and ran to the boat. Just as I pulled the rope from the post, Night stepped out of the mist that hung above the swamp, and onto the bank.

"I've loved you since we were both no older than baby chicks," she said. "I wish you weren't goin' away, but I hope you live a long, happy life." She threw her arms around me and kissed me on the lips. Then she vanished.

I rowed so fast across the swamp as the darkness of nightfall overtook the bayou that even Toothache, who raced after me, couldn't catch up to me.

⨯⫘⨯ ⨯⫘⨯ ⨯⫘⨯

Six months later I returned home to visit Pa and Ma. The unfinished quilts begun by the twins were piled in a corner.

"Auntie Grunn and the twins just disappeared," Ma said. "Most folks think they went back to the bayou where Auntie Grunn and the twins' mother came from. There's plates with rotten food on the table as if they left right in the middle of havin' supper. You should go take a look for yourself."

I never did.

~~~~~~~~~~~~~~~~~~~

Steve Carr, who lives in Richmond, Virginia, has had over 320 short stories published internationally in print and online magazines, literary journals and anthologies since June 2016. Four collections of his short stories, *Sand, Rain, Heat,* and *The Tales of Talker Knock,* have been published. Visit him at stevecarr960.com.
~~~~~~~~~~~~~~~~~~~

The Twofer Compendium

Roommates

Donna Cuttress

I was sweating when I finished. She was perfect. Just how I had always envisioned her. She had my face, but slightly different. I straightened the wig and neatened the edge of the paint on her lips with the cuff of my sleeve. I had dressed her in some of my clothes, the good ones of course. Now, I just had to wait.

I sat in the chair opposite her at the kitchen table.

'Say something, then. It's not like you to be so quiet.'

She was silent. Those flat blue eyes stared through me, just like when we were kids and she was annoyed.

'Fine! Sulk all you like. I'm off to bed.' I pushed the chair over behind me as I stood, she hated that, '... and don't make any noise! We don't want to piss off the landlady in the apartment below ours.'

That night I was unable to sleep. This was the first night since I was a child that I hadn't had my twin sister rattling on and on, usually about how much she hated someone or what she would do to them if she could. Mum would burst into the room, switch on the bedroom light, and tell me to be quiet.

'It's her!' I would shout. 'It's Melanie!'

Mum would get angry.

'You know it's not Melanie, *Sarah*. How *could* you? Go to sleep!'

She would switch off the light and slam the door after her. Melanie would pull a face and the light would flick back on. She would laugh so hard she almost screamed down my ear. Then I would hear her crawl under my bed and go to sleep. Sometimes she would kick me, punch at the mattress; just for fun she said. Not tonight though; she was very quiet tonight. I checked under the bed just to make sure she was not there.

Next morning, I ignored her as I got ready for work, and left the apartment without saying 'goodbye.' I passed Mrs. Cribb at the front door of the building. She was unashamedly examining the envelopes of her tenants' mail before she slipped them into the various locked post boxes. She looked at me with the usual irritation.

'Nothing for you, Sarah.'

'There never is.' I said.

She grabbed my arm; her long fingernails poked through the sleeve of my blouse.

'You got a visitor?'

I stopped.

'Only, I could hear someone laughing and walking around. Through the ceiling.' She pointed upward, with a long red nail. 'It didn't sound like you.'

'Sorry. I'll tell my sister to be quiet.'

She looked surprised, then smiled. Her big toothy grin showed how delighted she was at discovering gossip.

'Didn't know you had a sister. I thought you were alone.'

I opened the main door.

'I've *never* been alone Mrs. Cribb. She's my twin. We've never been apart.'

The look on her face was a picture.

When I returned home that evening, Melanie was still sitting at the kitchen table. Her wig had slipped again. The place looked messy. There were books scattered on the floor, ripped magazines, and a couple of smashed cups, tea still running down the wall. The TV was switched on with the volume turned up loud. I could hear it when I came into the building.

'Melanie! Mrs. Cribb will be complaining again. Turn that down!'

She didn't move. Just stayed still in the chair. One of her hands had come loose and was hanging at a weird angle, like she'd been in an accident. I pushed it back into place, straightened her wig, and opened both eyes. The right one kept sticking halfway as though she were winking. I tipped the head back slightly, letting her eyes close, then straightened her up. The eyes opened with a 'thunk' as the black plastic lashes flipped up.

I tidied the room and began to prepare dinner. I would have to cook what she liked, otherwise she wouldn't eat. We ate in silence. I could feel she was angry with me, but I didn't want to ask why. Instead, I went to bed early again, and fell asleep quickly. I was getting used to not hearing her chattering.

I woke up when the light went on. The blinding brightness frightened me. I sat up; my head was fuzzy. I thought for one moment I was back in my childhood bedroom. Then I heard a clicking sound. It became louder, agitated almost. I had to catch my breath. For the first time, I felt scared, fearful of what was in the room with me.

It was Melanie. She was trying to get my attention. After a few seconds, I slowly leaned over the side of the bed. Melanie was underneath. Those blue plastic eyes stared at me, her hands were twisted painfully, and her wig had now slipped off.

'Hah hah. Very funny,' I said, trying to hide the shakiness of my voice, and fell back onto my bed. I tried to go back to sleep, but the clicking of her eyes kept me awake.

At breakfast we sat facing each other across the kitchen table. I chewed my cereal very slowly. This had always annoyed her. Melanie just stared at me. I was beginning to regret giving her a body. She was better off being just a voice. I could ignore her then. When we were kids she was my 'imaginary friend;' some people thought it was sweet that I would talk to my dead twin. Mother didn't, though. She couldn't wait to get rid of me ... us.

There was a knock at the door. I could hear Mrs. Cribb singing outside. I tried to ignore her, but she knocked again and said, 'I've got your post, dear.' Melanie's eyes blinked.

'Don't let her in!'

It was the first time Melanie had spoken since I had made her.

'I have to. She knows we're here.'

I opened the door. Mrs. Cribb looked over my shoulder and stepped inside. She stopped when she saw Melanie.

'What's that?'

She dropped the junk mail on the floor.

'It's Melanie, my twin.'

She looked at me like I was deranged. The way people had looked at me my whole life, ever since I was a child.

'But it's a doll! A mannequin. ... It's grotesque!'

Melanie's head swivelled around slowly with a grinding, scratching sound. As she faced Mrs. Cribb, her eyes flicked open.

'Get rid of her, Sarah!'

Mrs. Cribb looked confused; her mouth opened in a grimace as she grabbed my arm. Those nails dug into my flesh again. Her head trembled slightly as she backed away.

'Who said that?'

I felt angry. She was just like mother!

'Melanie of course! Who else?'

I pushed Mrs. Cribb out of our apartment. Then I pushed her again, down the stairs.

I could hear Melanie screaming with laughter as Mrs. Cribb's neck cracked. I think it was another tenant who came to check their post who found her. We sent flowers to her funeral. I signed the card, 'With deepest sympathies. Sarah and Melanie. xx'

~~~~~~~~~~~~~~~~~~~

Donna Cuttress is from Liverpool, UK. Her work has been published by *Crooked Cat*, *FoF Publishing, Firbolg Publishing, Flame Tree Publishing*, and *Sirens Call*. Her work for The Patchwork Raven's *Twelve Days* is available as an art book. She has also been a speaker at the London Book Fair. Visit her at donnacuttress.wordpress.com.
~~~~~~~~~~~~~~~~~~~

The Twofer Compendium

Mirror Image

Emily Martha Sorensen

It was all my reflection's fault that I got grounded for two weeks.

I woke up early on Saturday morning, and I was eager to have the whole apartment to myself while Mama and Papa were still asleep. I tiptoed past the hall mirror, thinking I could make myself some cocoa and maybe even watch cartoons before my parents stirred.

Then a sound like tinkling glass made me spin around, my heart pounding.

Lying sprawled on the ground in front of me, looking like she'd just rolled through the mirror, was . . . me.

I stared at her, my mouth open.

"Who are you?!" I squeaked.

"Airam," she said, "what's your name?" She shook out her hair. It was long in the front and ragged in the back, just like mine. It had been an accidental haircut, and it was hideous. Surely nobody else in the whole world had a haircut like me.

"Maria," I said shakily. "Where—where did you come from?"

"There," she said, pointing.

I swallowed and looked in the mirror. I could see the carpet, threadbare and stained, the wall behind me, and . . .

The wall *behind* me?

"Where's my reflection?!" I shrieked.

"Shhhhhh!" Airam looked alarmed. "If you wake up your parents, mine are going to wake up, too. And I'll get in humongous trouble. It's, well, it's sort of forbidden."

"What is?" I hissed, barely believing I was doing what she said.

"Crossing through to reality." She bit her lip and looked innocent. "I've heard rumors that it's deadly . . . only it's not, is it? Look! I'm here! I made it safely!"

She raised her arms in a cheering position.

"You mean you're my reflection?" I asked stupidly.

"Uh huh," she nodded. Then she squealed. "Oh, wow! I've never seen that section of the hallway! Nothing's ever reflecting it, so on my side it's totally empty!"

She ran down the hallway to the kitchen. I ran after her, not sure what else to do. She stopped abruptly, and I stumbled and fell right through her.

"The *kitchen,*" she breathed. "All we ever get are pieces that are warped and blurry. You know, from pots and spoons and things. This is amazing."

I didn't even spare a glance at the kitchen. It was cramped and tiny and boring. What I couldn't believe was that I had just run *through* somebody.

"Oh," she gasped, pointing at the cereal boxes on top of the fridge. "Can I have some? Please, please, *please*? In my world, we have no sense of taste."

With misgivings, I fetched the stool from under the sink. Then I reached the corn flakes box, opened the top, and held it out to her.

She reached in and pulled out a translucent corn flake. She popped it in her mouth and closed her eyes, savoring it.

"Mmmm," she said. "I can't believe I have a real sense of taste."

"What did you do?" I blurted out. "I've never seen a corn flake go see-through like that!"

"I can't touch solid things," she said, like it was obvious. "Here, look. See?"

She ran her hand through the refrigerator. My flesh crawled as it came out unscathed.

"What I ate was the image," she said happily. "Somewhere in that box, there's now an invisible corn flake."

I looked at the box, shivering. I didn't think I'd be eating cereal today.

"What's next?" she asked eagerly. "Can we go outside? I've *never* seen the outside, *never*. I've heard, in this world, you guys play all sorts of games. . . ."

I opened the window to the kitchen so that she could look out. We were up seven stories.

"I'm not allowed to go outside without permission," I explained.

"Oh." In the bright sunlight, she looked disappointed. That, and dingy. "Then what can we play?"

I frowned, squinting. Maybe it was just my imagination, but it seemed like she was starting to fade a little bit.

"Umm . . ." I said. "Are you supposed to be see-through?"

She looked down at her arm, puzzled. Then she yelped.

"*That's* what they mean when they say it's deadly! I— I think I'm disappearing!"

"Then how do we get you back?" I asked urgently. "Will you just go back if you disappear here entirely?"

She gulped. "I . . . I don't know," she said in a small voice. "I don't think so. I think I'd die for good if I disappeared here."

Oh, great. I pounded my forehead with my fist. That was the last thing I wanted. I got teased enough at school as it was—I didn't need to add, "Ooh, she's got no reflection! She must be a vampire!" on top of it.

Airam ran back to the hallway mirror.

"It got me here, so it might get me back," she called, stepping through it.

For a moment, there was silence. Then she returned through the wall, looking ashen.

"There was no image to step through," she said, quavering. "Because we're both here. I'm going to be stuck here forever!"

My throat seized with panic. "What about a picture of me? Do you think that would work?"

She brightened up. "A picture," she breathed. "An image of you, just like me . . . yes, it may!"

I ran back to my bedroom and found my old school picture buried under a pile of homework from last year.

"Will this do?" I panted, holding it out to her.

She reached for it, her fingers trembling.

For a moment, things seemed hopeful. She flickered, kind of like a candle flame. Then she dropped it and started wailing.

"It's *too* similar!" she bawled. "I won't fit! I'm never going to get back home again! I'm going to die here!"

I bit my lower lip. We had to think of something.

"We need something that's completely different," Airam said. "But what's the opposite of a reflection?"

I shook my head. "I don't know."

"Take me back to the kitchen," she said in despair. "At least I can eat one last thing before I disappear forever."

I spilled half of the cereal boxes as I got them down for her, but we didn't have time to worry about that. In the sunlight streaming from the window, she seemed more see-through than before.

Airam gulped down handfuls of images, leaving invisible cereal strewn all over the kitchen. I sat on the stool, head in my hands, staring at the window.

What was the opposite of a reflection? Images were just light bouncing away; I knew that from science class. The opposite would absorb it.

What absorbed light? Darkness.

Where would I find a dark version of me?

I stared at the floor, which looked nearly empty because Airam was eating images so quickly. A dark shape stretched out behind me.

Wait a minute.

"Airam!" I cried. "Jump into my *shadow!*"

She stared at me for a moment, her mouth open. Then she dropped a handful of Cheerios and dove for the shape behind me.

I held my breath, waiting. There was a sound like slurping.

"WHY IS ALL THIS CEREAL ALL OVER THE FLOOR?!"

I spun around, eyes wide. Mama stood there in her bathrobe, looking furious.

I gulped. I tried to explain.

"It was my reflection, You see —"

My explanation didn't go over too well. Even after I swept the floor, Mama kept stepping on cereal, and she didn't believe me when I tried to explain that there was even more than she could see—half of them were invisible. In the end, because she was "sick of me lying," I ended up getting grounded for two weeks.

But it was OK. Because I had a mirror in my bedroom, and that gave me time to practice backwards writing.

Are you real? I wrote, holding the sign up clearly so that my reflection could see it. *It wasn't just a dream, was it?*

For a moment, there was nothing. Just my own face staring at me.

Then slowly, deliberately, Airam winked.
I smiled and wrote another sign backwards.
You'll have to come back tomorrow.
There were worse ways to spend a grounding.

~~~~~~~~~~~~~~~~~~~~

Emily Martha Sorensen writes clean fantasy and science fiction adventures with clever characters, fun plots, and lots of humor. Her most popular series is about baby dragons; she's also been known to write about children of prophecy, magical girls, and alien changelings. Read more at emilymarthasorensen.com.
~~~~~~~~~~~~~~~~~~~~

The Entwisles

George Young

"They're *where*?" Arlene Meyer, Metropolitan Productions' Executive Producer asked.

"London," I replied. "And through the summer."

Arlene stared at me. She made that chipmunk chewing motion with her mouth and leaned back in her office chair. She slapped her hands down on the desk and shook out her black hair, which caused a forgotten bobby pin to fly across the office and land on an unoccupied desk.

"The Entwisle twins are in London?"

"Yes, Arlene," I said. "And through the summer. Mom and Dad shipped them off to avoid having to pick them up at the police station or the nightclub in New York City at 4 a.m. Smart move, don't ya think, because London doesn't have a nightclub scene where two gorgeous blonde twenty-year-old party girls could get in trouble, does it?"

"Then why did they do it?"

"Their mother's sister, the twins' aunt, is a former commander in the IDF. Rumor has it that her husband was, or might still be, Mossad. The twins are staying with them."

"The parents think that's going to keep those two inside all summer?"

"Evidently," I replied and turned back to my computer screen. "Do you think I should tip them off about the security we hired to make sure they didn't leave their apartment before the AMEX shoot? You do know one of them started dating one of the guards shortly thereafter."

Arlene dropped her head back and mimed putting a noose around her neck. She laughed that maniacal laugh I liked. A stress reaction, but a good one. She sat up.

"Max is not going to –"

"Max is not going to what?"

Metropolitan Productions' mercurial director, Max Lieberman, bounded into the mezzanine office occupied by Arlene, the company's production manager (me), and Chris Wilson, our accountant, who was currently on vacation and not occupying the desk with the bobby pin on it.

"Max," said Arlene. "The Entwisle twins are in London for the summer. We're going to have to cast some other pair for the Mead BOGO spots."

Lieberman shot all 145 pounds on his 5'7" frame into the chair in front of Arlene's desk. He took off his black-rimmed glasses, and I waited for his mustache and eyebrows to come with them, but again I was disappointed. He put them back on his cartoon character face.

"I'm not doing the spot without them," he declared. "We have to get them back here for a day." Arlene chewed like a chipmunk. Max frowned. I wrote some gibberish on a legal pad.

"Max, when they're in the US we can't get them to our studio on time and they live two blocks from here on Gramercy Park. I cannot imagine coordinating a flight from London to NYC and expecting them to get on board and arrive here," Arlene proclaimed through her chewing.

"Not my problem," said Max. "I'm not doing the spot without them."

He vaulted out of the chair and walked over to the spiral staircase just as Pete McBride, the staff producer, finished climbing up to the mezzanine.

"Without who?" asked Pete.

"The Entwisle twins are in London," I said.

"Really? I'm surprised their passports haven't been confiscated."

"You do know their dad works for the State Department?" I asked.

"Oh, yeah," he said. "That's right!"

Max hustled down the staircase yelling, "Fix this!" or something like that as he hit the studio floor and left a vapor trail when he crossed to the opposite side. We watched until we knew he couldn't hear us.

"This is a million-dollar spot," said Arlene. "And there's no way Mead is going to wait until September to shoot something for school supplies."

"That makes sense," I said.

"You're not helping," replied Arlene.

"Send Max to London," offered Pete.

We both turned and looked at Pete, who played with the bobby pin. He looked up.

"What?" he asked.

"How do you do that?" I asked.

"Do what?"

"You know what. Come up with the easiest solution while the rest of us are overreacting. I guess you're going to London," said Arlene.

"Can't. I came up here to tell you that the tests on my inner ear came back. I can't fly for the next six months. Something's out of whack in there."

"Outta whack here, too."

Arlene turned her attention to me.

"Pack your bags."

"What? Wait a darned minute. I'm not a producer."

"That's right," she said. "But you are a P.M. Find us a producer over there. Put a studio on hold and find out who Max might want to shoot this sucker."

☓⬭☓⬭☓ ☓⬭☓⬭☓ ☓⬭☓⬭☓

That's how I found myself in London, in the upscale home of Kyla and Eitan Israelson, in a sitting room the size of my current digs in Manhattan, at 9 a.m. after a redeye flight from NYC. Kyla, a beautiful woman of about 45, sporting short black hair that curved around her cheekbones, sat with her athletic legs crossed in a Max Mara skirt both au courant and au sexy. Her equally attractive husband who introduced himself as "Eitan, not Ethan," sat next to her in a John Phillips or a Savile Row or some suit that looked like they took his measurements with an electron microscope.

"Two days ago," continued Mrs. Israelson. I hadn't heard anything since I started concentrating on the good looks of my hosts.

"Sorry," I said. "Jet lag. You'll have to forgive me. You said they haven't been back for two days?"

"That's correct," said Eitan not Ethan. "I've said it and now my wife has said it. I think we're out of people in this room."

He delivered the last line while surveying an original Chagall on the opposite wall, a painting worth the gross national product of Dubai.

"Except for me," I volunteered.

Eitan not Ethan gave me a look reserved for reluctant hirsute types strapped to metal chairs and sitting in some windowless bunker in Blacksite-istan. I cleared my throat.

"OK." I stood up. "You have no idea where they are and when they might be back?" I added with a laugh. "Aren't you both MI6 or something like that?"

I swear I saw Eitan's hand reach inside his perfectly fitted suit jacket, but all he did was pull out a cardholder and hand me one of its contents. I wouldn't remember to exhale until I got outside.

"Mr. Jackson," he said. "Here is my card. Give me one of yours; I'll be happy to contact you when the girls return, and they will. My brother's daughters are spirited young ladies, who, at this very moment might be at the

Georges V in Paris, or the Adlon in Berlin. But make no mistake, they will be back. It's just a question of when."

I swallowed and we exchanged cards. Some guy in a tuxedo showed me out.

ⅣⅣ ⅣⅣ ⅣⅣ

I walked out the front door of Castle Israelson and back toward the Airbnb I'd rented. It was a good 30-minute trip by foot, but if I took the tube or a taxi, I'd fall asleep and end up in Manchester. Max was at some stupidly overpriced hotel, and if I knew him, he was out photographing half of London. He'd get the other half tomorrow and ignore any prep time on the job I had left. Of course, if I didn't find the Entwisle twins all that would be—

"Well, Pauline, look who's in London."

"It's that somewhat officious type who works for that photographer."

Two melodious laughs filled the morning air and in front of me stood the two otherworldly gorgeous Entwisle twins. I tripped over nothing and heard the laughter repeat itself. Two sets of soft hands, smelling of Eau de Estrogen, lifted me off the London pavement.

The Entwisle twins were not identical. Their faces, hair, and skin yes, but below the neck the ladies struck two very different figures. Pauline, built like a ballerina, had her mother's legs, athletic shoulders, a waist with a built-in corset, two symmetrical hips, and an . . . well, if you've been to the ballet, I don't need to go any further.

Eleanor, about three inches taller, had just as hypnotizing a build, but more along the lines of Katy Perry or Scarlett Johannessen. More bosom, wider hips. The same gorgeous legs of her mother, but on steroids. Calves and thighs more muscular than her sister. If these two had been on a throne in Greece around 700 B.C., there would have been two thousand ships headed for Troy.

Both faced me, front-lit by the morning wash, cocktail dresses of same make and blush pink color. Short. Fabric hugging their lack of body fat, even Eleanor. Two-inch stiletto, sling-back shoes of the same hue. Dressed for dancing.

"Uh," I said, finding my voice. "Just getting back from a bar mitzvah?"

The laughter more subdued this time.

"We're staking out Kyla and Eitan's place," said Pauline.

"Yes. We think the last place they'd look for us is in front of their house," offered Eleanor.

"After meeting them I can imagine why you might want to do that, but where do you, uh, sleep, not that you seem to need much of it? Change clothes? Have clothes?"

Eleanor winked at me. I swear.

"That's not been a problem."

"Got it. Any interest in why I'm here?" I asked, walking past them. "Perhaps we should put just a block or two between us and your aunt and uncle?"

"Oh, don't bother," said Pauline. "Eitan and Kyla almost never leave. It might not be safe for them on the street. Something about their previous employers."

I'd been holding my breath again, but managed to let it out slowly enough to not attract any further scrutiny. I opened my mouth to say something, but Eleanor beat me to it.

"We know why you're here," she said. "Max's here too. He wants us to be in a commercial for some paper products company the day after tomorrow. Our agent called us from New York yesterday." I took the opportunity to say nothing.

"We'll be there. Nine a.m. sharp. Covent Studios. We know it," said Pauline. She reached into a purse the size of an iPhone and pulled out a card.

"Our London cell numbers. We're not sure where we're staying tomorrow night, but don't worry, we'll be there on Thursday. We'll bring our own clothes, as usual."

"That's it?"

"How hard would you like it to be?"

"Oh, I don't know. Other than getting on an eight-hour flight. Talking my way into your aunt and uncle's house." I had stopped, but since I had their attention, decided to continue. "Finding a crew. Locating the D.P. Max would like to use. Dealing with the unions, the stage, the equipment houses. All on no sleep and with a whole ..." I paused and glanced at my iPhone. "... thirty-six hours to prep. I'd like it to be a little easier. But that's just me."

The Entwisle twins looked at each other and laughed. They positioned themselves on either side of me and planted big, wet, juicy kisses on each of my cheeks. Pauline pinched my arm.

"Oh, but you'll have us there. So much fun."

They waved and walked in the opposite direction of where I needed to go.

⋈⋈⋈ ⋈⋈⋈ ⋈⋈⋈

I drank more black tea that one day than I did during the course of my life, but found it to be a much better way to push myself through the workday and line up everything for the shoot. More or less. The D.P. balked at the money and insisted on a prep day so he could get over to the studio and drink whiskey with the stage manager. I acquiesced, since I'd asked him to take no more than three hours to light the scene with the Entwisles.

My cellphone rang. Max.

"I'm back. You don't need to take me to dinner because I don't like you and you don't like me."

"The twins are in, and so is your overpriced D.P."

"Great. Good night."

I called Arlene and gave her the good news about the D.P. and the Entwisle twins. I also explained their nomadic existence in London and the strange pair of humans passing themselves off as their aunt and uncle.

"The twins are going to show on time?" she asked. "They said that?"

"Yep."

"Do you believe them?"

"Nope."

"What will you do when they don't show?"

"I guess I'll come home."

"You don't have a backup?"

"Hey, cut me some slack. I just got here. I put together a crew with the I-Know-He's-Not-Worth-the-Money, Flavor-of-the-Month D.P. Got a verbal commitment from two of the bigger party girls since Paris Hilton. And sat in what was probably the vestibule to the panic room owned by the modern-day versions of Bonnie and Clyde."

"So you don't have a backup?" asked Arlene, and I heard her smile all the way across the Atlantic.

"You've been waiting to use that, haven't you?"

"Yes, I have."

"I am going to sleep now. Tomorrow, I will find a casting agent in London. I heard a rumor they have them here. I will ask for identical twin women in their early 20s, who cause men to leave their wives and families only to find themselves broken-hearted, sitting in a gutter outside a trendy nightclub in some urban setting. Abandoned by the treachery of beauty."

"So, you do have a backup?"

"Absolutely."

"Thought so. Did you invite the aunt and uncle to the set?"

"Are you insane? I'd have to order body bags if I did that." She hung up.

I fell asleep before Arlene's office phone handset found its cradle.

ⵊⵊⵊ ⵊⵊⵊ ⵊⵊⵊ

The day before the shoot I got the obligatory call from Max blowing me off for the only prep time we would have on the job. All he cared about was whether the Entwisles were going to be there. He didn't want to look at any backups.

"If they don't show, there's no sense in shooting the spot," he said.

I reminded him of the $100K in crew and travel expenses, and I could hear him waving his hand in the direction of my Airbnb. He hung up muttering something about St. Paul's or Westminster or some other church and I pushed through another day of jetlag.

Max rang at the end of the workday, first insisting that we not meet for dinner, then asking, "What's my call time?"

"General crew is eight a.m. D.P. will be there at that time to light the set. Entwisles are due in for wardrobe, makeup and lighting tests starting at nine a.m."

"Why are you bringing the D.P. in with the crew? What if we go into overtime?"

"Oh, now you want to produce the job?" I asked. "Six p.m. the night before?"

"What if we go into overtime?"

"Max, we spent thousands of dollars schlepping us over here because there are no other sets of drop-dead gorgeous twin females looking for work as actresses in New York City. We're paying way too much money for the D.P. And, let me finish, if the Entwisles are even remotely on time, we'll be out of there by three p.m."

"See you at nine a.m."

※ ※ ※

As nursemaid to the film crew, I arrived at 7 a.m. with the usual overblown purveyor of breakfast and craft services, who set up to deliver another 6000-calorie day of haute cuisine meals to a bunch of people who can't make a peanut butter sandwich on a day off.

At 8 a.m., Alexei Yudenich, the D.P. from Bosnia showed, as did the crew. Unfortunately, since no one eats anything for days before a film shoot, I lost them all for a half hour while they powerlifted blintzes and held their heads under the coffee urns and opened the spigots.

And at *exactly* 9 a.m., the Entwisles, fresh off one more evening of sending blood flow away from the brains of young men and into a smaller organ, floated into the studio. They looked like I could have walked them straight onto the set.

The A.D., an annoying "chap" named Roderick, hustled them into the Vanities Department. He then cut off the caffeine and carb surge at craft services, and the crew, to my utter surprise, got to work. I took advantage of Max's usual fashionably fifteen-minutes-lateness to check on hair and makeup and see what clothes the Entwisles had with them.

The twins, never shy about wearing only underwear in dressing rooms, again surprised me as I found them both sitting in makeup chairs wearing matching robes. Vanities had already started their hair.

"Wardrobe choices are on the rack," said the stylist, Claire, a cliché of purple hair and more than enough tattoos, all on prominent display due to her choice of a tank top, white denim shorts that would have cut off the lower body circulation of a member of the Lullaby League from *The Wizard of Oz*, and nothing else except for the rolls of excess flesh. She pointed an index finger with a cross embedded in the nail in the direction of a single garment rack.

"Told you we'd be here," said Pauline.

"So you did," I replied. I cleared my throat and checked my watch. "I'll pop back out to the stage. Max's fifteen minutes of directorial lateness are up. I'll bring him back and he can charm the two of you without me." I said the last line with visions of coffee and biscuits dancing in my head.

"We ran into Max at the club last night. He was having dinner," said Eleanor.

"Yes, and Kyla and Eitan just happened to be there as well," said Pauline. The vision disappeared.

"Yes, they got along famously," said Pauline. "So well, in fact, that they all decided to take Eitan's private plane to Tel Aviv for a few beach days."

"Uh."

"I think Max said something – it was hard to tell with all the laughing the three were doing – about starting without him," said Eleanor.

"Anything else?"

"Yes. He said you could finish without him, too."

~~~~~~~~~~~~~~~~~~

George Young is a former dancer and 35-year veteran of the film industry. His nonfiction book, *Try Not to Annoy the Kangaroo*, is represented by Bill Gladstone of Waterside Productions. He has two novels in development, *The Google Earth Murders* and *DracuLAND*! Visit him on Facebook at George.Young.965.
~~~~~~~~~~~~~~~~~~

Second Thoughts

Gary Zenker

People who aren't twins can't understand how special it is to be one. So let *me* tell *you*. It's like living in your own body and living outside it at the same time. It's like having a best friend who is just like you ... with whom you can swap clothing and copy homework and compare boyfriends without judgment.

And there's an inexplicable psychic connection, an intuition. I can tell when my sister is happy, or stressed, or threatened. There's no logical explanation why the sharing of genetic material before birth should result in this. I share genes with both my father and mother, but have none of that same connection.

My dad is the exact opposite of me, if that's possible. Unemotional, gruff, uncaring about how he makes other people feel, even to those he presumably loves—assuming he's capable of that.

Mom is at the other end of the spectrum, loving and emotional and supportive. Over-the-top dramatic, the yin to Dad's yang in many ways. What they do share is the way they view twins as more of a pair than as individuals.

Parents like mine think it's charming or cute to do everything in twos. That means always buying us identical toys, meals—parity in everything. Why should you need the privacy of your own room when you can share it with your identical twin? And birthdays, a celebration of individuality to nearly everyone else, ends up more about being sisters than being individuals. You learn that lesson early and are made to feel guilty when you put yourself above the privilege of the shared duality everyone else wishes they had.

It also means our parents dressing twins the same, to emphasize that we are twins, as if people couldn't tell from the matching faces and haircuts. Maybe they do it because it places themselves in the unique position of being able to tell us apart. Maybe they believe it gives them power, or maybe it just means they don't have to work as hard to understand us as individuals. In the beginning, it bonded us closer, homogenizing our differences. As a twin, you play it for a while. It's like having a naughty secret that you only have to share with one other person.

But when you reach middle school, even your friends tire of that game and invent their own differentiators for you. They stereotype you and assign the traits they want to assign you, even if you don't own them. Individuality is thrust upon you. The artsy one, the quiet one, the smart one, the bitchy self-centered, stuck-up one. And there's nothing you can do about it. Her friends are your friends' friends.

By the time you hit high school, you're pretty much branded with no available escape hatch. Other girls have created the label you are forced to wear. Boys, on the other hand, see twins as a conquest, to contrast and compare in every way. Any positive feelings about being a twin takes second place to feeling trapped in a way no one else can fathom.

You become an identical image, forever trying to measure up but failing in ways you can't understand to an outside image that doesn't match the inside. All for the dumb luck of early division.

And if you are the sister who benefits from it, you let it happen without regard to the one who has been literally by your side since birth. You stand by and watch it envelope and crush your other half, inch by agonizing inch, because you don't want it to touch you and drag you down in the same way. And you can see, with all clarity, what it would look like if it did.

Tomorrow night I'll smother the bitch with her own pillow and be done with her nonsense. Then I'll be the nice, fun friend of everyone, the one deserving of the attention and compliments. I bet they'll hardly notice the difference.

~~~~~~~~~~~~~~~~~~~

By day, Gary Zenker is a marketing strategist and copywriter. By night he writes flash fiction stories that explore characters and their motivations. He is the founder and President of the Main Line Writers Group and of Noir at a Bar, hosting local author readings. Visit him on Facebook.
~~~~~~~~~~~~~~~~~~~

- 324 -

The Last Hallowe'en

Tony Conaway

Alexander Mertz went to bed stuffed with Halloween candy. This was his last chance. After all, he was 12 years old now – he was getting too big for trick-or-treat.

He woke up late to a beautiful, crisp day. Alex attended a parochial school that was closed on November 1st, All Saints Day. He listened to the thump of a squirrel landing on the roof and skittering away. He lay there with his eyes closed, thinking about all the other things he'd started noticing. He'd noticed that middle school wasn't nearly as scary as he'd been led to believe. He'd recently noticed that, compared to his friends, his family was relatively poor. Although he hadn't quite reached puberty, he was starting to notice girls.

He also noticed that he was a little warmer than he expected. His bedroom tended to get cool in chilly weather, and there was frost last night. Alex liked to sleep in the nude, covered by several blankets. One of his arms was elevated upon what he assumed was a lumpy mass of blankets. A *warm* mass.

Then he opened his eyes and noticed something else: There was a warm body next to him—a naked boy, about his size and age.

No, not just next to him.

Attached to him.

That's when he started screaming. No one came to help. His mother, a single parent, had already left for work. So had her father, who lived with them. There was no one else in the house. The body attached to Alex was breathing, but unconscious. It was too heavy for Alex to move, so he couldn't get to his cellphone. The phone was still in his jeans, on the floor across the room.

Alex was fortunate that his home was near the start of his postman's route. About thirty minutes later, that postman approached the Mertz home. He heard the boy's now-hoarse screams and called the police.

One of the EMTs had dated Alex's mother, and knew that Alex was not a conjoined twin. Yet now he was, attached at the torso to an unconscious twin, just like the famous Siamese twins, Chang and Eng.

On a different day, the fate of Alexander Mertz would have been a media sensation. As it happened, it didn't even make the top ten.

⋈⋈⋈ ⋈⋈⋈ ⋈⋈⋈

The following winter was brutally cold in the Northern Hemisphere. Even though it was only 40 miles away, Dr. Max Cuddhy could barely make it through the half-plowed snow from Philadelphia to Kennett Square. To his surprise, the New Bolton Veterinary Center still had power. He parked and went inside.

Two armed National Guardsmen greeted him. They were unshaven and not at all friendly. He showed them his I.D. and told them that he was expected.

The surlier of the guardsmen examined his I.D. and checked it against a list. Cuddhy noticed the ubiquitous radiation monitor by the door. Ever since the North Koreans had gone crazy and nuked Hawaii, there were radiation monitors everywhere. Of course, most of the radiation in the atmosphere was from the USA's response, which was to turn all of North Korea into a radioactive hellhole.

The surly guard handed back his I.D. The other one tossed him a brush.

"Go back outside and brush off the snow. We got enough to do without mopping up after you." Then the guardsman got on an intercom and mumbled some orders.

Cuddhy made a point of not arguing with armed men. He dutifully went back outside, stood under a concrete awning, and brushed off the fallout-laden snow. By the time he got back inside, a female member of the guard was waiting to escort him.

"Dr. Cuddhy?" she asked. "I'll take you to Director Maerov." The woman didn't offer to shake hands. With all the diseases about, no one shook hands anymore. The woman was young and looked healthy, but she limped as if she were in constant pain.

They walked down several corridors, deep into the building. Most of the offices they passed seemed empty. The entire place smelled of disinfectant.

Finally, the guardswoman led him into a sizable observation room.

"Director Maerov? This is Dr. Cuddhy."

"We've met," said a woman in a motorized wheelchair. "That will be all, Grace."

The Guardswoman nodded and limped out.

The woman touched a control knob, and the wheelchair turned to face Cuddhy. "Max," she said. "Thank you for coming. I was so sorry to hear about Emily."

"Thank you," Cuddhy said. He had first met Dr. Maerov at his late wife's fifteen-year high school reunion, and the three of them had gotten together several times since. When they last met, Miryam Maerov had been a pretty, energetic woman in her mid-thirties. Now she looked twice her age and needed a wheelchair to get around.

"We still have coffee," she said. "Would you like a cup?"

"It took me four hours to drive here through the snow. At this point, I'll take anything warm."

She rolled her wheelchair to a side table. The motor on her wheelchair whined, as if it weren't working correctly.

She poured coffee into a cup and held it out to him.

"Here. Don't worry, what I have isn't contagious. It's a new form of adult-onset Tay-Sachs. You have to be genetically predisposed—a mutation in the HEXA gene on chromosome 15. Mostly Ashkenazi Jews seem to get it."

He nodded and took the cup. Of course, the scabies that had ravaged his once-handsome face *were* contagious. But most people had that nowadays, or something worse.

"There's artificial sweetener by the coffeepot," she said. He knew better than to ask for real sugar or cream. No one was delivering those anymore.

She rolled her wheelchair over to a huge observation window that took up most of one wall. "The young man in there is the reason I asked you here. I understand you're related to him."

There were two attached medical beds in the room. On one of them a boy lay, reading comic books. Next to him, an identical boy slept.

Dr. Cuddhy stifled a cough, covering his mouth.

"The boy was actually a distant relative of Emily's. I met him at a few family holiday functions, but I never said more than a dozen words to him. They sat him at the children's table during Thanksgivings."

"As far as we know, you're now the boy's next of kin. We've all lost so many ..."

"Why is he – they – here? Instead of in a hospital, I mean."

She gave a slight laugh.

"There aren't any hospitals still operating. So many sick people, with so many new, contagious diseases. The hospitals were overwhelmed, and their staffs died or fled. We barely got the boy out of Philadelphia in time. This veterinary facility was one of the best in the country, and it was still operational. Also, standard MRI machines weren't built to accommodate conjoined twins. This veterinary facility had an MRI big enough for a horse. So we brought him here."

"I'll help in any way I can, but I don't see what I can do. I'm not a medical doctor. I'm a theoretical physicist, specializing in cosmology."

"I know. But what happened to the boy is impossible by any known causative agent. I wanted the opinion of someone who's used to thinking about ... other possibilities."

She picked up a clipboard filled with medical notations.

"The boy – Alexander Mertz – was an ordinary middle school student from a working-class home. The only child of a single mother. No other family members lived with them, except for her father. Both the mother and grandfather had left for work when the boy woke up on November first of last year. That's when he found out he'd become, inexplicably, a conjoined twin."

"That must have been terrifying for him."

"It was. By the time the EMTs had arrived, he'd screamed for so long he'd lost his voice. Once they verified what had happened, they airlifted him from his home upstate—some town near Scranton—to the Hospital of the University of Pennsylvania. Unfortunately, the best doctors in Philadelphia had no idea what caused this or how to treat it. His vitals were dangerously erratic, so the best they could come up with was to put the boy into a medically induced coma while they figured it out."

"Did they get any clue from his mother or grandfather?"

"His relatives were as baffled as everyone else. They're all dead now. That entire area was wiped out by the aphasia plague. You remember?"

He shook his head. He didn't pay much attention to the news while his wife was dying from a new, unknown disease. Unbidden, the smell of the truck full of corpses came back to him. His last sight of Emily: carrying her from their home and putting her in a bring-out-the-dead truck, like in a medieval movie.

"So tragic! Entire towns of people that suddenly couldn't understand speech or writing. Mass panic, people killing each other. The military quarantined the area. But the victims couldn't understand the soldiers who ordered them not to flee. They were shot down by the thousands. We believe it was caused by some new airborne pathogen, possibly a prion. At least it killed them within a few weeks. There are worse ways to die." She looked down at her withered left hand.

"My disease, for instance. I'm hoping my body will lose the ability to breathe before my mind goes."

They were both silent for a minute.

"The entire human species seems to be in a death spiral," he said. "This boy is an unusual case, but I don't understand why you're expending limited resources on him."

She referred again to the notes on her clipboard.

"November first of last year about 8 a.m. Eastern Time, Alexander Mertz woke up and discovered he now had a conjoined twin. At 8:06 a.m. there was an earthquake measuring 8.6 on the Richter scale in New Madrid, Missouri. Tens of thousands of people were killed in and around St. Louis, and there were floods up and down the Mississippi. Some ten minutes later, a massive typhoon appeared out of nowhere and devastated Taiwan. At approximately the same time, half the glaciers in Greenland plunged into the sea, causing a tsunami that inundated much of the coastline of Iceland, the UK, and Northern Europe." She coughed several times, then took a sip from a water bottle.

"By noon," she continued, "the entire population of

the northern part of the island of New Zealand was dead. We still don't know what killed them. And that was just the beginning. The plagues may have started at that time as well, but it took longer for us to identify them."

"You think," Cuddhy asked, "that whatever's happened to the whole world somehow started with … with a boy in Scranton, Pennsylvania?"

"You tell me. I remember you talking about the Kardashev scale at the reunion. If you could turn an ordinary twelve-year-old-boy suddenly into a conjoined twin, where would you be on that scale?"

"I … I don't know. It's fantastic."

"Nothing we know could have caused it. His body couldn't have somehow *grown* an identical twin overnight. Something did this to him."

Cuddhy looked at the boy—boys—in their attached beds.

"How long has Alex been out of his coma?"

"We started waking him up two weeks ago. We've given him some anti-anxiety drugs to keep him from panic, but otherwise he's stable and off medication. Do you want to talk to him?"

For lack of anything else to say, Cuddhy said, "Yes."

⚕ ⚕ ⚕

Alexander Mertz looked up from his comic book as they entered the room. His eyes had a dull expression. *From the anti-anxiety drugs*, Cuddhy guessed.

"Alex," said Dr. Maerov. "This is Dr. Cuddhy, a relative of yours. He's come to see you."

"How are you feeling today, Alex?" said Cuddhy.

"OK," said the boy. "I wish I could move around. If Sasha's going to be attached to me, I wish he would wake up."

"Sasha?"

"That's what we named the twin," said Maerov. "*Sasha* is a Russian nickname for *Alexander*."

"It's kind of like when I broke my leg and had to wear a cast," said Alex. "I couldn't move around much then, either."

"So Sasha never wakes up?"

"Um," said Alex. He looked at Dr. Maerov.

"We've tracked increasing brain activity from Sasha in the past few days."

"Sometimes, it's almost like I know what he's thinking," Alex said.

"I see," said Cuddhy. He picked up one of the gaudy magazines. "Does Sasha like comic books, too?"

Alex looked down.

"No. The comics are for me. I like to imagine that a superhero—someone really powerful like Green Lantern or Doctor Strange—could make Sasha go away. Make the internet work again. Bring back my mom and grandpa. Make things like they used to be, y'know."

Then the boy's voice seemed to change, grow more forceful.

"But that's not going to happen. Dr. Maerov asked you a question, Dr. Cuddhy. Answer it. What kind of civilization could make a twin of a boy appear overnight?"

Cuddhy started to ask how Alex could possibly know about a conversation that occurred outside his room. But he saw Maerov mouth the word "Sasha" to him. Was the twin communicating through Alex?

"Well," Cuddhy said. "I did my Master's thesis on something called the Kardashev proposition. It's a way of categorizing the technological level of future civilizations. A scale, of sorts. Right now, we're not even on the scale. We're at Level Zero."

"What's next?" asked the boy.

"Well, Level One is a civilization that has mastered

fusion energy and uses it. Fusion energy always seems to be about twenty-five years off, so we aren't there yet. It could be a hundred years away." *More, with all the disasters and diseases,* he thought.

"Next is Level Two, which is a civilization that has colonized a number of planets in different solar systems. They do massive engineering projects, like a Dyson Sphere. That's—"

"I read," the boy said. "I know what a Dyson Sphere is. Get to the point. What level of civilization could bring Sasha here?"

"My best guess would be the highest level, Level Five. A civilization of that sophistication hasn't just mastered space travel and colonized a galaxy, it's gone beyond that. You know what the Multiverse is?"

"Again, I read. Multiple universes, some of them very like this one, others far behind or far more advanced."

"Right," Cuddhy said. "The only way I can imagine Sasha appearing is that he came from another universe. If that's the case, he looks like you because he's a *version* of you, Alex. A version from another universe. The people who sent him here have mastered the Multiverse."

"If they're so advanced, then why are the two of us attached to each other?"

Cuddhy thought for a minute.

"Well, one possibility is that even a Level Five civilization isn't perfect. When they made Sasha appear in your bedroom, he was too close and somehow merged with you, partway. Like a transporter accident on *Star Trek.*"

"And the other possibility?"

Cuddhy didn't want to say it in front of Alex.

"Dr. Cuddhy?" said Maerov.

"SAY IT!" Alex's voice was suddenly loud and commanding. Or was this Sasha speaking through Alex?

"It's possible," Cuddhy said slowly, "that travel to

another universe is very draining. And the only way someone could survive is to become a sort of parasite. The traveler has to attach itself to a compatible body in order to survive. And what could be more compatible than an identical body?"

"Thank you," said the boy. His voice was back to its usual lethargic level. "I'm tired now. Let me sleep."

Without another word, Alex closed his eyes and lay back. Cuddhy and Maerov exited the room.

"I'm glad I asked you here," Maerov said. "At least we have a theory now. That's more than we had before."

"It's just a theory."

"But it fits the facts," she said. "Sasha may have been sent here by a civilization that's far more technologically advanced that we are, from some sort of parallel universe. The next question is, *why* would they send him here?"

Cuddhy stared through the glass at the boys on their attached beds. Ever since his wife died in the plagues, his mind went to the darkest places imaginable.

"If all the bad things that have happened recently are really connected, then all I can think of is that some civilization in another universe is getting rid of its bad things by dumping them on us."

"So Sasha—the twin—is a bad thing, too?"

Cuddhy squinted at the boys.

"Wait. Look at Alex. Is something happening to him?"

It looked as if Alex was growing older. He was wrinkled, like he was being hollowed out from inside. Or having the life sucked out of him.

Maerov looked at her instruments.

"My God, his vitals are flatlining!"

She shouted into an intercom.

"Code blue, code blue! Observation room! Bring the crash cart!"

Cuddhy just stared at the boys. He heard the noise of medics arriving behind him.

At that moment, the twin opened his eyes—and smirked.

And, somehow, Dr. Cuddhy knew that things were about to *really* get bad.

~~~~~~~~~~~~~~~~~~~

Tony Conaway has cowritten nonfiction books for such publishers as Macmillan, Prentice Hall, and McGraw-Hill. His fiction has been published in many magazines and anthologies. His odder work includes cowriting the script for a planetarium production and selling jokes to Jay Leno that were performed on *The Tonight Show*. Connect with him on Facebook at Too.Hip.For.The.Room.
~~~~~~~~~~~~~~~~~~~

The Twofer Compendium

Reprints

"Skippy" by Danielle Ackley-McPhail was originally published in *Transcendence* 2012, 2018.

"Double Exposure" by John H. Dromey was originally published online in *Saturday Night Reader* in 2014.

"Mirror Image" by Emily Martha Sorensen was originally published in *Spellbound* 2013 Spring Issue, and also in *Magic and Mischief*, 2018.

"Last Hallowe'en" by Tony Conaway was originally published in *Twilight Madhouse #4*, 2018.

Thanks for buying *The Twofer Compendium.*

We hope you've enjoyed reading this anthology as much as we've enjoyed compiling it.

Check out geminiwordsmiths.com/publishing for our future submission calls.

And like us on Facebook at Celestial Echo Press and Gemini Wordsmiths, along with all of our fabulous authors!

The Twofer Compendium

About the Editors

Ruth Littner

Ruth earned a B.A. in English from SUNY at Buffalo and a teaching certification in secondary English. She holds an M.A. in administration from Goddard College in Vermont. She is a twice-contributing author to the anthology series *Not Your Mother's Book....*, published by the same folks who created the *Chicken Soup for the Soul* series, and *Until the Neighborhood Changed*, a Young Adult coming-of-age short story. She is the author of (as-yet-unpublished) *Living with Ghosts*, a nonfiction narrative that examines the PTSS legacy of the Holocaust through three generations. She is a graduate of *New York Times* best-selling author Jonathan Maberry's Short Story Class.

Ann Stolinsky

Ann's first publishing credit was a poem in an anthology titled, *Male and Female Under 18*. Ann received a certificate in editing from Manor College and is a graduate of *New York Times* best-selling author Jonathan Maberry's Short Story class. Her editing skills have been honed on PR materials, websites, newsletters, short stories, poems, game rules, articles, and more. Her writing skills have developed while creating poetry, short stories, content for websites, game rules, tweets, PR materials, articles, newsletters, and more. Several of her short stories have been published in various magazines. Ann is the owner of Gontza Games (www.gontzagames.com), an independent board and card game company, in operation since July 2002. Ann is the proud mother of two daughters, two sons-in-law, and one incredibly beautiful and smart granddaughter.

About Gemini Wordsmiths

- 343 -

Gemini Wordsmiths, a women-owned editing, copywriting, and proofreading business, was founded in 2011 in Willow Grove, Pennsylvania. As karma would have it, Ruth, Ann, and Gemini Wordsmiths were all born under the astrological sign of Gemini.

Every project is given the same intense review, regardless of whether it is a one-page document or a 100,000-word novel. And instead of getting one editor for their dollars, our clients receive a second set of eyes at the same cost, as both editors review each project separately and then collaboratively.

For more information about Gemini Wordsmiths, call 215-605-5231 or visit geminiwordsmiths.com.

www.ingramcontent.com/pod-product-compliance
Lightning Source LLC
Chambersburg PA
CBHW032209180726
48284CB00001B/250